Sipped

C. T. Collier

The Penningtons Investigate, Book Two

Asdee Press

Cover design by Dave Fymbo
Imprint logo by Karen Sorce
Series logo by Lia Rees

To my Great Grandmother
Martha Dowding Burroughs
who set me on a spiritual path and,
even now, watches over my journey

The author gratefully acknowledges the following persons. Lourdes Venard, editor. The Lilac City Rochester Writers group, the Canandaigua Writers Group, and the Guppies and Murder on Ice Chapters of Sisters in Crime.

Chapter 1

Certain the forecast had said nothing about snow, Lyssa Pennington huffed at the fat flakes whirling in the pools of light around the quad. Her students' noisy debate—pizza versus Chinese—faded into murmurs before the heavy teak door of the classroom building thudded shut behind them. Frigid air from their exodus enveloped her.

One glance at the walkways thick with snow cover, another at her new leather heels, and she palmed her cell phone.

"Looking for a ride?" a cultured British voice called from the far end of the corridor.

She startled before turning to him with a warm smile.

"A bit jumpy?" he teased. "Thanks for not triggering that Perv Alert thing."

She laughed. "Catch up, Kyle. At Tompkins College it's a Creeper Beeper." All the students and employees carried the devices to summon Campus Security. There had been talk lately about attacks on students. Though their friend Tony Pinelli, head of security, said the numbers were below average for the fall semester, rumors took on a life of their own at this institution.

"Interested in a steak at the Manse Grill?"

"Perfect. And thanks for the rescue. These shoes were not going to survive the half mile home." Her high heels clicked on the old terrazzo floor.

"A bit wobbly on those things, are you?"

She gave him a playful punch on the arm. "Tell me you're not parked out back." It was a faculty-only lot. "Stan Block's on tonight, and he holds the record for dispensing the most parking tickets in a single night."

Together they made new tracks in the snowy walkway. Lyssa spotted Kyle's Lexus halfway down the row, its red flashers barely visible under a fresh coating of flakes.

"No!" A woman's scream carried from the far corner of the lot. "Stop!"

Kyle sprang into action, shouting, "Need help over there?" The slippery surface slowed his sprint and turned it into a battle for traction.

"Get away! Leave me alone!" The woman's voice was panicky now. Lyssa was sure it was Marguerite LaCroix.

She pressed her Creeper Beeper. Immediately, an emergency alarm wailed and two blue lights flashed, one above the Call Box near the classroom building they'd just exited, the other on the wooded path leading from the parking lot to the Tompkins College administration building.

Just as Kyle rounded the end of the row, Lyssa's cell phone rang, the next step in the emergency protocol. "Faculty D lot," she told the operator. "A woman's screaming at someone to leave her alone. My husband is running to help her."

She paused as the dispatcher insisted she confirm her own identity. "Yes, I'm Lyssa Pennington. I can't see the woman or her attacker, but I'm sure it's Professor LaCroix." There was no mistaking Marguerite's lilting French accent.

Lyssa was walking from row to row, tracking Kyle's progress at the other end. At the third lane, she spotted him just as a hulking figure tackled him.

"Kyle!" She dumped her tote bag and the Creeper Beeper. Phone in hand, she slipped and slid toward the spot where Kyle had gone down. "He's attacked my husband. Send help," she told the dispatcher.

"Professor, stay clear of the scene. Do you understand?"

"No way." Kyle wasn't moving. Was he seriously hurt? "I have to help."

"Where is the attacker now?"

Movement in the snow-laden shrubs beyond the lot betrayed the location. "He's heading toward the Admin building but going through the woods," she told the operator. "He's a big man, wearing dark clothing. Please send help."

Pocketing her phone, she squatted beside Kyle, who had risen to a sitting position and was holding his head in his hands. What had happened here? He was normally a fit and wily opponent. "You're hurt?"

"No, just got the wind knocked out of me. See to Marguerite, eh?"

Lyssa started toward the far corner. She'd heard a car door slammed, and now a small engine caught.

"Sounds like she's all right." Kyle came up behind her. With a dry laugh, he said, "Chap must have played rugby in his day. Flew out from behind that last SUV and flattened me. I was so focused on helping Marguerite I never saw him coming."

"He's disappeared. Can you describe him at all?"

"Size of a small lorry. Head as thick as a battering ram. I might be losing my edge, love."

"You're bleeding from your chin." She touched it with a gentle finger, and he hissed through his teeth. Bits of gravel stuck to the blood. "Road rash, Kyle. Not a good look for you. We'll swing by Urgent Care, get you cleaned up, make sure your teeth are where they should be."

A small car shot out of the last lane and fishtailed on the campus road. Gears ground as the Mini Cooper navigated the campus roadway. Kyle observed, "So Marguerite's okay, but very angry, I should say. That was her car?"

"Yes, her blue-and-white mini."

Shouting came from Lyssa's phone. "Sorry, ma'am." She gave the operator an update.

"I'll leave you with the security officer now." The response made no sense.

"What officer?" Lyssa shouted. Both paths were deserted, and snow had covered Kyle's tracks and her own. "No one has come."

"My screen indicates the alarm has been turned off and the blue emergency lights, too. Is that correct?"

"Uh, yes, but no one came to help us." The operator had disconnected. She growled. "Tony is going to hear about this."

Kyle squeezed her shoulder. "Can you drive us, my love? I may need some tape on this wrist." He had his left hand tucked under his right arm.

"Sure, let me find my tote."

The bag was where she'd dropped it, but there was no sign of her security device in the thickening snow. She'd lost her scarf somewhere, too, she realized, as the snowflakes on her bare neck melted and quickly froze in the icy wind.

"Lyssa?" Kyle called.

She abandoned the search for the lost items and cut through the rows to his Lexus. He had started the engine and was sitting in the passenger seat.

"Tony's going to be furious about no one showing up at the scene," she told him. "And my shoes are ruined."

"I may bring it up with Justin as well." Justin Cushman, Kyle's longtime friend, was president of the college. "Who did you say was on duty tonight?"

"I'm completely serious." Kyle told Tony Pinelli. Though he'd promised the hostess at the Manse Grill he would end his call shortly, her thin-lipped frown conveyed censure. He and Lyssa grudgingly accepted their placement at a small table away from the windows. In fairness, the restaurant was busy on this Friday evening the week before Thanksgiving.

"Your dispatcher can tell you the events as she experienced them," he told Tony, "but *I'm* telling you no one came to our aid, and, worse still, no one came to help Marguerite LaCroix. If we hadn't come along, Lord knows what might have happened."

Tony's answering exhale was so loud Lyssa looked up from across the table. "Yeah, well, there's bad blood between her and one of my officers," Tony said. "She called me from outside her office last week. She'd caught him rummaging through her files and personal papers. Probably let himself in while she was in class and didn't leave fast enough. He gave her some bull about responding to a distress call from a student who'd seen someone fiddling with the lock on her door. No record of any such a call to security."

"Do you think the same officer was tonight's attacker?" Kyle asked. Lyssa set down the menu, her eyes alight with a question, and he held up one finger for patience.

Tony was saying, "I don't know, pal, but you can bet I'm going to find out."

Kyle told him, "Lyssa thought someone named Stan was on duty tonight."

"Stan Block. He's been here longer than God."

"And he's the officer at odds with Professor LaCroix?" He took Tony's silence as affirmation and gave Lyssa a nod.

"Hey, buddy, since you're already involved in this, I've been wanting to dig deeper into the guy's emails. I have a hunch he's got some coercion or extortion going on. Maybe even toward Professor LaCroix. Are you available to do that?"

Kyle hesitated. He knew from experience that eavesdropping on individuals and monitoring or mining computer accounts was a touchy subject at the college, as well it should be. Still, it was one of his areas of expertise. "Assuming the college administrators bless that work, yes."

Lyssa tapped his wrist, and he realized the waiter was shifting from foot to foot, awaiting his order. "Tony, how about we continue this discussion tomorrow first thing?"

He pocketed his phone. To the waiter, he said, "The scallops. No potato. Small house salad with lemon thyme dressing. No bread or dessert for me tonight." He lifted his elbow and the bandaged wrist to free the menu.

As soon as the waiter left, Lyssa said, her tone urgent, "Marguerite texted me right before she took off. I didn't see it until just now. She said she needed to talk and to call her. Kyle, I've been trying her number and there's no answer. I also called Gianessa and Gwen to see if she'd shown up at a meeting tonight or called them. They both said no." All four women were recovering in AA and had formed a tight support group. "Gwen is going to ask Peter to swing by Marguerite's house when he gets on duty later." Gwen's husband, Officer Peter Shaughnessy, was on the night shift for the Tompkins Falls police.

"He'll make sure she's all right," Kyle assured her. "She's probably turned off her phone. You know she does that when students are calling too late. Here's our salad." He sat back as the plates were set before them. He automatically reached for his fork and winced at the pain. "Blast. This had better heal overnight."

"Or at least in the next four days. Fiona will never forgive you if you pass on her Thanksgiving meal for us."

They had plans to fly to the UK four days hence for a short stay at Pennington House, Kyle's estate in Cornwall. The family's housekeeper adored Lyssa and always roasted a bird and prepared root vegetables and tart sauces for the occasion.

"You did clear it with Justin to reschedule your Wednesday classes?" he asked her.

She held up one finger.

"Is he going to fire you?" he teased.

She smiled as she chewed and swallowed. "My job is safe. But something's bothering you, isn't it?"

"If I hadn't parked illegally Marguerite would have been on her own in the parking lot, and who knows what would have happened. I wish I'd seen the attacker's face."

"You can't describe him at all?"

"I never saw him coming, and I was eating gravel when he ran off. Supersized but quick on his feet. Tony said Marguerite recently had words with a security officer, the same one who was on duty tonight, Stan Block. I'll wager he reset the alarm without coming to our aid, and he'll probably file a report claiming he'd handled the matter."

As she pushed the plate aside for the busboy, Kyle saw that she'd left the croutons, tomatoes, onions, and peppers. Why had she bothered to order salad?

"What was Tony asking you to do?" Her question startled him.

"He wants me to look into Stan Block's record of communication with Marguerite. I gather he's building a case against him."

"Can you do that while we're in Cornwall?"

"Easily, but I shan't cut into our time together."

She played with her spoon, flipping it over and back. "Why wouldn't Marguerite have stayed to talk? She must have recognized your voice, and her text to me said she needed to talk."

"Sweetheart, she was probably too shaken to notice who we were. Her attacker ran off and she bolted. End of story."

"But there was a delay, a minute at least, between her car starting and leaving the lot. During which she did what? If she was injured, she shouldn't have gone off like that."

"In which case we'd have seen her at Urgent Care ahead of us, don't you think?"

"Maybe. Something's not right." She pressed her thumb and one finger against her forehead with a grimace of pain.

"Headache? Or are you having one of your intuitions?" His wife had some kind of sixth sense that operated from time to time, typically at a crime scene.

"Both. I'm her AA sponsor. She's never said anything about trouble with Stan Block."

"When did you last talk with her?"

Her fingernails tapped against her glass, and he reached over to still them.

"Sorry, I know you hate that. Actually, since summer break, she has put me off every time I've called or tried to schedule with her. *'Too busy to meet this week.' 'Can't talk now.' 'I'll let you know when things ease up.'*"

He felt momentary guilt that his face-plant had diverted her attention from Marguerite. Another baseless reassurance formed on his tongue, but the pain etched into her lovely face stopped him. He reached for her hand. "We'll swing by her house after our meal."

They hadn't seen lights at Marguerite's, though, and her car was nowhere in evidence. Lyssa had even peeked in the garage. After one more unsuccessful call to Marguerite's phone, she took her headache to bed while Kyle read the latest Louise Penny.

Sirens woke her from a sound sleep. When she sat up, though, there was no sound at all. Had she dreamed the wailing? Just before waking, she'd seen a flash of Marguerite's beautiful face stilled in death, the hair on the left side of her head caked with dried blood, but only a trickle of blood on her forehead. Had that really happened to their friend?

When a shudder convulsed her body, Kyle stirred but did not awaken. One glance at the clock told her it was nearly six in the morning. Leaving him to sleep, she wrapped herself in her thick terry robe and padded through the kitchen to a French door that opened to the apartment's lakeside porch. It was too cold to venture out in bare feet, so she simply watched the scene and let it soothe her.

A crescent moon hung above the eastern horizon. Chestnut Lake was a shimmering silver ribbon stretching from north to south, the shoreline dark except for a light directly across the water. Trooper Moran's home, she thought. They'd worked together—she, Kyle, and Hank—on two murders.

"Yes, hello?" Kyle's voice sounded from the bedroom. She hadn't heard his phone ring. "Hold on, Peter." He joined her in the kitchen and put the phone on speaker. "It's Peter Shaughnessy."

Peter's strained voice scared her. "We've been looking all night and finally got a tip. A driver who stopped on the shoulder to use his cell saw lights under the snow in a deep ditch. Evidently your friend's car went off the highway. I'm sorry to tell you she's dead. We'll need both of you to come downtown this morning to make statements about whatever you saw at the college last night."

"Now?" she asked. But Peter's shift would end at seven, and she'd rather tell it to him and his partner, Sam Pinelli, Tony's younger brother.

Kyle answered for them, "We'll be there straightaway."

"I didn't want you to hear it on the morning news," the officer said.

"We're grateful, Peter."

"I can see a light at Hank's," Lyssa said without thinking.

Peter hesitated. Finally, he said, "We're investigating."

Chapter 2

At dawn the next Wednesday morning, Kyle surveyed the nearly full chapel. The police were treating Marguerite's death as suspicious and, although the tight-lipped investigation could go on for days, the college needed some kind of closure before grieving students and colleagues left for the Thanksgiving holiday.

In an executive session, the senior college officers had put together a predawn candlelight memorial service to honor her. Flowers filled the sanctuary. Marguerite's devastated students, each wearing a black armband, filled the first rows on both sides of the aisle.

He'd had to move heaven and earth to reschedule their reservations from Tuesday to the eve of Thanksgiving, the busiest travel day of the year. "I'll stay back here, where I can watch for our ride to the airport." They would arrive in the UK before midnight, where a private limo would deliver them to Pennington House.

Thoughts of his beloved Cornwall were his only defense against the sorrow he felt at their friend's death.

"Looks like we're getting underway." He nodded toward the sanctuary, where the college chaplain swept to the podium, his vestments floating behind him. "We need to make a quick exit if we're to make our flight," Kyle reminded Lyssa.

"How much time?" Lyssa asked.

"Eighteen minutes."

She hurried away and ducked into a seat on the faculty side.

Silence descended on the congregation.

The chaplain intoned, "Friends, we are gathered this morning to remember our dear friend Marguerite LaCroix. Scholar, professor, department chair, and beloved wife of William. It's particularly hard for us to bid farewell today, as we prepare for Thanksgiving celebrations with our loved ones."

Paper rattled over the sound system as the chaplain unfolded his notes. He read off Marguerite's impressive accomplishments. Her degrees from Vassar and Brown University. Her scholarly papers and books. Her annual travel to French speaking areas around the world. Her commitment to engaging her students with French literature representing many cultures, particularly African nations. Her politic handling of her role as chair of Languages at Tompkins College.

Following the chaplain's tribute, the student choir sang a medley of French songs and hymns, and two of Marguerite's students gave tearful testimonies to her teaching and her sponsorship of the semester-abroad program for Language majors.

Mourners on both sides of the aisle sniffled and fished in their purses for tissues.

The chaplain announced, "Next we'll hear a few words from William." A well-dressed middle-aged man stepped to the lectern and adjusted the microphone to accommodate his height. "I'm Marguerite's husband, Billy Warren," he said with a gentle smile.

Well over six feet, and Marguerite had been tall for a woman. They'd been a striking couple—Billy with rugged good looks and muscles that filled his suit jacket and Marguerite, slender, stylish, and bookish with those round eyeglass frames. Kyle dropped his gaze for a moment and gathered himself. Those spectacles had always brought a smile to his face. He'd finally caught on she had multiple pairs, color-coordinated for every outfit. He'd wondered if she'd worn them just for show, but he'd never had the gumption to ask.

Now he couldn't ask. She was gone.

He lifted his eyes as Billy went on, "You know, when I met Marguerite I couldn't imagine that a beauty like her, with a PhD and all, could be interested in a businessman and carpenter like me. But when I asked her for a date, she said yes. And when she insisted on calling me William, not Billy, I knew I would love and protect her forever." His jaw tightened and his gaze went to the AA contingent across the aisle from the faculty. "Most of you know she struggled with alcoholism, and that was hard for us. When she got sober a few years back, I thought it would be smooth sailing from then on." He ducked his head, and his shoulders shook with a stifled sob.

Many in the pews exchanged worried looks, and the chaplain leaned forward at the edge of his chair.

Soon, though, the man straightened his spine and lifted his face to the rafters. His gaze again searched the AA audience, and a frown creased his brow. Had he been seeking someone and not found the person? "One of you knows she uncovered something that put our marriage in jeopardy."

Kyle snapped to attention. Billy must be talking about Lyssa, something only she knew as Marguerite's AA sponsor. Had Billy done something illegal? Nonsense, why would he hint at it in public?

He checked the time. Three minutes until their car would arrive. They could not chance missing their flight. He and Lyssa desperately needed this break at Pennington House. For Lyssa, the end of the semester would be pressure-filled, and he had an unresolved lawsuit waiting for him in London.

Billy's gaze now swung to the far aisle, where several uniformed officers stood. "Some of you know my wife was attacked hours before she was found dead at the side of the road." A collective gasp rose from the congregation. Billy's voice had hardened. "Know this, whoever you are. You who terrorized her to her death on Friday evening, you will burn in hell."

Kyle sucked in his breath. The officers straightened and cast their gaze over the crowd. Shocked silence gave way to whispered conversations and restless shuffling of programs.

Kyle checked his phone. *Almost time.* Someone tapped his left shoulder, his brother-in-law. "Outside," Joel whispered.

The rising sun nearly blinded Kyle. He asked, "Did you expect that bit about burning in hell?"

"I'm not surprised he said what he did. Billy was crushed by whatever Marguerite told him last summer. They'd been separated since then. Someone was harassing her lately, and she wouldn't let Billy intervene."

"In heaven's name, why? And what secret?"

Joel just shook his head. Kyle did a slow burn. "Stop being so mysterious."

"It's not for me to tell Marguerite's story, even if I knew it, which I don't." He lifted his chin toward the campus roadway. "Is that your limo?"

Kyle spotted the black Lincoln cruising toward them. "Lyssa's phone may be off, Joel. She's halfway up the aisle on the faculty side. While I get our bags, would you give her a tap on the shoulder? Thanks."

He hailed the car and ducked back into the foyer for the luggage.

She appeared seconds later and held open the outer door for him. "Will we make it?"

He nodded. "We've just enough time, assuming no delays."

But as she descended the steps, Billy Warren stepped in her path. "A word, Mrs. Pennington."

Since Lyssa's expression was open and sympathetic, Kyle moved past and assisted the driver with loading the car.

With no warning, Billy shouted, "You had no right to encourage her to"—he spat on the pavement—"pursue her passion."

"I did no such thing," Lyssa snarled. "Get out of my way."

Kyle whipped around as Billy Warren gripped Lyssa's shoulders with both hands.

Billy hissed, "And no right to give her—"

"Let her go." Kyle lunged for Warren.

Peter Shaughnessy, out of uniform, raced down the chapel steps toward them. "Back off, Warren."

Billy hesitated a moment, seething, before raising his hands, palms out, and stepping back with an affable smile. Kyle's momentum had carried him within striking distance of Billy before he could check it. "Kyle," Peter barked, "I've got this."

The three men froze in place. Into the standoff, Lyssa's shaky voice said, "We can't miss our flight, Kyle." She cut straight through their triangle and discreetly tugged the sleeve of Kyle's jacket as she passed.

With his arm around her shoulders and hers around his waist, they walked away. Though she looked cool, he could feel her vibrating. He held the car door for her to slide across the bench seat, then climbed in after her and double-tapped the seatback. The limo rolled toward the college's main entrance.

"Thank you." Lyssa leaned into him.

One backward glance showed Peter Shaughnessy talking with the widower, his stance wide.

14

"What the—" His voice betrayed his bottled-up rage. "What was that about?"

"He blames me for everything that happened." She shook her head. "Everything that went wrong in their marriage, I mean, not for the attack on campus."

"Surely you're not to blame?"

"No, I'm not. My job was to point out how the Twelve Steps could help with every aspect of her life, including marital difficulties. I'd never sponsored anyone before, so Gianessa guided me constantly, plus her sponsor, Carole, and Gwen Shaughnessy. And, yes, I *will* call Gianessa from the airport to talk about what just happened with Billy."

"You're saying you didn't do anything wrong, but I'm asking what the issue was that rocked Marguerite and Billy's marriage." He doubted she'd tell him, but he wanted—no, he *needed* to know, though he couldn't have given a good reason at the moment.

"All I can say is, some of us used alcohol to block out a fact of our early life that we had found impossible to deal with. Something so disturbing we drank to suppress it so we could function normally." She sandwiched his hand between hers. "And when we got sober we couldn't deny it anymore. That happened with me, and Marguerite saw that I had moved beyond it. So she chose me as her sponsor to help her do the same."

It struck him as far too much responsibility. Was she feeling like she'd failed? "You did all that for her?"

"Yes, I did, and it was hard work. Knowing the truth tore her life apart." Her eyes brimmed with tears. "Over the past few months she'd seemed happier, like she'd made a new beginning."

"Did Joel know the secret?"

"Of course not. How could he?"

"He's married to your sister. All of you alcoholics are part of the same club."

A laugh escaped her. "Sorry, I'm not making fun, but AA's not a club. Tell me what you're thinking."

"You know what I mean. You have your own language and all those sayings."

"Like 'First Things First,' you mean?"

"Precisely. And you smile at the most unlikely people when we're shopping at Wegman's or walking on campus."

"True."

He tried again. "Just my opinion. Now that Marguerite's dead, there's no need to keep her secret, and it would make it easier for us to talk about it."

"But it's nothing to do with us."

"I'm not so sure." He snapped the words.

She shifted on the seat to face him. "What's bothering you?"

He cast a meaningful look toward their driver, whose gaze briefly met his in the rearview mirror before returning to the road. Quietly he told her, "It's what Billy said up there at the lectern. His wife stopped drinking and realized something about herself that ended their marriage. Is that about to happen to us?"

Lyssa entwined her fingers with his.

"I promise I don't have any secrets you don't already know. God knows there were some horrible revelations early on in recovery, but you know all about that." Perhaps he'd looked skeptical, for she tipped her head. "Don't you?"

With a cautionary nod toward the driver, he told her, "Tomorrow on our walk, let's talk through all of this."

Chapter 3

Over breakfast in the sunny morning room at Pennington House, Lyssa and Kyle caught up on news of the north coast of Cornwall. While Kyle's preferred source was the stack of newspapers his mother had been saving for him, Lyssa went right to the expert.

Between spoonfuls of fruit, she peppered the eighty-four-year-old widow with questions and listened with rapt attention to the responses. They'd nearly lost her a year ago to pneumonia, and Moira Pennington qualified every answer with, "Of course, I don't get out much these days, but ..." Regardless, she demonstrated keen insight into Cornwall's business climate, the Padstow area's social scene, and matters of concern on the Pennington estate.

"You don't miss a thing, Mum." Lyssa reached over to give her thin hand a gentle pat. "How do you do it?"

"Newspapers, Facebook, minutes of all the council meetings, that sort of thing. And I'm well enough now to visit our tenants and get out with my friends for lunch or a drive."

Moira had a twinkle in her eye as Fiona, the cook and housekeeper, set a full breakfast and a plate of sticky buns in front of Kyle. "And our Fiona, while I would never call her a gossip, has a way with every delivery person and shopkeeper."

Fiona puffed out her chest. "Just keeping me ears open, ma'am." She carried a smaller plate topped with scrambled eggs and toast to Moira's place, then deposited an assortment of jams between Moira and Lyssa.

Moira squeezed her daughter-in-law's hand. "You're a bit peaky, my dear. And much thinner than I remember from summer." There was the faintest rebuke in her tone.

"Am I?" Lyssa asked.

"Yes." The response came at triple volume from Moira, Kyle, and Fiona together.

Lyssa's face was hot.

In the ensuing silence, Fiona placed breakfast potatoes and eggs sunny-side up in front of Lyssa, along with a basket of the Pennington kitchen's specialty, Irish brown bread and butter.

Moira pointed a finger at Lyssa's food. "You'll eat every bite, eh?"

Lyssa nodded meekly and lifted her fork. "Beautiful meal, Fiona. Thank you."

They ate without speaking, Lyssa's eyes straying between bites to the birds flitting in the boxwood border of the rose garden just past the windowpanes. This past month, while they'd been in exile from their house while repairs were done to the first floor, she had missed the view of her own rose garden from her kitchen in Tompkins Falls.

Maybe if they were back in the house she'd feel more like cooking meals. Especially when Kyle was in London for business, she hadn't taken good care of herself. She hated that they could see it, too.

She'd finished her eggs and slathered a chunk of brown bread with butter and blackberry jam when Moira proclaimed, "Kyle, you're still squinting. Isn't he squinting, Lyssa?"

Lyssa laughed. "Your turn, darling. Yes, Moira, he always looks like he's mad at me."

Moira spread apricot jam on her toast. "Have you seen your eye specialist, as I asked last time you were home?"

"I don't believe I have one." Kyle selected a sticky bun from the plate. "Ah, still warm."

"Manda has a terrific ophthalmologist," Lyssa told him. "We'll get you an appointment."

"That's settled," Moira said brightly. "Where are you two off to today? No doubt we'll have rain at some point."

Kyle raised an eyebrow in Lyssa's direction. "Up to the cliffs?"

Lyssa nodded happily, not just because the interrogation was finished. She wanted nothing more than to throw herself into the complete change of scene offered by the estate on the wild coast of Cornwall. A bracing walk would let her cast aside her guilt and sadness about Marguerite's death and, along with it, her curiosity about the police investigation into the accident.

Or at least she could try.

Kyle watched Lyssa for any sign of hesitation as they laced up their hiking boots and grabbed their waterproof anoraks for the promised rain. He wasn't entirely sure she was up for a strenuous walk, let alone the tricky footing and punishing wind they would face if they came home by way of her favorite cliff path.

But she jumped to her feet and sported a wide smile. "I am *so* ready for that view from the cliff." Her sapphire eyes sparkled as they stepped into the bracing wind of a Cornish winter morning. They held hands crossing the formal lawn, then cut through a stand of trees to the stony dirt track that ran along the backside of the cliffs.

Bleats and tinkling bells greeted them as they trudged uphill. His shoulders relaxed and he sucked in a lungful of ocean air mixed with pasture smell.

"How many sheep do we have in all?" Lyssa asked.

"A hundred or so." They rounded a bend to see a grassy field with twenty or so black-faced sheep and, beyond, a high pasture dotted with still more. "Maybe two hundred. Why, love?"

"They're handsome, aren't they, with their tan coats and black stockings and black faces?"

He laughed. Honestly, he had no idea how his wife's mind worked. "Suffolk sheep. Bred more for meat than wool. They're none of them yours and mine, you know."

"No?"

"They belong to two different farmers on Pennington land. If you look closely, you'll see some have blue marks and some red."

"You don't mind them chomping on the greenery and leaving their calling cards?"

"Not in the least. It saves Padraig having to mow the whole lot. Does it bother you?"

She balanced on one foot while showing off her sturdy waterproof boot. "Not when I'm wearing these and the wind's blowing the other way."

"Spoken like a true Cornish wife." He gave her one of his quirky smiles—every Cornish lad had mastered the art—a tug at one side of his mouth and the lift of an eyebrow. He knew even now, a month short of their first anniversary, the expression could melt her heart. Sure enough, she gave him a wink, and they picked up the pace.

But she was puffing a good bit when they reached the highest point of the stony track, not something she'd done in the past. "Are you game for more this first time out?" He gestured to the chest-high wall of stony earth and scrub to their right and the field rising beyond.

"Absolutely. Let's cross to the cliffs." She let him help her up the bank. Once on top, a fierce wind off the ocean buffeted them. He slung an arm around her shoulders, and she wrapped her arm around his waist as they bent their heads for the trek across to the cliff edge.

He shouted against the roar of the wind and waves, "Other than admiring the sheep, you've been quiet since we left the house."

She lifted her mouth close to his ear, and he reveled in the feel of her breath on his neck. "I keep replaying what Billy Warren said yesterday about someone terrorizing Marguerite."

Blast. He'd hoped they could leave it behind for a few days.

"I'm worried someone had a hand in her death," she said. "Why else would the police still be investigating? Have you heard anything more?"

"Only from Tony that they haven't ruled on the death." He massaged the area over his heart to ease the ache. There was something about Marguerite that had captivated him. When he'd met her at faculty parties, she'd seemed shy, like him, but possessed a dignity that allowed her slender form to stand firm among her backbiting colleagues.

Once he understood she was sober in AA, like Lyssa, he felt protective toward her. Her humor blossomed once Lyssa became her sponsor. Only a month ago, she'd coaxed him to converse in French with her and dissolved in giggles at his pronunciation. "I can't imagine who would want to harm her." He shuddered. "You don't think we stopped a rapist from doing his worst?"

"Probably not. If she didn't know the person, she would have used her Creeper Beeper. But why wouldn't she stick around for us to help her?"

He wished she would let it go. There was no bringing back their friend. "It's a dreadful loss, my love. It's going to take us time."

"And remember the way her car shot out of the parking lot? Are we even sure she was at the wheel?"

"You're thinking someone cracked her skull, drove her body to the site of the crash, propped her up behind the wheel, and helped the car into the ditch?" He glanced behind them. "I hope no one's listening or they'll think we're ghouls." It was their style, though, when confronted with a suspicious death, to talk over the circumstances and brainstorm explanations.

"I don't buy that. Remember the dream I was having when the sirens woke me? There was only a trickle of blood on her forehead. Besides, if someone knocked her out and drove her car off the road on that deserted stretch, they'd have had a cold walk home."

Kyle set his face to the wind. "I suppose they're testing for alcohol or drugs in her system." He felt Lyssa shiver and drew her closer.

"I don't think she picked up a drink. She's been at meetings and looking happy and content. I suppose I should have reached out to her, but my sponsor always says it's up to the sponsee to reach out."

"Is all this talk helping or making it worse for you?"

"Helping. Could the attacker have slipped her some drug? And when it took effect, she passed out, veered off the road, and died on impact?"

"I should think if you're intent on killing someone, there's no guarantee a drug would make a person drive off the road and die."

"Kyle, could Billy be the attacker?"

Until the scene outside the memorial service, Kyle had respected, even admired, Marguerite's husband. Now, not so much. "I suppose it's possible, given the way he manhandled you on the steps of the chapel." He felt the heat rise in his chest.

"That was hard to take, but I know he was really torn up about their separation. And now she's gone he's got to be hurting."

The heat crept up his neck. "How can you defend the man? There's no excuse for directing his venom at you. I was put out enough to make some calls about it between flights."

"What did you find out?"

"Officer Shaughnessy filed a report with the city about your incident, which I'll support if I'm called upon. And Trooper Hank Moran is the one investigating Marguerite's death, though I don't know why that should be necessary."

She shook her head. "I'm sure they're not looking at Billy. He loved her and wanted things to work out for them, until … It must have been someone on the faculty or staff. Maybe Stan Block. Scary to think a Campus Security officer is harassing a woman on the faculty."

They'd reached the edge of the cliff with the full drama of the wild Atlantic before them. Lyssa exhaled with a *whoosh*.

"So we'll leave off this discussion and enjoy the view, eh?"

"Gladly."

He gave her a boost onto a broad flat rock, where they huddled together and let the wind whirl around them and the waves of the gray Atlantic crash into the base of the cliff and shoot white foam high into the air.

When Lyssa heard him calling her name, she hopped off their giant boulder and strolled to meet him at the top of the three stone steps that marked the start of the cliff path. He'd gone ahead to check the conditions.

"Is it safe?" He wasn't meeting her eyes, though, and she lost hope for a thrilling hike along the face of the cliff.

"I got as far as the narrowest point, but beyond that it's muddy and slick from spray. We'll not try it today."

Disappointed, she pulled out a smile for him. "We'll return by way of the sheep."

He grinned. "The sheep it is, my love."

She loved getting a laugh out of him, but something was bothering him, probably to do with Marguerite. He'd been dancing around the couple's separation since they'd left the memorial service. She knew how the split had come about, but she couldn't tell Kyle without betraying the secret Marguerite asked her to hold in confidence. She drew in a calming breath and sent up a silent prayer.

Once they'd descended the steep bank and settled into a rhythm on the dirt track through the fields of sheep, she nudged his elbow and gave him a bright smile. "Tell me what's on your mind."

"You always could read me." With no preface, Kyle said, "I need you to tell me Marguerite's secret."

"I—" She licked her lips and gathered her thoughts. Maybe the right thing was to get it into the open. "Only if you promise to keep this totally and absolutely confidential."

"Agreed. Totally and absolutely."

"Don't tease," she said with a laugh. "It's very sensitive, and it may shock you."

"Try me."

"Okay. When she got sober and her head cleared, Marguerite realized why she'd started drinking in the first place." *God, I don't think I can do this.*

"Which was what?"

"It was because when she was thirteen she realized she had feelings for girls, not for boys." She gulped in a breath and stole a look at his face. Frozen in a squint. "*Strong* feelings for girls."

He tipped his head and met her gaze. "You're saying her sexual orientation was lesbian. I'm surprised, yes, but why did that pose a problem for her? Weren't we open-minded on the subject twenty-five or so years ago, whenever it was she discovered the truth about herself at thirteen?"

"Her family lived in a very conservative Minnesota town where anyone who was gay or lesbian was shunned or worse. She couldn't even *think* she might be lesbian, let alone tell anyone. So she drank to forget and to fit in, like a lot of us did for entirely different reasons. And it worked for a long time. Until the alcohol stopped working and became a problem of its own."

"And when she stopped drinking, what?"

"It all came back—the knowing, the fear, the shame. She couldn't deny her sexual orientation anymore."

Kyle muttered *bloody hell* under his breath and his hands tightened into fists. "Evidently the booze worked long enough for her to marry Billy Warren, who impressed me as a manly man."

She raised a defense. "Long enough to marry a man she loved, yes. You blame her, don't you?" Aware she was shouting, she glanced around. A few sheep had edged away from them. No humans on the horizon.

"How could I not? That's a horrible deception. Don't you agree?"

"She didn't intentionally deceive Billy."

"You must be joking." He came to a halt and faced her.

"I'm not joking. I'm sure she was in complete denial. It happens that way for some of us. We completely suppress things we can't deal with and keep them out of our consciousness by drinking."

"First, I don't see how that's possible. Second, what kind of marriage could they have had? And anyway, why would a virile gent like Billy stay in the marriage under the circumstances?"

"I don't know the details of their sex life, but I know they had one."

He pressed his point. "There were no children, right?"

She shook her head and brushed the tears from her cheeks.

"I'm making this worse for you, aren't I? But I can't imagine how Marguerite could perpetrate such a fraud. It doesn't tally with anything I know about her. And how could she *not* have known at the time of her marriage what she'd obviously known about herself at thirteen?"

Lyssa shifted her focus to the sky. The uniformly gray cloud cover had given way to storm clouds. She and Kyle were about to be deluged. She drew on her anorak.

Kyle shook out his own anorak and weatherproofed himself. "So what happened? When she realized the truth a year or so ago, she told him and they divorced?"

"Not exactly. When she told him, he was horrified. I guess he didn't want to talk about it for a long time, and she finally asked him if he wanted a divorce or to have the marriage annulled. That was more than a year ago in late spring. It was awful, Kyle. She was sobbing whenever we talked about it, just in total agony."

"I shouldn't wonder."

His tone, unrelentingly cold, made her shiver. Or was it from the fat icy drops of rain splashing her face? Lyssa added, "He didn't want to go through the ordeal of annulment. They stayed together for another year. He only moved out last summer. I honestly don't know what precipitated that."

"I thought she told you everything."

"Until last spring, she did, but she didn't contact me at all after spring semester. We were here and she was on vacation in France. Maybe Billy found someone else."

"She said nothing to you about him leaving her?"

Lyssa hesitated, trying to remember. "She texted me when she got back from her vacation, wanting to get together. I was still here, so I offered to call her or Skype with her, but she didn't respond. When I got home and saw her at a meeting sometime in September, she said Billy was gone and she couldn't talk then, maybe later. We never got together."

Tears flowed down her hot cheeks, mixing with the icy rain. She didn't wipe them away. "Why didn't I call her?"

He squeezed her shoulders. "It's done, sweetheart. Let's get ourselves home."

With Lyssa snuggled next to him on the library sofa, Kyle stared into the wood fire, still tied in knots from their conversation on the walk home. Yet, he was reluctant to ask Lyssa more about Marguerite's deception. He wanted their time together at Pennington House to be upbeat and restorative.

"You're so quiet." Her voice startled him. "What's up?"

"Tell me something."

She sat up and curled her legs under her. "Anything."

He leaned forward with his elbows on his knees. "You seem so certain that Marguerite was in complete denial about her sexual orientation when she married."

"Yes."

"And you based that conclusion on your own experience, correct?" She nodded. "I believe you said pot and booze helped you repress memories."

"Exactly."

"You've told me about your parents being alcoholics and being killed when you were in high school. I know your father was given to violence when he'd had too much to drink. Are those the memories you meant?"

"Uh ..."

What further trauma had she'd lived through? "Perhaps if you share what else you suppressed, I'll understand why you say Marguerite was in denial, not perpetrating a fraud."

She had paled. "Okay, but it may involve tears."

He raised his hand in a solemn vow. "I promise I can handle tears." He'd hoped the hand-raising would lighten things, but it didn't.

She hugged her knees to her chest. "What I've never told anyone, including Manda, is that our father got into trouble on his job by taking advantage of a student who had a huge crush on him."

"Took advantage how?" He dreaded the answer. Already his shoulders were tight with anger.

"He had a sexual relationship with her for a semester. She boasted about it to her friends and eventually some other girl turned him in. He should have lost his job, but he didn't."

"Why ever not?" Kyle sputtered. "That's a horrible violation of the faculty code at any college."

"Agreed, but my charming father somehow persuaded the girl he was sleeping with to lie for him and deny the whole thing. Plus, my father had been on the faculty a long time and had lots of supporters who pretended to be outraged that the tattletale would lie about him and try to ruin his reputation. I don't know if some of the protestors were her professors, too, but the girl who'd told on him took a lot of flak and finally recanted her accusation."

"I'm disgusted he got away with it."

"Well, yes, but there were consequences."

He could see from the crease of pain in her forehead that she was not as calm as her voice sounded. "Did the girl get pregnant?"

"No, thank God, but my mother knew all about it, long before the other girl turned him in, and I'd hear my parents arguing about it when they thought I was at a friend's house studying. It really shook me, and I never trusted my father after that." She'd hesitated with that last bit before lapsing into silence.

"Couldn't trust him how, love?"

"I ... " She lowered her gaze and hugged her knees tight to her chest. "I made sure I was never alone in the house with him, especially when he was drunk. And I made Manda promise she wouldn't be either."

She'd said it so fast he wasn't sure he'd got it right. Every muscle in his body had tensed. Well, he'd asked for it, hadn't he? "Correct me if I'm wrong, but I take that to mean you were afraid he might molest you or your sister."

Her eyes shifted, suggesting there was more to the story, but she simply nodded without making eye contact.

He let it rest a moment, wondering if she would add anything. When she didn't, he asked, "How old were you when this happened?"

"I was seventeen, and Manda was sixteen. The student he was sleeping with graduated that semester, and that was the end of it, as far as the college was concerned."

"Did you ever confront your father about it?"

A shudder ran through her. "I went to his office at the college one day, and I took two guy friends with me. I asked them to wait in the hall, and I didn't close the door all the way. And I told my father I knew what he'd done and thought it was despicable the way he'd betrayed my mother, and I told him if he ever came near me or Manda that way I'd kill him. And—" She choked on the word.

"Catch your breath, sweetheart."

She nodded and gulped in two deep breaths before continuing. "And I would have. And he knew it. Then I left, and he tried to follow me, but the two guys stopped him."

She was trembling and, when he reached for her, she let him wrap her tight in his arms. With his own rage barely contained, he somehow kept his voice gentle. "I'm so sorry, my love."

Her tears finally ran their course. She sat apart from him. "I don't think Manda ever knew what he'd done, or maybe it just didn't bother her as much. Anyway they died. I mean my parents died soon after." She sat up straighter and tossed her head. "Then I put everything into getting my doctorate, and I drank and did pot to forget about all the bad stuff he'd done to us."

"I suppose it was important to forget, eh?"

She turned her tear-streaked face to him, her eyes like liquid sapphires. "Absolutely. All that shame and anger got in the way of studying. I wanted to be like him but only in the good ways. I really believed deep inside that I was meant to be an economics professor, like he was, but I would *never* treat any student the way he did. He abused his power and it made me sick."

He placed his hand on the back of her neck. The cords were so tight, she moaned before letting go some of the tension.

"Thank you."

"So you buried it deep to stay on course with your goals?"

"Exactly. I made my own path and followed my own interests in financial literacy, especially for women and young adults. And I'm proud of that."

"You didn't remember any of what you've just told me until you got sober?"

"I did not." She snuffled her nose, and he searched his pockets for a handkerchief.

She laughed at her own seriousness. "So, that was a long story, but my point is that's how I know alcohol and other mind-altering substances, in sufficient quantities, can block memories and block feelings very effectively. For years."

He handed her the handkerchief, and she cleaned up her face and saw to her nose. She was hiccupping now. "And I believed Marguerite when she told me she was in denial about her sexual orientation when she married Billy. Not deceiving him."

"I'm making a bit more sense of it now." He hadn't the heart to tell her he still thought Marguerite had known her sexual orientation, on some level, when she married. Ultimately, it was none of his business. She'd found the courage to talk with Billy about it once she'd got sober, and Lyssa had helped her take that step.

It struck him as a weighty responsibility for his wife to take on. He admired her for that, but she really did take on far too much. That was a subject for another conversation. "When did you finally remember what your father had done?"

"The whole ugly truth revealed itself to me when I was maybe six months sober. I had a really good alcoholism counselor who helped me through it."

She looked at him straight on. "Do you think less of me now that you know all that about my father?"

"Lord, no." He had his own family secrets that were best left in the closet. He stroked her cheek. "You are my world."

She held his gaze for several seconds, then gave him a smile that softened his insides. They talked a few minutes longer until yawns overtook her.

"You need sleep," he said.

"Are you coming up, too?"

"Soon." Though some of his tension had eased, he needed half an hour at the piano. He walked her to the foot of the stairs and watched her to their bedroom door, where she turned and blew him a kiss.

He closed the door to the library and rummaged in the piano bench for sheet music. Any one of the Bach *Inventions* would surely see Lyssa gently to sleep in the bedroom above.

After the third piece, he left the keyboard and poured a short brandy for himself. Standing close to the dying fire, he swirled the liquid and inhaled the fragrance. He hoped the telling of that particular secret after ten years or more had helped the love of his life to heal in some way.

But what was the secret their friend Marguerite had been keeping for the past several months? And why hadn't she shared it with the one person she'd trusted, Lyssa, her sponsor? Whatever it was had made her race out of the parking lot rather than accept the help they'd both offered. And hours later she was dead.

Something had transpired over the summer that Marguerite wouldn't talk about, even with Lyssa, and it had made Billy Warren, who had loved her and vowed to protect her, step away from their marriage and their home.

With a crack and a spray of sparks, the last log of any size broke apart. Kyle lifted his glass in a pledge to Marguerite LaCroix. "We'll find the truth, my friend, so you can rest in peace."

Chapter 4

Lyssa had managed not to cry when she and Kyle parted at Heathrow Sunday morning—he to tend to his business in London, she to finish her semester at Tompkins College—but she'd been weepy that night, alone in the apartment on Lakeside Terrace. Would she feel any less alone in their master suite at the house on Seneca Street? Probably not, but she was missing both her husband and her pretty little home.

Over coffee Monday morning, she vowed to check on the repairs at the house before the week was over. A drug-crazed teenage vandal had wrecked the first floor of their home, smashing furniture, dishes, and glassware; ripping a closet door off his hinges; and slashing coats and jackets.

Justin had generously handled the repairs. The last report from him said they were on track to move-in-ready by the first week of December. If she could count on that, she could schedule the movers to deliver all the replacement furniture and housewares the various vendors had been keeping in storage for a month.

But first things first. She needed to rally her students through their final exams and get their semester grades posted by the second Monday of the month. Then a few days to settle into the house, and she'd be off once again to London and Cornwall. Already overwhelmed, she puffed out a breath. Maybe she'd swing by the Bagel Depot for something to fuel her first day back.

She'd just set out her bagel breakfast on her desk at Tompkins College when a phone call summoned her to the president's office. After racing down the stairs, and before entering the well-appointed office, she reminded herself that in the presidential suite it didn't matter that President Justin Cushman was family, specifically, her sister's husband's uncle. What mattered was the man was her ultimate boss, and her career was in his hands.

"Any idea what this is about?" Lyssa asked his assistant, who merely raised her eyebrows and gestured her into the inner sanctum.

Justin Cushman took thirty seconds to inquire about her Thanksgiving in Cornwall and three minutes to saddle her with a short-term assignment. "Know that I am grateful, my dear, and understand that this is in addition to wrapping up your semester grades and preparing for your spring semester."

She swallowed and asked, "What exactly do you mean I'm the coordinator of the search committee for Marguerite's replacement?" At the president's glower, Lyssa tuned into her own facial expression. She replaced her put-upon scowl with a cool professional smile. "Let me rephrase that. Since I've never been on a search committee, I don't know what a coordinator does, and I don't want to fail out of ignorance."

Justin came around his massive desk to stand as her equal, as if six-foot-two could ever be equal to five-foot-seven. "The search committee will consist of your interim dean, the department chair from Communications, and assorted faculty from several departments."

That made no sense. She could see having a department chair from a different department, but why faculty as well? She shrugged. It wasn't her job to pick the committee or to critique its makeup.

Justin was saying, "As resumé s stream into the posted email address, each needs to be logged in, given a cursory screening, and, unless they're completely unacceptable for the position, forwarded to the committee for their consideration."

"Unacceptable might mean the candidate doesn't have a PhD?"

"Correct. However, this position is also for department chair, so the candidate must have tenure at his or her institution or enough teaching, service, and publications to qualify for tenure at Tompkins College."

"Got it." She'd have to study the faculty handbook to know the details. "Am I expected to check candidate references?"

"No, that's handled by committee members on assignment from the committee chair, whose name will be revealed within the hour. As the committee identifies and vets its short list, up to three candidates will be brought to campus. You'll coordinate the interview schedule and see to the candidate's formal dinner." One raised finger stifled her imminent protest "The dean's assistant will support you throughout. She's been through this many times, including your own interview two years ago."

Lyssa cleared her throat. "So I should talk with her today and make a game plan."

"She's expecting you in ten minutes. We want Professor LaCroix's replacement to start in January."

"Two months from now?" Her voice had risen an octave in four syllables.

He nodded. "Seven weeks from today. The ad is live on the internet, and it appeared in print over the weekend."

"You're aware Kyle and I will be in Cornwall for the holiday break. How—"

"The coordinator's job is entirely electronic, and you're a wizard with technology. No one else on the committee is capable of pulling this off in the timeframe."

My reward for competence. She kept that impertinent thought to herself, but tested, "I'm not sure I can manage dinner reservations and menus from a distance."

"The dean's office will do the heavy lifting with the candidates' dinners and lodging. You'll just manage information like food allergies, schedule conflicts, and personal requests."

"Personal requests?"

He harrumphed. "Such as, 'Can I bring my spouse and children and the dog?'"

"What—?"

"The answer is spouse, yes; children and pets, no."

"I suppose there's a Frequently Asked Questions out there on the college intranet I can consult."

He brightened. "Excellent idea. Get one started, we'll all thank you."

Maybe she'd quit while she was ahead. With a smile, she saluted him. "Onward. Thank you for trusting me with this, Justin."

He wasn't smiling. "What you're doing, Lyssa, will help us all move past Marguerite's death."

She swallowed the lump in her throat.

"One cautionary note," the president added. "Our adjunct for Languages , Nicole Dutois, will apply. She's not qualified to be department chair; nevertheless, we'll give her a courtesy interview, including an exceptionally nice dinner. You're not to give any indication, to her or to anyone, that we've spoken of her unsuitability for the position."

"Understood."

Justin nodded his dismissal, and she trudged back to her office, certain her bagel sandwich was now mushy and cold.

Kyle perched on the corner of his desk at the end of his workday, listening to the unanswered buzz at Lyssa's end. Until their fireside discussion about her father's indiscretion and, before that, her revelation about all she'd done for Marguerite, he hadn't fully appreciated that her sunny disposition served to blind him to the difficulties she faced.

He had resolved since their parting at the airport to be proactive concerning her needs. The tricky thing was, that would only work if she didn't feel coddled by the increased attention. This long-distance-marriage business was harder than he'd ever imagined.

He wished he were at her side, wished he were anywhere but London tonight, where rain poured from the heavens and the temperature hovered just above freezing. No way would he walk the ten blocks to his loft this evening, but he'd have a deuce of a time getting a taxi for another hour or so.

He had his finger on the end button when Lyssa answered, her breath coming in gasps. "Caught it in time. Hi, darling. What's up?"

"Tony just phoned me with the news. I suppose you've heard already?"

"I've been swamped with students freaking about finals next week, and I've already fielded a dozen replies to the ad for Marguerite's replacement. Did I tell you Justin appointed me coordinator of the search process?"

"No." *Blast.* "I'm sorry about that, sweetheart." He had hoped for an uneventful time for her, leading up to her return to the UK. "Couldn't the college have waited a couple of months to start a search? It almost indecent, isn't it?"

"Justin wants someone in place as professor and chair starting in January. I know it's ridiculous, but that's what's happening. Have I heard what, darling?"

He drew a blank, and she prompted, "What was the news Tony gave you on the phone just now that you thought I'd already heard?"

"Ah. The autopsy shows Marguerite suffered head trauma, internal bleeding, exposure to excessive cold, and ultimately shock. However, they can't explain why her car simply left the highway and dove nose-first into a deep ditch."

His wife was rarely speechless. "Are you all right?" he asked.

"Yes. You're saying there were no brake marks?"

"Correct, nor skid marks. It was not a weather-related accident." He told her the rest. "The saddest thing is she must have lain there for hours before someone stopped on the shoulder to answer a text message and saw the light from her car down below." He heard her gasp. *Lord, why did I tell her that?* "The authorities are saying she was almost certainly unconscious from the moment of impact."

At her silence, he told her, "I'm so sorry to be the bearer of all this sadness. I thought you probably knew already and were in need of support. Are you in your office?"

"Um, yes, I just finished office hours and have class in fifteen—make that seven minutes. Another class after lunch and a review class after that."

"Promise me you'll eat lunch and at least get a snack before the review session."

"I will. And, honestly, I'd rather hear the bad news from you, so thank you for telling me. How are things there?"

"Other than the weather looking like the Second Coming, things are swimming."

She exhaled a laugh. "Punny."

He chuckled. "The solicitor and I spent a few hours going over the evidence in Geoffrey's case, and we'll go at it again Wednesday and Friday. If I can get away next week, would it be helpful to have me there?"

"I'd love it, of course, but I think I'll be underwater myself with students and finals, not to mention applications and details for the Languages position. I plan to get everything done as soon as possible. But I realized, when I met with the dean's assistant, they want to hold the interviews immediately, and, if necessary, up through the week before holiday break."

He squawked, "The week before Christmas? We're planning on you coming to the UK shortly after you post your semester grades. Surely you don't have to participate in the interviews?"

"I hope not. Gotta go, darling. Love you, talk to you later."

And she was gone. With his finger, he traced a raindrop's path down the window.

Lyssa stopped at her office after class just long enough to drop off a set of quizzes. Her next stop would be the college cafeteria for that meal she'd promised Kyle.

As she raced down the hall, someone larger than she rounded the corner into her path. Hand on her chest, Lyssa said, "Natalie, you scared me."

Her neighbor and friend Professor Natalie Horowitz might have a voluptuous figure but she never apologized for her size. She held up two bags from a whole-foods take-out place. "I've got the perfect post-holiday lunch. Salad with grilled salmon, anyone?"

Lyssa reversed direction. "You're wonderful. Let's use my office." She made space on her round table for their lunches and helped unpack the bags.

Natalie tucked her napkin into the V of her sweater "I still haven't shopped for groceries after my long weekend in"—she cleared her throat—"Manhattan."

"Oh my gosh. How could I forget? You spent Thanksgiving with Norman." Art history professor Natalie had met gallery owner Norman—both of them widowed—earlier in the fall, and the two had started a long-distance romance. "Tell me *everything*."

39

Halfway through their abundant salads, Lyssa's head was spinning with the Broadway shows they'd seen together and the museums, galleries, and shopping Natalie had managed on her own while Norman operated his gallery every day of the holiday shopping rush.

Without stopping for a breath, Natalie added, "Be honest, did you have any idea Marguerite had a heart condition?"

Shaken by the question, Lyssa dropped her fork. Rather than pick it up, she pushed her salad bowl away. "Why do you think she had a heart condition?"

"That's what the rumor mill is saying." Natalie wiggled in her chair. "And I'm feeling guilty. She'd been complaining about a little pain in her chest, and I thought it was heartburn. I never suspected a heart condition." She shook her head. "However, I *do* know she was afraid of someone. That can give anybody heartburn, right? If I'd suspected anything worse I'd have told her to see her doctor."

"Afraid of whom?" Lyssa asked.

"I don't know. She clammed up when I pressed her about it."

"But you were friends with Marguerite?"

Natalie nodded with a mouthful of lettuce.

Lyssa hadn't realized that. She'd kept her own relationship as Marguerite's sponsor strictly confidential at the college level. Maybe Natalie had information about what was going on with Marguerite since spring semester, something that would explain why she'd been assaulted the night she died.

"So you probably heard all about her trip to France last summer. I'll bet she had a good time."

A smile spread across Natalie's face as she finished chewing and swallowed. "She had a blast. I think she met someone." Natalie winked. "Maybe even had a little fling."

"Seriously? She told you that?"

"Not in so many words. But there were a few photos on her Facebook that included their guide, who was a hottie, and the posts were all about him taking them to clubs to meet artists and walking on the beach in the lingering twilight and yada yada."

Why hadn't she thought to check Marguerite's Facebook? "You're not saying she had an affair?"

"No way." Natalie's fork, loaded with salad, waved in an arc over the table, thankfully dropping nothing. "She would never go behind Billy's back no matter how hot some guy was. She loved Billy. But a flirtation? That would have put roses in her cheeks, and you have to admit she was *glowing* when she got back in August."

"Yes, she was." The first time Lyssa had run into Marguerite on campus, she'd been dreamy-eyed, but the moment Lyssa had spoken to her, Marguerite had wiped her face clean of all emotion and rushed off, claiming she had an urgent meeting.

She let out her breath in a steady stream. Natalie apparently didn't know Marguerite was lesbian. *Interesting.* She recalled a conversation with Marguerite months ago, probably in April, about her reluctance to come out to the faculty.

Though she and Marguerite had both thought the students would be cool with it, Marguerite insisted the faculty, as a whole, were known for their vicious backbiting toward one another. In spite of her firm footing as tenured professor and department chair, Marguerite refused to open herself to their gossip, let alone possible cruelty toward her. Nor did she want to cause Billy embarrassment in the community. Lyssa had supported her decision.

She asked Natalie, "Just between us, were you aware someone assaulted Marguerite on campus the night she died?

"My God, no."

"Kyle and I came out to the parking lot and heard her scream. The guy took off then, and Marguerite raced away."

"Scary." Natalie pointed a fork at Lyssa's abandoned salad bowl. "Are you going to finish that?"

When Lyssa shook her head, Natalie consolidated the contents of the two bowls, popped on the lid, and packed everything in her shopping bag. "And I thought I was always ahead of you with the gossip. Who was the guy?"

"We couldn't tell. But that's why the police initially treated her death as suspicious." Did they still? Kyle would have told her if they'd made a final ruling. What was the holdup? Lyssa rubbed her arms, suddenly freezing cold.

"Are you all right?" Natalie asked.

"I just ... I worry Marguerite doesn't rest easy and there's more to come, causes and consequences we can't see yet."

"Is this one of your psychic things? Those premonitions you get?"

Lyssa hated that "psychic thing" of hers. "You're right, that's probably all it is."

"Lyssa Pennington, do not take your premonitions lightly." Natalie jabbed Lyssa's forearm with one manicured fingernail. "They've been frighteningly accurate in the past."

Chapter 5

The dreaded knock repeated, more insistent this time. Lyssa reached her fingers into her copper waves and yanked. It was Friday, and grades were due Monday.

She was twenty minutes away from finishing the last set of final exams, but to get this far she'd had to shut off her cell phone, silence her email and the ringer on her office phone, and position her laptop so it blocked the flashing light for her voicemail.

She hissed as the doorknob turned and the door swung open.

"A moment, Lyssa." It was a presidential command.

God, help me out here. "What can I do for you, Justin?"

Justin strode to her desk. No apology for interrupting. No inquiry about her progress with grades. "My email to you ten minutes ago, with the attached resumé?"

She hadn't seen it, of course, but she wasn't going to admit that. She scrolled through her inbox and opened the message. Justin had forwarded it from some woman's personal email. Her name was not one she recognized as affiliated with Tompkins College.

The subtext of the message was the woman wanted a favor on behalf of a potential candidate and had gone right to the top.

She displayed the attachment. "Emile Duval," she read aloud the name on the *curriculum vitae*. "Has he filed an application?"

Justin retorted, "You would know that better than I."

She stretched her shoulders and back while she waited for her applicant-tracking program to open, the one that organized all the formal applications, supporting documents, interactions, and determinations for the candidates. "Yes, he submitted five minutes ago." She checked the timestamp on Justin's forwarded email. Half an hour earlier. Someone wanted Marguerite LaCroix's job very badly, someone who knew Justin Cushman well enough to expedite the hiring process.

She bit back a sarcastic, *Friend of yours?*

As she read through the CV, Justin nudged aside a student essay to make himself comfortable on the edge of her desk and inadvertently sent a dozen others fluttering to the floor. She gritted her teeth.

"How's the grading?" he asked.

"Almost done."

"I want him here for an interview ASAP."

"He's impressive, isn't he?" And he was. PhD from Harvard to start.

"Emile Duval is a *star*. The kind of person we want to showcase as the new Tompkins College faculty. Quality in every dimension."

The document Dr. Duval had fashioned for them highlighted his extensive travel in multiple countries. *Six continents, seriously?* Fluent in six languages, including Arabic. *Wow.* A little thin on the publications for full professor, but his three years of experience as department chair made him a good fit for Marguerite's position. She found herself nodding with approval, even as alarm bells sounded in the dark recesses of her mind.

44

"Really impressive on paper." With another glance at the forwarded message, she asked Justin, "Who's the woman who sent you his CV from her personal email?"

"She called me this morning, introduced herself as dean of Humanities at Duval's college in the Bronx. She said she'd gotten my number from an old friend of mine, Sydney Shorey, who is president of Immaculata College Manhattan."

"Why did she circumvent our application process?" Asking that was a risk, but someone had to put the brakes on Justin long enough to check the guy's references.

Justin scowled. "She's rightly concerned his paperwork will be set aside, given that it's difficult to validate references this time of year. Colleges are posting grades and closing down for the holiday break."

"So we're bringing him in without vetting him?"

The president made a noise in his throat. "It's late morning on the Friday before the close of fall semester at most colleges around the country, my dear. We can go through the motions of calling the candidate's references, but chances are they've left the building." He chuckled at his own witty phrase.

"Wouldn't he have alerted them to the urgency and asked them—"

"Call them if you like." He accompanied the retort with a lofty wave of his hand. As he vacated his perch, another set of essays cascaded to the floor. "I've instructed the committee to fast track this candidate. I want him here no later than Thursday next week for the full two-day interview."

Her heart was in her throat. "My flight to the UK is Thursday morning."

President Cushman stood with his hand the doorknob. His voice was dangerously low-pitched. "Then bring him in Monday or Tuesday. Or change your flight." With that, he exited with a bang of her office door. Its window quivered.

She counted to twenty, long enough for him to turn the corner out of hearing, then let loose a string of expletives, followed by foot stomping and a good hard throw of her neon green sponge ball at the wall between her windows. *I will* not *change my flight.* With a glare at the closed door, she resolved to check Duval's references or die trying.

Kyle's mind was in turmoil as he left the solicitor's office. True, they'd built a solid case against his former employee Geoffrey, a case so strong Geoffrey would be a fool not to negotiate a deal for himself, rather than risk a costly trial. Still, Kyle was deeply saddened by the swift decline of the young man he'd once trusted as his second-in-command.

Just a few weeks ago Geoffrey had accosted him on the street, and he'd seen for himself the radical change in his appearance over the few months since he'd given him the sack. Worse—and the police had verified this—he'd been under the influence of drugs at the time.

His phone sounded with Lyssa's tune. He halted on the sidewalk to let a flood of office workers flow around him. Her greeting sounded nasal, as if she'd been crying. "Hi, darling, I'm so glad I caught you. Did Justin tell you what he's done?"

Justin. It figured. "No, what's happening?" He listened with growing irritation as she explained Justin's power drive to bring in a candidate without going through channels. "He'll get what he deserves, won't he? And it's not your problem, is it, love?"

"I feel responsible, though. I'm going to check every one of the references myself whether Justin wants me to or not."

"Lyssa, that's *not your job.*"

"There's an even bigger problem. Justin told me if the guy's not here to start his two-day round of interviews by next Tuesday at the latest, I'll have to delay my trip." Her voice rose in pitch and volume. "The arrogance! I will *not* change my flights."

"Sweetheart, you know as well as I do Justin has done this precisely to make you move heaven and earth to get the fellow in for an interview on the earliest possible day. Why not take charge?"

"What?"

His wife was brilliant beyond measure but, in many ways, unsophisticated. "Instead of giving the candidate options, declare he *must* come Monday. Tuesday at the latest."

"I didn't know I could do that. You're a genius. Thank you."

"You're welcome, sweetheart."

"Still, it's not like we don't have a good candidate already. Sure, everyone totally agrees the adjunct, Nicole Dutois, isn't up to the job. But why can't Justin be satisfied with Danika McGregor, the woman we've just had to campus? She's hugely qualified, and everyone loved her. But, no, Justin wants this *star*—that's what he called this guy, a star—who'll show the world the caliber of faculty Tompkins College is hiring."

"That's Justin for you. And he is your president." Truthfully, he wanted to take his old friend by the shoulders and tell him to get over himself.

"Added problem, the dean's assistant is so swamped with her end-of-semester responsibilities she can't help me find a venue and a caterer for the dinner. It's the holidays, darling. Everything's booked."

He grinned, delighted to have one piece of knowledge that could make her load easier. "I happen to know just the place. Perfect for a star's dinner."

"You do?" Her voice brightened.

"You'll have to look up the building's name, but think back to when my nemesis Rand Cunningham was vying for your hand. I recall one night you had dinner with me instead of attending a faculty reception with him, some obscure place on campus, catered by someone or other. It was a huge hit and you missed it." More important, Rand had been livid.

"Oh my gosh. The President's Dining Room in Westerlee Hall. That's *brilliant*. It's right here on campus, Kyle. No one can possibly have booked it this late in the semester. And someone will know who catered that event. Darling, you've saved our vacation in Cornwall. Love you. Bye."

Astonishing. Lyssa had welcomed his help. He pocketed his phone and grinned at his fellow pedestrians all the way to his loft.

Monday evening, Lyssa told Natalie Horowitz, "Thanks to my wonderful husband, everything is ready for the last, the ultimate, candidate's dinner tomorrow night. And I get to play hostess and eat all the wonderful food I've ordered." They were at Natalie's house for supper to celebrate submitting fall semester grades on time.

"Then I'm packing and taking off for the cultural delights of London and our family Christmas in Cornwall." While she prepared a salad from the ingredients she'd brought, Natalie sipped red wine and kept an eye on a pan of lasagna in the oven. "What's new with you, Professor Horowitz?"

Natalie hummed a self-satisfied tune. "Wait until I tell you who's staying at the Manse."

"Who? Tell me." This was just what she needed— lighthearted confidences, free of consequences.

"You *can't* tell a soul. Promise?"

Lyssa had so many details competing for attention in her weary mind she was in no danger of remembering it, let along repeating it. Nevertheless, she thumbed a cross over her heart.

"It's Vivienne." Natalie's wide eager smile fell flat at Lyssa's non-response.

"Help me out. Vivienne who?"

"Think celebrity, no last name."

"I know Adele. Lady Gaga. Halsey. No Vivienne, sorry."

"Vivienne is the hottest runway model for women of a certain size." Natalie shifted her shoulders as she surveyed her own generous assets. "Such as *moi*."

"And she's staying at the Manse?" Lyssa had serious doubts, but she was not about to spoil the fun.

"Don't. Tell. Anyone." Natalie gestured with her wineglass, the liquid swilling within millimeters of the rim. "She's here to get the goods on her husband."

Lyssa chuckled at Natalie's dramatics. "Come on, tell me. How's she going to do it?"

"I'm not sure yet, but I'm going to help."

Lyssa's forehead throbbed with a sudden headache. "So her straying husband isn't here with her?"

"Naughty hubby is someplace in North Africa— Morocco, I think she said—setting up for a big fashion shoot next week. *Their* fashion shoot. They work together. And they're married. To each other."

Lyssa squinted through her headache at the radishes in front of her and tried her best to thin-slice them in perfect rounds. Natalie was normally a strong, intelligent woman. She wasn't really planning to help this Vivienne person, was she?

"Say something, Lyssa."

"I-I don't know what to say."

Natalie sniffed. "I can see you don't believe me."

"It's more that I think this woman, whoever she is, is taking advantage of you. Or maybe even putting you on." Or maybe Natalie was just suffering end-of-semester insanity. Come to think of it, Natalie had been on the flaky side since she'd met Norman a few months ago. Maybe all those years of mourning her husband's death and building a serious new career had turned a corner, and her humor was blossoming. *Going wild is more like it.*

"It's the God's honest truth, Lyssa Pennington. We both got massages at the Manse Spa this afternoon, and we happened to use the sauna at the same time. I spotted the dragonfly tattoo on her right butt cheek and blurted out her name. I thought she'd have a heart attack. That's when she swore me to secrecy."

"But couldn't it be someone who knows about Vivienne's tattoo and is mimicking her?"

"The woman is six feet tall, her skin is an unmistakable shade of cocoa, and her eyes are amber-flecked with gold. There's no way some pretender could fake all that. *The* Vivienne is staying at the Manse, under an assumed name, which I will not share with you."

"And you're saying the husband of this supermodel did something—like had an affair or something—*in Tompkins Falls* of all places?"

"You got it." Natalie beamed at her, and Lyssa mumbled something she hoped passed for *astonishing*. She really didn't want to ruin Natalie's fun.

She gave her full attention to the salad while Natalie prattled on about Vivienne discovering an X-rated love letter from some woman, with a return address of Tompkins Falls. "Of course Vivienne has already destroyed the letters written by That Woman to her husband, and now she's on a mission to find and destroy the letters her husband admitted writing to *her*. While he's out of the country, this is her opportunity."

Lyssa licked her lips. Didn't that almost certainly involved burglarizing someone's home? "Why wouldn't she just divorce the guy?"

"Because as long as the letters exist, Vivienne's reputation could be ruined. She's incredibly sexy, you know, and she'd lose that power-woman mystique if her fans knew her husband cheated on her."

And getting caught breaking into someone's home would not? One radish rolled off the counter and Lyssa kicked it away.

"Plus, if she threatens divorce, That Woman can hold those letters over her head."

Did that make sense? Lyssa heaved a sigh. "Complicated lives, these celebrities lead." She stood back from the counter as another thought occurred to her. "Tell me she's not planning to kill this woman."

"Really, Lyssa? I trust this woman completely or I wouldn't have offered to help her."

"I wish you wouldn't." Lyssa tossed the knife onto the chopping block, scattering slices of radish and cucumber across the counter. "If you get into trouble, there goes your bid for tenure."

"No one is better at staying out of trouble than I am." Natalie splashed more wine in her glass.

Maybe she was making this up, but Lyssa didn't think so. *I can't worry about this now. I won't.*

"And as my reward, she's arranging tickets for me and a guest to her runway appearance this spring in New York City." Natalie laughed low in her throat. "I'm going to take Norman and see if he'll buy me one of the outfits."

Lyssa, having given up, nodded and smiled. She scooped together the vegetable slices, added them to the bowl, and grabbed for the dressing and salad utensils. "Let's eat."

The next evening, Lyssa was counting down the final hour before the star candidate's dinner when Kyle called to wish her luck as hostess. "My darling, you are so sweet. I'll give you the full report tomorrow morning, but right now I still haven't dressed or done my makeup, and you know how slow I am."

"I do, indeed. I shan't keep you. Have fun."

"Love you. Talk to you soon."

Having already consulted her wardrobe mentor and AA sponsor, Gianessa Cushman, she chose a navy knit dress with sequins across the chest. She took care with her makeup and stood tall in her strappy heels, but even her appearance in the mirror didn't ease the anxiety about the event.

It's not about you, she kept telling herself. Really, she just needed to suit up, show up, and do the hostess thing.

As she entered Westerlee Hall, the warm glow of wall sconces led her along a hallway toward the dining room, where walnut wood paneling and a pair of sparkling chandeliers set a formal party mood. At the sight of the beautifully set table, her shoulders finally relaxed into place. For ten seconds.

Male voices reached her from the end of the hall, and she looked back the way she'd come. A group of three surged toward her—Bob Winthrop, interim department chair from Communications; Rand Cunningham, interim dean of Arts and Sciences; and, between them, Emile Duval, the candidate himself. Right behind that trio came the remaining guests: three faculty.

Panic rose in Lyssa's chest. Everyone was early. She hadn't planned any appetizers. How long until dinner was ready?

As fast as she could in a straight skirt and high heels, she crossed the dining room and pushed open the swinging door to the kitchen. She was just in time to see someone wearing a dark coat and leather gloves slip through the outside door to a staff parking lot. The catering staff paid no attention to the woman. "Who—" Lyssa started to ask.

"Help you, honey?" The question came from a woman whose black pants and crisp white shirt identified her as a caterer. Three helpers buzzed around her, filling baskets with dinner rolls, plating rosettes of butter, and checking the ovens.

"Who was that, the person who just left?"

The caterer scanned the room. "No one here but us worker bees."

It couldn't be important. She put on a smile. "I'm Lyssa Pennington."

"Ah, the voice on the phone. Six besides you, right?" The caterer pointed in turn to each of seven bowls heaped with greens and colorful salad toppings.

"Seven of us, yes, and they're all here. Early."

"Relax, honey. We've got this."

"Anything I can do to help?"

"You just leave everything to us, honey." The caterer took her by the arm and hustled her back toward the swinging door.

Before the woman could push her out of the caterer's domain, Lyssa eyeballed the two bottles of red wine and two of white positioned on the counter beside the door. She'd seen one red and one white on the table, and that tallied with the six bottles of wine she'd ordered. However, it didn't explain the small wine bottle that stood by itself just beyond the four larger bottles.

She leaned closer to study the label. "This split of Beaujolais isn't on the menu. Where did it come from?"

The caterer shrugged. "First I've seen it. What does the card say?"

"Card? Oh." Lyssa picked up a handwritten card propped against the bottle and read it aloud. "To my darling Emile, from your beloved Loire Valley." Duval's resumé had ended with a clever remark about his hometown in the Loire Valley of France. "That's an odd way to sign a card." She flipped it over. "No name."

The caterer placed her hands firmly on Lyssa's shoulders and reoriented her to the swinging door. "Must be his wife," she said. "Isn't that sweet?"

"No, remember, she's—"

"Make sure your people have the correct name cards, honey. We don't want to mess up on the food sensitivities." A firm hand on her back propelled her forward.

The door whiffed behind her, and she smoothed the skirt of her dress to calm her nerves, just as laughter erupted from the other diners.

"Good one, Emile," Bob Winthrop said. Apparently the candidate had scored a hit with a joke.

Lyssa put on a festive smile and called out, "I can tell we're going to have fun tonight. Is everyone hungry?" As if this were a game of musical chairs, all six adults dropped into place. Two people slyly swapped name cards.

Conversations resumed. Lyssa circled the table, greeting each one by name.

Becca Dillingsworth had changed places with Bob Winthrop and now sat between Bob and Rand Cunningham. Lyssa wondered about that. Was the pretty mathematics professor, Becca, interested in killer-handsome Rand, or was it just that she was up for tenure this year and Rand was her interim dean? Regardless, both Bob and Rand looked happy with the rearrangement and all three had the right name cards.

The candidate and the two Languages faculty—Jeanne Marie Pruitt and José Guzman—were engaged in a lively discussion in Spanish. The only word Lyssa was sure of was *fútbol*, which she thought was soccer.

Emile seemed to be eyeing the red wine in front of him, and she couldn't blame him for wanting a drink after his two-day ordeal. How nice that someone had arranged for a bottle of his favorite wine. As she passed behind him, she touched his shoulder and whispered, "You have a surprise coming, a special wine." He nodded without interrupting his conversation.

Lyssa finished checking the name cards, gave a thumbs-up to the caterer standing in the doorway, and took her place at the far end of the table, opposite the guest of honor. Jeanne Marie had already reached for the bottle of red wine in front of Emile and was tipping it toward José's glass. Lyssa grabbed for her spoon. Crystal rang as she tapped her water glass. Six happy faces turned expectantly. *Showtime.*

She beamed a smile to each person in turn as she said, "To bring this interview for professor and chair of Languages to a conclusion, Tompkins College is proud to break bread with Emile Duval here in the President's Dining Room at historic Westerlee Hall. I understand you've arranged a special wine for him." She motioned to the young waitress hovering at the door.

Rand gave Lyssa a puzzled look.

What? she mouthed, but he only shrugged.

Duval placed his hand on his heart and tipped his head. "How very thoughtful. I thank you all." Everyone looked puzzled. Evidently the committee hadn't provided the special wine.

While the waitress poured for the guest of honor, the others helped themselves to red or white, and Lyssa gulped half her glass of ice water. Becca's happy smile as she reached for a bright blue bottle assured Lyssa she had done well to insist on Saratoga water for nondrinkers, like herself.

Rand Cunningham rose. "A toast," he announced. "We thank Emile for submitting to our two days of grilling. There will be no more of that tonight. We're here to enjoy a stress-free meal of delicious food and drink arranged by our tireless hostess, Dr. Lyssa Pennington." He bestowed a wink on her before saluting the candidate with a glass of his favorite Riesling. Lyssa knew from dating Rand more than a year ago that he'd probably drink a bottle all by himself and charm the caterers into letting him take another bottle home.

She slid her linen napkin from its college signet ring and draped it on her lap, reflecting that this meal would be the perfect end to a perfect interview. The consensus was Duval truly was an exceptional match for the position and would be a shining star for Tompkins College. If you believed the grapevine, he'd even dazzled the provost.

Always interested in the money story, she wondered how generous an offer he'd be getting from the college. Her own experience told her when Justin Cushman wanted a candidate he was willing to set aside conventional limits.

Emile was lifting his glass. Had he already done the ritual—sniffing the cork, swirling a smidgeon in the glass and then sloshing it around in his mouth—and she'd missed it? Maybe he'd skipped it, since the bottle had been open before it was brought to the table. Come to think of it, there was no cork on the table near him, nor had she seen a cork lying on the counter in the kitchen.

The candidate held his wineglass aloft, made eye contact with each person around the table, and tipped the glass back for a sizable swallow. He then smoothly followed his first gulp with a small sip and made a face.

Jeanne Marie, to his right, said something that made him chuckle. She reached for the bottle of red wine and offered to pour for him, since he obviously didn't think much of his Beaujolais.

Whatever witty response he'd been about to make died on his lips. His glass jerked out of his hand, flipped onto the linen tablecloth, and spilled its contents. His terror-filled eyes sought Lyssa at the end of the table. "You—" he croaked, his face contorted in obvious agony, before a convulsion sent his body crashing to the floor.

Lyssa sprang to her feet and stood rooted in terror at her end of the table. Though she couldn't see his body, she heard the thuds of ongoing spasms. *God help us.*

Jeanne Marie screamed, while José flailed his arms and shouted, "Help him, someone."

Rand had rushed to Duval's aid but retreated, backed against the paneled wall, his panicked eyes on Lyssa. The convulsions wracking Duval's body echoed in the wood-paneled space.

Bob bolted to the hallway, and the sound of his retching snapped Lyssa to attention.

She fumbled for her purse on the table near her place setting. While she dug out her phone, she said in a firm teacher voice, "Rand, I'm calling 911. I need you to call Campus Security and stop everyone from leaving the building, including Bob."

To cool-headed Becca Dillingsworth she said, "Tell the caterers to secure the kitchen. *No one* may leave. *No one* is to touch the little wine bottle."

Chapter 6

It was after midnight in London when Kyle awoke from a sound sleep. Lyssa's dinner with the star candidate should be wrapping up shortly. He chanced a call, but it went to voicemail. Evidently her phone was still silenced. Rather than leave a message, he trusted she'd see the missed call when she picked it up again and give him a ring.

Still, he felt uneasy, for no obvious reason, and wanted to stay awake until her call. He opened his laptop and got back to his audit of the Tompkins College email system. Tony had asked him to focus on Stan Block's communication going back some years. Kyle had gone at it as time permitted over the past week, and by now he'd seen enough to discern the pattern of threats to certain individuals, worded in a style that changed only slightly over a seven-year period.

Tony had said he suspected extortion, and it appeared he was correct. Until three and a half years ago, Stan's threats were characterized by the phrases, *I know what you did*, *I'll make you pay*, and *Don't forget, you owe me*. Sums of money were mentioned in about a dozen cases. Stan had been collecting money or coercing favors from employees at the college for quite some time.

Although Marguerite LaCroix had not surfaced as one of Block's victims, Kyle had enough data to prepare a report for Tony and President Cushman to use in ousting the man from the Campus Security force. For each target of extortion,

Kyle had recorded the target employee's name, email address, and whatever information he could extract about the alleged wrongdoing that Stan was exploiting. He'd also noted the sums of money and frequency of payment or, in some cases, the nature of the favor Stan had demanded.

He paused as he looked at the rough draft of the report his software had produced. There were really two categories—offenses against the college, such as falsifying grades or stealing computer equipment; and entirely personal matters, such as extramarital affairs. For those employees in the first category, the college president was certain to want the details. Most likely he would compare the employee names to those who'd been fired in the past few years and take special interest in those still employed by the college.

As for the personal indiscretions, Kyle could not in good conscience report the details. To his way of thinking, that would be a violation of privacy that had no bearing on the college's case against Stan Block. He quickly substituted the code Personal in the report for those matters. Should the need arise, he could refer to his raw data for further information.

The case against Stan Block hinged on the college policy every employee signed regarding acceptable use of the campus network. Kyle had been reminded of it when he'd noted a change in Stan's method of communication dating from three and a half years ago.

At that time the CIO had broadcast and paper-mailed a memo to all employees reminding them the college network services were strictly for college business and, as of the date of the memo, the college could and would exercise its right to monitor network use by any employee at any time. Each employee had been required to sign and date their commitment to uphold the policy and return it to the college for the employee's personnel file. The same requirement applied to new hires regardless of position.

Stan may have been a bully, but he was not stupid. He'd found a way around the letter of the law. He stopped using his campus email for his blackmail operation and started using his personal email for the job. However, he'd made the mistake of addressing his messages to his victims' campus email addresses. He'd made no changes to the wording or tone of his bold threats.

Not only was his use of the victim's college email address still against policy, it had made things much easier for Kyle's query to continue tracking and documenting Stan's ongoing extortion. From a policy perspective, Stan's switch to his personal email at the time he'd signed the memo was an admission on Stan's part that he knew he was in violation. With Kyle's report in hand, the college would have ample grounds for firing.

The only thing missing from his data collection was Stan's newest victims, the ones he'd added since the switchover to his personal address. Since the new victims might include Marguerite LaCroix, Kyle was determined to capture that data.

He modified his query to start with Stan's personal email within the campus email system, narrowing the results to messages containing Stan's characteristic phrases. The search would take time.

As he pushed back from the desk, a crick in his neck told him he'd sat too long hunched over the task. Worse, his eyes burned, and his forehead throbbed.

Eye strain again. Perhaps Lyssa and Mum were correct that he needed spectacles. He was, after all, approaching forty. He sent a quick email to Lyssa's sister, Manda, asking for the name of her eye specialist. She replied in under two minutes with the information. He chuckled. Manda had cc'd Lyssa on the reply. The women were on his case.

He tried Lyssa's phone again, planning to leave a cheery message for her to call him back, but her device gave him a busy signal. She was using the phone but she hadn't called him back. She had to have seen the missed call from him. Technically that wasn't cause for alarm, yet the hairs on the back of his neck were tingling. He checked his messages. Nothing more from Lyssa. No texts, no emails, no voicemails.

Unable to shake his disquiet, he called Tony Pinelli's direct line and was sent to voicemail. He left word about having hard evidence of Stan's blackmail activity in the past seven years and described the search still in progress for new victims. He added, "By the way, is everything all right there?"

He'd done all he could do for now, but it didn't feel like enough. Phone in hand, he paced.

In a moment of stillness after Emile Duval's body ceased its spasms, Lyssa became aware of her own noisy breaths and the trembling she couldn't seem to control. "God, help us," she blurted out loud, then silently prayed for Emile. Dreading the ordeal ahead, she prayed for her colleagues in the President's Dining Room at Westerlee Hall.

She sent a quick text to Kyle: candidate poisoned maybe dead, I need your strength.

Tears welled up and she wanted to give in to them, but shouts and wailing from the kitchen demanded action.

She left her phone on the table and cautiously opened the kitchen door to find Becca shouting words of reassurance to the four caterers, while two of them bombarded her with angry questions and another offered comfort to the youngest one, who was in hysterics; she had served the wine to Emile Duval.

"How can I help?" Lyssa said and was surprised by how loud and calm her voice sounded.

"Thank God you're here." Becca maneuvered behind her as if she were a shield.

Lyssa whispered over her shoulder, "Do *not* leave without me. Promise." Becca's fingers dug into her arm and she took it as a pledge of solidarity.

She held up placating hands to the four black-and-white-clad women. "Ladies, you're not at fault; we know that."

Fists relaxed. The youngest hiccupped, while the other three exchanged glances. The head caterer challenged Lyssa, "You'll make sure the police know that?"

"I'll tell them, of course, but you'll need to answer their questions. That's all you need to do, answer thoroughly and honestly. The college and I will vouch for you."

"It was that stupid little bottle of wine, wasn't it?" The head caterer spat the words, still belligerent, though she'd taken a step back from Lyssa and Becca. She stuck her hand in her pants pocket. Out came a pack of cigarettes and a lighter.

Lyssa shut her eyes. *It's not my job to enforce the Smoke Free Campus policy.*

"We didn't bring that bottle, Professor Pennington. It wasn't even on our menu, was it?"

"Correct, it was *not* on our menu. I don't know where it came from. The police will analyze the bottle and the card that came with it. What's most important here is that a man has fallen ill, the emergency medical technicians are on their way, and so are the police. We *all* have to cooperate. Can I count on you—all four of you—for that?"

She looked each of them in the eye, one after the other, but only three of them gave her tentative nods. The youngest had her face buried in the linen serving towel she'd worn over her arm to serve the wine. The woman who'd been comforting her told Lyssa, "I'll make sure she understands. It would help if I could be with her when she's questioned."

"Be sure you say that to the police, okay?"

The head caterer had sucked in a lungful of smoke. As she released it in a cloud above their heads, she nodded emphatically. "We'll all cooperate."

Lyssa thanked them. Becca coughed.

"Are they going to arrest me?" the young caterer whimpered. She looked about fourteen and wore braces on her teeth. Why had they chosen her to serve the wine? She couldn't be legal age to drink or serve alcohol. One more issue Lyssa chose to ignore for the moment.

She gave the girl a warm smile. "No. Just tell the police the truth as you know it. Nothing more, nothing less."

In the doorway, Rand called, "EMTs and police have arrived, Lyssa. You're needed in here."

"Coming." She told the women, "Sit tight, okay? No sneaking out through the back door?" This time all four gave firm nods.

Becca preceded Lyssa through the swinging door to the dining room. Someone had pulled Lyssa's chair away from the table to the wall farthest from the body. A white-faced Bob was hunched on it, staring at his hands in his lap. Jeanne Marie and José hovered behind him, speaking to each other barely above a whisper. Becca grabbed her own chair, dragged it next to Bob, and handed him a glass of water.

Their tableau of nervous quiet contrasted with the intensity at the far end of the table, where EMTs worked over Emile, shouting each step of their protocol, shocking him with paddles, carrying on static-filled communication with some remote party.

Rand hovered at the hallway door, and Lyssa headed toward him, "I'm needed for what?"

"Tell you in a sec."

Two police officers rushed in. Officer Peter Shaughnessy took an authoritative stance, hands on his utility belt, and informed the faculty, "This college is on lockdown. No one may leave the premises until we say so."

To Lyssa he said, "Backup officers are on the way. The caterers are where?"

She gestured to the swinging door. "They're expecting you, and they're not to blame for this."

"We'll make that determination." He signaled his partner, and Sam strode into the kitchen, the door whiffing shut behind him.

Peter touched her elbow. "You holding up okay?"

With a rush of gratitude that he was a personal friend as well as an officer on the TFPD, she answered, "I think I'm in shock. I thought your shift didn't start until eleven."

"Sam and I were called in when the campus went on lockdown. Lucky for everyone the students have all left for break."

He was right. This could be much worse.

Peter nodded toward the hallway. "I've asked Cunningham to stand at that door and direct traffic in here." Rand gave them a jaunty salute from his post. "State Police are on their way with the coroner and crime scene techs."

"Is he still alive, Peter?"

The grim set of his mouth was her only answer.

"Wait. I guess if the coroner's coming ..." A shiver passed through her. "So he was murdered? Poisoned?"

Peter cleared his throat, pointed unobtrusively to the huddle of faculty, and mimed locking his lips with a key.

"I'll shut up now."

"We'll need to speak with everyone. We can interview the catering staff in the kitchen, but they'll need to wait in here with all of you. I want everyone gathered at this end of the room, nowhere else, even if the EMTs leave ahead of you."

Lyssa was glad to see Peter taking charge. She'd heard he was studying for the rank of detective, and investigating this death would be a challenge. But he'd said the state police were on the way, too. Probably he'd partner with Trooper Hank Moran.

"You'll need more chairs," Peter was saying.

"They've moved some of the chairs from the table. Can we take the rest?"

"Yes, but leave the table exactly as it is. Name cards, water glasses, wine bottles, everything stays just as it was."

"Um." She gestured toward the cluster of faculty. "Except what's already been taken." Bob sat sipping his water, and a half-full pitcher sat on the floor beside his chair. Jeanne Marie and José were passing a bottle of red wine between them. Becca had appropriated the bottle of Saratoga water.

Peter barked, loud enough for everyone to hear, "See that nothing else is disturbed." Bob looked sheepish and clutched his glass. Becca shifted the blue bottle out of sight. José lowered the wine bottle from his mouth and ran the back of his wrist across his chin.

Rand, in the doorway, winked at Lyssa.

Peter wasn't done with her. "And we'll need a small room to interview your people. See what you can find."

Me? Peter had moved off to confer with Sam who had returned from the kitchen.

Maybe Campus Security could help when they arrived. She closed her eyes and prayed Stan Block wasn't on duty tonight.

There must be an anteroom, probably near the main entrance. Westerlee Hall, originally a dorm, had been renovated as a posh residence for visiting faculty and distinguished guests. Had Emile been staying here? She'd never heard the details about his lodging.

But first things first. She dragged Bob's abandoned chair away from the table and nearer to the knot of faculty. Jeanne Marie dragged José's chair. When Lyssa went back for Rand's chair, she steeled herself not to look at the activity around the body, but the smells and sounds left her too shaky to go back for Jeanne Marie's and Emile's chairs, which had been flung aside by the emergency techs.

She plunked down on the empty chair next to Becca, grabbed the blue bottle Becca held out to her, and took three glugs. The tiny bubbles shocked her mouth and esophagus and made her cough.

Rand straightened suddenly and announced, "Officers, your backup's here." He waved his arm to direct four additional Tompkins Falls police officers into the dining room. As the last one entered, Rand took a phone call and listened a few moments before wading through the swarm of uniformed men to address the faculty. "Listen up, guys. New York State Trooper Hank Moran is on his way. He's in charge of this investigation. He's given all of us an order. If you took any photos or videos of what happened here, absolutely nothing can go on social media. Or else." He glared at them. Everyone nodded.

"But don't erase anything," Rand continued. "The police will need it for evidence." To Lyssa he whispered, "Someone needs to tell the president what happened, from our point of view, and I don't want it to be me."

"I'll do it."

Rand crooked his finger at Jeanne Marie, and the two went after the remaining chairs. Lyssa scrolled through her contacts for Justin's cell number and sent a high-priority text.

Emile dead. Everyone else okay. Police here. Pls tell Kyle what's happening.

Kyle was at that moment on the phone with Gianessa Cushman, the president's wife, who had called him the moment Justin was summoned to campus.

"All I know is Duval is dead and the campus is on lockdown," Gianessa told him. "Lyssa won't be able to call you, at least not without a reprimand."

"Good Lord." His heart hammered in his chest.

"Justin is sick about it, Kyle. He had high hopes for Duval as a leader for language study in the new global economics concentration."

Kyle had no idea why she focused on that at a time like this. "Do we know if everyone else at the dinner is all right?"

"We just know Lyssa is the one who placed the 911 call and Rand Cunningham called Campus Security."

"That's good. They're all right anyway."

"Justin heard it was something in a special bottle of wine just for the candidate."

"Lyssa wouldn't touch alcohol. She wouldn't have drunk a drop of it."

"But the others might."

"But if the bottle was special for him ... No, you're right, he might have been in a sharing mood." In which case, some of Lyssa's colleagues could have been affected, too. "Did they say what poison?"

"I think it's too early to know. And no one has said if it was intentional."

"How could it not be?" Still, Gianessa hadn't said the word murder and he didn't say it either. They'd know soon enough. "Who had it in for Emile Duval, eh? You'll let me know if you hear anything else?"

"I will. Kyle, Justin wanted me to ask you. Did Lyssa have any concerns about anyone or anything as she coordinated the search?"

"Other than possibly missing her flight to the UK Thursday morning, no." Would she be allowed to travel if they hadn't solved the murder by then? If not, he'd go to Tompkins Falls and stand by her. The thought calmed him. Should he book a flight anyway? Perhaps.

He remembered then. "She was also upset no one was checking Duval's references, knowing how costly that mistake has been in the past. There may be some clue in that line of investigation."

"I'll communicate that to Justin."

He chuckled. "Good luck with that." Justin would not want to hear he'd made a mistake.

Her answering laugh was a clear middle-C followed by another note a fifth higher.

"Will you do something for me, you and Justin?"

"Anything. You know that."

"I want Lyssa to stay with you at your home for the next couple days. Don't let her fight you on this. I don't feel she's safe anywhere alone until we know who's done this. The killer may think she knows something that will identify him or her."

Lyssa's text to Justin Cushman had gone unanswered. Why? *Duh*. Probably he already knew.

A challenge from José returned her attention to the group of faculty. "Who would want to kill Emile Duval? He was perfect for us."

"I can't imagine, José," she answered with honesty.

José glared at her and opened his mouth.

"Enough." Rand cut off whatever nasty remark José had about to make. He held out his hands for silence. "Look, everyone. The police don't want us talking among ourselves."

"Why the hell not?" Bob snapped.

"Because it messes up our memory of what we saw and heard. They need to interview us first, before we start sharing what we saw." At Jeanne Marie's defiant look, he added, "Communications theory supports that."

Rand was a communications scholar, and his appeal to scholarship seemed to convince Bob and Jeanne Marie, but José jumped from his chair and blustered, "Who made you king?"

Rand stood his ground. "The president appointed me interim dean of Arts and Sciences a few weeks ago, and I'm the college's official contact for this shindig, which is why the police are funneling their orders through me."

"Then what's *she* doing here?" José pointed a fat finger at Lyssa. "Playing hostess for you?"

Lyssa lifted her lip in a sneer any sixteen-year-old would be proud of.

Rand stepped closer to José. "Shut. Up."

José flipped his fingers along the bottom of his chin, and shifted his chair until it faced away from the group, the bottle of red wine still in his grip. Lyssa hoped it was nearly empty. She took another swig of the Saratoga water and offered the bottle to Becca, who shook her head.

Jeanne Marie rose and began pacing, phone in hand, along the wall at their end of the room.

Lyssa whispered to Rand, "Are we allowed to use our phones?"

"Probably not, but I'm not fighting that battle." He sniffed the air. "Do I smell smoke?"

"The head caterer lit up a cigarette. Since it wasn't a joint, I ignored it."

He gave her a knuckle bump, and the knot in her stomach eased. So she had exactly two allies, Becca and Rand.

Keeping her phone low, between her chair and Rand's, she checked her messages for anything from Kyle. Two missed calls from him. Half a dozen texts from Natalie Horowitz who, Lyssa remembered, was on a mission with the woman claiming to be the famous model, the one who'd come to Tompkins Falls looking for damning love letters from her husband to his lover.

Make me laugh, Natalie. The first few bulletins told her: Heading to campus. We're pumped. V looks like Catwoman.

Lyssa covered her mouth to stifle a laugh. She read on: Me in black jeans, hair stuffed in hoodie. Leather gloves. Lock picks in back pocket.

Lock picks, seriously? The drama continued: Sneaking through woods to Admin. You're not the only sleuth, Lyssa Pennington!

Lyssa groaned. She'd warned Natalie not to do this. Had she taken it as a challenge instead? She could get in serious trouble for breaking into someone's office in the administration building. Besides the C-level offices and Information Technology on the first floor, the garden level housed Student Services, Alumni Relations, and Financial Aid. Upper floors had most of the faculty offices, including Lyssa's.

They must have determined the identity of Vivienne's husband's lover: V won't even hint who M is. Definitely a professor. I figure 14 possibles.

Rand put a cautionary hand on Lyssa's arm. "Security zeroing in on you."

She'd barely tucked her phone behind her when Tony Pinelli planted himself in front of her. "Speak with you?" It was an order, not an invitation, and she jumped to her feet.

"Easy there," he said when she swayed a little. "Sure you're okay?"

She wasn't exactly dizzy. More like disoriented. No wonder, switching from Emile's cruel death to Natalie's escapade and back again. She slipped the phone into her tiny clutch bag. "Absolutely. How can I help?"

"So, what kind of space do you need for the faculty interviews?" Tony asked once they reached the hall.

Peter must have filled him in on the plan. "Small. Is there an anteroom?"

They headed down the long hallway that had looked so romantic and inviting an hour or so ago.

She told him, "And we'll need some more chairs in the dining room for the caterers to wait. Sam is using the kitchen for their interviews."

"How many chairs?"

"Four." Actually, with Emile out of the picture ... She shook her head and let the order stand at four.

"You happen to know who lit up the cigarette?" he grumbled.

She chose her words with care. "I didn't see anyone light up."

He mumbled something that sounded like, *The heck you didn't*. When she didn't rise to the bait, he heaved a sigh and said, "Your people look like they're in shock. Maybe we can get some food for them. What's good?"

She thought longingly of the filet mignon, del Monaco potatoes, and colorful vegetables on the evening's menu. "Maybe chicken salad wraps and chips. Bottles of water, one for each person. Depending on how long you think this will take, maybe two bottles each. Big ones."

He relayed the request to someone, using his two-way communicator, before fitting a key in the door of the last room on the left.

She watched the operation, thinking of Natalie breaking into someone's office. Lyssa really didn't care which woman professor had indulged in an affair with Vivienne's husband. She cared that Natalie was jeopardizing her tenure. Maybe Natalie was in danger herself playing sidekick to this out-for-vengeance supermodel. How stable was Vivienne?

Tony swung open the door to the anteroom, and Lyssa shivered in the chill of the unused space. Actually, it was a relief after the stifling dining room. She told him, "The room where everyone's waiting is way too hot with all those people. If you can dial down the temperature, that might help the tempers."

Tony made another call while Lyssa examined the anteroom. Its dim overhead light showed a settee, two straight chairs, a small desk with a padded five-wheel chair, and two side tables with lamps. She swiveled the desk chair to face the room, moved one of the tables in front of it, and placed a straight chair on the other side.

Tony grunted. "Think it will work for Trooper Moran?"

She shook her head at him. "Peter Shaughnessy is doing the faculty interviews."

"Nope." Tony gave an evil chuckle. "The big guy's gonna make you all sweat."

"Thanks a bunch, Tony." She wondered how Peter felt about that.

Tony was already out the door.

She had just switched off the overhead light when the double door of the main entry burst open, admitting an arctic blast. She shrank back out of sight and watched as Trooper Hank Moran, a tall straight man in a Smokey the Bear hat, led the new arrivals. On his heels was a slight man carrying a black bag, whom Lyssa recognized as the coroner. Next came three men and a woman, all juggling cases and equipment.

The crime scene team had arrived.

Lyssa took deep breaths as they traveled the long hallway. After they'd vanished into the dining room, she made the trek back to the scene of the crime.

Kyle paced his loft, crazed with the powerless of his situation. His wife was in lockdown with a dead candidate poisoned during the festive dinner she had worked so hard to arrange. He should be at her side.

Instead he was stuck in London, restricted not so much by the demands of running Pennington Secure Networks but by the unfolding legal action against Geoffrey St. John, who'd cleverly defrauded his company of five million pounds, more or less, in the space of two years. Was the money really more important than being with Lyssa at this critical time?

Even if he only netted half from the lawsuit, he wanted that money for the family he and Lyssa planned to start, God willing, in the coming year. And if they had all of the six children Lyssa wanted, two and a half million, compounded annually, would fund their educations.

Perhaps he'd call the solicitor in the morning and see how much wiggle room he had in the proceedings.

No. Wrong. As his wise mum had told him on more than one occasion, *It won't do to be so responsible to others that you neglect your own needs.*

He reached for the phone and left word for his travel agent to book him on a flight out of London as soon as possible, spare no expense. His well-paid solicitor would just have to work around his absence.

While he waited for the callback, he packed a few essentials. Somewhere between the socks and the shirts, a what-if scenario took shape in his mind. What if Duval were somehow another victim in one of Stan Block's blackmail schemes and he'd *really* come to Tompkins Falls to do in the blackmailer? And, instead, Stan had turned the tables.

He wouldn't put anything past Stan Block, even rat poison. He and Lyssa were fairly certain Stan was the one tormenting Marguerite in the faculty parking lot minutes before her car plunged off the highway into a ditch. Kyle's mouth twitched with bitterness at the thought of their lovely friend's unwarranted death.

And now Justin's star candidate was dead. Two unwarranted deaths in a few weeks' time. Probably not coincidence.

Kyle took his musing to the wall of windows in the living area of his loft. Low clouds hid the tops of the taller structures. Just as well, as some of the newer ones were hideous. Yes, he could picture Stan Block keeping poison around the house for pests. Stan could easily have found out Duval was coming to Tompkins Falls, since the star candidate's identity and credentials had been floating on the desktops of the search committee members and a few administrators for several days. As a security officer, Stan had access to everything including Westerlee Hall and could have positioned a tainted bottle of wine with the others.

Have I gone mad? Kyle laughed at his crazy thinking. Duval had no assurance his bid for Marguerite's position would lead to an interview. And if his goal was to put a stop to Stan Block's blackmail, why would he arrive with fanfare and interview for a highly visible job at the college where his blackmailer was employed? It was ludicrous. And where would Duval find time in two busy days of interviews to hunt down Stan and beat him up or whatever he'd been planning?

Ridiculous as it was, though, Kyle couldn't let his theory go.

What if Duval's first objective was to find a plum job close to someone in Tompkins Falls—a lover, perhaps? And, second, to be rid of the blackmailer who had plagued that special someone? "That's it," he said out loud.

Stan had been victimizing Duval's lover at Tompkins College. Duval, star that he was, had come to town to save his ladylove from the bad guy. And what underestimated Stan? Exactly.

Sure that he was on to something, Kyle returned to his computer and reviewed the report he'd prepared for Tony Pinelli and Justin Cushman. Most of Stan's victims were men, not one of whom fit Emile Duval's profile. Of the women, Kyle rejected the much-older woman with gambling debts and the younger one who'd been stealing new computers.

He nodded as he read through Stan's communication with the next woman on the list. He'd found a match. A woman professor at Tompkins College by the name of

Melissa Rossini had been having a long-term affair with a man in New York City.

Salaries for professors did not leave much room for payments to blackmailers, yet Melissa had apparently been making payments for several years, always pleading for time to arrange for the money. Perhaps Duval was the lover and was co-paying the blackmailer's demands. Perhaps they'd both grown tired of the extortion. Or perhaps Duval was finally divorcing his wife and ready to move closer to his beloved. Or both.

How could he test his theory without looking the fool or damaging someone's reputation? He couldn't very well ask Duval. He was dead.

Kyle's phone dinged and he grabbed it. His travel agent had booked him in business class on a flight out of Gatwick late morning. He thanked her, finished his packing, and called Gianessa Cushman for an update.

Chapter 7

Two hours into the post-murder interviews, Lyssa and Becca took a bio break. Becca stayed in the ladies' room to make a few illicit phone calls, but Lyssa was trying her best to play by the rules. It was late enough in London that, she hoped, Kyle was sleeping rather than freaking out about his wife's involvement with another murder.

She was on her way back to the dining room, halfway down the hall, when an officer and two EMTs emerged from the dining room wheeling a giant black bag. *Oh, God, it's the body.*

She shrank back into a recessed doorway and tried to pray, but she was too rattled by the tormenting squeak of one wheel as Emile's body rolled past and by the irreverent banter between the first responders. How had this happened? Who had done this to Emile Duval? Why?

She gave in to tears for a moment and sank down to the floor. The little nook gave her some comfort and quiet, away from the squabbling faculty and the sounds of the crime scene team. But it wasn't enough. With no hesitation this time, she called Kyle.

When he didn't answer by the third ring, she knew she should stop. But then he was saying, "Lyssa, are you all right?"

"I'm sorry to wake you, darling. I just needed to hear your voice."

"I'm so glad you called, and I wasn't sleeping. I've been on with Gianessa getting updates from her."

She couldn't speak for a moment, too upset by the impact this was having on so many people.

Kyle yelled, "Lyssa, can you hear me?"

"Y-yes." She shifted her body so her back pressed against the solid wooden door. "When they went past me with the body a few minutes ago I lost it." She took a cleansing breath.

"I should be there with you. In fact—"

"Hank's interviewing everyone, and it's taking forever. Thank God Tony and Peter are here, too. It was hideous, Kyle." A wave of horror made her squeeze her eyes shut. "There was nothing we could do for him."

"I'm truly sorry, sweetheart. Justin is on campus somewhere. Besides being presidential, he's making sure you're taken care of tonight. And I'll—"

"Why do I need Justin taking care of me? What do you mean?"

Someone cleared a throat. She looked up into Hank Moran's steely gaze. "Oh God, no. Hank's here. Love you. Gotta go."

Trooper Moran held out his hand. "Your phone, Mrs. Pennington."

She bit back what she really wanted to say and delivered her lifeline to him. Her whole body trembled when he whipped it out of her sight. At least she'd connected with Kyle for a moment. And Gianessa was funneling information to him. That was good.

Hank told her, with a flash of compassion in his eyes, "I'll return this after our talk, Mrs. Pennington. You're last on my list. Stay with the others until then. An officer will make any necessary phone calls for you and your friends." She stayed in her cozy spot while he strode toward the dining room.

By the time he passed her going the other way, she'd gotten to her feet and regained some composure. Bob Winthrop was with him this time.

"Good luck, Bob," she said, but Bob hissed through his teeth at her.

She told herself that, in times of stress, people reverted to their worst behaviors. First José, now Bob. *I will not let them make me cry.* Only Emile Duval merited her tears. She took a few fortifying breaths before stepping out of her niche and walking with her head high to the dining room.

Rand greeted her with a nod and put his arm around her shoulders. "Hang in. You and I will be the last people called. Until then, we'll tough it out together. Deal?"

"Deal." Camera flashes caught her attention, the technicians still recording and bagging items from the dining table and surrounding area. So much had been removed she could now see the red stain on the ecru linen tablecloth where Emile's glass has spilled its contents. A wave of nausea made her fold her arms around her middle.

"Their quiet intensity is unnerving, I know." Leave it to Rand to put a poetic spin on the situation.

"No kidding."

"It was worse when the body was still here, believe me. I keep reminding myself they're working hard for justice for Emile."

"Good thought. I hope they get a fingerprint off that little wine bottle or the card that came with it. It was poison in that wine don't you think?"

"I assume so, but no one has really said." Rand searched her face. "Lyssa, I've got to know. Was it your idea to get him the special wine?"

"Not the Beaujolais, no. The menu called for three bottles of your favorite Riesling and three bottles of red, the Merlot. Nothing more, nothing less. When I got here, the little bottle was already uncorked and sitting on the kitchen

counter near our wine, with a cute little white card that said
..."

Rand's eyes had glazed over. "Didn't the committee order it?" she asked him.

"No. I chaired the committee, and that never came up. What did Justin say when you told him about Emile?"

"I texted him. He didn't reply. I think he already knew, and he's probably dealing with a million things."

"This has to be a PR nightmare." And Rand would know. His family operated a PR business for high-profile clients in and around New York City.

"Kyle just told me Justin is on campus somewhere." At his puzzled look, she explained, "Gianessa's been on the phone with Kyle in London, passing along information."

"So hubby knows you're all right." He glanced behind her. "Officer approaching." He sidestepped around her and silently rejoined the assembled faculty and catering staff.

When Lyssa tried to do the same, Peter Shaughnessy blocked her passage. She expected a scolding for holding a forbidden conversation. Instead, he asked quietly, "Any idea who did this and why?"

"I swear when I came into the kitchen someone was leaving by the back door. The kitchen people said they didn't see anyone. And the extra bottle was a surprise to me and to them. You've got to make sure they get fingerprints from the doorknob, the little bottle, and the gift card with it."

"So you think someone slipped in with the bottle, left it with the other wine, and slipped out?"

"Exactly, but it was set apart from the others by about a foot, already open, and had that sweet little card with it."

"Card?"

She described it, but he shook his head.

"Peter, I saw it. I picked it up and read it out loud to the head caterer. She saw it. It's got my fingerprints on it, and it should have prints of the person who brought the bottle, too."

"Whose name was on it?"

"There was no name. I even turned it over, looking." She recited the message on both sides, but Peter only shook his head.

Frustrated, she gestured to the table. "It's the size of a place card." But the name cards had been removed. "It had a little sketch of grapes on the face in the top left corner, purple grapes and green leaves and a curly vine. Our name cards were plain except for our name on both sides."

"No one's seen a card with a grape design, Lyssa."

She stamped her foot. "Wrong. The caterer and I saw it. Maybe she tossed it. Come on, we'll check the trash. It has to be there." She started toward the kitchen, but a deep voice stopped her.

Lyssa and Peter turned in unison. Trooper Moran darkened the doorway from the hall. "Mrs. Pennington, I asked you to wait with the faculty. Officer Shaughnessy, I believe it's my job to interrogate the witnesses."

Interrogate? She'd thought these were brief but formal interviews. Was that why it was taking forever?

"Yes, sir." Peter moved silently away but not before Lyssa saw a spot of color on each cheek. Hank and Peter had been colleagues and friends for years, so why was Hank reprimanding him? And hogging all the interviews?

"Dillingsworth, you're next," Hank barked.

Becca jumped to her feet and hurried forward, her eyes wide with fear.

Hank did an about-face.

Becca licked her lips, and Lyssa gave her a quick hug. "Just tell him what you know. That's all any of us can do."

"Thanks." It came out in a squeak.

Bob still hadn't returned to the dining room after his interview. It must be Hank was letting people leave once they'd been interviewed. Or maybe he was eating them alive.

She sank down on the chair next to Rand's. "Hank gave me the evil eye before he confiscated my phone. I think he's going to give me a hard time when he questions me. Any chance you can stay until I'm allowed to leave?"

He gave her hand a squeeze. "I will stay as long as you do, no matter what anyone says."

It seemed like hours later when Trooper Moran loomed in the doorway and summoned Rand at long last. Without her phone, Lyssa had no way of knowing the time.

Rand gave her a hug and murmured, "I'm not deserting, remember. Not until you leave."

She gave him the best smile she could. "Good luck," she told him.

The caterers had all departed. Trooper Moran had nixed the TFPD's plan to interview the catering staff in the kitchen. Instead, he had talked with the four himself in the anteroom, one after another, starting after Becca, and followed by the Languages professors, Jeanne Marie and José.

Now only Lyssa and the technicians remained in the dining room. Hunger assaulted her. Tony's effort to get them sandwiches and water had gone nowhere.

It was no consolation that she had her pick of the haphazard grouping of dining chairs. Besides, she'd been sitting too long. She righted the chair that had toppled over in José's wake when he'd answered his call, twenty or so minutes ago.

She busied herself arranging the chairs in a two straight rows. The exercise helped her to think logically about who had wanted to kill Emile Duval. The how was obvious to her; something had been added to the Beaujolais, but what? And how had they pulled it off?

She kept coming back to the little gift card, its message so deceptive and enticing. The killer had to have seen Duval's CV. How else could they know about his love for the Loire Valley?

The resumé had been sent only to the search committee members, with the usual reminders about candidate privacy. Ethics aside, there was nothing to prevent someone from forwarding it or carelessly leaving it out in the open. Still, didn't that limit the pool of potential murderers to someone at the college?

Assuming the mystery person she'd seen leaving the kitchen had delivered the Beaujolais, was that person necessarily the killer? It could have been a delivery person, but what kind of delivery person transported an uncorked bottle of wine? Therefore, the mystery person leaving the kitchen was probably the killer.

"It's a wrap."

Lyssa startled.

The statement had come from one of the technicians. The team began packing up their evidence and their gear. Lyssa kicked off her shoes and tried a few yoga poses, only to find there were very few she could do in her dress without revealing too much thigh. Not that the men were looking.

In fact, they were so unconcerned with her, maybe she could sneak into the kitchen and hunt for the missing gift card.

Using Bob's empty water glass as an excuse, she ambled toward the swinging door. No one stopped her. She pushed on the door, and it squeaked as it opened. Four men in uniform swiveled for a look. Peter Shaughnessy, Sam Pinelli, and two more of Tompkins Falls' finest.

So that's where they'd disappeared to.

Peter had a laptop open on the kitchen island. The screen was at an angle to her, but she saw he was filling out a complicated form. Probably a report. The other three had their phones in hand, thumbs tapping even as they eyed her.

She put on her most flirtatious smile and made for the sink closest to her, the small one near Peter on the island. "Sorry, just desperate for some water." She rinsed the glass and filled it, then struck a pose. "So how's it going, guys?"

Sam nodded and went back to his phone.

With a wink, Peter told her, "You're too late to go through the trash."

She didn't deny that had been her intent. A quick look around showed surfaces cleared of anything that might explain the candidate's death. "They've taken everything?"

"Yes, ma'am. Photographed, bagged, and tagged. No little gift card."

"Seriously?"

He nodded, his gaze back on the report.

"The trash is gone, too?" Another nod.

She noticed fingerprint dust all over the counter where the wine bottle had stood. "Did they fingerprint the doorknobs?

"Probably."

She had to trust they'd done a thorough job. "How long do you guys have to hang around?"

Sam's communication device squawked. "Yeah, Tony," he answered.

They all heard the director of Campus Security's words. "You seen Lyssa?"

"Yep, she's in here with us." Sam grinned at her. "Just getting a glass of water, she says."

Lyssa couldn't make out the reply, but Sam hooked the device on his belt and motioned her to precede him out of the kitchen.

"I'll take her." Peter's offer took his partner by surprise. Sam raised his hands in a no-contest gesture.

Did Peter have something to tell her or was he looking for information from her?

The dining room was now deserted and, as they started down the hallway, the crime scene team was maneuvering their gear through the double doors to the parking lot where a van stood open, exhaust pouring from its back end.

Beside her, Peter was silent. She asked the question that had been bothering her since Hank had chewed him out earlier for daring to talk to her. "So, why is Hank doing all the interviews?"

"Between you and me, the last homicide investigation he didn't get all the information he should have from the department. That made the job harder than it had to be."

"But aren't you studying for detective? I would think Hank would split the interviews with you."

She sensed him stiffen.

"Theoretically maybe. I don't know what's with him tonight, but he's ticked off about something. Let's not take it personally."

"Meaning he's taking it out on everyone?" When Peter didn't answer, she asked, "Why did he make me last in line to interview?"

"Don't know." But he'd hesitated before answering.

Panic rose, making it hard to breathe. She forced it down. "What did Tony want? Where are you taking me?"

"He wants you where he can see you."

As they neared the end of the hall, she saw it was Tony holding the door open for the crew. With only his uniform for cover, he must be freezing.

"Can I go back for my coat? It's hanging inside the door to the dining room."

"I'll bring it to you. You're to wait here until Hank calls you." He pointed directly across from the door to the anteroom, then hustled back down the hallway.

She rubbed her arms to keep warm. Peter didn't return with her coat.

Tony had disappeared into the parking lot after the crime scene team exited, letting the doors shut behind him.

She discovered the anteroom was not soundproof, but even with her ear to the door she couldn't make out the words Hank and Rand were saying. Probably if Hank were shouting, she'd get the message loud and clear. Probably she shouldn't be caught with her ear against the door.

There were no chairs and she grew too tired to stand. Another recessed doorway would have to do. She chose the nearest one, ten feet down the hall, and sank to the floor. With the door supporting her back, she stretched her legs out straight. Hank would have no trouble seeing her and, if someone wanted to get by, they could step over her.

"Kyle, why aren't you talking this over with Tony?" Hoarseness in Gianessa Cushman's voice hinted at the perpetual exhaustion of a mother of twin toddlers and the strain she must be feeling with her husband's college on lockdown. A second later she laughed those bright musical notes that lifted Kyle's spirits. "Silly question," she answered herself. "Tony's tied up with a murder on campus, just as Justin is."

"Precisely. And he'd be horrified I was revisiting the questionable lives of faculty to find a motive to kill our candidate Emile Duval."

"Why horrified?"

"Our agreement was for me to search Stan Block's emails for evidence of blackmail, not to find a killer, but I can't help thinking there's a connection."

She didn't laugh, but she also didn't ask for details. "Since Justin authorized you to do an investigation, I don't see the problem."

"True. However, if one of our faculty who's being blackmailed is also our killer, and other faculty were to discover we've been investigating their email accounts, it wouldn't go well for any of us."

"It the first place, it's crazy to think one of Stan's victim is the killer. In the second place, it's Justin's job to handle faculty complaints. He's good at it."

"Any idea when he'll be back home?"

"Last I heard Hank still had not interviewed Lyssa. She's last in the queue, and Justin will stay until he collects her. Why not leave your conversation with Justin until morning, and use me as a sounding board for now?"

He told her about sifting through all the blackmail victims for a paramour, someone Duval might care about enough to come to Tompkins Falls, perhaps with the goal of ending Stan's extortion once and for all and, possibly, convincing the woman to leave her spouse. "And it went horribly wrong. By showing his face here, Duval opened himself to retaliation from the extortionist." The ensuing silence deflated his ego. "You're not buying this, are you?"

Gianessa told him, "If you're saying Stan Block killed our candidate, you're grasping at straws. You know that, right?"

"But it fits."

"What paramour are we talking about?"

"Strictest confidence, Mrs. Cushman?"

"Strictest confidents, Dr. Pennington." Her voice was a mix of skepticism and impatience.

"We're talking about a full professor at Tompkins College who's having a long-running affair with a well-to-do gentleman in New York City."

Gianessa chuckled. "You really are very good at what you do. By any chance, are we talking about Missy Rossini?"

"Good Lord, how do you know about her affair?"

"Justin and I occasionally play bridge with Missy and Roger. They asked us to join their couples' league, but Justin

86

chooses to keep his distance from faculty groups. Roger's a banking executive, a wonderful provider for their family, and a dedicated father to their teen boys. Missy's vivacious and passionate about the arts, but Roger couldn't care less. She confided once that her twice-yearly trips to the city for ballet and museums might be a little more than just cultural in nature."

"She met someone?"

"Yes. She noticed Jack by himself at several performances and struck up a conversation. The friendship turned into something more. It suits them both."

Everything fit except the lover's name. "Does Roger know about this?"

"If he does, he's not concerned. But *I am* concerned she's being blackmailed. I had no idea."

Kyle's pacing had brought him to the cabinet with the brandy snifters and Courvoisier. He splashed half his usual amount and swirled the glass in the palm of his hand. He inhaled the aroma, took a sip, and sighed as the liquid heated his insides.

"Are you still there, Kyle?"

"Sorry, yes. You were saying you're concerned about her being blackmailed."

"I can't imagine where she's getting the money to pay for someone's silence. I hope she's not raiding the kid's college fund."

Kyle remembered the woman's habitual plea for more time to come up with payment. "She may be tapping her lover for it, and maybe he's had enough and wants it ended."

"Stop." Her voice was harsh now and demanding. "Kyle, I want you to let go of this line of inquiry. You're going in the wrong direction. At least I hope you are, and I don't want to see Missy hurt by it. She and Roger don't deserve an inquiry."

"You're *sure* she's not involved with Duval, are you?"

"Not unless Emile Duval isn't his real name. Her lover's Jack Something. I've heard the last name. It's nothing like Duval. I think he's Eastern European. Drop it, Kyle."

Kyle paused with the glass halfway to his lips. Anger was so unlike her. He wanted to agree, but he needed one more piece of information. "I will if you can you find out where she was tonight. Her husband, too."

By the time Hank Moran called Lyssa in for her interview, she was sound asleep with her head resting against the recessed wall of her niche and her mouth hanging open. Someone, probably Peter, had draped her coat over her. The building was quiet.

"Let's wrap this up, Mrs. Pennington." He pointed with his chin to the anteroom and reached a hand down to her.

She wasn't sure her stiff legs would carry her that far, but she made it. She took a seat at the small table, poured herself a glass of water, and drank it down.

"You look like you need coffee."

She shook her head. "I'm just thirsty."

With Hank's coaching, they stepped through her actions from the moment she parked her car in the lot. She answered his questions as completely and honestly as she could, but one of them had her stumped. She simply couldn't remember what she'd whispered to Emile Duval before dinner as she'd made her circuit of the table to verify the name cards.

After the third time putting the same question to her, each time louder than before, Trooper Hank Moran barked, "Just answer the question so we can all go home."

Lyssa scrubbed her face with her palms. "Hank, *if* I could remember I'd tell you." She looked him straight in the eye. "No offense, but if you'd move on instead of hammering me with the same question, the answer might come to me." The twitch in his left cheek told her he hadn't cared for her remark. She shook her head. "Why can't I remember?"

"Maybe you *do* remember, Mrs. Pennington, and you're just protecting yourself."

Lyssa felt her face flame. Was he accusing her of something? "Wrong. But you have a point. Maybe my brain's protecting itself from what happened after." Elbows on the table, she clasped her hands, rested her forehead on them and prayed out loud, "God, let this nightmare end." If she could just clear her mind ...

Hank slapped the surface of the table. "Answer the question, Mrs. Pennington."

Frightened, she jumped to her feet. "I can't answer it, Hank. I *don't know* what I told him. It was probably something like congratulations or glad you're here or something obvious. I don't remember. Please believe me."

His skeptical look annoyed her.

"Do you want me to make something up?"

With a snarl of disgust, he rose and towered over her. "Sit down."

She did. And folded her hands to stop their shaking.

"All right, let's go back to your conversation with the caterer in the kitchen. When did that take place and why?"

Lyssa swallowed her exhaustion and fear. Her throat was dry again, and she poured another glass of water and took a sip. "Everyone—the faculty and the candidate—all arrived together, minutes after I did, ten or so minutes ahead of schedule. As they came down the hallway toward the dining room, I hung my coat on one of the hooks by the door and ducked into the kitchen to see how long until the meal was ready. The caterers were absorbed in their work. Someone was exiting by the back door, pulling it shut behind them." She squinted. "I asked who had just left, and the caterer—the head caterer, I mean—said there hadn't been anyone else in the kitchen."

Hank scribbled something in his notebook. "*Was* someone at the back door?"

"*Yes.* I saw a gloved hand on the doorknob, the outside doorknob, pulling the door shut." Rats. If the person had worn gloves, there wouldn't be any fingerprint on the gift card. Just her own.

"Ah, so the door opened *into* the kitchen." Hank said.

"Yes." The significance hit her this time through. "Oh. Outside doors usually open outward, don't they? And there was no blast of cold air." She nodded at Hank. "Maybe that door led to a hallway, not to a back parking lot, as I thought."

"It's easily checked. What happened next?"

So there was a method to his browbeating. She was remembering more detail, and it helped that he wasn't shouting this time. Her breathing settled into a rhythm. "I asked who had just left, and the caterer said no one had been there. She said, *Just us worker bees*, or something like that."

Hank scribbled.

"Aren't you voice recording this?"

"Yes."

"Then why are you taking notes?"

"What came next, Mrs. Pennington?"

A pounding pain took up residence in her forehead. "Then I think I asked about dinner. Or maybe she just told me dinner was ready. Anyway, she hustled me back toward the dining room, but I stopped at the wine bottles and did a quick tally to make sure we had six, three of each."

"Why was that important?"

"Because we'd budgeted for six, three red and three white."

"Why were you concerned about the budget at that moment?"

"I'm an economist. I've never been asked to host a meal, and I didn't want to screw up."

"Why did you pick the wine to worry about?"

Because I'm a recovering alcoholic and I zero in on the alcohol? "I-I guess because it was in front of me."

"I don't follow."

"Like, when the caterer verified with me there were seven people for dinner, she finger-counted seven bowls of salad. She didn't open up the basket of rolls and count them. She counted the bowls in front of her on the counter. I was standing next to the wine bottles, and I counted them."

"And there were six?"

"Yes, between the wine already on the table and the four bottles in the kitchen, there were six bottles of wine, three red—"

"And three white." He nodded. "Go on."

She'd stolen a second for another sip of water. "Then I asked her why there was also a separate small bottle of wine on the counter. I hadn't ordered it. She said she didn't know." Lyssa rapped her knuckles on the tabletop. "No, sorry, she said it was the first she'd seen it." She nodded to Hank. "And I wondered if the person at the back door had brought it. I mean, wouldn't the caterer have seen the person delivering a split of Beaujolais and arranging the card with it?"

"Why Beaujolais?"

The question confused her. "I don't know what you're asking."

"Why did you say the small bottle was Beaujolais?"

"Because when I looked at the label, it said Beaujolais. And at the same time the caterer noticed the card next to the bottle."

"You hadn't noticed the card yourself?"

"Not until she pointed it out. I hoped it would have information about who'd sent the wine and why. So I picked it up to read it. It said, from the Loire Valley, not a person's name. She said—"

"Who said?"

"The caterer said it must be from Duval's wife and wasn't that sweet. Or something like that. And she took hold of my shoulders to push me out of her kitchen." She caught a half smile on Hank's face. "It really wasn't funny."

He shook his head. "So you left the kitchen."

"First, she asked me to check everyone's name card because some people had food sensitivities."

"Which ones did?"

Lyssa studied the clock on the wall. Ten o'clock, but it had said ten o'clock each time she'd looked. *Stuck like we are.*

But this was a new question, and she knew the answer. "José is lactose intolerant. Becca and I don't touch alcohol, even in cooked food. Bob requested low sodium."

"And you know this how?"

"It was my job to know."

"These people volunteered the information to you?"

"Not directly to me, no." She exhaled loudly and pressed her fingertips to her aching forehead. "It was already in the database for each search committee member when I started as coordinator. And it was an optional question we put to short-listed candidates before we brought them to campus. Nicole, the adjunct who interviewed, is lactose intolerant. The woman candidate from the Midwest, Danika McGregor, had nut allergies."

"And Duval?"

"He said he preferred gluten-free but it wasn't an allergy. The caterer said at the last minute they weren't able to get any gluten-free rolls for him."

"She told you that when you were talking in the kitchen before dinner?"

"No, I think it was in an email sometime late that afternoon. I mean, this afternoon." She puffed out her breath. "I'd have to look at my campus email to be sure."

"I'll need the entire record of your communication with the caterer and with each candidate."

"Understood. It's easy enough." Even if it would take hours to put together for him. She closed her eyes against the throbbing in her head.

He checked his notes. "So you came into the dining room. The other six were milling around the table. What did you do next?"

"I invited people to take their seats and noticed two of them switching place cards, so I walked around the table saying hi and making sure each place had the right name. And they did."

"Who had swapped places?"

"Becca and Bob. So Bob was now next to me, and Becca was between Bob and Rand."

"Draw that, please. Last names, too." He handed her a black Sharpie and a piece of ruled paper. She sketched the table and chairs and added the seven names by the chairs. The moment she set the pen down, he grabbed the paper and positioned it between them on the table.

"Who had determined the placement?"

"I did. I wanted Emile at the head of the table and me, as hostess, opposite him." She pointed with her finger. "He and I would have the least to say to each other. I wanted the two Languages people, Jeanne Marie and José, next to each other and nearest him. And Rand, as interim dean, next to Emile in case he had questions only Rand could answer."

"Why did you originally have Becca sitting next to you, Mrs. Pennington?"

"Because she wasn't drinking alcohol. Nor was I. And I was nervous about being hostess and I wanted a sober person next to me for support. And, no, I hadn't asked for her support or told her that's what I had in mind. Nor did she ask. When she took the chair next to Rand, I didn't want to make her switch back."

"Why not?"

"I thought maybe she saw a chance to get closer to the interim dean and maybe score some points. This is her tenure year and he'll weigh in on her portfolio. And, yes, a good hostess would have thought of that when planning the seating, but I didn't. Like I said, I've never been a hostess."

This round of questions had gone so much better her headache had eased, but she felt a little dizzy. She reached for the pitcher to replenish her water, but it was empty.

"Why were you hostess for this dinner?"

Her vision was a little fuzzy, too. *So tired.* She reached her fingers into her hair and tugged to keep herself in the game. "Because whoever had been assigned that role had airline tickets somewhere and bailed on the responsibility. By default as search coordinator, I was stuck with the job."

"And when you came to Duval during your name-checking circuit of the table, what did you say to him?"

"I said there was a special wine for him and I thought it was from his wife." She sat with her mouth open and locked eyes with Hank. "Wow, I remembered." She held up one finger. "No, wait. The first part's right, but I didn't add the thing about his wife because I really didn't know, and anyway he was talking with Jeanne Marie and José. I'd said enough."

"Enough for what? And what were they talking about?"

"The conversation was in Spanish, and I just know a little. It sounded like sports, soccer, nothing to do with the college."

Hank stretched his neck. "Why did you say anything at all to Duval?"

"Because he was eyeing the bottle of red wine between him and Jeanne Marie, and I wanted him not to pour that wine into his glass before the waitress delivered his special bottle."

"Why was that important enough to interrupt what he was saying?"

"He only had one wineglass. Everyone did. And I didn't really interrupt. He went right on with his conversation. He nodded to me and inched his glass back toward himself." She'd missed something. "Oh, you asked what I meant by 'I'd said enough.' That's what I meant—Emile stopped before pouring the Merlot into his glass."

Hank leaned forward and placed his palms on the table. "Any more detail you can provide, Mrs. Pennington?"

"Yes, but I have a question first. Why were you so focused on what I said to Emile?"

"Because everyone at the table remarked on the fact you stopped him from drinking the regular wine and made him drink from the small bottle. Which he did and subsequently died."

Her headache was back with a vengeance. She shook her head to clear it. "I didn't *make* him drink from the small bottle. Why did they see it that way?"

"It's simple, Mrs. Pennington." He ticked off the reasons on his fingers. "*You're* the only one who noticed the small bottle of wine on the counter in the kitchen. *You* called it to the caterer's attention. *You* redirected Duval from pouring the untainted wine into his glass. *You* motioned for the waitress to serve him from the small bottle."

She scraped back her chair rose on shaky legs, so dizzy she nearly lost her balance. "Everyone thinks I *brought* that bottle? To poison him? Everyone thinks I made an underage girl serve poison to the candidate at a celebratory dinner? So he would *die* before our eyes?"

Hank picked at the corner of his notebook. "The two Languages people think you brought the wine. At this point in our investigation, everything points to that small bottle containing poison."

"They think I *killed* him?" She was screeching now. "You do, too, don't you?"

Hank rose once again to his full height and stared down his nose at her. "Sit down, Mrs. Pennington."

"It's not my job to *kill* candidates, Inspector Moran." Her voice shook with outrage. "And if you think I'm going to let them scapegoat me, you are out of your mind."

Cold air rushed in around her, and Hank scowled. A door slammed shut behind her. Hank shouted over Lyssa's shoulder, "Mr. Cunningham, you need to leave."

She sent up a prayer of thanks that Rand had stayed for her.

"With all due respect, sir, that's not happening."

Hank gripped the back of his chair, his knuckles white. "Then sit by the door and don't say a word. Mrs. Pennington, I advise you to think carefully before you say another word. Now sit down."

Still on her feet, Lyssa broke out in a cold sweat. "Not if you're going to blame me for killing Emile."

Rand's strong hands gripped her shoulders from behind, and he told her, "Lyssa, no one's blaming you for anything."

"The hell they're not." She wrenched away from him and looked with panicked eyes at the two men. "Hank just said everyone remarked on the fact that I said something to Emile to *make* him drink the wine that apparently someone had poisoned."

"Well, you did." Rand shrugged.

She squawked, "I—"

"Except you didn't know it was poisoned. The point was, you knew there was a bottle with his name on it. We didn't."

"Jeanne Marie and José are saying I killed him."

"They're beside themselves that he's dead. They don't really—"

"Who brought the stupid little bottle?" Lyssa shouted. "*That's* the right question, not 'what did Lyssa whisper?' The caterer said it was probably from his wife. I know Mrs. Duval never showed up on campus, but she was traveling with him, right?"

"No, she wasn't," Rand answered. His voice came from far away.

"I'm sure he said she was. That's why I made the original dinner request for eight. And then she backed out of the dinner and I told the caterer we would pay her for eight anyway." Rand was getting fuzzier all the time. "Tell me what you know about the wine." She sucked in a breath to counter the light-headedness. Searching behind her for a chair, she touched only air. *Oh, God, don't let me pass out.*

Rand grabbed her around the waist, seated her, and pressed her head between her knees. "My sister Chrissie gets panic attacks all the time." He stroked her back. "Just breathe for a minute."

She choked out, "This isn't a panic attack, and I didn't kill anyone. Are you sure she wasn't traveling with him?"

"She never showed. And we all know you didn't kill anyone. *Right*, Trooper Moran?"

No answer, but the noise Hank made in his throat sounded more like censure than agreement.

Rand's voice soothed her. "Forget about him. Just breathe."

Her inhales and exhales gradually settled into a rhythm and grew quiet enough for them to hear shouting in the hall, a deep male voice blustering, "I'll do what I damn well please. This is *my* college. Out of my way." The door to the room was flung open with such force it cracked against the wall. "Moran, you're finished here. I'm taking this woman into my protection."

Lyssa lifted her head just long enough to see President Justin Cushman come nose-to-nose with Trooper Hank Moran.

"Best show in town," Rand whispered as he squatted next to her. She tried to sit up straight, but his hand on her back discouraged that. "Stay down."

So she stayed—bent over, arms crossed on her knees, chin on her wrists—and watched as Justin rattled off all she had done to coordinate the search and her over-and-above commitment when others bowed out of their responsibilities.

Hank challenged, "Then why the histrionics?"

Justin laughed in his face. "Professor Pennington may have panic attacks, like the one you've *provoked* in her tonight, but she does *not* engage in histrionics."

Rand put his mouth close to Lyssa's ear and whispered, "Oops, I think Moran meant Justin's histrionics, don't you?"

Lyssa clapped her hand over her mouth before a hysterical laugh could slip out.

"Look, Moran," Justin was saying, "Professor Pennington can help you solve this crime. If you want her on your team, don't hold her here like she's the criminal."

Hank's cheek twitched. Gradually, his face lost its hard combative lines. His gaze turned to Lyssa. A flash of remorse gave way to a frown. "Mrs. Pennington, we will talk again later this morning. For now, you're free to go."

Chapter 8

Kyle was watching the street for his car to the airport when he received a phone call from the director of Campus Security. It was seven Wednesday morning London time, and he guessed Tony was still on campus following the murder at Tompkins College.

Without his usual *Hey, buddy*, Tony started in, "I tell you, Kyle, Officer Stan Block is trouble and I need him off my force."

"Agreed. I hope the report I've sent you and Justin will help your case for firing him."

"Sure, sure." Tony's voice trailed off. He probably hadn't read it yet.

"What's he done that's made you call me at this ungodly hour?"

"He removed all the evidence I'd found in his office, that's what." In the background at Tony's end were thuds and squeals. Kyle imagined him dropping piles of paperwork from his desk and plunking himself down in a squeaky old desk chair. There was nothing appealing about the Campus Security offices.

"What evidence, Tony? Did I know about this?"

"No, you didn't and that's my fault. You'll see why in a minute. Here's the thing. Officer Block clocked into work right on time three o'clock this afternoon. Well, yesterday now."

"So Tuesday, the day our murder went down, Stan showed up to work on time." He wanted to hurry this along.

"Right. He did his job until around six o'clock. Then he locked himself in his office."

"Stan has his own office—walls, doors, all that?"

"Yep, always has, far as I know. Even has his own closet. Which is where I was searching a couple days ago when I found the evidence."

Kyle reined him in. "You searched Stan's closet looking for evidence of what, my friend?"

"Extortion. And stuff he took from Professor LaCroix's office."

"Ah, so he *was* blackmailing Marguerite?" Why hadn't Tony been up front about that after Kyle and Lyssa rushed to her aid in the parking lot last week?

Tony snorted. "He tried anyway. But knowing the lady, I don't think she'd ever fork over money to him. That's probably why he cornered her in the parking lot. Tried to scare her to death." Tony swore under his breath. "Sorry, bad choice of words."

"Though it could be the truth. Hold on thirty seconds, Tony." His car for the airport had arrived. Kyle hoisted his carry-on, tossed it onto the seat beside him, and confirmed his destination with the driver. "Okay, Tony, start with the evidence on Marguerite."

"I only copped onto it when she emailed me, which I didn't tell you about because I didn't want to violate her privacy."

"And you hadn't returned the items to her?"

"I just found them yesterday." The director's tone was defensive. "She was already dead,"

The reminder of Marguerite's death took the wind out of Kyle. "I don't believe I've seen her message to you."

"She told me Stan Block had stolen something very personal of hers. She wouldn't tell me what, and Stan denied he'd taken anything. Anyway, this Monday before anyone was around was the first chance I had to search. I found some boxes in his closet. You know those fiberboard things that hold a stack of paper the size of a book?"

"Like document boxes, you mean?"

"Yeah, gray ones, eight of them piled on each other on a shelf behind his coats. And where the label goes, in that metal slot on the front, he'd written just initials. The top one said ML, so I opened it. Sure enough it's Marguerite LaCroix's stuff." His voice had gotten tight.

"Tell me what was in the box." No answer. "Are you there, Tony?"

"Yeah, Kyle. It's ... this is hard. I would never have believed it about her. It was a packet of letters, personal letters, tied up with a ribbon. They were addressed to her but at a PO box, not her house, not her office."

Interesting. "You're thinking they're love letters?" They could be anything.

"That's what I'm thinking, but I didn't go reading them. And there was something else in there, too. A snapshot of a bunch of people laughing for the camera. They're at the ocean, maybe the Caribbean. The water's all shades of turquoise and purple."

"Marguerite's in the picture?"

"Yeah, she's got the short blond haircut, so it's real recent. And here's the thing. Some guy's got his arm around her, and he looks like a Boy Toy, if you catch my drift?"

Kyle was willing to bet the handsome young man was the group's tour guide or program director and, more important, Tony apparently didn't know about Marguerite's sexual orientation. If they were love letters, they had been written by someone else, quite probably one of the women in the photograph. "Nothing else in the box?"

"No." Tony's effort to clear his throat came out as a growl. "Wish I hadn't had to tell you."

"I understand. You know how much I cared for Marguerite. This doesn't change that." He heard a *whoosh* from Tony. "Tell me about the other boxes."

"Okay, first you need to know, as soon as I got that email from her about Stan stealing her personal property, I asked around a little. About Stan, like had anyone had trouble with him? Anyone have concerns about him? I got some funny answers that started to add up. Like the guy had been blackmailing a bunch of people for longer than I've been at the college. That's when I knew we had to have you dig into his communication."

"I'd been wondering how you came to suspect Stan of extortion. And now we have a report substantiating the history of threatening emails from him to more than a dozen faculty. I think when you have a moment to read the report you'll agree we've got him dead to rights, Tony."

"Except I just looked, and all the boxes are gone."

And that's what had prompted Tony's phone call at two in the morning Tompkins Falls time. "I see." That the boxes were gone was bad news, but only if Tony hadn't investigated the other seven boxes and somehow recorded their contents. "Had you checked—"

"Just a sec." Tony yelled to someone that he was on an important call and needed five more minutes. "Sorry. Yeah, so back to your question, I opened the other boxes Monday morning, just like I did the ML box. Seven different people, besides LaCroix."

Kyle puzzled about that. He'd documented at least a dozen. Maybe some were old business, people who'd left the college or quit their immoral conduct. Or maybe Stan had another stash of incriminating evidence somewhere else. "So, you opened all eight boxes, and what were the contents?"

"It's all stuff nobody wants to make public, let's put it that way."

"I don't suppose you took pictures of the contents, eh, Tony? For documentation purposes, of course."

"All I did was take one picture of each box, one shot looking straight down at the contents. And I named each picture with the initials on the box. End of story."

"Well that's good, right?"

"Yep." Tony laughed, an evil chuckle. "And then I put the boxes back in exactly the opposite order, so Marguerite's ended up on the bottom. Figured sooner or later Stan'd realize somebody'd been messing around with his stash of dirty little secrets. Pretty sure that's what happened."

Kyle would have preferred that Tony confiscate the boxes and call Stan into his office for an accounting. But Tony had preferred to throw it in Stan's face and see what happened. Well, they'd lost the evidence, that's what had happened.

He summarized for himself, "Stan came to work Tuesday, the day after you played your trick, which was also the day the candidate Emile Duval died, correct?"

"Correct. Stan came in at three o'clock, his usual time, and in minutes he was spitting nails, soon as he hung up his coat. That's why I stayed around later than my usual five o'clock, to keep an eye on him. So I was still here at six fifteen, when the call came from Westerlee Hall about Duval going down."

"Was Stan around when the call came in?"

"Nope, he had slipped out of his office some time between six and six thirty. One of the guys told me that instead of taking his LL Bean lunch cooler, like he usually does when he's going for his supper, Stan was carrying a duffel stuffed full of something. So I figured that's when he moved the boxes someplace safer."

"You don't suppose he had a bottle of poison wine in that duffel, Tony?" A Campus Security officer would have no trouble getting into the kitchen where the caterers were preparing the meal.

"What? No way. Why would he want to mess with a candidate for a faculty job?"

Kyle hadn't told Tony his theory about Duval coming to Tompkins College to stop Stan Block's extortion, but now he wondered if he'd been right after all. "I can't imagine, but the timing is certainly interesting. Between five thirty and six, probably closer to six, is when someone dropped off the bottle of poisoned wine for the candidate's dinner. When your call came from Westerlee Hall at six fifteen Duval was already dying or dead. And Stan was out of his office carrying a duffel."

"I don't see a connection. If you ask me, Stan left campus with the boxes in his duffel and stashed them somewhere. My dispatcher said Stan came back around seven, empty-handed. Nobody saw him after that."

It wasn't quite adding up. "Okay, Tony. Listen, I need to see that photo you took of the ML box."

"Sure thing, pal, but it goes nowhere, right? No point in smearing the good lady's reputation."

"It goes nowhere, I agree." *Unless there's a connection to the murder.* Kyle's email dinged with the arrival of the photo.

Wrapped in the thick terry robe she'd found in the guest bathroom, Lyssa entered the Cushman's kitchen at five thirty Wednesday morning and did a double-take. She'd smelled coffee from her lower-floor guest suite and assumed Gianessa was up early. Instead, it was Justin pouring the first cup for himself. The house was otherwise silent.

"When do the twins wake up?" she whispered.

"Soon." His wink cautioned her, and she put a finger to her lips in a *Shhh* gesture. Justin crooked his finger at her. "My office."

She nodded eagerly. She had questions only he could answer, and she was curious how he was handling the fallout from the murder on campus.

With the office door shut behind them, Justin gestured to a pair of chairs facing east, out to Chestnut Lake. Though the moon was not in their sight, it cast enough brightness on the water for her to make out the full twenty miles of shoreline, from the public park at the north end of the lake, to the southernmost end. "You have the best view up here." Lyssa sank into her chair, mesmerized by the churning silvery water. Whitecaps told her the south wind hadn't let up from last night.

Justin pointed to the northeast corner of the lake where a cluster of gumdrop-shaped islands, unique to Chestnut Lake, huddled in the predawn mist. "Did you know Joel owns the islands now?"

Lyssa had no idea why Justin had brought that up. "He's not planning to develop them, right?"

"Never." Justin's brusque tone dismissed the insult. The Cushmans loved their lake and their property on its shores. "They'll be protected as forever wild."

They gazed solemnly at the twenty or more evergreen-covered mounds jutting from the water, some thirty feet high, none of them larger than an acre. It was said only one or two offered any kind of landing for a boat, and, if you believed the rumors, one island somewhere in the middle had a tiny sand beach.

Lyssa, not a boater, had never wanted to venture into the labyrinth. What she did want were some answers. Before she could speak, though, Justin asked, "How's your examination of Emile Duval's CV going? Have you found any clues to his murderer?"

"How did you know I was digging into his resumé ?" She'd awakened two hours ago and used the iPad provided with the suite to log into her campus network account, with the goal of finding a clue to Duval's murderer in his CV.

He chuckled. "I know *you*, my dear. And I'm certain that's one line of questioning Hank Moran will want to pursue. How far have you gotten?"

"You won't like the answer. I started with his publications, thinking one of his co-authors might have had it in for him. Turns out every publication is bogus."

Justin made a strangled noise in his throat.

"It's really clever how he did it. The journal names are valid, and the volume and issue date are valid, but there are no articles in those issues with those titles or authors. So that was a dead end for finding the murderer, except it tells us Emile wasn't legitimate. I tried to email the people he used as professional references, but the names don't match up with the institutions. So far only one of them looks like a real person but at a different college. I suspect they're all fake."

"Thank you for not saying *I told you so*."

She laughed. It felt good to be working with Justin on this. Normally she walked on eggshells around him, her ultimate boss. She dared to ask, "How are you handling the media and the internal repercussions?"

"I'm leaving the news channels to my PR person, Betsy, who will earn a fat bonus for her tireless effort and creative genius. Her story is the death was probably due to poison in a bottle of wine Duval and his wife had brought with them and that he'd drunk with her on a one-hour break between his daylong interview and the dinner at Westerlee Hall."

"Funny she didn't die, too. I thought she didn't come with him."

"She came."

Lyssa stared at him. Rand had been certain she hadn't come. If the wife being in Tompkins Falls was the party line she could live with it. "You know he didn't take a break, right?"

"I realize that, but the first story on the airwaves determines the ensuing conversation. Those minor tweaks Betsy is making to the facts will buy us time to determine the truth."

Lyssa had never thought about it like that. "What are you planning to do about Marguerite's replacement now that our star candidate is dead?"

"You're probably not surprised we're poised to offer the position to Danika McGregor, whom everyone liked. That's pending Hank Moran's thorough review of her as a possible suspect."

"Good. Justin, what can you tell me about that very first contact you had, the person who sent Emile's CV?"

"I didn't know the woman who called me. A couple hours ago I checked the website for the college she said she was from, and there's no one with that name at the college."

"Didn't she claim to know some other woman you knew? A college president?"

"She claimed she'd gotten my name from Sydney Shorey at Immaculata College. I called Syd earlier, too. She's a personal friend of mine and an advisor to me. She's never heard of anyone by that name. Nor did she know Emile Duval."

Syd must be a very close friend to have answered a call from him in the middle of the night. "So, the original call to you was pure fiction."

Justin nodded, his gaze on the lake. "I'd like to know why she chose Syd Shorey's name as the hook. She must have known Syd somehow. Or known her connection to me."

Lyssa narrowed her eyes. His method of digging into every point of connection had probably served him well in the years he'd run his own venture capital business. He'd probably had to do a lot of probing in pursuit of his billions.

He leaned closer to her and lowered his voice. "I've done something else Moran disapproves of."

She raised her eyebrows at him.

"I've posted Duval's headshot to my higher-education leadership circles with an urgent request for information about the individual who called himself Emile Duval, seeking a leadership position in languages in TC's cutting-edge global business curriculum."

Justin was really into this. "That's brilliant. When did you do that?"

"Shortly after you and I arrived home from the murder scene, as soon as Hank told me Duval's contact information was inaccurate."

"Wait. What?" Was their candidate a total fraud?

Justin had twisted in his chair, his face turned to the door. A smile of delight stole over his face. She heard it, too, the sweet sound of small children's voices.

She laughed softly. "The twins are up."

Justin asked her, "Is there more we can do with his headshot?"

"Definitely. I'll get right on it."

He held up both hands. "No. First, you'll eat breakfast with us. Kyle will be cross if we don't feed you properly and, forgive me for saying so, but lately you've looked too thin."

Her heart sank. She had no comeback for that.

"Frankly," he went on, "it's how you looked when you first came to Tompkins Falls. Emaciated, and still using pot to deal with life."

That hurt. But he was partly right. She was an unhealthy size four and the same weight she'd been when she entered rehab. She hadn't intended to lose twenty-five pounds; it had happened gradually over the past year, but mostly this semester. Dealing with one murder after another while newly married to a man rarely on the same continent as her had taken their toll. But that was her life now, and she needed to handle it a lot better than she had been.

"I'm not doing well with the stress, Justin, or the violence. Yoga is helping and Gianessa is a good teacher, but I'm a slow learner. Can I ask you one more question before breakfast?" He gave her a nod. "Did you ever speak directly with Duval?"

"I daresay I was the first person to do so." Justin's chin rose so his patrician profile was on display for her. "We had breakfast together Monday morning and talked, not about the position *per se*, but about his take on our global business curriculum and my desire for the Languages department to play a major role in it. He had a slew of good ideas about raising awareness with global corporations about the value of language-savvy new hires. Duval, if that's even his name, had a strong business sense, a good command of the market our graduates will be walking into. He backed up his ideas with interesting examples from fashion and retail."

"Really, fashion and retail?"

A knock sounded at the door. "Coming," he called. In a quieter voice he asked, "Lyssa, if Duval's CV is, indeed, the masterpiece of fiction your investigation so far suggests, what do you make of that?"

"Either he, or someone he hired, knew exactly what you wanted to hear to bring him in for an interview and make him an offer."

Justin was nodding now, tapping his empty mug with both index fingers as he cradled it in his hands. ""I have a sense I've met him before. And I agree he wanted the interview. I doubt he cared about the job." Without a word of explanation, he stood and motioned Lyssa ahead of him out of the study.

Kyle slept for an hour or two after he'd consumed British Air's quite decent eggs benedict. On waking, he tried one more time to contact Lyssa, but her phone went directly to voicemail, the way it had ever since he'd talked with her last evening when the body was removed from Westerlee Hall. A seed of worry took hold. Should he call the Cushmans' landline?

The ensuing internal debate convinced him of three things. One, he knew beyond any doubt she was safe with Justin and Gianessa and would remain so until he picked her up there later today. Two, a family with two rambunctious toddlers didn't need him interrupting their hectic day. And three, Lyssa would somehow be in touch with him if she needed him for anything.

He opted to send an email to her personal account letting her know his flight information and that he'd booked a car from the Syracuse airport to Tompkins Falls. Just before he sent it, he added a request for her to acknowledge the message.

That done, he opened his laptop and gave his attention to the photograph Tony had sent. In full screen mode, he examined the top-down view of Stan Block's stash of evidence against Professor Marguerite LaCroix. The packet of letters was, indeed, tied with a pale purple ribbon, and it appeared all the items in the packet were uniform in size, each likely to be a handwritten letter on fine stationery, rather than an assortment of quick notes and greeting cards. There looked to be nearly a dozen items in all. Assuming the correspondence was between Marguerite and someone she'd just met on her summer trip to Brittany, they'd exchanged letters at least biweekly.

Only the top item in the packet was visible, addressed to Marguerite LaCroix, not to Mrs. William Warren or Professor LaCroix or any other variation on her name. As Tony had said, the address was a post office box in Tompkins Falls. Unfortunately, the other piece of evidence visible in Tony's photo—the snapshot of the eight vacationers at the shore—covered the return address label of the letter.

He studied the stamp's cancellation mark. The date was the same week Marguerite had died. The location of the sending post office was, according to a postal code lookup site, someplace called Old Westbury in New York State. Wikipedia told him the town was deemed the wealthiest on Long Island and was within commuting distance of New York City. He whistled through his teeth at the median home price.

"Everything all right, sir?" the cabin attendant asked him.

Kyle looked up to see alarm on the uniformed woman's face. He *had* whistled rather loudly and now saw that his hand was pressed over his heart. "Sorry, yes." He pulled out a smile for her. "Photo of a friend's who's just passed. Perhaps some tea when you have a moment?"

He declined her offer of a scone to go with his tea and gave his attention back to the photo of the eight smiling vacationers. The photographer had arranged them in two tiers on the shore. There was Marguerite, front and center next to a rakishly handsome dark-haired man who'd slung his arm around her shoulders. Two blond women flanked them.

The exceptionally thin blond on the left posed with one hand on her hip, her head at an angle. Might be a model. In contrast, the forty-something blond on the right looked like a professional sportswoman with her muscular legs and form-fitting shorts. Perhaps a cyclist.

The couple centered in the back row were bookish, both wearing spectacles, she with the palest of British skin, while the clean-shaven man beside her, probably her husband, kept a close eye on her. Watching for sunburn? A curvy woman to the man's right had skin the same chocolate color as Tompkins College's provost, and she sported a wide-brimmed white hat that shaded her face and bare shoulders.

In spite of the shadow over her face, he saw she was flirting with the camera. Or with the picture-taker.

"Your tea, sir. I'm glad to see you smiling now," the attendant told him as she nudged aside Kyle's laptop to make room for the tray laden with a proper teapot, creamer, sugar bowl, and china mug. "Anything else?"

He shook his head. Back to the photo for one last detail, he squinted at the chap on the far left in the back row, distinguished by a full gray beard and bushy eyebrows. Kyle was fairly sure he was a mystery author from Scotland whose name he couldn't recall. Perhaps the woman next to him with the white skin was the author's wife and the chap to her right was simply admiring her. Might be a love triangle there. He shook his head and resisted the temptation to run the author's face through an image-match search. Instead, he stashed his laptop, poured a cuppa, and turned his attention to the legal thriller he'd picked up at the airport.

After breakfast and a fascinating conversation with the Cushmans' toddlers, Lyssa showered and shampooed away the horrors of Tuesday night. She emerged to find on the bed her own laptop, a few changes of clothes, and her pink down puffer jacket. On top was a note from her sister, Manda. "Sam says your apartment is safe and secure. Thought you could use these. Good luck with Hank."

Manda must have gone with Officer Pinelli to the apartment. *How sweet.* She reached automatically to send a thank-you text but growled in frustration. Her phone was still in Hank's possession. He had said he'd return it to her after her interview, but her meltdown must have overturned that.

She set up her laptop, used the Cushman's secure connection to log into her campus email, and got to work for Hank assembling the record of her communication with Emile Duval. Almost three hours into it, she spotted some information she hadn't seen in her headlong rush to bring Duval to Tompkins Falls for his two-day interview.

A lengthy chain of messages between interim dean Rand Cunningham's assistant and Emile implied the candidate was bringing his wife, Jacqueline, with him. The second-to-last message from Emile said, "*We'll be staying at a resort in Canandaigua. Jacqueline will not participate in any events at the college but will, instead, arrange a tour for herself of the campus and nearby housing.*"

So, she'd been correct that Jacqueline had been planning all along to accompany her husband, and that's why Lyssa had assumed she'd be coming to the final dinner. She dug into the preceding messages and saw that Emile had never acknowledged the fact Rand's assistant had already booked the Duvals into the Manse Inn and Spa. The assistant had replied to his news about Jacqueline's agenda and the Canandaigua resort by graciously asking Emile to clarify if Jacqueline would join him and the committee at the closing dinner Tuesday evening.

"Solo for dinner," had been the terse response on Tuesday late morning. The assistant had at that point forwarded the entire string of messages to Lyssa without comment. *They couldn't pay me enough to do her job.*

Lyssa tapped her fingernail against the edge of her laptop. Had Emile treated all the staff at the college with the same dismissive tone? He hadn't been openly rude to Lyssa, but he had created more work for her at several points in the process, without explanation or apology. In the case of cancelling Jacqueline's place at dinner at the last minute, she had cringed at having to tell the caterer about the reduced headcount, and the college had eaten the cost for the wasted food.

Had Duval angered someone else in Tompkins Falls enough to kill him? Okay, that was a long shot, but there was something important in the exchange she'd just read, something she didn't want to overlook. She just couldn't get a handle on it.

She finished her compilation for Hank an hour later, issued a print command to the guest suite's printer. Bundled in her puffer, she wandered onto her private patio. The wind had died down now and the waters of Chestnut Lake reflected the intense blue of the sky. A pair of cardinals chittered on their perch in the evergreen to her left. "Hi guys," she said. "I am so glad that job's done." Hank would have to be satisfied with what she'd put together for him.

By the time the printer went quiet, Lyssa realized what she'd nearly missed. "So, guys," she asked her feathered friends, "what do you think Jacqueline Duval was up to while her husband was dying from poisoned wine at his final dinner? And where do you think she is now?"

Chapter 9

With her hand reaching for the front door of the Chestnut Lake Café, Lyssa took a moment to gather her courage. *God, help me out here.* The moment she yanked the handle, the warmth and good breakfast smells of Lynnie's rushed to enfold her.

At a table in the back corner, Trooper Moran was thanking a waitress for delivering a carafe and two mugs. He looked up as Lyssa's entry set off jingle bells. No smile, no frown, just a steady assessing look.

I can do this. Keeping the promise of fresh coffee uppermost in her thoughts, she zigzagged among the filled tables until she reached the one Hank had staked out. He rose until he towered over her. She gulped. *It's just Hank.*

Although her breathing faltered, she kept her gaze steady and stuck out her hand to meet his firm shake. "I apologize for the meltdown last night, Trooper Moran. It won't be repeated."

"Good." With a gentle squeeze he released her hand.

"Okay then." She shrugged out of her pink puffer, rested it on the back of her chair, and slid onto the seat. "Where do we start?" she asked.

Hank poured them coffee. A frenzy of steam above the liquid cautioned her it was scalding. She set the mug aside and gave him her full attention.

When he finished pouring half a pitcher of what looked like skim milk into his coffee, he remarked, "I understand from Justin some of the information in Duval's resumé was false."

She nodded and filled him in on her early-morning investigation.

"Good work. Our efforts to verify his identity and communicate with next of kin have so far failed. Evidently, Emile Duval was not even his name."

Lyssa paled. "Who was he really?"

"We don't know yet, and we need your help with this in a very specific way."

She rubbed the fabric of her jeans to stop the trembling in her hands. "Okay, but first, how do you know he wasn't Emile Duval?"

"We found the driver's license, the one he used when he checked into the resort in Canandaigua, on the body. Forged. No one has a New York State license in that name or at that address or with that number."

"What about his credit card?"

"He paid cash up front, which is why they insisted on seeing his driver's license."

"But didn't he give a credit card number to hold the reservation?"

"No reservation. We're thinking he and his wife checked online for availability and just showed up. All of that, plus the work you've done so far, corroborates he was perpetrating an elaborate fiction. We don't know why. First question: do candidates provide a social security number as part of the application process?"

She had to think about that. "When I applied at the college, they only asked for it when they made the offer, so I doubt it, but I'll check." Without her phone, she resorted to a pen from her tote and the napkin in front of her to jot a reminder. "Didn't he have to use a passport for his flight?"

"No one named Duval took a flight to any of our airports. The hotel says they arrived in a private car. We checked limos serving airports in Rochester, Syracuse, Elmira, and Buffalo. None of them delivered passengers to Canandaigua. The security camera at the hotel recorded a small limo arriving at the time of the Duvals' check-in, but the license plate was obscured."

"What about his phone?"

"It was a throwaway. And his fingerprints don't match anyone in our system."

She gave a silent whistle. "So he's not a criminal. Maybe not even an academic, in which case somebody had to coach him or invent those false documents, don't you think?"

"Most likely. We have a statewide BOLO on the wife, who has disappeared. All her things were gone from the hotel by the time we examined the room last night. We're still going through Duval's own things."

Lyssa lifted her mug. After blowing across the surface, she took a sip followed by another. "So maybe it really was the wife who brought the poisoned wine to the kitchen."

"Possibly. That's one of many questions we have for her. No one with the name Jacqueline Duval took a flight or rented a car leading up to or following the murder. The hotel is pretty sure she took a taxi Monday from the hotel around noon, but none of the cab companies took a credit card with that name. The only rides logged from the hotel Tuesday went to restaurants in Canandaigua."

"You guys have been busy."

"And we've still come up empty. This is where you come in, Mrs. Pennington. Justin has furnished the headshot from Duval's application, but all we have to go on for the wife's appearance is a grainy still from the hotel security camera, which suggests she's close to six feet and wears her hair close-cropped. Did you see her or speak with her at any time?"

"No. Besides hearing thirdhand that she wouldn't be at the dinner, the only information I ever had about her was in Emile's paperwork." She withdrew from her tote a thick folder with the printed compilation of the emails she'd prepared for him.

"You'll see, there's a long email exchange between Duval and the dean's office that includes a quick reference to making his own hotel arrangements. That whole thread was forwarded to me the afternoon of the murder. Other than the last message in the chain about the wife not coming to the big dinner, I hadn't read any of the messages leading up to that until this morning."

She set that aside and flipped to a document. "This is a copy I had on my laptop of his cover letter and resumé, which gives his wife's name and says they have two children. No names, no gender. Anything else is in the college's tracking program, and I have to be on campus to access it."

Hank wiggled his fingers in a bring-it gesture, and she handed over the stack. He riffled through. "No photo of the Duvals, together or separately?"

"Just the headshot of him."

Hank sat back and nailed her with a look. "Describe Emile Duval, big picture, looks, clothes, style."

She stretched her neck and shoulders as she lined up her thoughts. "He was handsome, probably late forties. He had an aura of power. At the dinner Tuesday evening, he was charming and attentive but reserved."

"Height, weight, style?"

"Not as tall as you or Justin. Fit; maybe a runner. His style was not one you'd associate with a college professor. His clothes and grooming were much more like Justin Cushman's. Very high-end suit, accessories on par with Kyle."

"Meaning?"

118

"Expensive cufflinks, platinum wedding band with a center diamond. One of those watches with seventeen dials and windows and buttons."

"And his looks?"

"Silver hair and brown eyes. The hairstyle probably cost hundreds at a male salon. I think the headshot he gave us was taken a few years back, because his face and neck were thinner then, maybe ten to twenty pounds."

Hank was nodding, his eyes switching back and forth as if he were recalculating his profile of Duval. She sipped more coffee. Finally, Hank laid out what he needed from her. "Mrs. Pennington, we're depending on you to provide any and all information you can pull out of every source available to you." He positioned the stack of printouts between them on the table. "Let's go through what you've brought and see what it tells us."

For the next half hour, they talked through page after page of Duval's correspondence. Hank posed questions and jotted notes in the margins. At one point he checked his watch. "I'll make another pass later," he told her. "You dig into every line of his application materials and find anything that helps us identify the victim and find his family. Understand, I'm not asking you to find his killer. If you do, that's a big win for us, but don't take any action on your own; tell us. At all times, proceed with caution. This is a murder case."

While he coaxed the pages into a stack neat for carrying, Lyssa sat back and thought about what he'd said. She wanted to do this work for him, and it felt good to be working collaboratively with him. Apparently they'd both moved past their disastrous exchange last night.

"Let me ask you this, Mrs. Pennington. Who might have purchased the split of Loire Valley Beaujolais?"

"Not me, not Rand Cunningham, and he says not the committee. But it had to be someone familiar with Duval's

CV." She directed him to the final page of Duval's resumé . "See that little section he added about personal interests? That's where he says he grew up in the Loire Valley."

"And you're sure the committee did not buy or bring the wine?"

"Not as a group, they didn't. Rand is sure of that."

"If you had to pick one individual from the committee who might have, who would that be?"

Lyssa's neck stiffened at the question. "I'm not going to accuse anyone, Trooper Moran. I know how it felt to have my colleagues do that to me last night."

"They—" Hank grimaced and closed his mouth. In a gentle tone, he continued, "We're just speculating here, Lyssa."

Why was he using her first name? It felt buddy-buddy but, instead of trusting him more, she chose to see it as tacit permission to call him Hank.

So who on the committee might have purchased the wine and doctored it? José had said outright that Emile Duval was perfect for the job, but his belligerence toward Rand—*Who made you king?*—also came to mind. She related all that to Hank, and he scribbled the information in his notebook. "I don't know if Jeanne Marie wanted to be chair," she added. "And I don't know any of the other faculty in Languages. Maybe one of them thought they deserved the job. Plus, I think the chair gets extra money, like a stipend over and above salary."

Hank tapped his pen. "Let's talk about the person you think you saw leaving the kitchen when you entered, the one who delivered the poisoned wine to the kitchen."

"I didn't just *think* I saw her. I did see her." She waited for him to nod. "She went out the back door to the parking lot."

"Correction. We've established that the door in question leads from Westerlee Hall's kitchen to a hallway, not directly outside. That hallway has three doors, all marked Authorized Use Only. One door goes to the staff parking lot, one to a supply closet, one to a side hall that gives access to the entire building. Your person could have left the building or disappeared into the hallways and upper floors."

"Why would she hang around?"

He shrugged one shoulder. "Maybe to make sure the poison did the job."

A shiver coursed through her. "And just maybe she came back later to retrieve the gift card? That would explain why the techs didn't find it."

"It would also explain why we didn't see anyone other than the caterers and security staff on the surveillance camera during that time frame."

Lyssa sat up straighter. "Which security staff?"

For a moment, Hank regarded her without speaking. She stared back, unblinking.

"Stan Block," he answered.

"Was he carrying anything?"

"Not that we could see on the video. He clocked into Westerlee's security station at 5:40 p.m., entered the building and—"

"Is that normal, entering the building?"

"It's not required, nor is it unusual. It was probably a bathroom stop. He was out of sight of the camera for just over two minutes, and reappeared briefly as he backtracked across the parking lot."

"Long enough to drop off a bottle of wine and set up a card."

Hank snorted. "I doubt if a gift card is his style."

Lyssa smiled. "Good point."

He returned the smile. "His next check-in was the library a few minutes later, and he returned to the security office at 6:02 p.m."

"Okay, but for sure it wasn't Stan I saw leaving the kitchen by the back door. And it was only ten minutes before dinner was supposed to start at six o'clock. I saw a woman, not a man. Maybe she came into the building earlier. Maybe she slipped in when the caterers arrived and hung around."

"Good thinking. Besides the caterers, two wineries delivered around the same time."

Lyssa nodded. "And a sweet shop from Geneva should have been there." *Terrible waste of a chocolate cheesecake.*

"We saw that van arrive seconds after the caterers. In fact, there was a flurry of activity right around five thirty, so we don't have good stills of each person."

"Even if you had a photo, I didn't see the woman's face or body, just her arm and hand, closing the door."

"Help me picture that."

Lyssa drew the scene on her napkin. She had stood at an angle to the door, which was already partially closed so the woman's body was out of sight, except for her arm reaching across the rapidly diminishing space, hand on the knob, pulling the door shut.

"You are the only one who remembers seeing her at all. She probably came with the crowd, hung out until things settled down some, then snuck into the kitchen and quickly left while the caterers were busy."

"That sounds right. They were totally engrossed in their prep when I came in and saw the door closing. I asked who had just left. If I hadn't spoken, they wouldn't have even known *I* was there."

"What do you remember about the woman's coat?"

"Not much. I must have seen some of her coat sleeve, though. I didn't give it any thought at the time. I was fixated on the gloves."

"Cloth coat? Down? Shiny? Colorful?"

"I think it was the kind of dark winter parka anyone around here would wear on a cold night, but that doesn't tally with the classy gloves."

"Think about the position of her arm. Think about the angle yours would make if you were closing the same door. Can you tell from that if she was taller than you, shorter?" Hank seemed to hold his breath.

Lyssa used her mental muscle to make her arm reach for the imaginary doorknob and compared it to what she'd seen. "Basically my height, maybe a little shorter."

He released his breath in a grunt. "That would make her much shorter than the hotel's shot of Jacqueline Duval. Did you see the woman's footwear?"

"No, just the gloved hand."

"Okay." Hank chuckled. "Tell me about the glove."

Her cheeks were hot. "I was memorizing every detail to tell Kyle, because I really *really* wanted a pair just like them for Christmas. The color is what they're calling 'saddle' this year. The woman's fingers were slender like mine, and the gloves fit her perfectly. From the way the leather moved, it was supple and high-end. I got just a glimpse of some decoration, maybe interlocking gold-tone circles on the back of the wrist."

Hank shook his head and grinned at her.

"So I'm not a trained detective," she joked. "There's some other detail I noticed about her appearance, but I just can't grab hold of it."

"Her head popping back for a look?"

She shook her head. "This woman didn't second-guess anything. I think she'd worked out every detail before Tuesday's dinner."

Kyle tried Lyssa's number the moment he arrived at JFK but, as had been the case since she'd called him last night, her phone service politely informed him she was not available. His next call to Tony Pinelli got an immediate pick-up.

"Hey, what's up, buddy? Where are you?"

"New York, en route to Tompkins Falls. How are things on campus? Nice and quiet now that the police have finished their work?"

"I wish. They're back, scouring the grounds and all the buildings for a missing person."

"Who's missing?"

"Our friend Stan Block disappeared from work Tuesday night before eight. Our dispatcher thinks he came back to the office around seven and went right out again, but she won't swear to it. The police wanted to interview him about the murder, and he was nowhere to be found. His car's not parked anywhere on campus. They sent a couple of guys to search his house sometime this morning and, like I said, now they're searching the whole campus for him."

"Did a bunk, did he?"

"Maybe, maybe not. With all the weird things happening around here, I don't know what to think. You heard Duval isn't really Duval?"

"Justin told me. I haven't been able to reach Lyssa. Apparently she's still meeting with Hank Moran."

"Before I forget, Hank's pressuring me to tell him what Stan had on Marguerite."

Kyle paused. How much did Tony know about Marguerite? "What have you told him so far?"

"That Stan was into blackmailing employees, which the college only recently learned. Justin's insisting the details are internal college business, and I'm on board with that. Unless we know for a fact Marguerite's death is something other than an accident or natural causes, the college is not going to reveal any details."

"Okay, that works until the police go into Stan's place of residence and find the eight boxes he removed from his office, full of blackmail material."

"We don't know where he took them. Maybe he destroyed them."

"True. Keep me posted, eh?"

"Need anything from the pastry case?" Hank asked Lyssa as they shrugged into their coats.

"If Kyle were home, I'd get a sticky bun for him, but I'm staying with Justin and Gianessa, and they're both gluten-free."

"Torie wants a couple loaves of Lynnie's rye bread. Maybe you'll see something for the Cushman twins."

Lyssa took to mean Hank was not finished picking her brain. As they stood in line for take-out baked goods, he told her, "I need you to compile a list of everyone Duval came in contact with while he was at Tompkins College. We may find he insulted the wrong person in a way that tipped them over the edge."

"He insulted a lot of the staff, which you'll see in those emails. It's safe to assume he treated most nonprofessionals the same way. I'll get you a list of every staff person who supported the two-day interview and the planning for it, plus a copy of the interview schedule."

"Very helpful. Did he treat faculty the same way?"

"Not exactly. He used his charm to manipulate us."

Rather than probing further, Hank was thoughtful. Maybe he was reviewing his interviews with the faculty. After he ordered his bread, he reached into his pocket. "You might need this."

When he drew out her iPhone, she snatched it from him. "Thanks. I can also touch base with Joel Cushman about the resort in Canandaigua where the Duvals stayed."

"I don't follow. What would Joel know?"

"It's not what he knows but what he can find out, innkeeper to innkeeper."

"I'll leave that to you. One more question: did you communicate with Duval by any means other than email? Besides at the dinner, I mean."

"Once, yes. He called me on my cell, and we had a long talk."

He pounced. "How did that happen? What was the number?"

She checked her phone and was reminded she'd powered it down before she'd surrendered it to him last night. While it initialized, she said, "I had emailed him about the gluten thing, and he wanted to have a conversation. I heard back from him after I'd left campus and asked him to call me on my cell."

When the device was ready, she scrolled through her call history. After many screens of missed calls, most from Kyle, she found it. "Got it. We talked seven minutes, four seconds." She flashed the display for Hank but kept a tight grip on the device. She wasn't letting him touch it ever again.

Hank scowled and acknowledged it was the number of Duval's throwaway cell phone. "I think you probably learned a lot about him in those seven minutes. Tell me about his voice—accent, manner, everything."

"Well-educated. On the pompous side. Never said please or thank you. He told me in maybe fifteen seconds that gluten-free was a preference, not an allergy. Then the rest of the time he asked about Tompkins Falls, things he, quote, couldn't find on the internet, end quote." Only now did that strike her as significant.

Hank apparently agreed. "Such as?"

"Where did most faculty live? What was the office situation at the college? You probably know it's ridiculous at most colleges—cubicles and centuries-old furniture. We're lucky to have our own space—four walls, a door, and at least one window. I told him he'd probably have Marguerite's office in the Admin building, which is where my office is."

Hank shifted on his feet.

"But I digress. He asked if the person he was replacing had lived alone and if the house was near campus, and I babbled about Marguerite being separated and living in a gorgeous house in College Heights. He wanted to know if the house would be coming up for sale." She paused and drew in a noisy breath.

"What is it, Mrs. Pennington?"

"I can't believe she's gone. Why didn't she let Kyle and me help her that night in the parking lot? She knew us." The lump in her throat was so big it hurt.

Hank leaned closer. "Look, Lyssa, you can either make yourself crazy with guilt or you can help us solve this thing. My gut tells me her death is connected to Duval's. I don't see how, not yet, but I'm convinced there's a connection."

"I'll do whatever I can." She owed it to Marguerite to understand what had happened and why.

Hank reached for his two bags of bread and turned toward the front door, gesturing for Lyssa to walk with him. "What do you make of Duval's interest in Professor LaCroix's office and home?"

"Now that I think about it, it's creepy. When he asked, I remember feeling angry, but I figured that was because her death was so recent and shocking." Hank stood perfectly still. She asked him, "Was there a reason you asked me about that?"

Instead of answering her question, he posed one of his own. "If you didn't mix with the Languages faculty, how did you know Marguerite LaCroix so well?"

The question caught her off guard. *I can't tell him. I won't tell him.* Her breath hitched and she felt lightheaded.

"Let's get some air." He pushed open the door and she exited while he held it for her. He repeated, "Tell me about your relationship with Marguerite LaCroix, Mrs. Pennington."

She licked her lips. "Why do you need to know?"

"Because you know more about her than you're telling, and it may help us understand how and why she died. And if there's a connection to Duval's death."

"Whatever I know was told to me in confidence and it has nothing to do with her death or your investigation of her accident. Or Duval's death."

"I'll be the judge of what's relevant."

"To be honest, Hank, I don't trust you to keep some details of her life—the very personal, totally irrelevant details of her life—from the media."

Hank drew himself up with the authority of a New York State trooper—back straight, head erect, jaw set—and his eyes bore into her. "Do not hamper the investigations into LaCroix's death or Duval's death, Mrs. Pennington. Do you understand this is a warning?"

Lyssa squeezed her eyes shut against the welling of tears. She kept her voice low. "I was her AA sponsor."

He relaxed his posture. "I see. That fact is not relevant."

"But that's not the secret." *Damn.* Why hadn't she stopped while she was ahead?

"Go on."

Why do I always blurt out the truth? "Last year was hard for her. She faced a truth about herself that changed her marriage forever and left her in doubt about how to—"

"What truth?" he barked. Quietly, he added, "No one is out here listening to us."

A blast of icy winter wind on her face helped her put logic over emotion. Maybe this information *was* important to the investigation. Even if she couldn't trust Hank, she should tell him.

"Mrs. Pennington?"

"She came to accept her sexual orientation is lesbian. Was lesbian."

With a lengthy exhale, he directed his gaze to the lakeshore on the far side of the highway. "So there's no chance she was having an affair with Duval?"

Lyssa puffed out a laugh. "No. Why would you even think that? Marguerite loved Billy and respected her marriage vows."

"It's my job to think of every possibility. Duval was here under false pretenses. We don't know why."

She turned pleading eyes to him. "Don't go digging into Marguerite's life looking for the answer. Let her rest in peace. Let the rest of us heal from her death."

"My job does not allow that." His mouth tightened. "Do you know any possible connection between our two victims?"

That was the first time he'd referred to Marguerite as a victim. Did he really suspect she'd been murdered? Rather than hound him to answer that question, she told him, "Other than Stan Block's appearance near each of them shortly before their deaths, no. It's freezing out here, Hank. May I leave?"

Hank stared at her, but she couldn't read his expression. "Lyssa, I need you to understand that, until the cause of these deaths is determined and the responsible person or persons apprehended, your life is in danger. You, more than anyone else, knew Professor LaCroix's secrets. Emile Duval was hiding something, too, and you may uncover it before we do."

She read grave concern in the lines by his eyes. "I will watch my back," she promised.

"Go one better. At all times, let someone know where you're heading or take a friend along." Hank waited for her to nod her agreement, then strode across the parking lot to his Jeep.

Safe in her second-hand Passat, she rested her forehead on the steering wheel for a moment. Was she really in danger? Maybe. She locked the doors.

She'd have to return to campus, where she'd have access to the candidate tracking system, in order to finish the work Hank wanted. Maybe then she could breathe without the tightness in her chest. She texted her destination to Hank and promised to lock herself into her office.

Phone in hand, she tried Kyle's number, but it went straight to voicemail. He must be in a meeting. She spoke her message, "Just got my phone back from the New York State police. I miss you, darling. Don't know yet if I can travel tomorrow as planned." Her voice caught. "Love you, bye." She'd sort through the backlog of messages and texts later.

She caught her lower lip in her teeth to stop the trembling. There was one thing she could check really quickly with her newly released phone. She opened her texts, filtered for Natalie, and whipped through to the last bulletin: Not that you deserve to know. At EWR. Mission accomplished. Reward awaits.

So Natalie had delivered Vivienne to the international airport in Newark, New Jersey, after completing the mission. They'd found the letters. And, most important, Natalie was okay.

And royally pissed at me. Hopefully, she'd be forgiven when she heard Lyssa hadn't shared her fun because her guest of honor, the star candidate, had been murdered and the police had confiscated her phone. But that, too, would have to wait.

Chapter 10

At the clang of metal on metal, Lyssa whirled toward the door. Hand over her racing heart, she listened as the jangling grew quieter. So did the accompanying footsteps. She breathed out a long *whoosh*.

It was just Campus Security passing her office. One look at the clock showed she'd been at it for two hours. She'd heard him pass by twice before this, but she still wasn't used to the racket he made. Still, he was protecting her.

As promised, she'd gone directly to campus from her meeting with Hank so she could log into the candidate tracking system. And he'd apparently arranged for her to have her own security detail.

She had nearly finished her analysis of Emile's application materials and, so far, she'd not found one clue to his real name. Everything about his application was fiction. She'd probed the veracity of his past appointments and the names and affiliations he'd given for his professional references. All were dead ends.

Someone had gone to a lot of trouble to construct the persona of Emile Duval, Star Candidate, and she didn't think Emile's alter ego had done it by himself. Why would someone want to block every avenue to his real identity? What was he really up to?

How and why had he managed in the space of a week to utterly deceive the brightest minds at Tompkins College, including super-savvy ultra-careful Justin Cushman? If they just checked any one major item on his CV, they'd have spared themselves the expense and the horror of Duval's death on their campus. *Too late now.*

As her final task, she turned her attention to the unofficial copies of transcripts Emile had scanned and forwarded electronically. As with all candidates, they served as placeholders for the official transcript until the college seriously considered making an offer. Then the real thing had to arrive.

Sure enough, when she looked closely, she could make out thin lines where someone had overlaid a real person's name with *Emile Henri Duval.* On the one from Dartmouth, supposedly his undergraduate college, she could even see the serrated edge of the tape.

There was probably big money to be had by a credentials mill that offered services ranging from resumé s to transcripts. *Focus, Lyssa.* She still had a few facts to check.

She visited the websites for Emile's supposed alma maters, dug around for commencement programs for his dates of graduation, and confirmed that Emile Duval had not been awarded any of the degrees he claimed. Done.

As she wrote up her notes for Hank, she shook her head. Though Emile had fooled all of them with his false pedigree and on-campus performance, someone hadn't bought it, someone who wanted him dead. But what motive, and why follow him to Tompkins Falls to kill him?

No, that was too complicated, and it didn't add up.

There was no reason to think the killer *hadn't* believed Duval's super-candidate persona. In fact, Duval's seemingly stellar qualifications for the job of professor and chair of Languages made him all the more threatening if the killer were one of the Languages faculty and that person wanted the job. Or felt they deserved the job. Or wanted the extra money. Or all of the above.

She shook her head. José might be a nasty piece of work, but murder, really?

That brought her back to Emile's game. Maybe Justin was right that he'd wanted the interview but not the job, but she couldn't fathom why Emile wanted the interview. Was it some kind of weird initiation rite? *Focus, Lyssa.*

She sent her notes to Hank and stood for a big stretch. She ought to spend time checking her campus email messages, but she really was too tired, and she could do that from home.

Her phone pinged with a text from Kyle: Leaving JFK, home around 3.

Thumbs flying, she answered: Wow, great surprise! and added a smiley and a dozen bright pink hearts.

She needed a bio break before she did anything else. She automatically checked for the Creeper Beeper that should be in her jacket pocket. It wasn't there. She remembered losing it in the snowy parking lot the night Marguerite died. Probably she should stop by Campus Security for a replacement.

She laughed. She already had her very own hall walking security officer. That task could wait until she got back from Christmas break.

Halfway back from the ladies' room, her phone startled her so badly that sweat broke out on her upper lip. *Get a grip.*

The caller was her brother-in-law. "Hi, Joel. Thanks for getting back to me." She had asked him to talk with the resort where the Duvals stayed.

"I got some strange answers to your questions about the Duvals. The wife didn't arrive with him when he checked in Sunday evening. She did come, but no one's sure when. The maid didn't see any women's clothing when she did the turndown Sunday evening, but the wife was definitely there by Monday late morning when the room was cleaned, because her stuff was strewn all over and the closet was jammed with her clothes."

"Did anyone on staff see her? Can they describe her?"

"Not at all. Her only interaction with staff was through the concierge, whom she called from her cell phone on Sunday, right after her husband checked in. She identified herself to the concierge as Jacqueline Duval and said she and her husband were staying for three nights in Room 314."

"But she wasn't actually at the hotel then, right? She just knew the room number because Emile had checked in and called her. Or texted or whatever."

"Looks that way."

"Sounds like she made it a point not to show her face, doesn't it?"

"Maybe. But listen, it gets better. She wanted to know from the concierge how she would find a person to show her the office situation at the college and to see houses near the college that might be available for sale or rent."

That tallied with one of Emile's messages in the long string of emails to the dean's assistant about Jacqueline's plans.

"He told her she would find information about real estate agents in the hotel room. And, yes, he was deliberately rude and unhelpful because she was demanding and snooty. I'd have fired him if he worked for me, but that's not my problem."

Lyssa had arrived at her office door, and she fished out her key. Joel's information hadn't told her much, and she'd already printed her notes for Hank. If Joel had anything important, she'd handle that separately.

So Jacqueline has defined her tasks as the candidate's wife as scoping out his office situation and finding a place he or they could live in Tompkins Falls. If you believed Duval actually wanted the job, that made sense. Lyssa was absolutely sure neither Emile nor Jacqueline had requested a tour from the college; if they had, she'd have been informed and added it to the formal schedule for the two-day Duval interview.

"Lyssa, did I lose you?"

"Sorry, Joel. Just thinking. You said it gets better. What did you mean?"

"I wasn't kidding, and this is important. Jacqueline Duval also asked for a recommendation for a full-service spa, and the concierge directed her here, to the Manse."

Lyssa smiled. *That* would only be important to Joel Cushman, proprietor of the Manse Inn and Spa. "Doesn't their resort have spa services?" She smiled. "Or was the guy just trying to get rid of her?"

"Turns out they're expanding their spa, but right now they're limited to facials and nails, which was news to me. We need to jump on that, advertise some packages for the next couple months."

"Good idea." *Focus, Joel.* "Did Jacqueline Duval actually come to the Spa at the Manse?"

"She did. The concierge called from the resort and Remy somehow got her in for the entire afternoon Monday."

Actually, this part was important for Hank's timeline of Duval's wife. Lyssa had to wonder, though, why Jacqueline had spent Monday at the spa, instead of going house hunting or checking out the college office situation.

"Joel, when she came to the Manse, did she make the same request for someone to show her houses?"

"She told Remy she was interested in looking properties but needed, quote, The Right Person to show her around. Remy thought the subtext was she would pay privately for that service."

"Seriously?"

"He politely told Mrs. Duval no one at the spa could help her with that. Mrs. Duval didn't push it, just went ahead with her scheduled services and when she came out to pay—in cash, by the way—she included an exorbitant tip and made it clear she expected everyone to protect her privacy. Who would even care that some professor's wife had spent the afternoon at the spa?"

But Lyssa's thinking had gone in a different direction. "An afternoon of services had to be hundreds of dollars."

He sniffed. "More than a thousand for Mrs. Duval, not including tip. You didn't hear that from me."

"How does a professor's wife have that kind of cash to burn? And Hank told me Emile had paid cash up front for their suite at the resort. I don't like this, Joel." Emile and Jacqueline had been working as a well-funded team, whatever they were up to. Hank would definitely want to know this. "Anything else?"

"It gets weirder. Sometime during her spa experience, she apparently found the right person from the college to show her around. Want to guess who?"

"No. Who?"

Her mouth dropped open when Joel told her, "Your friend Professor Natalie Horowitz signed out at exactly the same time as Jacqueline Duval, and Remy said they went off chatting like old friends."

"Oh my gosh." Her whole body tingled. "Oh my gosh, Joel." She'd thought Natalie was just spinning a story when she talked about meeting someone at the spa and agreeing to help her get the goods on her husband.

While she logged off her computer, dove for her tote, and slung it over her shoulder, she asked him, "Joel, are you sure the woman didn't give her name as Vivienne?" She left her office at a run. Too late, she realized she hadn't locked the office door. No problem; her personal bodyguard would take care of it.

"Nope. Jacqueline Duval."

This was bad. "I'll think she's the person who convinced Natalie she was some supermodel named Vivienne, whoever that is. Joel, I'm on my way to Natalie's house to check on her. I haven't heard from her since Tuesday night, and if this woman is as manipulative as her husband was, Natalie might be in trouble."

"Wait for me to pick you up. We'll go together. You shouldn't—"

"Talk to you later."

Kyle tipped his driver, hoisted his bag, and made the climb to their Lakeside Terrace apartment. He paused outside the door, keys in hand. Usually Lyssa heard his tread on the stairs and rushed him on their third-floor landing with a full body hug and a warm kiss. Today, silence. He fitted his key in the lock and entered. "Lyssa?"

He checked each room and both porches. No Lyssa. He pressed her cell number. No answer. *Where is my wife?*

A call to Tony Pinelli revealed she had left campus over an hour ago. "Sorry, buddy, I don't know where she went, but she didn't take her car."

"Maybe she needed a walk."

"I don't think so. The guy I posted in her wing of Admin said she flew out of there and left her door unlocked."

Lord, where is she? A call to Lyssa's sister revealed Joel had talked with Lyssa and said she'd gone off somewhere with Natalie Horowitz.

That didn't make sense. Lyssa had known he was on his way home. Why would she take off with a friend? *Bother.* He tossed his phone on the island. At the moment, there was only one thing he could usefully do.

He stripped off his travel clothes, and showered away the grunge and stiffness of the journey. Toweled dry, dressed in jeans and a cashmere top, he rummaged in the refrigerator for something to eat. Peanut butter and half a bagel that had outlived its ability to please the palate.

He'd just grabbed his phone to try Lyssa again when he heard feet pounding up the stairs and Lyssa calling a breathless, "I'm here."

He rushed her on the landing and folded her in his arms. "I was getting worried."

"I tried to call you earlier, but your phone went right to voicemail. Kyle, you won't—"

"Manda said you went off somewhere with Natalie?"

She laughed. "Manda's seven-and-a-half months pregnant, and you can't believe half of what she says. In this case, it was totally wrong. Natalie went off on a great adventure with Emile Duval's wife Tuesday night. I went to her house just now, hoping she was back, but her car's not in her driveway. I'm really worried. Hank thinks Jacqueline Duval is her husband's killer, which would mean Natalie could be in danger."

He pressed two fingers to his forehead. "Let's calm down. Natalie's probably in New York with Norman or—"

"I don't think so. Last I heard from her, she was at Newark airport dropping off Jacqueline Duval, whom she thought was a supermodel named Vivienne. She conned Natalie into driving her all over the place in return for an invitation to her next runway show."

His headache intensified. "Any chance we can get something to eat while we sort this?"

"Sure." She backtracked to the landing and returned with a sack from the deli. "Sandwiches okay?"

"That will do very nicely." He got out plates and silverware for the little table by the window. She spread out her purchases on the island: fresh-baked rye bread, Virginia-baked ham, Swiss cheese, Boston lettuce, apples, and condiments. "I stand corrected. This is a feast." That won him a charming smile and a kiss on the mouth.

Kyle fixed two sandwiches while she made one for herself, and they settled by the window. He set his elbows on the table, took a giant bite of his sandwich, and let his gaze wander to the lake. Dazzling sunshine played on water the color of his wife's eyes. It occurred to him, not for the first time, that home was where Lyssa was. He'd been thinking while he showered away the dust of travel they were doing this marriage thing all wrong.

Long-distance wasn't working for them, despite their commitment to make it work. They'd stay in close communication for a time and then get caught up in their own agendas, work intensely at their own locations, and not operate as a couple, in any sense. And when they came back together, both of them were stressed and exhausted.

And this time it was worse because Lyssa looked thinner and more worn out than he'd even seen her. It scared him. By the time he'd finished his first sandwich, Lyssa had made it through half hers. She smiled over at him, and he said, "We have a lot to catch up on, don't we, Mrs. Pennington?"

"Too much, I think." Her gaze was solemn. "It's good you're here, Mr. Pennington."

He nodded. "After we finish eating, let's talk about Natalie, eh?" He quirked his eyebrows, and she laughed.

They'd put away the cold cuts and fixings and were standing at the island chomping on apples when Lyssa said, "So Natalie could be in danger if Emile Duval's wife is his killer."

"Isn't she smart enough not to go off with a killer?"

"I've always thought so, but now I'm not sure. This woman Jacqueline is married to Emile Duval, who conned every one of us, and I'm thinking she's every bit as conniving as her husband. Natalie got sucked in. But the critical the question is, did Jacqueline kill her husband?"

"Evidence to the contrary?"

Lyssa brightened. "Thank you. Yes, there is. When I walked through the crime with Hank last night, we determined that the woman I saw leaving the kitchen, moments after the poisoned bottle of wine appeared on the counter, was about my height, maybe even a little shorter. The hotel video where the Duvals stayed got a picture of her that's very poor quality but shows Jacqueline is at least six feet tall and has very short hair."

"Not proof positive but very reassuring, I should say."

"Agreed. I can breathe again."

He took that to mean she was reasonably sure Natalie hadn't run off with a killer, but he wanted to know what Natalie and Jacqueline had been looking for. Something was familiar about the scenario she'd painted. "Next question, what had the two of them been doing that required driving to Newark airport?"

"It's crazy, totally. They were running around Tompkins Falls trying to get the goods on the woman's husband, who was masquerading as our star candidate, Emile Duval."

His pulse quickened. "Where exactly did they go and what do we know about the candidate's lover?"

"Well, Hank confiscated my phone, but before that I read a few texts from Natalie saying they were preparing to break into someone's office on campus, a woman whose name starts with M, who Jacqueline claimed had an affair with her husband. Their mission was to find the love letters the husband had written to this M person."

"Melissa Rossini."

Lyssa fumbled her apple and it dropped to the island. "You sound pretty sure about that." She rinsed off the apple and took a big bite.

"I can't believe I was right." He grinned at her.

"I can't believe you're saying this. Prim, proper Missy Rossini, every hair in place, never an offensive word out of her mouth, had an affair with Emile Duval? How do you figure?"

"After your candidate was killed, I had a hunch Duval had some other motive for being in Tompkins Falls."

"Sounds familiar. Your friend Justin thinks he wanted the interview but never really intended to take the job. You could both be right. But how—"'

"I knew from my work for Tony that Melissa Rossini was being blackmailed by Stan Block for having an affair with someone from New York City."

"Wow."

"Gianessa confirmed it. She couldn't remember the gentleman's name, except his first name is Jack."

"And we know Emile Duval is not the candidate's real name, but we don't know what it really is."

"What Gianessa said is Melissa has been periodically enjoying cultural events and fine dining in the Big Apple, while her husband's slaving away in Tompkins Falls. And my theory is Duval came to put an end to the blackmail, but his plan backfired and Stan Block got rid of him instead." Belatedly, he thought to add, "And that's absolutely confidential about your colleague's affair. Agreed?"

"Agreed, but those are two huge leaps. One, Missy was having an affair but maybe not with Emile. Two, Duval definitely is made of money, but I don't see him as someone who'd tolerate blackmail for thirty seconds, let alone years."

"Melissa always asked for more time to make the next payment, and I think she was hitting up her lover for the money each time. Duval's money."

She was squinting, shaking her head.

"You don't think it fits?"

"It's not that. Some clue is there, something about Missy's haircut ..." She shook her head and went back to her apple.

He gave her time, finished his apple.

After two bites of hers, Lyssa burst out with, "*That's* what I couldn't remember." She dropped her apple and reached for her phone. "Hank needs to know this, and—"

"Hold on." He waved his hands at her. "We're not telling him about Melissa. Absolutely not."

She backed up, phone in hand. "Agreed. This is something entirely different. I've been making myself crazy trying to remember this one tiny detail about the woman who delivered the poisoned wine." Her thumbs flew over the tiny keypad. "Done. Here, see for yourself."

He read: Woman leaving the kitchen wore her light brown hair exactly like Roberta Van Derzee.

"You remember her hair, right?" They'd worked together with Hank earlier in the fall to solve the murder of Roberta Van Derzee's husband. Lyssa reminded him, "That sophisticated cut, with the sharp edge that swung along her jaw whenever she turned her head." She slashed her hand at an angle along her jawline and tossed her head right and left. "I saw the killer's hair swinging just like that. Just for a second before the door shut and she vanished from view."

Her phone, still on the island, pinged with a text. It was Hank's saying: Who at the college has that haircut?

Lyssa answered: No idea, but I'll tell you when I figure it out.

Hank responded immediately: No confrontation.

She answered: I agree absolutely.

Kyle felt relieved at her response.

The phone stayed quiet. Lyssa set it aside.

"Where were we?"

She tipped her head. "There's another reason I don't think Missy Rossini could be Duval's paramour."

"Let's hear it."

She stroked his arm. "Sorry to spoil your theory. And I'm not saying you're wrong, but Missy is smarter than the average professor and her area of expertise is Ethics. Duval might have fooled us, but he was only here for two days and we were set up to believe he was a star. If Missy had been having an affair with him for any length of time she'd have seen through him."

"Maybe not."

"I really think so, and she wouldn't have tolerated his conniving."

"Done with that topic, are we?"

"Done with Missy for the moment, and I don't think Natalie has gone off with a killer. But I don't trust Jacqueline Duval and I am still a little worried about our friend Natalie. But she'll keep. Did you get enough to eat?"

"Thank you, yes, but you've not been eating properly, have you?"

She lowered her eyes. "No, except at the Cushmans this morning."

"You know I'm worried, and we need to address it."

"But not now." The sunny smile came back to her face. "Let's do something fun the rest of the day."

He knew just the thing. He grabbed for their coats. "Bundle up, my love."

Chapter 11

When Kyle suggested they bundle up for a walk to the cove, Lyssa tingled with happiness. The rocky cove on the Cushman grounds, where Kyle had first proposed, was where they dreamed of building their own little house, the one she would stay in whenever she was in Tompkins Falls during the semester. Justin had already bought into the concept of her teaching online from Cornwall and visiting campus two or three times a semester.

The new house was also where they'd come during holidays with their children in tow, to enjoy family and all the Finger Lakes had to offer. She loved the idea of all the little cousins spending time together: Justin and Gianessa's twin toddlers, Manda and Joel's first child, due in February, with more to come, they hoped. *We'll catch up soon.*

"Penny for your thoughts?" Kyle asked her. His arm came around her shoulder.

"Dreaming about our house, watching our children play on the lawn."

"Our children meaning the Cushman and Pennington clan?" When she smiled her answer, he proposed, "Just a thought. As long as you're stuck here for a bit, let's use the time to put some plans in place."

She squealed her delight. "There's nothing I'd rather be doing. I'm so sick of doing footwork for Hank."

"What does he have you working on?"

She told him about the tedious work she'd done already. "I've finished that analysis, thank God. Next is an image search using Emile's headshot. I really think all I need is one clue to open up the whole puzzle of his identity."

"If it's there to be found, you'll find it. Then you'll be finished, no more obligation to Hank's investigation?"

"I have a feeling, once he hears about Natalie driving Jacqueline Duval to an international airport, he'll want everything I have on Natalie's meetup with the woman and anything I might know about their crazy mission Tuesday night."

"The same night Emile was killed, eh? Pity Natalie's unreachable."

Gathering all her worry and frustration, Lyssa gave a mighty kick to a stone in their path and sent it tumbling downhill toward the edge of the bluff. Over it went and splashed a few seconds later. "I wish I knew where she is. Every time I try to imagine her enjoying a vacation somewhere, I get a headache that tells me she's not on vacation."

"And it will look bad to Hank, you're correct. She prowled around Tompkins Falls with a stranger she believed was her fashion idol. Her car's gone and the woman, who's suspected of murder, somehow coerced or enticed Natalie to drive her to her flight out of the country, which makes Natalie an accessory to murder. And where might Jacqueline Duval be traveling?" Kyle asked.

"I wondered that, too. Natalie said something about a photo shoot in the desert. Not around here. I know from her very last text the night of the murders that she and Vivienne made it to the airport okay, but I haven't yet looked at every text in between, and I haven't written down everything she said Monday night over lasagna at her house. Soon."

"And I'll be happy to help. Knowing Natalie, that could be the most entertaining task of the lot."

She laughed out loud, and it made her whole body feel better. "Your turn. Catch me up on your work in London." She slowed her steps, and he matched her stride.

"Did you slow down because you want every detail?"

"No, silly. How about the executive summary?"

He counted off the main points with his fingers. "Pennington Secure Networks is back on track financially, with a record quarter in progress."

"Awesome." She turned a bright smile up at him.

"There's my sunshine." He planted a kiss on her temple. "As for the lawsuit, I may be kidding myself, but I believe Geoffrey knows we've got him. There's a good chance he'll accept a settlement along with a reduced sentence. And don't fret, my love, the settlement would more than compensate the team of legal eagles working on PSN's behalf. We stand to net half of what the bugger stole from the company."

"That's only if Geoffrey has stashed the money somewhere and not blown it all on luxuries or substances."

"He cleverly deposited it offshore, and the lot of it has been frozen. And, mind you, the police say he's been operating a lucrative drug business on the side for some time, so he has plenty more assets he can use for his own defense." Kyle's harsh tone made her shudder.

"It's nearly over, then?'

"Yes, and we're approaching the site of our new home." They quickened their steps until they'd rounded a stand of pines at the border between Overlook Park and the Cushman grounds. Below them spread a rocky cove. Kyle mused, "Don't you think that indentation in the shoreline was made by the Creator especially for us?"

"Totally." She tugged at his hand and they followed the curve of the hill down the slope and came to a halt twenty feet away from a blue heron who stood regally in the shallows of their cove.

With his arm around Lyssa's shoulders, Kyle observed the heron hinge slowly forward.

In the blink of an eye, it thrust its head underwater and emerged with a fish in its beak. Two practiced maneuvers of head and neck positioned the prey, which slid down its throat.

Lyssa whispered, "We have our own blue heron?"

"So it would appear."

"Think he'll still come, even if we build here?"

"I should think so. We might find him on our deck one morning."

When her laughter rang out, the flap of giant wings heralded the bird's departure. "Or not." He joined in her laughter, and they watched their visitor glide out of sight.

Kyle pointed to a flat boulder on their right, and they sat side by side, hips and knees touching. "Tell me about your dream house on this cove, Mrs. Pennington."

He listened as she described a modest wood-and-glass structure, "with big open living space on the first floor and a suite for us. Upstairs two big bedrooms and a bath for the children." Her smile stretched ear to ear.

"Dormitory style?"

She nodded. "It's a vacation home, really."

"Six little Penningtons, you're thinking?"

"I'd like that, but I think you're right, God has a plan. We'll go with whatever that turns out to be."

"Wise thinking, my love."

"It's so peaceful here."

Even more important to him, the property was part of the Cushman grounds, and their home would be protected by the security team Justin employed.

"Where do we stand? Have you talked with Justin about our house?"

In fact, he and Justin had had several conversations about it over the past year. "Justin is delighted. He understands we'll make Cornwall our permanent home, but he's all too happy to have you living close by Gianessa and Manda, and he's pleased to have me, his good friend, in residence several times a year. And of course, he wants all the children to know each other."

"How free are we to design what we want?"

"It's understood we'll run the drawings past him. I think it's prudent to ask for his recommendation about architects. It appears he has only one restriction. The house will be ours but not the land it sits on."

She squinted. "Who'll pay the taxes?"

My wife, the economist. He'd actually been concerned she would insist on owning the land as well. "Justin will handle the taxes. The cove is on his half of the Cushman grounds."

She stretched her arms overhead and let out a sigh. "What's our next step, Mr. Pennington?"

"First, I need to tell you Billy Warren was the contractor for both Justin's house and Joel's house. I assume you'd prefer not to use him as ours?"

"Correct." She shivered and he stroked her back. "I'm sure he's not the only competent builder in the area."

"Agreed. Is your vision closer to Justin's wood-and-glass structure or to Joel's stone-and-glass ranch?"

"I think we should start with Justin's architect."

"Agreed."

She elbowed him playfully. "You're easy."

He winked and pulled her to her feet. "It's cold here. Let's head back for a warm-up."

Though it was windy going, they trekked along the edge of the bluff to enjoy the wind-whipped waves crashing against the rocks. The joy of it ended when a helicopter *whup-whup*ped overhead. "State police." They came to a halt.

"It's heading for the gumdrop islands."

He focused on the northeast corner of the lake where an indeterminate number of small boats appeared and disappeared among evergreen-covered mounds. It would be rough going for them, but they seemed determined to find something or someone. "I hope a child isn't lost on a day like this."

She drew out her phone. "Justin told me this morning Joel owns the islands now. He should know what's up." She shook her head. "No answer. I'll try Manda."

She put it on speaker, and he bent his head close. Manda sounded frantic, and he had trouble making sense of her words over the wind and waves.

Lyssa had a grip on his arm and was shaking her head and moaning. She whispered, *God help us*, as she ended the connection.

"I couldn't hear, sweetheart."

"They're looking for Stan Block's body. The police found blood, a lot of it, in his house."

In the warmth of the apartment Kyle hunted in the freezer and found two slices of Lyssa's homemade apple pie. He heated them while she made a pot of coffee. "Are they sure Stan didn't injure someone else and take off?" he asked.

"No, the police think it's his blood and someone dumped his body in the lake."

"Why do they think that?"

"I don't know. Manda didn't know." She was shaking and he let it go. She'd spilled coffee grounds on the counter. He steered her to a stool at the island and took over the job.

"Rest. Catch your breath, sweetheart."

She nodded and brushed away a few tears. "I didn't like the man, but I never wanted him dead."

"Nor I."

Their snack seemed to restore her equilibrium. When they'd finished, he brought out an eight-by-ten print of the photo Tony Pinelli had sent him. "Can we look at this together?"

"Is this what you sent me? I've barely glanced at it."

"It shows the contents of the blackmail box Stan Block had labeled with Marguerite's initials." He positioned it between them. "What do you make of it?"

Lyssa touched one finger to the snapshot of the eight vacationers where Marguerite's smiling face beamed from the front row.

"She was away for a month," Lyssa said. "July. She came home changed, happier than I'd ever seen her. Dreamy. Gianessa and I wondered if she'd started drinking again, but there was no evidence of that. I barely saw her except at meetings. Whenever she spoke up during discussions, she said how happy she was to be sober and to have the freedom to take her life in any direction she chose."

Kyle said with a catch in his voice, "She had a keen spirit, eh? The photographer has caught it in her eyes."

"You liked her, didn't you?" Lyssa touched his hand. "More than I realized."

"She was a grand girl once she put the drink down. That brilliant humor came out, and she started looking people in the eye rather than shrinking into silence after *hello*." Kyle stroked Lyssa's back. "You helped her become her best self, my love. Why did she choose Brittany for last summer's holiday?"

"She traveled every summer for a month to a French-speaking area. A different place each year, with a different research goal. This time she was researching food." Lyssa laughed at the memory. "She told me she wanted to write a cookbook about healthy French cooking."

"I didn't know there was such a thing."

"She intended to find it, get the recipes, and publish it for all the world."

"Marguerite was a cook?"

"No, that's why it's so funny. But she loved to eat healthy, and it bothered her that French cooking had such a bad reputation—all that cream and butter and *foie gras*. She wanted to extend the popular perception of French cooking to include healthy dishes. She thought she'd find lots of them in Brittany where starving artists lived off the fruit of the land and the sea. Her words."

"So she was looking for recipes?" He tapped the photo over the packet of letters, all of a uniform size. Perhaps she'd paid for the postal box to serve her research project. Would Stan Block blackmail her for that?

"Recipes and the cooks who made them. She wanted the story behind the ingredients. I wonder what she found."

"I suppose we'll never know." He needed to bring Lyssa back to the people in the photo. It was worth considering that one of them had shown up in Tompkins Falls and accosted Marguerite in the college parking lot before her death. "Tell me what you think of her fellow travelers and what might have brought them together."

Lyssa bent her head to the photo. "It's not obvious from the picture they had anything in common. I think Marguerite said the trip was some kind of small-group retreat. Seaweed was involved."

He let go a laugh from his belly. "Seaweed?"

"Probably a health thing. They made soup with it. Probably wrapped up in it, the seaweed, not the soup."

"Why on earth?"

"Seaweed has cleansing properties, didn't you know?" Her eyes, sparkling with humor, teased him.

Suddenly, the fatigue of the day's travel from the UK left him and he was glad he'd flown back to be with her. This was her holiday break and she shouldn't be working for Hank

Moran at all. They should be together, husband and wife, whether it was planning their house on the cove or enjoying London or hiking on the Pennington estate.

She bumped her shoulder against his. "I remember now. She said the locals in that village were known for their seaweed broth. That made Brittany and the health retreat a good starting point for her research, don't you think?"

"Mmm. So back to the eight merry travelers. She said something about choosing a new direction, did she?"

"Sort of. What are you thinking?"

"That she might have struck up a friendship with one or more of these people that somehow backfired on her."

"Hard to imagine," Lyssa said. "She was not naïve, and she was a seasoned traveler."

"Ah, but she may have been vulnerable as a newly admitted lesbian. She may have disclosed it to the wrong person."

"Someone homophobic, you mean?"

"Or someone who was also lesbian who latched onto her and stalked her all the way back to Tompkins Falls."

A spasm shook her body.

"Just saying. I wasn't wishing it on her."

She rested her chin on her fists. "Look at the man standing third in the back row, between the two women." She pointed.

"I see who you mean, with the spectacles. I couldn't decide if he was the husband of the woman with the very fair skin and he was worried about sunburn. Or if the chap on the left was her husband, and your fellow was ogling her for a possible liaison. That rather fits with him being the stalker type, eh?"

"I guess. What about your guy on the left? He looks a little dangerous, don't you think?"

He chuckled as he massaged her shoulders. "I'm pretty sure he's a mystery author from the wilds of Scotland. If I could remember his name, I'd Google him."

"Or do an image search on—oh my gosh, I completely forgot! I'm supposed to be working on that image search of Emile's headshot. I need to get that started." She tried to shove back her stool, but he hooked one leg of the stool with his foot to hold her in place.

"Leave it for morning, eh? Hank's got his hands full with Stan's death. Let's finish up with the photo and take ourselves out for a lovely dinner. The Manse Grill?"

"That is so perfect." She settled back into a relaxed position. "What else can we learn from this photograph?"

"One theory is that Marguerite kept this snapshot and a packet of letters because she had launched an exciting new research project on healthy French cooking. The letters all tied up in a pale purple ribbon may be recipe cards from a dozen or so people."

"But why would Stan Block try to blackmail her over recipes?"

So far they were on the same page. If he proceeded carefully, he might lead her to the truth. "Good point. Perhaps Stan just assumed they were passionate love letters from someone she met on the trip and had an affair with."

"Really, Kyle? He'd have opened at least one of them and seen they were recipes."

"But suppose they were written in French?"

"And what?" She snorted. "He assumed the list of ingredients were some weird list of techniques her lover wanted to be doing with her at that moment? Ee-u-w."

He stayed silent to see where she would go next.

"Kyle, you don't think Marguerite could have actually had a lesbian affair with one of the women, do you?"

She'd gotten to it on her own.

"I suppose none of us is immune to a summer fling."

She swiveled to face him, fists on her hips. "You wouldn't dare."

"I would not, under any circumstances. You are the love of my life."

"Good. And likewise. But if she did have a fling, chances are they *were* passionate love letters." Her hands trembled. "And if the lover were American, they could have been written in English and Stan knew exactly what they said. And if the lover were a woman, Stan would see a golden opportunity. What do you think?"

"I think you've found the key to Stan's harassment of her in the parking lot the night she died," he said, his voice as neutral as he could make it.

Lyssa took a deep breath. "And it would also explain why she kept the letters and the photo together, hidden in her office at the college, not at home. And why she had them sent to a post office box in the first place."

Her breathing had grown ragged. "Billy was still living with her when she first got back from the trip, and she wouldn't want Billy reading them." She glanced out the window.

He asked an easy question. "You're certain Billy and Marguerite normally received their mail at their home?"

"Yes. They had a brass mail slot in their front door, which Marguerite kept polished. She always came into the house through the front door, always picked up the mail first thing, and always read it with a *café au lait*."

"Which makes me think you're correct, they're letters of passion," he said.

"And somehow Billy found out about the affair, and that was the reason he moved out." She was nodding now.

"That says, for Billy Warren, it was one thing to learn her sexual orientation and something else entirely for her to have an active sex life with anyone, even if it wasn't another man."

"Yes. So Stan Block may have attacked her in the parking lot, or Billy Warren."

"And if Marguerite's lover also had a lover who was on the trip with her, that person might have attacked that night. It could be any of the three. Shall we tell Hank?" he asked her.

A vigorous shake of her head was the answer. "It's all guesswork at this point. I think we should wait for the results of the toxicology report. There's nothing else pending on the case."

"If he declares her death from natural causes, how would you feel about that?"

"I would be okay with that," she said. "I don't want to see her name dragged through the mud by our faculty or anyone else." She sighed heavily.

He massaged the back of her neck along with her shoulders. "We're both exhausted, aren't we?"

"This morning when I met with Hank at Lynnie's, I told him that Marguerite was gay. I had to stop him fishing for a connection between Marguerite and Emile Duval. I wish I hadn't told him."

He shivered for no reason. The apartment was toasty warm and cozy with the smell of Lyssa's apple pie and the coffee.

She stood and cleared the dishes from the island.

He tucked the eight-by-ten enlargement back in his briefcase.

"Kyle, I hate that Stan disrupted lives the way he did."

Chapter 12

Kyle paid a visit to Joel Cushman's home first thing Thursday morning. Manda greeted him at the door with a kiss and a hug. "Joel's got a fresh pot of coffee for you in the kitchen. I'm off to work."

He helped her on with her coat. "How are you and the baby?"

A smile lit her face and her hand went to her belly.

Exactly what I want for Lyssa, even if we have to wait.

"We're doing well. Six weeks to go." She wrapped and tied her navy wool coat. "I'm so glad Lyssa will be back from her break by then."

"We're very excited for you and Joel."

"So what's new, my favorite brother-in-law?" She touched the sleeve of his coat.

"We're planning our house on Justin's cove," he offered.

Both hands gripped his arm, and her eyes danced. "That's not just a dream?"

"I'm talking with Justin this morning about using his architect."

"That's the best news *ever*. Did you hear that, Joel?" she shouted before rushing out the door.

"Morning, Kyle," Joel called from the kitchen. "Drop your coat and join me."

"Does she ever slow down?" Kyle asked with a laugh as he entered the spacious high-end kitchen. Joel was settled by the window with the morning newspaper spread before him. Their house was halfway down the slope from Justin's but still had a dramatic view of Chestnut Lake.

"Only on weekends, when we have a no-work policy."

"How does that work?"

Joel told him. "We cook, walk, read, and catch up with each other."

"Sounds healthy." He followed the direction Joel was pointing to a rack of mugs on the counter. "Lyssa looks like death lately." The words were out before he could stop them. His hands shook enough to slop coffee as he poured. "Sorry." He grabbed a few paper towels.

"She's not pregnant?"

His stomach took a dive. "Lord, I hope not." That hadn't occurred to him. They'd agreed to hold off planning their family until over the winter break. She wouldn't have gone ahead, would she?

"No point worrying. Have her check it out with her doctor."

"Truth to tell, I don't think she has a doctor, and she should see one, you're correct." Kyle's throat tightened. Besides being far too thin, her shining copper hair had dulled over the past month and she had no color in her cheeks.

While he cleaned up his mess, Joel jotted something on a scrap of paper. "This is Manda's doctor. We trust her completely." He held out the contact information, and Kyle pocketed it with his thanks.

After a calming swallow of the fragrant brew, he nudged the conversation toward the reason he'd come. Though he wanted the inside scoop on the search for Stan Block's body, he knew the indirect approach worked best with Joel. "Lyssa says you've acquired the islands." He gestured toward the northeast corner of the lake, gray and quiet this morning under brooding clouds. "I assumed they were town or state property."

"Popular misconception." Joel shook his head. "They've always been privately held. My AA sponsor, Phil Phillips, inherited them when his wife passed half a dozen years ago. They'd been in his wife's family forever. When Phil needed more care and his pension wasn't stretching far enough, I offered to foot the bill for whatever care he needed, but he wouldn't hear of it. He sold me the islands for a dollar and my promise of continuing care right up to the end."

"Is there a benefit to you? Development, I suppose."

Joel snorted. "They're not habitable. Their main value is to the fishermen who live in the cottage community adjacent to Phil's property in the direction of town. They each have their favorite spots, and Phil has always supported their presence. I'm cool with that. Phil took me to meet them the day I signed the deed, and we told them they were welcome to fish there, just as they'd always been."

"We saw the boats and a helicopter yesterday afternoon. Have they turned up a body?"

"They're keeping it quiet but, yes, the fishermen found Stan Block's body, with a modicum of help from a state police helicopter. Whoever dumped him didn't weight the body enough, and it drifted with the wind and waves until a tree at the start of a rocky beach snagged it. Evidently the wave action had carried it up and over the rocks, so it was out of sight of the fishermen. The helicopter spotted it, and the boaters brought it in to Hank Moran's boat ramp."

"They were at it all day, sounds like."

"Hours of bone-chilling work in small boats. Most of the boat owners were running on empty at the end."

"I take it you were there?"

Joel nodded. "Hank had contacted me when the helicopter was summoned and asked me to stand by to thank the searchers and learn whatever I could from their talk. I arrived at his house just as Hank's wife was handing out blankets, making sure everyone wrapped up and ate a meal."

"How did it happen that the boaters were out before the helicopter? I'm asking because Tony Pinelli said Stan was nowhere to be found Tuesday night, midway through his shift, and that the police had gone looking for Stan Wednesday morning. Why didn't the police start searching then?"

"First I've heard it. The police aren't warmly welcome in that community. Possibly they knocked at Stan's front door early in the morning, got no answer, and left. One of the neighbors did call the police late morning because he started out to fish and found his boat was gone."

Kyle's gaze went to the lake where a few boats rested on the open water to the south and west of the islands, each boat carrying one or two fishermen. "They fish even this time of year?"

"Most of them are on public assistance. As long as the lake is free of ice, they fish from their boats. When the lake freezes hard enough, they set up huts and fish through the ice."

"So they can't ignore the theft of a boat. And, I'm guessing, when the police responded to the call about the stolen boat, they tried again to get a response at Stan's cottage."

"Makes sense because that's when they noticed Stan's Jeep parked behind his house and figured he was home. When Stan didn't answer they looked in the windows and saw the blood."

"Stan's blood, they think?"

"Most likely. There was a dried pool of it at the corner of the brick platform where his woodstove sits. And bloody footprints across the floor, plus drag marks leading away from the back door to the water and ending at the empty spot in the row of boats along the shore."

"That just says the killer stole the boat to get rid of the body. Why wouldn't the police assume Stan was the killer, not the victim? He might have left the Jeep there to fool them."

"The neighbors swore Stan would never have taken one of their boats. He's been a good neighbor for decades. When the police asked them about the blood, they stopped answering questions. Then, while the police were off conducting a door-to-door canvass of the properties on both sides of the cottages, the boaters organized a search for the missing boat and for Stan's body, totally against police orders."

"But why were they so sure the body had been taken into the islands?"

"As soon as the police asked Phil if he knew anything, he got in touch with the boaters. He'd heard a boat splashing by his place around eight o'clock Tuesday night and saw a man rowing the boat, heading into the islands. He hadn't called the cops because he figured it was kids who'd smoked a little too much weed and taken a boat out for some fun. When the boaters heard that, they knew to focus on the islands. They figured correctly that someone had dumped their neighbor's body in that maze of waterways."

Kyle had come to the right source. He hoped Hank Moran knew all this. "Interesting community, those boaters."

"True. The next break came when Hank's neighbor to the south got a visit from the police. He had looked out before midnight and had seen someone rowing out of the islands toward shore. The boat disappeared from his view but, come morning, he found it abandoned on his shore where an overgrown track leads back up to the highway. At the time he had no way of knowing whose boat it was and figured someone would come back for it."

Without thinking about it Kyle was fingering the rough patch on his chin where he'd hit the pavement the night Stan had flattened him in the faculty parking lot. "And the helicopter got into the act why?" he asked.

"The neighbor who found the missing boat finally called Hank when no one came back for it. Hank got the helicopter involved, which was a good thing because the boaters would never have seen the body." Joel asked him, "How did you get those scars on your chin?"

Kyle told him about the encounter with Stan the night Marguerite died and admitted he'd been doing a mental review of the people Stan had blackmailed. "If there was a moon Tuesday night, there'd have been enough light for the killer to see his way around the islands, but think about it, Joel. Stan was a tough guy, strong enough to blindside me and leave me winded. His killer must have taken a beating during their fight, and then he had to drag the body into a boat, row quite some distance, heave the body overboard, probably getting soaked in the process, and then row to shore and hike to his car wherever he'd left it. All in freezing temperatures."

"True."

"So Stan's killer had to be in top physical condition, would you agree?"

"Good point."

Which of Stan's victims could have handled the job? Or was it the spouse of a victim? Melissa Rossini's husband was a banker, but perhaps, like Kyle, he ran and worked out on a regular basis. He needed to confer with Tony Pinelli about the victims and narrow the field of possible killers.

Showered and dressed in fresh navy sweats, Lyssa sat at her laptop and uploaded Emile's headshot to an image search engine, determined to find the man she'd known as Emile Duval, as quickly as she could.

She rolled her eyes at the results of the first pass. Determination went a long way, but 526,782 results didn't cut it. She needed a better strategy to narrow the field. The well-groomed silver-haired gentlemen smiling from her laptop all looked alike to her. What distinguished Emile from all of them?

Since his resumé was bogus, she couldn't trust those facts. For all she knew, he was a career criminal who'd finally met his fate in the dining room of Westerlee Hall. *Wrong.* Hank had said Duval's fingerprints didn't match anyone in the system.

Her instinct told her he wasn't from any college but, before she could eliminate that as one of her criteria, she needed to test it out by restricting the next pass to EDU sites. This time there were fewer than two thousand hits.

With a timer set for fifteen minutes, she quickly determined the matches were primarily administrators at for-profit universities, VIPs at publishing ventures, and C-level officers for IT businesses that served collaboratives of schools and universities. Not one of them was the man who called himself Emile Duval.

She eliminated the EDU line of inquiry and, this time, drew on her belief that Emile was a successful businessman who, for whatever reason, had faked his way into an interview at Tompkins College. Restricting her search to commercial and business sites, she filtered for results containing the phrases and examples she and Justin had heard Emile use in conversation, mostly drawn from sports, fashion, and retail.

The new results were a manageable 4,281. After sorting by date to bring the most current to the top, she created a spreadsheet for possible matches, which would help consolidate information for duplicates.

Let's do this. She hunkered down to examine each of the silver-haired gentlemen.

She'd lost all sense of time and was stiff and thirsty when her phone sounded the theme from *Dragnet*. Ugh. Hank Moran's ringtone.

She reached for her phone, stood, and stretched. "What can I do for you, Trooper Moran?"

Hank barked, "Give me everything you've got on Natalie Horowitz since last weekend."

How had he learned about Natalie's involvement so soon? The Tompkins Falls rumor mill, probably. All it took was someone from the Spa at the Manse voicing a story about the two women meeting there and leaving as buddies.

She hesitated, asked herself how Kyle would handle this. "Okay, but right now I'm making good progress toward Duval's identity and I'm not going to stop until I have it. Besides, I'll have to piece together the Natalie stuff for you, which will take three or four hours minimum. Some is from memory and the rest is from bulletins she texted while my phone was out of my possession." She really shouldn't have added that dig about the phone.

Silence. Prompted by her own growling stomach, she suggested, "How about we meet for a late breakfast at Lynnie's tomorrow morning, like nine o'clock? I'll bring the Natalie stuff then, and I'll make sure it's readable."

Hank grumbled about the delay.

Tough. She wasn't going to drop everything and dive into a request that was second priority. She thought to ask him, "Have you found Natalie's car yet?"

"I'll update you on that when we talk at Lynnie's."

Okay, she deserved that. And Hank hadn't said *No* to her question. She wanted to believe they had found the car and that Natalie was safe somewhere. She meant it when she told him, "Thank you."

Hank's tone shifted, too. He sounded more like a collaborator when he said, "To help us create an accurate timeline of the wife's movements around the time Duval was killed, I need you to include the time of each individual communication from your friend. Follow that through until after the time Stan Block was killed, which was shortly before eight o'clock Tuesday night."

She wondered how they knew that. They must have found Stan's body. Was there a witness? Figuring Hank would only answer one more question, she asked, "You're thinking Jacqueline Duval killed her husband *and* Stan Block, aren't you?"

"It's one possibility." With that, he ended the call.

She really should fix a bagel and peanut butter, but she knew any one of her active search results might lead her to the real name of Emile Duval. She grabbed an apple, set it on the island, and went back to work.

One hour more of clicking, skimming, and copying-pasting everything that might be useful, she felt goose bumps on her arms. She knew it wasn't suddenly colder in the room. She wondered if this was a psychic sensation, like the others she'd had when she was closing in on a clue. Emile's true identity had to be within reach.

Kyle and Justin Cushman had been friends for twenty years and, until this morning, Kyle had always felt Justin had the greater power. *That ends today*, Kyle vowed as he strode into Justin's office and helped himself to a chair across the oversized mahogany desk from the president.

Kyle had called for this morning's meeting and he deliberately opened by asking for the name of Justin's architect. With that information in hand, he lambasted the president of Tompkins College for his exploitation of Dr. Lyssa Pennington. "It has to stop, Justin."

Stunned, the president sat back in his cushy chair and listened.

"You forced her to serve you at the worst possible time in the semester to support a search for a candidate outside her area of expertise. You required her to organize and be present at the candidate's dinner, where he was murdered.

As a result, she was frivolously accused of murder and is now confined to Tompkins Falls when she should be in Cornwall with me."

"Kyle—"

"She has since slaved for hours fact-checking a resumé that should have been vetted upfront by the committee. And now she's hunched over a computer giving further support to the murder investigation, on your suggestion. And, Justin, it all points back to your unreasonable demands on her time and on her good nature."

"I—"

"Your insistence that she save your college by performing one outrageous task after another must stop. Have you looked at her lately, at what all this is doing to my lovely wife?" He stopped at that, simply because his throat had closed with fear about Lyssa's health. In the ensuing silence, he swallowed and regained his composure.

After puffing out his cheeks and popping a breath, Justin confessed, "You're right. I saw her faint while Hank Moran was browbeating her."

Kyle stiffened. Why hadn't Lyssa told him that? His emotions got the better of him. He half rose and, with his fists on the edge of the desk, stared down at the man. "Hank wouldn't have been doing any such thing if you hadn't gotten her and the committee into that mess in the first place." A muscle in his jaw twitched.

"You are correct. And I apologized to Lyssa immediately when I drove her back to the house after res—after securing her release from Westerlee Hall."

Kyle glared, certain Justin had been about to say *rescuing* her. Justin *would* think of himself as her savior.

The president's voice was maddeningly calm. "And I apologize to you, my good friend, for that egregious error and also for ruining your holiday in Cornwall. You both need the break right now and need the time together, away from your work and hers."

"Well, if you must know, we *were* planning to have a conversation over the holiday about starting our family." Kyle pushed away from the desk and paced the width of the office. "I'm not at all sure she's healthy enough to carry a child. Pregnancy and fainting are orthogonal."

"Are what?"

He pivoted and faced Justin. "At odds with each other."

Eyes lowered, Justin stared at his hands. "I believe there's a New Year's resolution in this for both of us."

"And what might that be?"

"Revisit our priorities." Justin stood then and held out his hand. "I have another meeting."

Kyle met the president's strong grip. "Don't ever do this to her again."

"Understood. Since you're stuck in Tompkins Falls, let's plan on dinner for the four of us at the house."

Despite Justin's conciliatory tone, Kyle shrugged. "I'll see if Lyssa's interested."

He strode toward the exit of Tompkins College's administration building, his footfalls echoing in the hallowed hall. The fresh air cleared his head. There was one more thing he had to do for Lyssa this morning.

Lyssa quenched her thirst by gnawing her apple to the quick and setting aside the mangled core. Then it was back to her search. Ten clicks in, the image on her screen made her sit up straighter. She clicked the accompanying View Page button, and up popped a two-year-old news story about a charity fundraiser on Long Island. One of the article's photos showed a handsome tuxedoed Emile Duval lookalike with a strikingly beautiful woman on his arm. Lyssa had seen the woman's eyes before, in shadow beneath a wide-brimmed beach hat, flirting with the camera. *Oh my gosh.*

It couldn't be, could it? Was this the real Emile Duval accompanied by the woman in the snapshot of Marguerite's fellow travelers? *Or have I completely lost my mind?*

She ignored her nagging thirst, bookmarked the link, and rubbed her hands together. After reading and rereading every line of the article, she could not find a name for the man or the woman. Nor was there a caption for the grainy photo, and her inspector function merely gave the dimensions and resolution of the image.

She scrolled back for the story's byline and used the newspaper's contact form to request more information. It was worth a try.

She then issued a Google search for the same fundraiser and also an image search for the same grainy photo of the wealthy couple. Neither produced additional information, but she returned with renewed energy to the tedious task of examining the roughly 2,000 remaining hits. She was sure now she would get another lead, one that would produce the real name of Emile Duval.

Within the hour she found another news story about a fundraiser two months earlier in the same year, which included the picture of a man she'd swear was Emile, posing in front of garlands and red ribbons and artificial snow. This time he was flanked by two beautifully coifed women, neither of whom had been his companion in the other story.

The trio held their champagne flutes aloft and showed perfect white teeth for the camera. The caption referred to the man as a fashion mogul; no names for any of the three people. Although she scrutinized the article, she found no additional clues.

Her hands trembling with fatigue and excitement, it took her multiple tries to simply copy and paste the URL of the article, type in the phrase fashion mogul, and download the image to her spreadsheet.

She'd forgotten something important, though. Before moving on, she backtracked to the previous story with an Emile Duval lookalike, the one where his partner might be Marguerite's fellow traveler. She added its URL and downloaded its photo.

Aware that her work had grown sloppy and she was too shaky to continue, she pushed back from her computer.

As he fitted the key in the lock for their third-floor apartment, Kyle hummed a passage from a chamber piece performed at their wedding a year ago. Surely, if Lyssa were home, she would have rushed to greet him this time. Maybe she was getting some fresh air. He juggled his two bulging grocery bags as he pushed open the door with one hip.

He stood with his mouth open for a full five seconds, wondering why Lyssa was leaning heavily on the kitchen counter with one hand, while the other hand gripped the handle of the refrigerator door. He hadn't been far off when he'd told Joel she looked like death. The sweatshirt hung on her thin frame, and her skin and hair were lifeless.

He dumped the grocery sacks on the island and got his arm around her waist. "What's wrong, sweetheart?"

She turned to him in slow motion. "I was hungry and thirsty. I got this far but I'm dizzy."

"Come, sit down. Can you?" She leaned into him and he steered her to a chair at the table by the window. "Let's get some food into you. I've brought your favorites."

Though she landed heavily on the chair, she did have a spark of interest in the bags on the island. With shaking hands, he unloaded the bounty. "Stop when you see something that appeals."

She croaked out, "Crackers and cheese. You're wonderful."

He passed her the box, but she struggled to open the glued top flap. "Here, let me." He couldn't keep the fear out of his tone. He opened the box and the inner package and plunked a handful of crackers on a plate. "Been working too hard and too long, eh?" He'd been gone four hours and all he saw by way of nourishment was a tooth-marked apple core.

"What kind is the cheese?"

He had removed it from its sealed covering and set it on another plate next to the crackers. "It's that cheddar Fiona likes from Ireland. They carry it at Wegman's, did you know?" He sliced half the brick, arranged the slices, and set the lot in front of her. "No more questions until you've finished this off."

"Water, please."

He brought her a tall glass of it, which she drank down, then handed back the glass.

"More, please."

When the plate was bare, he asked, "Any better?"

She nodded. "That was scary." Her voice was stronger now. "But I found him, Kyle."

"Found? Your murdered candidate?"

"I'm pretty sure."

"Sweetheart—"

"Can you grab those two pages I printed?"

That her response focused strictly on work bothered him, as if what had just happened was all in a day's work. With a sinking feeling, he wondered if it was.

Perhaps this was how she operated when they were apart, putting her students and her semester responsibilities ahead of her health, taking on Justin's special jobs, and dealing with whatever fallout might occur. Like murder.

No wonder her appearance had changed so radically, so quickly. He lifted the two sheets from the printer and studied the photo of a black tie affair, a man with two society ladies. "So our candidate is in reality a wealthy society donor, is he?" The people's clothing was very high-end and the jewelry, assuming it was real, worth tens of thousands.

He glanced up to see her watching him while she munched another cracker from the package. He set the page face up on the counter and squinted at the next photo, which showed the same man with a different woman. His eyes switched back and forth between the man and woman in the second photo.

Lyssa asked him, "Do you think it's the same man in both photos?"

"Yes, I do. But in this photo of the couple, I swear I've seen the woman on his arm." He locked eyes with Lyssa. When she smiled, he asked her. "You think so, too, don't you, love?"

"Think what?" she said with an innocent grin.

"That she's a dressed-up version of the flirt in the lineup of Marguerite's fellow travelers." Lyssa merely raised her eyebrows. "Come on, you know who I mean."

When she made a move toward her laptop, he held up his hand to stop. "Stay where you are and keep eating. Out of cheese, are you?" She nodded wordlessly and he sliced the rest of the package for her.

"Thanks." Her voice cracked, and she had tears on her cheeks.

The tears gave him all the incentive he needed to take over the mind-numbing task of sorting through search results one by one. While he slogged through them, dutifully checking the context for each successive photo in her results list, he resolved to get Lyssa into the hands of Manda's physician before they left for their holiday, whatever it took. The problem was convincing her she needed to be seen.

If he could get her to Cornwall, Fiona and Moira would do their part to feed her healthy meals, insist on rest and exercise, and cluck at her about exhausting herself. But those were only quick fixes. Lyssa herself had to take responsibility for turning around the unhealthy habits she'd fallen into.

He had processed several hundred more results—some of them obviously not relevant, others finance articles or society news with photos of their unnamed man. It finally occurred to him that Justin's star candidate made it a point to keep his name out of the media. Why? And how much was he paying out of pocket to ensure his privacy?

He glanced up at Lyssa at that point. She'd given up the cheese and crackers and was staring out the window. She ought to be in bed, and he ought to be making her a hot meal. Yet, he was in striking distance of finishing with the search results.

He stretched his neck and vowed to keep going until he turned up a name for their devious fashion mogul. He'd no sooner made that decision than a financial article identified the gentleman as Charles Drayton. Kyle flexed his fingers and, rather than exhausting the search results, took a direct route to the man. It paid off.

"Aha, Old Westbury, indeed," he shouted. "We were correct." Lyssa was up from the table before he could stop her. She came behind him and looked over his shoulder.

"Read it to me," she requested. She probably had eyestrain on top of everything else.

She settled on the next stool. He summarized the Wikipedia article as he scanned it. "Charles Drayton, born 1970, lives Old Westbury, New York." He pointed across the island to Tony's snapshot of Stan Block's blackmail box for Marguerite. "If you look very closely at the postmark of the topmost letter in the packet Marguerite tied up with a purple ribbon, you'll see that's where the letter was posted."

"Keep reading," Lyssa implored.

"Sorry, yes. Educated Harvard, MBA Cornell. Founder and CEO of Drayton Textiles, which produces two clothing lines favoring full-figured women—"

"Ohmigosh, Kyle." Her fingers dug into his forearm. "It's all coming together, isn't it?"

Not sure what she meant, he continued the narrative. "Two clothing lines, one retail, one couture."

She interrupted again. "I'm not sure I know what that means."

He was certain that she, an economics professor, knew exactly what it meant, but he answered, "Retail is clothing sold on the rack at a store. Couture is very high-end dressmaking, custom to each client's taste and measurements."

"Okay, but what does it say his wife's name is?"

"Why is that important?"

"*Because* if Emile Duval's real name is Charles Drayton, his wife might really be the model Vivienne that Natalie says she met at the Spa at the Manse on Monday afternoon." She rested both elbows on the island and pressed her palms against either side of her head. "All the puzzle pieces are crashing together. My head's spinning."

"You think she's the woman the police are looking for, and I think she's the woman in the photo with Marguerite and her fellow travelers in Brittany last summer."

"She's *both* those things, Kyle. Don't you see?"

"Go easy, sweetheart. Is this a panic attack?"

"*No*, it's just—Can you *please* find the name of his wife in the article? Please." Still holding her head, she inhaled deeply, held the breath, exhaled completely, and then repeated the sequence.

"I'm looking," he said, desperate now to find the answer for her. *Lord, are we insane? Should I take her to the hospital?* The answer popped on the screen. "Here. Drayton is married to supermodel Vivienne. And there's a link."

He clicked the link, tapping his fingers in a tricky pattern while he sorted through the Drayton Textiles' website for more about their supermodel. He heard the tension and excitement in his own voice when he told her, "No question she's the one in the picture with Marguerite in Brittany last summer *and* in the photo with Charles Drayton at the fundraiser. Want to see?"

With one hand he blindly swiveled the computer toward her and, with the other hand, reached halfway across the island for the photo showing the Brittany travelers. "I'm right. In the Brittany photo, the woman is *not* flirting with the camera at all, is she? Or with the cameraman. She's flirting with the woman who *kept* the photo—Marguerite. That's why our girl kept *that* photo. Here, take a look."

But Lyssa had rested her head on her arms, and she mumbled, "But what if we're wrong and the woman at the spa forced Natalie to drive her somewhere and she's in danger?"

"I'm sure Natalie's fine." He snapped his fingers. "And something else that's obvious: the letters addressed to Marguerite came from Vivienne, and they're love letters to Marguerite, which Stan found and used to extort money from her. The rotter. I'm sending the link for these articles to Hank, and—"

But Lyssa had slid off the stool and lay on the floor on her back, pressing her hands against her face. Trembling with alarm, he knelt at her side and touched a gentle hand to her arm. "Can you tell me what's wrong?"

She whispered, "I don't know. I'm scared."

He grabbed for his phone and called 911.

Chapter 13

Kyle glanced up from testing the doneness of their jacket potatoes. Lyssa was stirring in the next room. She'd scared the life out of him when she fainted. A call to 911 brought the emergency medical technicians within minutes. Her blood pressure was low, and Kyle's description of symptoms indicated dehydration. When Lyssa came to, she admitted that, until Kyle fed her crackers and cheese, she hadn't eaten more than an apple since dinner the previous night.

Kyle hung back while they gave her a lecture on the importance of nutrition and hydration. Her blood pressure slowly improved during the tutorial, and Lyssa agreed to get plenty of liquids and rest, a hot meal, and a good night's sleep, in that order. When Kyle told them of her other recent fainting spells, they directed Lyssa to see her primary care physician within twenty-four hours.

Her admission that she didn't have one met with scowls. Kyle produced the phone number for Manda's doctor. When he asked if they knew of her, they gave Dr. Bowes and her clinic a strong endorsement. With Lyssa's permission, they called the clinic's after-hours line with their findings and requested that Lyssa be seen the next day.

The rest was up to Lyssa.

As they packed up their equipment, she narrowed her eyes at Kyle and asked how he'd come to have the phone number. He told her frankly about his conversation with Joel that morning. "You realize everyone's been worried about you, eh?" She'd closed her eyes at that.

After seeing the EMTs to the door, he'd carried her to bed with an order to sleep. Each time he checked on her, her pulse was steady and strong and she sat up for another glass of water. Still, he sensed something was very wrong that would take more than one hot meal to fix.

The potatoes tested done. Perhaps Lyssa had smelled the good food, for he heard the bathroom door click shut and water running in the shower. He waited until the shower noises stopped, then plated a meal for each of them.

She gave him a sleepy smile as she emerged from the bedroom, still pale-faced, dressed in blue jeans and a Cornwall sweatshirt.

"Feeling okay?"

She nodded, picked up her phone, and settled at the island.

"Meal's hot, love. Chicken, potatoes, and vege. I've set the table for us."

She merely nodded and made a phone call. He stood with his arms folded. He'd give her sixty seconds.

Evidently, her dreams that night had popped up some new insight, for she was now verifying that the person she was speaking with was Charles Drayton's assistant. She crooked a finger at him, put the conversation on speaker, and set the phone on the island. He reached for a pad and pencil and joined her.

Lyssa stated her name using a professional tone of voice. "If Charles has returned from his trip, I need to speak with him about the few items he left with us Tuesday. Can you help me contact him? I assume he's at the photo shoot."

Kyle was certain *the few items he left with us* was pure fiction. It took him a moment to realize what she'd put together. Natalie had told Lyssa her new friend Vivienne was on her way to a fashion photo shoot after her visit to

Tompkins Falls. And they now knew that Vivienne was Charles Drayton's wife, as well as the top model for Drayton Textile's line of clothing. Charles's assistant would know where the photo shoot was taking place and how to reach Vivienne.

Clever girl. Her ruse would only work if the authorities had not yet contacted Drayton's office with the news of Charles's death. They'd given the information to Hank just four or five hour ago.

The assistant replied, "He didn't return to the office, Dr. Pennington. May I be of assistance?"

"After our inhospitable weather here"—Lyssa interjected a laugh—"he's probably gone right on to Morocco. I can't blame him for wanting the heat of the desert."

"You're right about that, but there's been a tiny little change in the plan." Kyle held his breath. "Too much sand blowing around. The models and crew are still booked into the Four Seasons in Agadir but they're shooting on the beaches north of the city."

He jotted a few words on his pad—*She doesn't know he's dead*—and tapped Lyssa's hand. She read the note and nodded.

The assistant sighed. "I really wish Charles had swung by New York and taken me with him this time."

So Charles had planned all along to join his wife, the supermodel, in Africa after his two-day performance as Professor Emile Duval at Tompkins College. Kyle picked up his phone and texted the new information, first to President Justin Cushman, and then to Hank Moran.

Beside him, Lyssa was listening to the information offered by Charles's assistant, using Kyle's pad and pencil to note the details of the hotel in Agadir and the expected timeline and locations for the shoot.

Kyle was sure Hank would be over the moon to have all this information handed to him. Hank was convinced the murderer was the candidate's wife and, despite the complication of Stan Block's murder, his highest priority was undoubtedly to bring Duval's killer back to Tompkins Falls to answer for the man's death.

Lyssa ended her call with a self-satisfied smile. "Done."

"Pure genius," he told her.

Lyssa shut off her phone. "I feel so much better," she told Kyle.

"Hungry?"

"Starved." The herbal aroma of the roast chicken made her salivate. "The whole apartment smells good. What can I do?"

"Sit yourself at the table and tuck in your napkin."

With a kitchen towel draped over his arm, he delivered his masterpiece to the table. Flanking the bird on its platter were steaming baked potatoes and artfully arranged green beans. He went back for a dish of toasted sliced almonds and a larger bowl of mashed butternut squash.

Lyssa laughed with delight. "Comfort food. How did you learn to cook like this?"

"You thought my repertoire was limited to scallops and spinach, giant healthy salads, and foods of that sort?"

"Yes."

"Actually, I called Fiona and had her instruct me. She's terribly worried about you. We all are."

"Me, too." She met his gaze. "I'm deeply sorry for worrying everyone."

"As you should be. You can't keep doing this."

She nodded. "I've been neglecting my health all semester. Whenever you're away I go back to my old habits, and I can't be doing that."

She was filling her plate when he asked, "Was that a panic attack you had earlier?"

"I don't think so." She reached for the dish of whole-berry cranberry sauce and deposited a spoonful next to her pieces of chicken. "I agree with the EMTs I was dehydrated, and maybe that's what caused the headache and the light-headedness, but the same thing happened when Hank was grilling me after the murder, and I'd been drinking lots of water that night."

"So you really did faint then, just as Justin told me this morning?"

He'd talked to both Joel and Justin about her? Her cheeks felt hot. Over a loaded forkful, she answered his question. "I almost fainted, yes. Sorry for not telling you, but the whole night was such a nightmare. Hank grilled me forever, and when he said two of the faculty had accused me of the murder I lost it. I would have passed out if Rand hadn't come into the room and sat me down and got my head between my knees. I knew you'd be upset. Needlessly."

"I wouldn't say 'needlessly.' My former rival, Rand Cunningham, putting his hands on you and forcing anything between your knees? That's something I need to know about."

She winced at the image. *Touched a nerve with that, didn't I?*

Kyle was busy layering squash and cranberries on the back of his fork.

She took a moment to savor the moist chicken. "What are these herbs?"

"Rosemary, fennel seed, and a blend from Provence. That's quite a spice rack Joel left for us."

"This is really good."

"Have there been other occasions when you've fainted or nearly fainted?"

She fought with herself not to shut down at his stern tone. He had cause to be upset. Angry, too, for that matter. "The only other time was at Fritz Van Derzee's memorial service earlier this fall. Someone socked me in the jaw and I went down."

"Did I know about that?"

"Probably not. I know you're angry."

"I'm afraid for you." His volume rose with each statement. "And for me. And for our dreams of a family." He forced out his breath.

She reached around the bird to touch his hand. "I will do whatever I have to do to get my health back."

"I will hold you to that." He blinked back tears. "And I will help in whatever way I can."

Her fork slipped out of her hand. Berry juice spattered on the fresh blue linen Kyle had chosen for the table. "Sorry, I'm shaky."

"Eating will help with that. Let's just enjoy the food for a few minutes, eh?" His tight smile didn't fool her.

She sat up straighter and followed his lead combining the squash and cranberry in one bite. "It's really good."

Once the protein hit her system, she felt some energy coming back. In rehab three years ago, they'd taught her something she'd completely forgotten, that a healthy snack or meal was the answer to most episodes of emotional turmoil and that she should remember to HALT. That is, never get too Hungry, Angry, Lonely, or Tired. "I'm my own worst enemy, aren't I?"

"I'd say so, yes." He set down his fork. "Sweetheart, I want you to see Manda's doctor and get a thorough checkup, as your highest priority. Straightaway. We can go together, if you like."

"I agree to the physical, and I'll call first thing tomorrow for the earliest possible appointment. But I'm not sure about having you come this time."

"And why is that?"

"It would feel like you're holding my hand for something that's my responsibility. I'll see if Gianessa will come so we can talk woman-to-woman."

"I see." His tone was clipped, but he'd relaxed a little. "If you change your mind, the offer stands."

"Thanks." She attempted a sunny smile. "You know what I'd really like your help with tonight?"

A raised eyebrow was her answer.

"I'm meeting Hank at nine o'clock tomorrow morning. I have homework, and it will take me hours if I do it alone. It's the very last thing he's asked me for, and together we could knock it off in a couple hours."

"I'm game. If I recall, this task involves consolidating all of Natalie's great adventure with Vivienne."

"Correct. And I think you're right. It could be entertaining."

Kyle's flashed one of his Cornish smiles. "You're getting your spirit back, eh?"

After dinner, Kyle typed while Lyssa recalled the substance of her dinner conversation with Natalie the evening after they posted semester grades. Lyssa reviewed and approved his report.

"That would have taken me hours," she told him.

The relief in her voice partially made up for the headache he'd acquired in the process. Natalie, high on most of a bottle of wine, had giggled and gushed the entire time, and what she and Vivienne were planning sounded reckless to him.

He hoped their transcription of Natalie's text bulletins would go much faster. And it did, though their walk-through of the activities the night of Drayton's and Block's murders made it clear the adventure was not the lark Natalie had been expecting.

He and Lyssa also saw why Natalie was not replying to any of Lyssa's frantic texts or voicemails since getting her phone back. Natalie believed Lyssa had deserted her in her hour of need.

Kyle got a chuckle out of Natalie's description of the cat burglar costumes Natalie and Vivienne had worn, but the entertainment gave way to sobering reality once the women entered M's office looking for love letters from Vivienne's husband. In Natalie's words:

OMG. M is Marguerite? No way.

V like a machine looking everywhere. Killing me to see all Marguerite's travel treasures on the shelves and walls. Can't believe she's gone.

I KNOW Marguerite loved Billy, but try arguing with V?!! She's a screamer. Afraid we'll get caught. Hate this.

Bombshell. V had the affair with Marguerite, not V's hubby. What was she thinking??? CALL ME!!!

No letters. V upping reward. We're off to Marguerite's house. Wish I'd never started this mission. CALL ME!!!

"She was in over her head from the start," Lyssa said.

"So it would seem. I can't imagine any reward the woman offered was worth the risk."

"I think, like her husband, Vivienne was a master manipulator." Lyssa shook her head. "And you know what's ironic? If my phone hadn't been with Hank I might have known what she was going through and figured out sooner who Duval really was."

"This is upsetting, sweetheart. Shall I finish the job alone?"

"No, I need to see the rest or I won't get any sleep tonight."

But the updates from Marguerite's house were gut wrenching:

V sobbing in M's bedroom. She has my keys now. Don't ask.

I've looked everywhere. No letters.

V raging now, wants to know where Stan Block lives. Says he tried to blackmail Marguerite.

I tell her she'll miss her flight. OMG what if he's home? I don't trust her. She's out for blood.

But she's right Stan can ruin Marguerite's good name. Can't quit until we find the *#@##@ letters.

"So Vivienne told Natalie about Stan's blackmail of Marguerite?" Lyssa said.

"Apparently, though I don't think Natalie put it together with the attack on Marguerite in the parking lot." Kyle scrolled back through the messages to make sure he'd got the correct timestamps. There were only cryptic bulletins from Stan Block's cottage before they'd taken off for Newark airport:

V tearing apart closets and drawers. Glad I'm wearing gloves.

You won't believe what I found in his entertainment center. CALL ME!!!

On Thruway. V driving like a maniac, has to make the flight.

Can't think who was sitting in that beatup car behind Stan's. Creeped me out the way he watched us leave. I need to talk!!!

Furious you haven't called.

Seriously- she wants to read them? Now?? At least I get to drive the rest of the way.

V has no heart. Says she'll burn them in the desert.

Not that you deserve to know. At EWR. Mission accomplished. Reward awaits.

And that was the lot of them. "What do you make of that comment about wearing gloves?" Kyle asked.

Lyssa was scrolling back through the texts and double-checking their report for accuracy. "Either Stan was a lousy housekeeper or she was looking through some of the other blackmail boxes and felt dirty at what she was seeing."

"I suppose either could be true. Are you cold, love?"

She was rubbing her arms. "No, it's that stuff about some guy watching them from a car behind Stan's house. That was probably Stan's killer."

Kyle felt chills of his own at that. "You may be right." Perhaps one of Stan's blackmail victims drove a beat-up car. Tony would have information about the vehicles driven by each employee.

After he'd seen Lyssa off to bed, he realized a text had come for him from Gianessa Cushman, insisting that they meet at first light.

Chapter 14

Kyle assumed the summons from Gianessa Cushman was about Lyssa. Yet, when she greeted him with a megawatt smile at the Cushman's front door wearing her down coat, his instinct told him otherwise. There was an edge to her he'd never seen.

She flipped up the hood of her coat and gestured him back outside. "Let's walk. It's a glorious day."

"It's minus ten Celsius," he grumbled. He turned up the collar of his cashmere coat, wrapped his muffler tighter, and stuffed his hands in the pockets. Perhaps he should get one of those long puffer coats like Gianessa's. "Down is it? Your coat?"

"Yes, from LL Bean. The store is right next to Eastview Mall. I heard you gave Lyssa an ultimatum to see my doctor."

"Dr. Bowes is your physician, too?"

"She saved our lives when the twins were born, but that's a story for another time."

Kyle bowed his head at the words *saved our lives* and let the emotions pour over him. "She is desperately ill, Gianessa. Haven't any of you seen that?"

"Of course we have and we've been after her to take better care of herself, but she laughs it off or turns a deaf ear."

"While Justin hounds her to do more and more work." He hated the bitterness in his tone.

"I heard about your confrontation with him."

"And there's Hank, who needs her to solve his case for him."

"Both Justin and Hank Moran are masters of the guilt trip. Right now, she's doing their bidding because she feels responsible for Marguerite's death."

"She's not—" He halted and held up his hands. "Let's leave that for the moment. I wanted to ask you if you'd learned anything about Melissa and Roger Rossini, specifically their alibis for the night of the two murders, Drayton's and Block's."

She paused, narrowed her eyes at him, then race-walked ahead. He rushed to catch up.

"It's of paramount importance, Gianessa."

"You and Lyssa get on a case and nothing else matters," she hissed. "Not common sense. Not common courtesy. Nothing but answers."

"Sorry."

"Save it for someone who believes you. Yes, I talked with Missy. In fact, that's why I called you. And, yes, they have alibis."

"Say more."

"She and Roger hosted their bridge group Tuesday night from six o'clock dinner right through the last hand at ten thirty. Another couple, whose names I will not tell you, stayed behind, as they usually do, until after midnight to help clean up and to have a long friendly conversation."

"Did—?"

"No. I did not interrogate the other couple. I'm satisfied Missy and Roger had nothing to do with Duval's—I mean, Drayton's—death. Or Stan Block's either. But it's entirely possible their marriage will suffer if the police start poking into their private lives. Missy sobbed the whole time we talked. Does that satisfy your curiosity, Dr. Pennington?"

"Hold on." Kyle put a hand on her arm. She jerked away from him and marched ahead. "Gianessa, I'm not a monster." He struggled along behind her, his loafers slipping on the snow-packed drive. "And it's not my job to mess up people's lives. Missy took a risk when she started the affair, and now she may have to face the consequences. Two men are dead, and all of us are in pain because we've lost our dear friend Marguerite. Many people are suffering about all of this, and I'm one of the good guys here." He'd run out of breath, and he slowed his pace.

She faced him, vapor from her nostrils forming tiny clouds in the frigid morning. "Well, so am I, and I hated doing what you asked me to do."

"I regret involving you. I shan't do it again."

Her jaw set. "Don't make promises you can't keep. Now talk to me about Lyssa. How can I help?"

Lyssa shook out the paper napkin and placed it on her lap. "Thanks for meeting me here, Hank. It's easier for me to think when we talk like this." Although it was mid-morning, breakfast traffic at Lynnie's was still brisk.

"I'm here as Trooper Moran, not as Hank."

"I know, but if I remember you're human, I have a shot at getting through this interrogation without a meltdown. I intend to be helpful."

Their waitress interrupted to pour coffee. "The usual, Trooper?"

Hank nodded. Lyssa ordered a Mediterranean omelet. When she asked for separate checks, Hank scowled but didn't comment.

She patted her tote. "I've brought a summary of what Natalie told me Monday when we had dinner at her house to celebrate turning in our semester grades." At Hank's blank look, she added, "Natalie Horowitz. Monday night, the night before the murders, is when she first told me about her encounter with her idol, supermodel Vivienne, AKA Jacqueline Duval, AKA Mrs. Charles Drayton. I'd never heard of Vivienne and frankly didn't believe she'd met a supermodel who happened to be her idol."

Trooper Moran blew on his coffee and tested the temperature with a small sip.

"Plus, I have printouts of all the text messages from Natalie on the night of the murders, including the times and some annotations that might be useful. Kyle was a huge help putting the whole thing together."

"We'll talk through your report after we eat, but right now I need to make you aware, in confidence, that Stan Block's body was airlifted to Albany for autopsy, and they've determined the cause of death is a fractured skull with external and intracranial bleeding." Hank gave her a hard look. "Which he received by cracking his head against the brick woodstove surround when he fell or was pushed in a fight in his living room."

"Why are you glaring at me? You know I had nothing to do with his death. He was a blackmailer and he'd led a life that invited violence. If he'd been physically threatening Marguerite, he'd probably been harassing his other victims, too. It wasn't necessarily connected to Emile's—I mean Charles Drayton's—murder."

"We intend to check the alibis of the blackmail victims as soon as the college releases their identities."

"Wait, don't you have the boxes Stan kept with the evidence of his victims' crimes? Or bad behavior or whatever they did?"

"The what?"

She closed her eyes. Hadn't the police searched Stan's place and found the boxes? "Tony told Kyle that Stan took eight boxes full of blackmail stuff, one each for eight of his victims, out of his office at the college the night of Drayton's murder. As you'll see in the report, Kyle and I found out for sure last night that he stashed the boxes at his house."

Why hadn't the police told Hank? Interagency rivalry, maybe? Hank made an angry phone call to someone ordering them to search Stan's cottage again and report back as soon as the boxes were in hand.

"Back to my point," he said. Though his voice was stern, his hand shook just enough for Lyssa to notice. "A woman could have caused the fracture to his skull by tripping him or joining forces with a sidekick to rush him into a fall, which brings me back to your buddy Horowitz and Mrs. Drayton. The intent may not have been murder, but the result is Officer Block is dead."

"You're assuming they were at Stan's when he was killed and, therefore, are responsible for his death. You're wrong. Natalie made no mention of Stan being present, and I don't believe for a moment that she would leave Stan Block unconscious and bleeding, let alone try to dump his body in Chestnut Lake. Frankly, I'm not sure Vivienne had much of a moral compass, but she and Natalie left together. No Stan."

"At the moment we want the wife for both murders." His eyes narrowed at her. "And we want to talk with your friend Horowitz about her role."

Lyssa summoned up her strongest voice. "You'll see her role when we go through the stuff I brought. I don't believe either of them had anything to do with either death, but I am fully cooperating with your investigation." Now she was especially glad Kyle had helped her compile the documents for Hank. He could testify to the objectivity used in transcribing the texts that documented Natalie's movements the night Stan Block was killed.

"Good choice." Hank's tone was wry. "I believe you're aware the two women have fled the country together and—"

"Wrong." She hit the table with her fists. "I called the hotel in Agadir, and Natalie Horowitz is not there. I thought you knew that."

"She may not be registered under her own name, Mrs. Pennington, but I'm confident the authorities who are raiding the hotel as we speak will find both women in Agadir or the vicinity."

She sucked in a breath and offered a silent prayer for Vivienne and Natalie, wherever they were. "Where was Natalie's car found?" He'd never said it was found, but if she pretended to know, she might get farther.

The waitress gave them a cheery, "Here you go," and set down their breakfasts. Lyssa took a long drink of coffee and held out her cup for a refill. "Thank you," she said, making a mental note that the waitress probably knew more about people in Tompkins Falls than she ever would.

While Trooper Moran was intent on slicing a banana onto his steaming oatmeal, Lyssa dug into her omelet. It was heavy on the olives today, and she picked out most of them.

Halfway through his breakfast, he rested his forearms on the table. "As you know, the local police came up empty at Dr. Horowitz's house. We tracked the two women via Horowitz's EZ-pass. They traveled nonstop by interstate highway to Newark airport, but the car then left the airport and continued to a subway stop near the George Washington Bridge, where it has been parked since shortly after midnight Wednesday morning."

"So Natalie has probably gone into New York City. That's good."

"Or doubled back to the airport." He spooned his oatmeal.

"That doesn't make sense. If she were flying somewhere she'd park it at the airport, wouldn't she?"

Hank ignored her question and ate another spoonful.

"What about her credit card?"

189

He dabbed a spot of milk from his lower lip. "Hasn't been used. However, a first-class ticket on the same flight as Mrs. Drayton's was purchased by electronic check, within minutes of departure time. The airline has so far refused to reveal the passenger's name or the name of the person who purchased the ticket."

Lyssa sat open-mouthed. *Seriously? That was thousands of dollars.* "Hank, who has that kind of cash sitting around?" When the state trooper only smiled in response, she answered her own question, "Someone who's rich and who knows how to pay for privacy." When she looked up, he was nodding. "Maybe it was an employee of Drayton Textiles who accompanied her?" She snorted at her own suggestion. "Employees don't go first class, Lyssa. Cancel that."

Hank set down his mug. "Around the time Professor Marguerite LaCroix died, Mrs. Drayton rebooked her own ticket. She delayed her departure one day and upgraded it from business class to first class. Does that mean something to you?"

Lyssa nodded thoughtfully. She was guessing about this. "I think she had originally planned for Marguerite to accompany her to the shoot." She narrowed her eyes at Hank. "But Natalie Horowitz has *not* taken Marguerite's place in Vivienne's life, Hank. Natalie is as straight as they come."

"I wasn't suggesting that. But think about it. I know what my wife would say if someone offered to pay *her* way to that photo shoot."

Ohmigosh, he's right. Torie Moran had given birth to the couple's four children and made no apology for the extra weight she carried. Like Torie, Natalie would be all over the opportunity to accompany her idol Vivienne—first class, no less—and hang out on a beach watching a parade of the latest curvy woman fashions.

Hank had gone back to his oatmeal.

Lyssa drained her coffee. "But ten thousand dollars, maybe more, out of pocket? Why would Vivienne lay out that kind of cash for someone she'd just met?"

He drilled her with a look. "Maybe as payment for helping her escape the country after she'd murdered two people?"

Lyssa shook her head. "That doesn't hold up. Even if Natalie helped a criminal, which she wouldn't, not knowingly, why would they go exactly where Vivienne was expected to be for her work?"

"You make a good point. However, I suspect she planned to shift the blame to Horowitz."

"Whoa." If he was right, Natalie was in major trouble. Lyssa's hand shook too badly to hold onto the fork. She let it drop on the plate and flattened her hand on the table.

"We'll continue our efforts to learn the identity of the last-minute ticket-holder." He set aside the empty cereal bowl. "Thanks to you we know the connection between Vivienne Drayton and Marguerite LaCroix, which you caught on to from the photograph of Ms. LaCroix's merry band of travelers to Brittany last summer. Have you given any thought to the possible involvement of others in the photograph?"

"Kyle and I recognized Vivienne as the model in the top right of the group. I suppose the other model, the rail-thin blond standing next to Marguerite in the front row, might have been a friend of Vivienne's, but I think she was too thin to be modeling for Drayton Textiles. They design for a different figure type."

"Could she have been another of Mrs. Drayton's lovers, angry about LaCroix moving in on her territory?"

Lyssa only shrugged at the suggestion. "Then why would she wait to kill Marguerite until months later in Tompkins Falls? And then days later kill Vivienne's husband when the

Draytons arrived in Tompkins Falls? And then Stan Block? None of that makes sense to me, Hank."

"Does anyone else in that snapshot strike you as a suspect?"

"No, but Kyle thinks the guy with the facial hair and wild eyebrows is a thriller writer."

Hank chuckled and Lyssa remarked, "He probably doesn't need to murder people to come up with his next plot."

"Not to put too fine a point on it," Hank said, "we don't know that LaCroix's or Block's deaths were murder."

"I understand."

"Back to Ms. Horowitz's role. You sound certain she went with the wife willingly."

"Absolutely. Natalie's too savvy to be coerced. Well, not physically anyway. Her husband was a career soldier, and she's had lots of training in self-defense. Basically, she idolized Vivienne. At least at the start, this was a lark for her."

"If she's so savvy, why isn't she responding to your texts and emails? Surely she knows how worried you are."

Lyssa choked on a sob. "You'll see. She was upset with me that I didn't respond to any of her texts during their mission to find the love letters." She cleared her throat. "And I would have responded if someone hadn't confiscated my phone."

Hank barked a laugh.

She felt her face flame with anger. After a cooling gulp of ice water, she said the nastiest thing she dared. "Like I said in my email last night, when I talked with the Four Seasons in Agadir, they assured me Natalie was *not* there, had never been, and wasn't expected to be."

Hank growled.

She drew in a calming breath. "And I need to eat this nutritious breakfast right now." She picked up her fork and, with her eyes focused on her plate, calmly worked through the entire omelet. She could almost feel Kyle's strong hand on her shoulder and hear him whisper, *Good show*.

Kyle parked his Lexus at the curb outside the Penningtons' house on Seneca Street. Lyssa had stopped by from time to time to collect warm clothes, which were housed in the upstairs closets and mercifully saved from their vandal's destruction, and to check on the progress with the repairs, but he hadn't been inside in more than a month. Unlike his last visit here, when police cars lined the street, the home looked peaceful and inviting today with its gray shingles, dark blue shutters, and rose-colored front door.

He locked the car and walked the length of the narrow driveway, noting with satisfaction that their yard service had kept up with the mowing and snow removal in their absence. He'd started toward the garage to check on it, before remembering both their automobiles were elsewhere. He cancelled that move, rather than ruin yet another pair of leather loafers in the four inches of snow on the back lawn. Instead, he crossed the patio and let himself into the house. After deactivating the security system, he glanced around their kitchen.

The repairs had been completed with such skill he wouldn't have known the young vandal had destroyed every cupboard door, every plate, cup, saucer, and tumbler. Unblemished cupboards stood empty now, waiting for the replacement dishes and glassware Lyssa had ordered weeks ago, along with replacement furniture for their dining nook and living room.

Likewise, the living room looked fresh, all the wreckage cleared away and a smooth coat of paint on the walls. The closet door was new, but only he and Lyssa would know that. The room begged for comfortable seating, and the closet for warm jackets, walking sticks, and other signs of their life together.

Next he visited the dining room, which housed his baby grand piano, untouched by the rampage, thank the Lord. Unable to resist, he seated himself at the keyboard and ran through his usual practice scales, followed by a Brahms piece.

The playing relaxed him and let his mind sort an issue that burned and bothered him, Lyssa's health. Possibly the root of the fainting was stress from the two murders that had come soon after the nightmare of Marguerite's death.

Still, he wanted her to see a physician for a good checkup and for a serious talk about her anxiety attacks, her poor nutrition, and her punishing work habits. They couldn't very well start a family the way things stood.

Aha. And Lyssa knew that, and that's why she'd "forgotten" or "been too busy" to tell him about her health scares. They needed to deepen their trust and work on their communication. How were they going to manage that with him working in London and her in Tompkins Falls?

As he replaced his sheet music and headed upstairs to inspect those rooms, he weighed the pros and cons of moving the two of them back here, to the house on Seneca Street, now that it was ready for occupancy. Lyssa loved the house and it was walking distance to campus. But living there alone, with him in London, meant less protection than she had in Joel's third-floor apartment, with a young policeman living on the floor below. That was one of the reasons he was so keen to build on the Cushman grounds and share the security force guarding that property.

Granted, their house had an excellent security system, but the elderly neighbor on one side, the oblivious neighbor on the other, and the empty house across the street meant no one would hear her if she screamed for help. The thought made him ill.

Resolving to leave that discussion with Lyssa until they were in Cornwall, he reset the security system and ambled out the drive only to find a Warren Construction van parked at the curb behind his Lexus. He hadn't counted on another confrontation with Marguerite's husband, Billy, but the man himself stood at the foot of the Penningtons' driveway, hands in his jacket pockets, watching Kyle.

Anger surged. He wanted nothing more at that moment than to avenge Billy's attack on Lyssa after Marguerite's memorial service. With effort and several prayers, he cleared his throat and asked, "What brings you to 57 Seneca Street this morning, Mr. Warren?"

"Call me Billy. Everyone does. I was just talking with Joel Cushman about the big job we're planning, the renovation of the mill buildings along with river. He mentioned a residential project I might be able to fit in around that work."

Kyle's eye twitched.

Billy shifted on his feet. "He says you're planning a new house on the cove of the Cushman grounds. I'd like to talk with you about that. Got a minute now?"

What cheek. "After your abusive treatment of my wife at your wife's memorial service, why do you imagine I'd let you near my home and my family?"

Billy shrugged, cast his gaze over the house behind them, and said, "Maybe no one told you. Justin Cushman hired me to do the work here last month." He puffed out his chest. "I also did the renovation for the previous owners—your master suite and the kitchen and patio."

Kyle's blood boiled. That was all news to him. He'd been glad to let Justin handle the repair job and hadn't thought to ask for the contractor's name. Much as he and Lyssa loved the master suite and the kitchen, knowing that it was Warren who'd created them, he never wanted to set foot inside the home again. Through clenched teeth, he said, "Nice work. Have you been paid?"

Billy's head jerked as though he'd been slapped, but he put on an easy smile. "Justin has more than generously settled with me for the job. So about the house on Justin's cove?" He hooked a thumb toward their vehicles. "We could drive there right now, kick around your ideas."

"That's not happening, Mr. Warren. I'll hire my own contractor for the cove house. All the best to you and Joel with the mill renovation. If you'll excuse me."

"Not so fast, Pennington. I have a score to settle with you and your wife."

"I can't imagine what that might be."

"The pills your wife gave my wife." Warren had tensed like an animal ready to strike.

"I've no idea what you're talking about." But his stomach was doing somersaults.

"Ask your wife. Are AA sponsors supposed to medicate their sponsees? Because that's what she did. And Marguerite died of a heart attack because of it."

The hate in the man's eyes chilled Kyle to the bone.

Warren flipped his keys, caught them, and backtracked to his vehicle.

"That's a damn lie," Kyle shouted after him.

"Ask her," Billy flung over his shoulder. He slammed the driver's door, started the van, and revved the engine.

Kyle dug his keys out of his pocket as the van squealed away from the curb and roared past the Lexus. It sailed through two stop signs before taking the corner onto College Boulevard, sideswiping an SUV packed with kids. The mother at the wheel blared her horn, swerved, and slammed to a stop crosswise in the intersection, one front wheel up on the grass.

Phone at the ready, Kyle raced on foot to the scene to assist the driver and her children. When he was close enough to hear the children's screams and see the mom, eyeglasses askew, temple bleeding from a cut she'd received when the airbag exploded in her face, he called 911 with their location.

Lyssa sat back and let the waitress clear their dishes. "I've got this," Hank told her and placed his credit card on top of both checks.

"Thank you. It was delicious," Lyssa told him. She'd eaten the whole meal, minus half the olives, and felt stronger for it.

"How do you see it, Mrs. Pennington? Why did the Draytons come to Tompkins Falls?"

She dropped her wallet back in her tote to buy time to think. "One possibility. Charles's interview was nothing more than a cover for Vivienne to come to Tompkins Falls and retrieve her own letters to Marguerite. Which means Charles Drayton knew all about the affair, and one or both of them were worried the exposure would damage her career. Or both their careers. Totally strange marriage, don't you think?"

Trooper Moran harrumphed.

"And if they were still in communication, maybe Vivienne knew Stan Block had been trying to blackmail Marguerite and had stolen the letters."

"Gives her a motive to murder Stan Block, don't you think?"

"But the same is true for all his other victims over the years. If I can finish what I started to say, Charles had no intention of taking the job even though he pretended to be supremely qualified for it. I give him credit for a brilliant snow job that got him and his wife to Tompkins Falls with a legitimate purpose, long enough for her to find the letters. His interviews were the cover for her sneaking around. Killing Charles was not in the plan. That would have been supremely bad for business."

Hank gave her a wry smile.

"That's just my take. I don't really know who killed him or why."

She reached into her tote for the material she and Kyle had assembled for the meeting. "This is what you wanted. And you'll see, with Natalie's help, Vivienne did retrieve the letters she'd come for and then beat it out of town to catch her flight to the photo shoot in Morocco. At which point, I don't think she had any idea her husband had been murdered." She held out the folder.

He positioned it between them, facing him, and began paging through.

After a few minutes of silent reading, Hank told Lyssa, "I see your point."

"Sorry, which point is that?" She leaned forward to see which page he was on.

"The one about Horowitz seeing Tuesday night as a lark. And if the wife didn't kill Drayton, you may be right she didn't know her husband was dead. We hadn't notified anyone yet because we didn't know his identity. Or hers. And due to the college's PR misinformation, the media never mentioned the victim's name; nor did they represent the death as murder."

"Hank, who's communicating his death to Vivienne?"

"The authorities in Agadir, and if we're lucky there's a representative from the American Embassy with them. Hold on." He held up a finger and answered his cell.

It was probably the police at Stan's house reporting on the blackmail boxes. Lyssa picked up the carafe and jiggled it. Empty. Just as well. She needed to leave soon for her doctor's appointment. She stood and stretched her back. Her phone buzzed with a text from Kyle saying he would be at Lynnie's shortly, and could she hold Hank there until he arrived so he could ask a burning question.

Kyle stayed at the accident scene until the EMTs had patched up the woman's cut and determined none of the passengers had injuries. A tow truck arrived for her car. The woman's husband arrived on the scene in an identical SUV and swept away his wife and the children. No one offered Kyle a word of thanks.

Still angry at Billy Warren's recklessness, he made certain the city police had the facts about the accident, including Warren's name, license plate, and stop sign violations.

"How is it you saw the van's license plate?" the officer asked, his tone suspicious.

Kyle explained the sharp words he'd exchanged with Billy Warren at the foot of his driveway, his proximity to the rear end of the contractor's vehicle, and his eye for detail. A grunt was his only acknowledgement.

As he walked the two blocks back to his car, he got a return phone call from Tony Pinelli. "Yeah, Kyle, I got that information you wanted about the vehicles driven by each of the blackmail victims. What I have is the vehicle they registered with Campus Security, and no one's admitting they drive a wreck. Doesn't mean it's the only car they own. The police could dig deeper through Department of Motor Vehicle records."

"Good try, Tony. I'll let Hank's investigation take it from here. Tony, from what you know, did any of the blackmail victims have a strong motive to kill Stan Block?"

"Sure. Any one of them. I can see the woman with gambling debts going after him. She's close to retirement and doesn't want to lose her job at the college but, like I said, she's old. There's no way she could have dragged his body to a rowboat and hauled it out to the islands and dumped it."

"Anyone else you'd eliminate?"

"Personally, I don't see our lady professor as a killer. You didn't say what Stan had on her." The implied question mark indicated Tony didn't know about Missy Rossini's affair.

Kyle bit his tongue. His theory that the lady professor's husband could have done it had already been shot down when Gianessa told him both the Rossinis had alibis. "Agreed," he told Tony.

There'd been one more personal situation in his report, a young man with a drug habit. Without revealing the offense, he asked Tony about that victim's fitness level.

"You know, pal, I worry about that kid. He's skinny as a rail and shaking half the time. No way he could have removed the body."

"What about the chap who stole construction materials while the science building was in the works?"

Tony didn't have to think about it. "He could do it, no question. The guy works out. And he's a young accountant, just hired two years ago. He can't afford to have his reputation ruined."

"Do you think Hank will get all that from what's in the blackmail box with his initials on it?"

Tony gave an extended exhale. "Yeah, yeah, I think so. At least enough to make a call to one of us for more details." That was fair enough.

Kyle went through the rest of the list with him. The tech-savvy professor who'd taken money from students to fix their grades had been fired less than a year ago. So had the woman in the Business Office who'd falsified inventory records so her fiancé could steal a few computers from every lab in the new science building.

The elderly cafeteria worker who was helping herself to meat was, according to Tony, "probably feeding her family. She looks pretty feeble herself. I'd give her a pass. Let Justin decide if he wants to do anything about it." Kyle wondered how the woman could be paying blackmail.

He knew the eighth blackmail box had been labeled with Marguerite's initials.

That left four others who might or might not have a box of evidence somewhere. Tony confirmed all four of them had left the college in the past few years. None of the four was fit enough to have rowed Stan's body into the islands on a frigid night.

"That covers it, Tony."

"Okay, so I'll give Justin the go-ahead to release information to Moran for the two blackmail victims we think could have handled dumping Stan Block's body in the lake."

"Thanks ever so much." Kyle pocketed his phone and enjoyed the sunshine as he continued to his car.

He took one last look at the house Lyssa had so loved. Once she learned Billy Warren's hands were all over it, would she want anything more to do with it? That was for her to say.

For now, he needed answers from Hank about Warren's claim that Lyssa had given pills to Marguerite.

Chapter 15

Kyle arrived at Lynnie's Chestnut Lake Café just as Trooper Moran was leaving a tip on the table. Lyssa was on her feet and slinging her tote over one shoulder. Seeing Kyle approach the table, Lyssa put a restraining hand on Hank's arm. "Hank, I know you're responding to a call, but my husband urgently needs to talk with you."

"Quickly," Kyle promised as Trooper Moran glared at him. "What pills is Billy Warren referring to when he claims my wife provided her with a substance that caused a heart attack the night she died?"

"What?" Lyssa's face turned white, followed by blotchy red. She wheeled on Hank. "Billy Warren thinks I killed Marguerite, doesn't he?" She directed the next question to both of them. "That's what he was getting at outside the church, isn't it?"

Kyle recalled Billy's harangue after the memorial service when he'd started to say, *You were wrong to give her* .... At the time, Kyle had assumed Billy meant Lyssa had given his wife bad advice. But now he saw Warren had meant something different, something deadly. Neither of them had suspected what was behind the words.

Evidently Hank had known all along, for he put a hand under Lyssa's elbow. "Walk with me, both of you." He motioned them ahead of him out of the restaurant. Lyssa rushed ahead and threw her weight against the front door.

The assemblage of jingle bells clanged wildly and a blast of cold air rushed past her. Kyle hesitated just long enough to still the bells with a tug to their leather strap.

The slam of Lyssa's driver door signaled she was removing herself from whatever discussion Kyle planned to have with Hank. Too late, he remembered she was on her way to pick up Gianessa for her appointment at the clinic in Clifton Springs. Gianessa had told him that before he left the Cushman house early that morning.

Blast. His timing was all wrong, unforgivably so. He should have been wishing her well, not burdening her with an accusation from Warren.

"Will she be all right?" Hank asked as Lyssa's car spit gravel before merging onto the highway.

"Let's hope so. Fill me in on the drugs Warren is talking about."

"It's true there were pills in Mrs. LaCroix's vehicle, and the toxicology report identified nitroglycerine in her system. I briefly considered Lyssa as the source of the pills, but it's my understanding she was a pothead, not a pillhead."

"Quite right. Beer, pot, and the occasional Kir Royale. Hank, are you saying Marguerite had a heart condition?"

"I'm saying someone, not her physician, gave Mrs. LaCroix nitroglycerine tablets, and she'd taken one or more just before the accident. Several loose pills were found on the floor of her car along with an empty vial."

Kyle stuffed his hands in his pockets and put it together for himself. "Which explains the period of silence in the parking lot."

"I don't follow."

"The night she died, Marguerite had to have known it was Lyssa and me trying to help her. Yet she didn't call to us or come to us. There was a minute or so during which she might have done. Instead, she raced out of the parking lot, as Lyssa just did."

Hank filled in the rest. "You're thinking Mrs. LaCroix was popping a pill she shouldn't have been and didn't want her sponsor to know."

Kyle nodded. "Had she been drinking, too, Hank?"

"There was no sign of alcohol or other substances in her system. After the autopsy, we did check with her personal physician. No heart symptoms of any kind. Nor did the autopsy indicate heart trouble."

"Then where did the prescription come from? And why was she taking it?"

"The vial had come from an online Canadian pharmacy but the patient's name, what little we could make out, was not Marguerite LaCroix."

"So what's your thinking? She'd been having chest pain and mentioned it to an acquaintance? Who thought it might be angina and offered to share a few of her own pills?"

"Probably something like that. I doubt we'll ever know. The information on the bottle was blacked out. Our lab used a variety of techniques to recover it, but we know only the dosage, the postal code for the pharmacy, and the patient's first name, Shirley. Mean anything to you?"

Kyle shook his head and crossed his arms over his chest to quell sudden chills. "I doubt Lyssa knows either, but I'll ask her. Perhaps it's someone in her meetings. Could the pills have brought on a heart attack, as Warren claims?"

"The short answer is no, they did not cause a heart attack, and I don't know why Warren even thinks she had a heart attack."

"There was a rumor saying she'd died of a heart attack. You're saying she didn't?"

"She did not. However, the quantity of the drug found in her system may have caused dizziness, which could explain why her car went off the highway in good driving conditions and why we found no signs of braking or swerving to avoid an obstacle."

Kyle had to clear his throat to give voice to the next question. "You never considered suicide?"

"We ruled that out early on." Hank's tone warned him not to question it. "What I can tell you is, the car dove into the ditch at such an angle that her airbag did not completely protect her. She sustained a head injury and significant internal bleeding."

Kyle hated to ask, but he needed to know. "Was she conscious, Hank?"

"I don't believe so, no. Still, she lay unattended in her car in the ditch for hours, six at a minimum, in frigid temperatures."

"When all's said and done, are you calling it death from natural causes? Death by misadventure? Something else?"

"The investigation is continuing. We're still looking for the person who supplied the pills to her." He huffed out his breath, and Kyle took it as a signal to end the discussion.

"May I share all this with my wife?"

"With the caveat it goes no further than the two of you."

When Gianessa touched her hand, Lyssa jerked. Her body was rigid with tension, every nerve on edge. She didn't know how long she'd been in that state. Probably since her talk with Dr. Bowes, which had come at the end of her two-hour appointment.

"Your hands are ice," Gianessa said, her voice gentle. "I'm going to stop for something to warm you up."

Lyssa nodded and glanced out the window of the Cushmans' SUV. Downtown buildings came into view, one by one, but this wasn't Tompkins Falls. "Where are we?"

"Geneva." Gianessa signaled for the turn into a parking lot and maneuvered the car into a one-hour space. They crossed to a café and gift shop, where Lyssa took a seat at a bistro table near the front window, away from other customers.

She kept her coat wrapped around her. When Gianessa arrived with a tray, Lyssa offloaded a blue teapot, two mugs, and one giant piece of carrot cake. "Dr. Bowes would not approve," she told Gianessa.

"We're sharing." Gianessa positioned the dessert in the center of the table and put one fork in front of each of them before draping her long down coat over the third chair. "Let's start with an easy question. What did you think of the staff at her clinic?"

Lyssa savored a bite of the moist dessert and waited for her brain to switch on. "They're very kind and very smart about … pregnancy and motherhood."

Gianessa consumed two bites before prompting, "Are you saying you're pregnant?"

"No." Her test sip of tea made her wince. "But I want to be." She sighed.

"Eat while the tea cools," Gianessa ordered.

"I will. And I'll eat whatever you don't. It's delicious. But first, thank you for helping me rehearse all the way to the clinic and staying with me through the intake questions. Do you think I left out anything?"

"I think you gave them more information than they expected, and I was proud of you for putting it all on the table. The dizziness, the fainting, missing meals, sitting through long work sessions, not keeping up with hydration."

"I was irresponsible."

Gianessa continued the litany of causes. "Losing Marguerite, witnessing Drayton's death, the recurring stress of the various murders and investigations you've been dealing with." She took a third bite, set down her fork, and nudged the plate close to Lyssa. "And you were smart to acknowledge the danger you've been in, the pain from your gunshot wound last year, the strain of having Kyle away so much, the violation of having a stalker who vandalized your home."

Lyssa's tears welled up and spilled over. She used her napkin to blot them.

"I want you to finish that carrot cake before we go on. It is possibly the second best carrot cake I've ever eaten."

Lyssa took another bite followed by a deep breath. Her hands had warmed up, and she had enough energy to shed her coat and sit up straight.

Gianessa disappeared from the table and returned minutes later with a fistful of napkins. "Just in case you need a few more." Without another word, she smiled her Mona Lisa smile and waited silently until Lyssa had scraped the plate and licked her fork clean. "Ready to talk about your meeting with the doctor?"

Lyssa replied with one firm nod. "I like her. She asked right away if I still felt dizzy, and I was honest that I didn't." She explained to Gianessa that halfway through the blood draws, when her arm with the intravenous needle had gotten sore, the technician had asked her to squeeze a ball to keep the blood coming. She'd grown dizzy then and was made to lie down until the end. Graham crackers and apple juice had restored her equilibrium.

"So the techs reported that to her, plus she had read all the checklists and forms I'd filled out. She thanked me for being thorough and truthful in reporting the symptoms and causes. Until the blood tests come back she won't know all she needs to. She wants to see me as soon as the results are back, so I have an appointment in two days. She wants Kyle with me then."

"Good. And you're okay to include him this time?"

She thought about it. "It depends on how things go with him today." She told Gianessa about his bursting into Lynnie's and demanding an explanation about pills Marguerite had supposedly taken before her accident. She'd

207

known nothing about that. On top of being nervous about the appointment, that had completely overwhelmed her. "Maybe he didn't realize I was on my way to the doctor's," she said.

"He knew. I called to tell him I would be driving us."

Lyssa stiffened. She told herself they were just trying to support her, and she wasn't doing a good job of communicating on her own. "Thank you. So back to the doctor I have to eat three meals a day and document everything I eat between now and my next appointment."

Gianessa chuckled. "And the first item on your list is this carrot cake?"

Lyssa laughed and felt her whole body relax. "It will give us something to talk about, right? And I have to keep a log of all the ways I exercise. With work, I have to record how long I sit. When I drink water. Anything that stresses me out. And a bunch of other stuff." Her head ached and she pressed her fingers to her temples.

"Can you do all that?"

She nodded. "I told her I'd make a spreadsheet and add my own notes. I offered to send it to her if she needs to see it while we're in Cornwall. She's considering it."

"So she didn't tell you couldn't travel?"

Lyssa felt lightheaded. "No. Were you thinking she would?"

Gianessa pursed her mouth. "I just knew something she'd said had put you in a state of shock. Can you share it with me?"

Lyssa grabbed for the napkins and buried her face in them while she cried. After a minute, she mopped her face and told Gianessa, "She insists we not try to get pregnant for at least six months, maybe more. I don't know how to tell Kyle, and it's all my fault."

Following his talk with Trooper Moran, Kyle returned to the house on Seneca Street, parked in back, and made space for himself in the small room upstairs facing the street. They'd given the room over to their wedding gifts, still in boxes, and to his clothing, but the small desk under the window would serve his current purpose.

His primary objective was to catch up on affairs at Pennington Secure Networks and the case against Geoffrey. But his secondary objective was to watch for any return by Billy Warren to his and Lyssa's home. He didn't trust Warren, and he would not allow any more damage to happen to the house Lyssa loved.

Two hours of business phone calls and emails brought him up to date but resulted in an action list longer than he would have liked. Still, he didn't expect Lyssa to return to the apartment for another hour. She'd texted half an hour ago to say she and Gianessa had enjoyed dessert first and were now having a private lunch with Manda somewhere at the Manse.

He chafed at that, wondering why she preferred talking over her doctor's visit with them, rather than sharing it with him. He was, after all, the husband in the equation and this was as much about their future family as her current health.

As always, work was the best distraction, and he spent another hour sorting out the high-priority tasks on his list. Once he'd sent the final bit of information to his assistant, he realized his snit about the girls-only lunch had run its course.

Worry took its place. Maybe the verdict from the doctor was so dire they feared for Lyssa's sobriety. He'd half a mind to drive to the Manse and check on her.

He stuffed his papers and the laptop into his briefcase and rose to his feet, stiff from sitting so long. As he stretched, a white van cruised into view. Warren Construction again. The vehicle slowed. The driver focused first on Kyle's Lexus in the driveway, then leaned across the front seat for a better view of the house, and examined each window in turn. Kyle stepped closer to the glass and gave Billy Warren a cheery wave. The van sped away.

He texted Justin to confirm Warren had been paid for the job. When Justin replied in the affirmative, he thanked his friend for handling the repairs and offered to repay him and to pick up the key Warren had returned to Justin.

No reply.

Kyle already knew Justin did not expect a dime from the Penningtons for the repairs, and now he knew his hunch was correct. Warren still had the key and knew the code for the security system.

On his way out of the house, he checked all the windows and doors and reset the code, choosing something only he and Lyssa knew. Her sobriety date.

He had one more stop to make before joining Lyssa.

Full from a nutritious lunch and relaxed from conversation with her sister and her AA sponsor, Lyssa enjoyed fifteen minutes alone in the quiet of the third-floor apartment. When she heard Kyle's step on the stairs, she sent up a silent prayer, brushed impatiently at a few tears, and opened the door to their landing. The fragrance of roses drifted up to her, and she laughed with delight. "You are the very dearest husband a girl could ever have, Mr. Pennington."

Kyle raced up the remaining flight. "I believe there's a crystal vase that will fit these nicely." In his arms he cradled a tissue-wrapped bouquet of red roses, creamy white peace lilies, assorted greens, and baby's breath. In spite of his broad smile, she read strain in the lines of his brow.

"We'll figure it out together." The words just popped out of her mouth.

"Sounds right, love," he told her, his voice husky with emotion.

While he deposited the bouquet on the kitchen island, she stood on a chair to reach the Waterford vase that Joel had left at the apartment, one that belonged to his grandmother.

Side by side, she and Kyle snipped stems, arranged the flowers to their liking, and swept away the leavings. Lyssa tucked a few blooms with broken stems in a jar for their bedside. "Can we take a walk?" she asked him.

"If we dress warm. The wind's come up."

They headed out to Overlook Park, but instead of making directly for the cove, they explored every pathway in the woods and play areas of the park. She gave him the details of the morning's appointment. He shared the news from London and told her, "I have airline tickets for us to London a week from Sunday."

"Whether Hank approves or not?" She grinned at him.

"Precisely. We'll fly together, and meantime we can meet with your doctor, talk over our options, and perhaps have a pre-holiday celebration with our Cushman family."

"I like that." They had reached the edge of the bluff, and she felt her shoulders settle into place as she gazed at the dark blue waters of Chestnut Lake. With a steadying exhale, she told him, "And the bad news is we're advised to delay getting pregnant a minimum of six months." A sob slipped out. "I'm horribly sorry. I got us into this, and I'll do whatever it takes to get us out."

"Agreed, but it's not entirely on you." He drew her close, his hand firm on her back. "I've been absent too much, focused on my own business which, due to my neglect, had fallen into near ruin. You were the strong one supporting me through that, and I wrongly concluded you could handle anything that came your way, on your own. I regret the way I've handled our long-distance marriage."

"I've been thinking about that. This six-month delay could be the perfect time for me to get really good at teaching online. Then we'll all know I can make the UK my home base and still do my job for Tomkins College. We could live in Cornwall or London or both, whatever makes the most sense to you."

He placed a kiss on her temple. "I must say, one of the things I most admire about you is your flair for turning a bad situation into an opportunity. But how does that fit with the plans we're making for the house on the cove? Continue or not?"

"I say we move forward, for all the reasons we've talked about already. Security, family, the beauty of the cove and the lake. We'll still come with the children for family visits, and I'll need to be here periodically during the semester. Darling, will you take the lead planning the new house?"

"Music to my ears. I absolutely will."

Chapter 16

After a cozy evening with Kyle, Lyssa slept better than she had in a month and looked forward to her first day free from Hank's investigation. She had other priorities now and good health was at the top of her list.

Kyle was sound asleep beside her, but she was hungry for a big breakfast and a walk along the lakeshore. Quietly, she dressed in layers and headed to Lynnie's. After a veggie omelet (no cheese) and a blueberry muffin (no butter), she set out for a brisk walk on the willow path.

She'd gone just over a mile when fatigue claimed her. That gave her pause. A month ago, she'd been able to walk the full two miles, in both directions, at a fast pace without feeling winded. Rather than give into panic or push herself too hard, she opted to turn around and slow her pace back to the car.

There she sat sipping her now-cold takeaway coffee and contemplating the stillness of the lake. This morning a few fishing boats were out, probably Stan Block's neighbors. She wondered if they missed him, if anyone missed him. She hadn't heard anything about a service. Did he have any family? Why had he lived the way he did, extorting money from fellow employees, always on the lookout for a scandal or an infraction he could exploit? She had no answers.

Marguerite's death felt unresolved, though she couldn't think of a next step.

And she was still worried about her neighbor and friend Natalie Horowitz. She dug out her phone and tried Natalie's number one more time. It went right to voicemail, and she left a cheery hello. "Natalie, hope you get this soon. I want to know all about this adventure you're on, wherever you are. Kyle and I will be returning to Cornwall next weekend. Yes, he's here, because I've been stuck here, long story. Text me or call as soon as you're able, and let me know if you're okay."

As soon as she disconnected, a fleeting thought returned, one that had teased her during her talk with Hank yesterday at Lynnie's. Hank Moran wouldn't agree, but it was entirely possible that Vivienne, rather than invite Natalie to fly with her first class to Morocco, had rewarded Natalie with some extravagant gift from Drayton Textiles.

She vaguely remembered Natalie saying something about tickets to a runway show in the spring, but that wasn't something that would take her to Manhattan in December. She'd already texted Norman to see if Natalie was with him, and he'd answered: I wish.

She gave some thought to what other reward Vivienne might have bestowed. A private showing, maybe? A new outfit of her choosing? Some ravishing evening attire? "All of the above," Lyssa said out loud and laughed. Natalie would be all over it. There must be a way to find out.

Kyle awoke to an empty bed. When he discovered Lyssa's note about going out for breakfast, he assumed she'd gone to the Bagel Depot for an early AA meeting followed by bagels with her fellow AAs. While he'd prefer a leisurely breakfast with her each morning, as was their practice at Pennington House, he supported her meeting routine.

He arrived at the Bagel Depot to find the meeting still in progress in the back room behind closed doors. Officer Peter Shaughnessy sat by himself in the dining room, framed by a picture window that looked out to the old passenger platform and train tracks.

He'd probably just finished his night shift. His right hand held a half-eaten bagel sandwich, and his left rested on the morning newspaper opened to Sports.

"Got a minute for a few questions?" Kyle asked. It had occurred to him yesterday, during his vigil at the Seneca Street house, that he and Lyssa might want another option for their building plans, one not so dependent on Justin's architect and Warren Construction. He understood the Shaughnessys, Peter and Gwen, had built a home for their family on a cove several miles south of town.

"Sure." Peter stretched out his hand for a firm shake. "Join me. What's on your mind, Kyle?"

"Nothing to do with crime, I assure you. Lyssa and I are planning to build a home on a pretty cove on the Cushman grounds, and I understand you and Gwen did something similar."

"We did and we love the house. How can I help?"

Kyle peppered him with questions about the Shaughnessys' design, the contour of their cove, the architect and contractor for the job, everything he could think of including how they kept their children safe on the rocks and in the water. When he was out of questions, Peter offered, "Why don't the two of you come by the house to see our layout? I'm sure Gwen would be glad to talk about our decisions and how they've worked out."

"Nice of you. We'd love that." They exchanged phone numbers just as the door to the back room swung open and disgorged two dozen energized AA members. Lyssa was not among them.

Peter noticed the direction of his gaze. "You were expecting your wife?"

"I was, yes. She simply said she was going out for breakfast and a walk. She must have meant Lynnie's."

215

"I saw her on the willow path when my partner and I came back to the station after our shift, at least half an hour ago."

"Thanks, I'll swing by, see if she's still out in the cold."

"Before you go, let me ask you something." Peter cleared his throat. "I know Warren has been the contractor for all the Cushman projects. Does your interest in our builder have anything to do with the altercation with Billy Warren after Professor LaCroix's memorial service?"

"That's partly it, yes." His face had grown warm as he recalled the more recent encounters with the man.

Peter studied Kyle over the rim of his coffee cup. "I don't like the animosity between the two of you."

Kyle felt like he'd been scolded. He'd been expecting a suggestion along the lines of a restraining order against Warren. He countered with a question, though it came out more like an accusation. "Did you know about the drugs found in Marguerite's car?"

Peter set down his mug and straightened the unused knife beside his plate. "I did. I'm sure you understand we had our reasons for keeping that aspect of the case out of the public eye."

Kyle nodded slowly, his gaze on the winter scene outside the window. "Hank filled me in on the details."

"It goes a long way toward explaining Warren's rough handling of Lyssa after the memorial service, don't you think?" Peter asked.

Kyle narrowed his eyes. "It doesn't make his actions right."

Peter lowered his voice. "A word of advice, Kyle. Don't use Warren's bad behavior as an excuse to carry on a feud with him. That won't end well for anyone, including Lyssa."

"But—"

"Unlike Warren, you have a wife and an opportunity to build a home for your family on our beautiful lake. Try some compassion for him. Save your energy for your family."

Home again, Lyssa wondered where Kyle had gone. She hoped he wasn't worried about her and out searching. While she fixed a cup of hot cocoa in the apartment's gourmet kitchen, she ran through her strategy for the upcoming conversation with Charles Drayton's assistant. She planned to sidestep any questions about Drayton's death, if it came up. Her goal was to learn if Natalie had appeared at the showroom and if anyone knew her whereabouts.

She filled her mug to the brim with steaming chocolate and settled at the island to make the call. Just as Drayton's assistant answered, Kyle's footfalls sounded on the stairs. The moment he came through the door, she put the phone on speaker and pointed to the saucepan of cocoa.

"Drayton Textiles, Jocelyn speaking."

Hearing the introduction, Kyle's brow creased with questions, but he quietly filled a mug for himself and took a seat beside her.

"Yes, hello Jocelyn, this is Professor Lyssa Pennington. I spoke with you a few days ago and you were very helpful connecting me with the photo shoot in Agadir."

There was only a gasp at the other end. Lyssa waited, hoping the woman would say something to inform her next step. Kyle put a reassuring hand on her back. After some throat clearing from Drayton's office in New York, the assistant said, "I'm glad I was able to help, Professor. You probably know Charles is dead?"

"I did hear that, and I'm very sorry for your loss. I don't mean to intrude, Jocelyn. I have a very specific question for you today. My colleague, Professor Natalie Horowitz, met Mrs. Drayton during the Draytons' visit to Tompkins Falls, and I haven't been able to reach Natalie for several days. I'm worried."

God, what do I say next? "I thought maybe she'd gone to Agadir with Vivienne, but I've contacted the hotel, and they assure me she has not checked in. It's possible she's in New York City shopping. By any chance, has she visited Drayton Textiles to see your beautiful fashions?"

"Yes, she's been here."

It was Lyssa's turn to gasp. "Then she's okay?"

Jocelyn chuckled. "She's more than okay, Professor Pennington. She has charmed everyone here and has given us something to smile about. Your friend has reminded us how important our fashions are to American women."

While Lyssa got control of her emotions, Kyle introduced himself to Jocelyn and said with a laugh, "That sounds like our Natalie. Will she be back? Or do you know where she's staying?"

"She's at some five-star hotel with an amazing spa, but that's all I know. She said something about hiding out and indulging herself." Jocelyn laughed. "I think she doesn't want anyone to know she's in the city buying holiday gifts just for her."

Kyle told her, "Sounds like she's having a luxurious vacation for herself. If she comes back or if you're in touch with her, Jocelyn, please have her call us."

After their goodbyes, Lyssa said, "I wonder if Natalie even knows that the much-mourned head of Drayton Textiles was Vivienne's husband?"

"I would think so by now. If they love her as much as Jocelyn implied, they'd have talked with her some about it. But she and they may not know he died in Tompkins Falls during the dinner you had planned for him. And apparently no one knows the police want Vivienne in connection with the murder."

They had barely finished the pan of hot chocolate when Lyssa's phone rang. "That's a New York City area code," she told Kyle before answering, "Pennington residence."

The caller was a salesperson in the couture division of Drayton Textiles. "Lyssa, please?"

"Hi, I'm Lyssa, thanks for calling. Is this about my friend Natalie?"

"Exactly. She's due back here tomorrow at four in the afternoon to pick up her gifts. The outfits will look fabulous on her. I'll be sure to have her get in touch with you then or soon after." The connection ended.

Lyssa and Kyle exchanged glances and laughed. "At least we captured the woman's phone number," Kyle pointed out. "We can plug in all the clues and determine where the couture operation is located. Shall we go to New York, my love, and surprise Natalie?"

"I've got a better idea. Let's have Norman do it." She placed a call to him.

His greeting was an abrupt, "Lyssa, honey, I'd love to hug my Natalie, but she and I have an agreement. Thanksgiving night through Christmas Eve are all about my gallery and my customers. Plus, if she's in the city, she has not deigned to call me." This last came out as a sulky rebuff before he disconnected.

"I guess he told me." Lyssa scowled.

"Good idea, bad timing. Shall we tell Hank Natalie is in New York?"

"No."

"You're serious?"

"I'm pretty sure I don't work for Hank any more. And we don't actually know where Natalie is, do we?"

Kyle squinted at her. "I'm not convinced that's the right thing to do, love. I know you're angry with him for eating up so many hours of your time, but …"

Lyssa's neck grew warm, and she averted her face. *Am I being petty?*

At her silence, Kyle went on, his voice strained. "I'll leave it to you, but I'm pretty sure you haven't been to an AA meeting lately. Perhaps we can go together this evening. Joel says there's a good meeting downtown, at seven this evening, and guests are welcome. What do you say?"

Lyssa hated that he'd been talking with Joel about her. Again. She folded her arms across her chest. When she looked at him, he was regarding her with a steady gaze. The distance between them seemed to grow. She wanted to hang onto her resentment toward Hank for a while, especially if the trooper was planning to dump another job on her. And she especially didn't want Hank to preempt Natalie's fitting tomorrow. Natalie would see that as unforgivable, far worse than the negligence she imagined on Lyssa's part.

But a lot rode on the answer to Kyle's question. And, now that she thought about it, she couldn't remember when she'd last gone to a meeting. "You're right, darling. Let's go to tonight's meeting together."

"Splendid." His warm smile said so much more.

The seven o'clock meeting in the community room of a downtown church was set up with rows of wooden folding chairs facing a stage. An elderly gentleman in a wheelchair, pushed by Joel Cushman, rolled up the ramp. The man maneuvered his chair to face the group, while Joel lifted the mic from its gooseneck holder on the lectern. The assembly buzzed among themselves. A few called out, "Glad you're here tonight, Phil." Applause broke out.

It dawned on Kyle this was Joel's AA sponsor, Phil, who lived in the house between Stan Block's community of fishermen and Hank Moran's property. He'd like to hear firsthand what Phil had seen the night of the murders. Given the reception of the crowd, he doubted he could get near the man, both during the break and after the meeting.

The group quieted, and Phil told his story with humor, though there was no mistaking the devastation that occurred during his twenty-five years of active drinking. His health, his work, and his marriage had all suffered. Phil had come into recovery forty-two years ago. The impetus was an ultimatum from his wife. He hadn't had a drink since.

Kyle reflected how fortunate he and Lyssa were that she'd stopped using in her twenties. Yet her recent descent into self-neglect and obsession with the investigation made it clear to him that ongoing recovery required hard work and a continual connection to her fellow AAs. The disease could destroy her whether she was drinking or not, and the realization chilled him.

Her fingers brushed the back of his hand, and she whispered, "Thank you for bringing me tonight." He sandwiched her hand between both of his.

During the applause that followed Phil's talk, Kyle's phone vibrated in his pocket. A text from Tony Pinelli asked him to meet in the hall at the break. Kyle searched the room and found Tony standing at the back. He nodded his agreement.

Tony led with, "Nice to see you here with Lyssa."

"She and I both needed a meeting, my friend. What's up?"

"Just telling you I gave Hank Moran the names of the two blackmail victims we think are fit enough to row Stan's body out into the lake. Justin is meeting Hank tomorrow and giving him the other names but *not* saying what Stan had on each of them."

"Doesn't Hank have the eight boxes of evidence, the ones he'd moved to his house?" Kyle narrowed his eyes. "All he has to do is match the initials to the person, Tony."

"Exactly, but that's a lot different than the college volunteering that information about its employees."

"I see your point. And I'm to keep my mouth shut about any and all of this, correct?"

"You got it, buddy. Just wanted to give you the heads-up. How's Lyssa doing? She still fainting?"

He suspected word was out about her ill health, at least among the AA community. "Between us, she's under a doctor's care, and we're working together on it. We're off to the UK next weekend." As he said it, he thought perhaps they'd skip the holiday festivities in London and spend all their time at Pennington House. "The main thing is her health right now."

"Is Hank still pestering her to investigate for him?"

"He'd better not try." But as Tony gave him an easy smile and sauntered away, Kyle knew Lyssa had been right about one thing: it was just a matter of time before Hank came up with another urgent request for her. In fact, he thought he knew what Hank's next few moves would be.

Indeed, his phone vibrated with a call from the man before he could reenter the meeting room, Hank asking Kyle for the names and infractions of the remaining blackmail victims. He gave his standard answer about the college being the gatekeeper for that information. "I hear you're meeting with Justin tomorrow," he added just to let Hank know he was in the loop and was standing firm with the college.

Hank growled. Kyle countered with a question of his own, starting with the status of Vivienne's arrest and extradition. Hank replied, "All I can say is she's still our prime suspect."

He deserved that nonanswer. He wondered if Hank would use the information in the boxes of evidence Stan had amassed to interrogate Melissa Rossini and her husband. Gianessa would be cross with herself if she'd played a part in damaging the Rossini marriage. She'd be doubly upset with Kyle for involving her in the first place.

In fact, the more he thought about it, the more he regretted using Gianessa that way.

She was correct that, once he and Lyssa started a case, they were obsessed with their investigation. Focused on results *beyond common sense*, Gianessa had said. That perfectly described Lyssa's behavior and its consequences, and now he saw the same in himself.

Pressuring Gianessa to spy on her friend Missy had been *beyond human decency*. And it was no wonder that, just this morning, Peter Shaughnessy had called him on having no compassion for widower Billy Warren.

He owed Hank for the series of personal insights he'd just experienced. "You know, Hank, both Lyssa and I are certain Natalie Horowitz is in no way culpable in these murders, but I appreciate that you want to question her just the same. My money is on Natalie pampering herself in New York City, getting a jump on her spring wardrobe, and spending every free moment with her boyfriend, Norman Wischnowski." Before Hank could probe, Kyle ended the connection, certain Hank would follow up with Norman, whether Norman wanted to be involved or not. It struck him as silly that Norman and Natalie, lovebirds that they were, were just blocks away from each other, each not contacting the other because of some business agreement.

When he looked up, the meeting was back in session. Lyssa was craning her neck, searching for him. She spied him, phone in hand, at the entrance to the meeting room and started to rise, but he motioned her to stay.

"Sorry," he whispered as he retook the chair next to her and shut down his phone.

His attention, though, was not on the discussion among the members in response to Phil's story. Instead, he was questioning if he and Lyssa were doing more harm than good—to themselves and others—by their sleuthing. Intriguing as the chase could be, perhaps they ought to put the same zeal into their real jobs and their marriage and their future family.

Chapter 17

Lyssa's phone jingled during their breakfast the next morning. "Oh my gosh, it's Norman." Her heart fluttered with hope that Natalie was safe with her gentleman friend in Manhattan.

Kyle wanted in on the call, and she put it on speaker before answering with an excited, "Hi, Norman, what's the news?"

Norman snarled, "*Why* did the state police just invade my gallery?"

Across the table Kyle cleared his throat, and Lyssa gave him a mad face.

"Relax, Norman," Kyle told him. "They came before you were open for business, right? Be glad."

"Don't mess with me. Which of you is the Dr. Pennington that sent them in my direction?"

"My bad," Kyle admitted. "We'll tell you what we know, but first, what did the police say?"

Norman thundered, "You first."

"Very well. If Lyssa's intel is correct, Natalie's having a luxury vacation for herself in Manhattan. She's staying at some five-star hotel with a spa, though we don't know which one. However, we do know Drayton Textiles is custom-making something for her. Has she been in touch with you at all?"

"Back up. It's *Natalie* the police are looking for? *My* Natalie?"

"Precisely. Now, what did they tell you, Norman?"

"Two of them barged in here, said they'd gotten a tip from a Dr. Pennington upstate about my affiliation with a Dr. Horowitz. One of them backed me into a corner and browbeat me while the other set off the alarm system by poking into every niche and storage space in my gallery. What kind of game are you playing?"

"No game, I swear. They had a search warrant?"

"Don't know, but the big guy accused me of harboring a criminal. What this about?"

Lyssa filled him in on Charles Drayton's murder and Natalie's innocent friendship with Charles's wife, Vivienne, including the fact she'd driven Vivienne from Tompkins Falls to Newark airport for a flight out of the country.

Norman barked a laugh. "So the police think a famous model murdered her husband and my Natalie abetted the woman in fleeing the country? She's a wonder, isn't she? No worries, I'll find her." And he broke the connection.

"Wait—" Lyssa grabbed the phone and texted Norman the name and number of the saleswoman in the couture division of Drayton Textiles, its location, and the time of Natalie's appointment that afternoon.

"Good show," Kyle said.

Lyssa's tension let loose in tears.

"Sweetheart, I'm sorry. I thought it was wrong of us to withhold information, so I gave Hank our lead."

"It's not that." She shook her head. "I'm scared for her, and I want my friend back."

Kyle's arms came around her and she cried until there were no more tears. "You were right," she said, "and this way Norman will get to her before the police."

"Really, I was right?"

She gave him a playful punch on the arm.

"Glad you have your sense of humor. Why are you still worried? We know Hank's wrong."

"I guess you're right and it's pointless to worry about her. So, quick reset, what will we do with our day?"

"How about having fun? You remember fun."

She laughed. "What can we do that's fun and that brings our cove house closer to reality?"

"If you'll make some drawings of your dream house, I'll see how soon the architect can meet with us."

"Perfect." She grinned at him. "I'll get to work."

Kyle's effort to schedule with Justin's architect was both frustrating and discouraging. The earliest appointment for a new project was May. After saying he'd have to get back to them, Kyle moved on to the architect Peter Shaughnessy had recommended.

He had no idea whether it was the effect of his British accent or simply a different attitude at this office toward potential customers. Regardless, Pamela Kriegstein's assistant presented an upbeat and thoroughly professional voice.

Ms. Kriegstein could see the Penningtons at the site early in February and in the interim would welcome sketches, photos, or any visuals that would communicate their vision for the house. He gladly made an appointment, just weeks after their return from the UK and the start of Lyssa's semester.

"Wow," was Lyssa's response when he filled her in.

A brief discussion sent them in two directions. Since Lyssa had already seen Gwen and Peter's house, she went to work at the kitchen island on her sketches of the new home.

Kyle paid a visit to the Shaughnessys. There he plied Gwen with questions and took photographs of features he especially liked. The experience helped him to imagine what he and Lyssa might build on their smaller lot. And it pleased him to learn Billy Warren had not been the Shaughnessys' builder.

Before he left, Gwen made a quick phone call to Kriegstein & Kriegstein, Inc. Pamela could meet the Penningtons informally the next afternoon, but cautioned it would only be a productive conversation if husband and wife were on the same page with their design. "What shall I tell them?" Gwen asked him.

Kyle accepted and left with a wide smile.

Back at the apartment, though, when Lyssa showed him her drawings, he chewed on his lower lip. "I've got issues now that I see it on paper. We need to resolve them today if we're to meet with her tomorrow."

"Let's do it. And maybe tomorrow we can check on the work at the Seneca Street house to see if I can move back there for spring semester." Her eyes widened. "Good things are coming together, darling." She surprised him with a kiss. "Why don't we take a walk right now to work out the problems with the design?"

"Hold on."

"Something wrong?"

He hadn't yet told her about his confrontation with Billy Warren at the Seneca Street house and the fact Warren had done all the work there. That might change her mind about moving back, even for a semester. "I need to make you aware of something first."

"I'm not going to like this, am I?"

"Tell you what. Bundle up, and I'll explain the dilemma as we drive to the willow path. I'd like to have it out in the open before we look at the design together."

On the drive to the town parking lot, Kyle related his unpleasant encounter with Warren. "Now you know the whole story. Does it make a difference about moving back to the house versus relying on Joel's good graces to let us use his old apartment?"

"Fortunately, we don't have to worry about Joel kicking us out. He's not ever going to rent our place to anyone except family, and we're only paying a nominal rent."

"Good to know. But how do you feel about moving back to the house?"

"I'm not sure I can live in our pretty house again, knowing it was Billy Warren who created all those features we love so much, and that he did all the repairs we've needed this past year." Her mouth settled into a frown. "I'm not saying it isn't quality work. It is. But the anger in his voice when he came at me outside the chapel." She shuddered. "And knowing he blames me for Marguerite's death, I don't want to have that in the back of my mind all semester, especially when you're in London or traveling to your client locations. Am I overreacting?"

"Those are valid concerns. Like you, I'm of two minds about it. At first I was sure we'd have to abandon the house, knowing how proprietary he is about the work. But then Peter set me straight on a few things. Come on, let's walk and talk." While they did a quick warm-up at the start of the two-mile recreational path, he recapped his early-morning conversation with Peter at the Bagel Depot. She nodded thoughtfully but didn't offer a response.

Hands stuffed in their pockets, they set off at a leisurely pace. When she finally spoke, it was to say, "While we're talking about Billy, what about his accusation that I supplied pills to Marguerite? When you told Hank that, I was blown away. I had no idea drugs were found in Marguerite's car or that Billy was angry with me about giving them to her—which I didn't. I didn't even know she was taking anything. But it does explain why he was so aggressive after the memorial service. Kyle, you *do* know I had absolutely nothing to do with those drugs, don't you?"

"I never doubted you." He told her the details about the vial of nitroglycerin and the results of the toxicology test.

"They were able to see the prescription was written for someone named Shirley, but they couldn't make out a last name. The pharmacy was in Canada. Could she be someone in your AA group?"

"No. I'll bet you anything it's one of"—she paused for effect—"the seaweed people."

He laughed, glad that her spirit was reviving. Thank the Lord. "You're referring to Marguerite's fellows in Brittany?"

She nodded. "It was after that trip that she got so mysterious with me. Okay, maybe the affair made her secretive, but deep down I think it was the drug she was hiding from me."

"Why would she hide it if it wasn't a mind-altering substance?"

"Because she knew she shouldn't be taking someone else's prescription." She kicked a stone off the path. "How can I get the seaweed people's names?"

He wagged an admonishing finger. "No more investigating. Let's leave that one to Hank, eh?"

She drew herself up. He held his breath, expecting an argument. Instead, she turned her face to him and smiled. "Agreed. First things first for us. Let's review the drawings of the cove house and make them work for both of us. Tell me your vision and your concerns."

"I see the cove house as a classy holiday place, roomy enough for our brood, with sufficient privacy for the two of us and a kitchen to rival the one in our current apartment. You?"

"On most of those points I agree, but the kitchen has to be larger for a family, and we need a pantry. Joel's cupboards are jammed with pots and pans and cooking stuff I can't even identify, but I know he cooked most of his meals. I guess he had groceries delivered a couple times a week. I can't see us doing that."

Kyle chuckled. "Joel is so well known, he just snaps his fingers and whatever he needs arrives on his doorstep." When she laughed, he slung an arm around her shoulders. "How's this for a compromise? To keep the kitchen small but functional, we can limit ourselves to basic pots and pans, which will fit in fewer cabinets, and use the freed-up space to add a pantry. Same amount of floor space as Joel's."

"Clever," she agreed. "Keep going."

"About our master suite. I've given it a great deal of thought."

They had nearly settled on an expanded master suite when his phone interrupted. "Yes, Norman, are you with Natalie?"

"Is she all right?" Lyssa implored him, and Kyle switched to speaker.

"The lady in question is radiant from her spa treatments and magnificent in her new outfits. I'm lining up special events for us in the spring so she can show off her new evening attire. For now, though, I've put her on a train. She's coming by way of Albany, arriving in Rochester approximately ten tonight. In spite of my best efforts, she doesn't fully realize she's in big trouble with the law. Any chance you can fetch her from Rochester and take her directly to the local authorities and, obviously, prepare her for what's coming?"

"Why is she on a train?" Kyle asked.

"I thought it best that she avoid airport security checks. Her car has been impounded, and I will make it my job to get it out of hock. However, there's no way I can move on that before she's made her statement to the police and been cleared. Since I have a gallery to run and this is our busiest season, I am calling in a favor from Dr. Kyle Pennington, who owes me from this morning's police raid."

"Well played, Norman. We'll see to Natalie at this end and keep you posted."

"There she is, behind the pillar." Lyssa pointed at the shadowy figure of a woman huddled over a pile of shopping bags trying to shelter them from the wind.

"Best get her fast," Kyle said as he edged to the curb. "Police are taking an interest in every car, and we're about to harbor a wanted criminal."

Lyssa dashed from the car, grabbed six bags by their handles, and told a scowling Natalie, "I know you're mad at me, but we've got to get you out of here fast." With three bags on in each hand, she hustled her friend into the Lexus.

"Buckle up, Natalie," Kyle ordered.

"And hello to you, too," Natalie sniped.

Kyle countered, "The police are merciless tonight." In seconds, the car rolled smoothly into the flow of traffic away from the station.

"Good work, ladies," Kyle said and muttered to Lyssa, "No one's following."

She heard huffing and rustling in the backseat. Lyssa twisted around to see Natalie shed the dark pashmina that had shrouded her face and busying herself rearranging her purchases.

"Was the shawl Norman's idea?" she asked.

Natalie screwed up her face. "Honestly, that man! I've never seen him so protective. You'd think riding a train was the most dangerous thing in the world."

"We've all been scared for you, Natalie," Kyle told her as they glided through the EZ-Pass lane onto the New York State Thruway.

"I was perfectly fine, having the time of my life in the Big Apple, thanks to Vivienne's generosity. And then Norman barged into my fitting room at Drayton Textiles and, by the way, he loves the new outfits. Then he totally freaked me out on the way to dinner, telling me the dead CEO they were all mourning at Drayton Textiles, was Vivienne's husband. I had no idea. Neither did Vivienne, and she's off in Morocco on a photo shoot. She's the one to worry about, you guys."

"To be honest, I don't have a lot of sympathy for her," Lyssa said. Beside her, Kyle nodded.

"Seriously? Why?" Natalie's eyes darted back and forth between husband and wife. When neither answered, she said, "Long story, I guess. Anyway, thank you for coming all this way to scoop me off the sidewalk at this hour and drive me home. Norman made me take the train or I would have driven my car."

"Except your car's been impounded," Lyssa told her.

"That's not funny, Lyssa Pennington."

"It's true, Natalie." Kyle explained why the police had impounded the car and told her they'd be stopping at the police station on their way to her home.

"I don't understand." Natalie's voice betrayed unease. "Norman said something about a murder. Can one of you spell this out for me?"

"Allow me to connect the dots for you, Natalie," Kyle said. "Last Monday and Tuesday at Tompkins College, Vivienne's husband, the CEO of Drayton Textiles was pretending to be our star candidate for Marguerite's job, when someone murdered him."

"Murdered?"

"Poison in the wine designated just for him. The police think Vivienne killed her husband, which makes you an accessory."

"Vivienne didn't kill anyone. I was with her." She looked from Kyle to Lyssa.

"Precisely. Drayton was poisoned while you two were running around looking for the letters." Kyle enunciated each word. "And then you took off in your car to deliver the dead man's wife to the airport for a flight out of the country. You see how it looks."

Even in the dim light of the car's interior, Lyssa saw her turn pale. She reached a hand between the seatbacks, and Natalie grabbed for her like a lifeline, her hands icy.

"Oh. My. God."

"Which is why we're taking you directly to the police station to tell your side of the story." Lyssa's teacher voice brought Natalie to attention.

"And we have less than thirty minutes to prepare you for this," Kyle said, "so tell us what really happened. Don't edit and don't get distracted. This is your rehearsal for the interrogation."

"I'm scared. Tell me where to start."

Lyssa told her, "Focus. Tell us *everything* that happened with Vivienne. Explain this mission the two of you were on last Tuesday, while Charles was dying across the table from me in the dining room of Westerlee Hall." She wasn't surprised to see Natalie gulp. "Tell us all the places you and Vivienne went and why. What you found. And why you left town with Vivienne in such a hurry."

Natalie sucked in a deep breath and nodded on the exhale. "Here goes. Lyssa knows I met Vivienne in the Spa at the Manse on Monday and recognized her tattoo. She probably saw me as a gift from heaven because I knew how to find someone's office at the college, how to pick locks, and I had a car."

"You might want to leave out the lock picking when you tell the police," Lyssa said.

"Agreed," Kyle said. "Good start. Stay focused, Natalie."

She drew in another deep breath. "Vivienne had me convinced that her husband, who she said was in Morocco setting up for the photo shoot, had an affair with a faculty person, code named 'M,' at Tompkins College and the evidence was either in M's office or her home. She needed the evidence in case she ever filed for divorce but, more important, she wanted to steal it and hide it because, if the affair became known, her mystique as a powerful sexy woman would be destroyed and her career would go down the tubes."

"So you agreed to help her?"

"Made sense to me." Natalie shrugged. "I signed on to drive her around under cover of darkness, get her into the woman's office and, if necessary, her home, so she could find the letters. I picked her up at her hotel."

"When?"

"I figured the offices in the Admin building closed at four thirty and the place would be deserted by five thirty. So I picked her up at her resort in Canandaigua at five fifteen. While we drove to campus, I rattled off all the women on faculty whose names started with M, but she absolutely would not tell me the identity of the other woman. I never imagined she was talking about Marguerite and that, in reality, Vivienne and Marguerite had the affair, not Charles and some random other woman on the faculty. I can't believe Charles was masquerading as the superstar candidate Justin was hot to hire."

"Focus," Kyle said.

"Cheeky Brit," Natalie muttered.

Lyssa asked, "So your first clue about the other woman's identity was when Vivienne took you to Marguerite's office?" Lyssa asked.

"No, it wasn't until we were *in* Marguerite's office where—believe it or not—I'd never been before. I have no idea how but Vivienne had a master key and she already knew which office was Marguerite's. So there we were in my friend's office and I started recognizing photographs and possessions like the embroidered silk wrap she brought back from Paris a few years ago." Natalie let out an anguished breath. "I still can't believe she's gone."

"Stay focused, Natalie. You're doing great." Lyssa squeezed hard.

"Right. It was awful. I felt sick when I realized it was Marguerite she was targeting. I challenged her, knowing that Marguerite would never betray Billy. She really loved him. Don't you agree?"

"The fact is, Marguerite did have an affair. We know that now. Just not with another man."

Natalie wet her lips. "I know, but when Vivienne told me, I argued with her. We got really loud and I started to worry security would come after us so I shut up. Then she told me the details about hooking up with Marguerite in Brittany. I didn't know Marguerite was gay or bi or whatever she was. Did you?"

Lyssa nodded. "Keep going."

"I wanted to scream and deny it and throw Vivienne out the window into the snow. She laughed and told me not to be so naïve. I felt betrayed by both of them. I started opening drawers and flipping the pages of books looking for the letters, wanting them *not* to be there, because then none of it would be true."

"And Campus Security didn't come after you?" Lyssa asked.

"No one noticed. No one bothered us. We looked everywhere, and there were no letters. I was ready to quit at that point."

"Why didn't you?"

"Because I had said something about Stan Block being on duty and we better get out of there, and Vivienne went crazy, saying Stan was trying to blackmail Marguerite and probably Marguerite had taken the letters to her house for safekeeping. I didn't want Marguerite's name being ruined by Stan Block, so we went to Marguerite's house to find the letters."

"Just so you know," Kyle said, "Stan already had the letters. He'd stolen them from Marguerite's office before she died."

"That monster. That's what he was hassling her about in the parking lot, wasn't it? I could kill him."

"Whoa," Lyssa said. "Don't say anything like that to police."

"I'll say what I want to say. He's a monster."

"Don't say it, Natalie," Kyle warned. "Turns out someone killed Stan that same night while you and Vivienne were on the hunt for the letters."

Natalie's mouth formed a perfect O. "I am so screwed." Her voice was barely above a whisper.

"No you're not. Finish your story; let us coach you. So you went to Marguerite's house."

"Right, and we searched every room. No letters. Then Vivienne said Stan must have them and how could we find out where he lived. Before I could stop her, she grabbed the phone book. I didn't want to go there because, if he wasn't at work, he was probably home. But no one was at his house. The back door was unlocked. We went in. She searched the closets. I searched the shelves and drawers. And you won't believe what I found."

"Time's running out. Just tell us."

"This pissed me off. That stinker had a pile of boxes in his entertainment center and, when I opened one, it was packed full of incriminating evidence about a crime against the college. It was disgusting. When I started yelling and swearing, Vivienne came running and told me to stop wasting time. She pulled out a box with Marguerite's initials on the front—smart woman—and there were the letters. She stashed everything from the box in her tote, and we were out of there."

"Where did you go next?" Kyle's voice was urgent.

Lyssa looked out the windshield to see the turn to the police station two stoplights ahead.

"Wait, first, someone saw us leave Stan's. Some guy was sitting in a car behind the house, just watching us. I don't think it was Stan either. Doesn't he have a Jeep?"

"He does, yes," Kyle answered.

"This was a dilapidated Volkswagen Beetle, the kind of car some people drive all winter because their other car can't take the ice and snow or they don't want it to get rusty or—"

"Whatever," Kyle cut her off. "What happened then?"

"I'd already agreed to get Vivienne to her flight if I possibly could, and she'd already written out a promise to me for a week in Manhattan at her favorite hotel and spa and custom clothing from Drayton's."

"Do you still have that written promise?"

"In my purse, yes. We were in such a hurry, I didn't even think about stopping home for the bag I packed, but all her stuff from the hotel was already in my car, so we hopped on the Thruway and went straight to New Jersey. I dropped her off at Newark airport with minutes to spare for her flight and left my car at the subway stop. And you know the rest."

"So the bag you packed for the city is probably still in your house? That's good." Kyle pulled into the lot beside police headquarters and parked at the back. "Let's go."

Natalie grabbed for Lyssa's arm as they leaned into the wind. "Why did he say that was good?"

"Because," Lyssa said, "if you haven't been home and the bag you packed is still there, it lends credibility to your story."

"It's not a story, it's the truth. Don't you believe me?" She looked behind them. "Who's Kyle talking to?"

Ten feet back, Kyle spoke into his phone. "Yes, Hank. I'm on my way into the city police station with Natalie Horowitz."

"Traitor," Natalie hissed.

Chapter 18

"The nerve of them considering me a suspect!" Natalie railed the next morning when Lyssa picked her up at the police station. "I am furious with all of you." She folded her arms and glowered at the windshield.

"Look," Lyssa snapped, "*I'm* not the one who decided you should be in a holding cell all night while the police checked out your story."

Natalie huffed and shifted away.

"Natalie, Hank considered *me* a suspect for a while, too, and he confiscated my phone the night of the murders, which is why I couldn't communicate with you. And he grilled me so relentlessly I passed out."

"Beast."

"Exactly." Still, Natalie's gaze was directed out the side window.

So much for enlisting Natalie to scour Marguerite's Facebook for names of her fellow travelers in Brittany. She'd promised Kyle she wouldn't do it herself, even if Hank asked her to.

"So." She started the car and backed out of her parking space. "I can drive us to Lynnie's for breakfast, which was my original plan, or if you're just going to sulk, I can dump you at your house. Which is it?"

Natalie flounced the best she could within the confines of the seat belt. "Aren't you the bossy one."

239

Lyssa drove out of the lot and came to a stop at the traffic light. "I am not bossy. I am hungry. And I'm buying, if you're interested."

"I suppose, if you're buying." Natalie tossed it off with a shrug.

Lyssa switched on the left turn signal, and they drove in silence to the restaurant.

She had just turned off the engine when Natalie placed a gentle hand on her wrist. "I didn't know about the phone, and I didn't know what you were going through. I guess it was rough on you. And why aren't you and Kyle in Cornwall?"

Lyssa rallied her positive attitude. "New plan, we'll be flying to the UK together next weekend."

"You know, you don't look good."

Lyssa squeezed her eyes shut against the tears. "It's been horrible, and I've wrecked my health."

"So that's why Kyle is here instead of in London?"

"He's going with me to the doctor's in a couple of hours." She sucked in a breath. "And that's all I'm going to say about any of it."

After parking in the lot for Lynnie's it took two tries to get the key out of the ignition. She wished she could stop her body from trembling. She sent up a prayer that a hot meal would help.

"I won't pry anymore." Natalie made no move to leave the warmth of the car. "I don't want to lose you as a friend."

Unable to speak, Lyssa nodded and let herself out of the car. With a deep cleansing breath, she walked into Lynnie's and the welcome of jingle bells. She didn't care that her face was splotchy from crying. "Two of us," she told the waitress.

When Kyle swung by the apartment to collect his wife for their appointment in Clifton Springs, she was waiting for him in the entry on the first floor, dressed in the blue cashmere roll-neck he'd given her two years ago for Christmas, the one she wore whenever she was facing some daunting task.

Their appointment was worrisome for him as well. He fully expected to be drawn and quartered by Lyssa's doctor for leaving his wife behind in Tompkins Falls to deal single-handedly with murder and mayhem. Left her more than once the past year, while he gallivanted throughout Europe, staying at five-star hotels, and trying to salvage the business he'd built from scratch and nearly lost through his own neglect. *Fine husband I am.*

"Ready, my love?" he asked as she settled in the passenger seat.

Her answer was a gulp and a single nod. Her hands clutching the handles of her navy tote bag seemed to be all that was holding her together.

"Did you learn anything new from Hank this morning?" she asked him.

"Yes, quite a lot actually." If it helped her to talk about something entirely unrelated to her health, then he'd go along. "Vivienne is now in the hands of the state police on Long Island, near her home, and has given them a full accounting of her activities in Tompkins Falls and after."

"Did she throw Natalie under the bus?"

"Not at all. She took full responsibility for the break-ins and for removal of her personal property from Stan Block's house, and she insisted nothing else was taken from any of the places they visited."

"Did she really not know her husband had been murdered while she was running around trying to retrieve the packet of love letters?"

"Apparently not. She thinks it's absurd that he was poisoned with wine from France, as he's not even French and he never liked wine. The police now believe someone chose the wine based on the information in his bogus CV."

She laughed drily. "That was obvious on day one."

"Yes, well, they've caught up, and they're again questioning everyone on the search committee and all of the Languages faculty and staff."

"So, Vivienne was completely ignorant about his death until the authorities approached her in Agadir?" Her tone was incredulous.

"Indeed."

"How did she explain that?"

"Remember, there was a media blackout for twelve hours after the death. She'd have been in flight when the college's formal statement made the news, and it was purposely vague. They didn't know the identity of the victim at that point. Drayton Textiles was also unaware of the death for some time, since none of them knew he was in Tompkins Falls. The police had no way to inform them until you identified him and told Hank."

She shook her head. "I've been sitting here feeling like a total screw-up. It's good to remember I accomplished something this week."

Finally, she was sharing something of her feelings. "Why would you feel like a screw-up?"

"Marguerite didn't let us protect her in the parking lot. She took a drug on my watch, just before she died. Justin's star candidate was murdered at my table. Stan Block got himself killed. And no one, including me, can figure out who's behind any of it. I can't believe it's all one person doing this."

"Nor can I." He wanted to be done discussing the deaths, but the thought popped in his head, "Hank said Vivienne described a car outside Stan's house with an occupant who seemed to be watching her and Natalie. Her description was identical to Natalie's. You remember she said it was the sort of beat-up car someone would drive in the winter around here. Did that mean anything to you?"

She shook her head. "I'm just glad whoever it was didn't hurt the two of them. Probably the guy waited until Stan came back to the house and killed him. Can we set this aside and let Hank take it from here?"

"Absolutely. I totally agree."

"Careful, darling, you're starting to sound like a Yank."

He laughed and noticed a grin on her face. Yet aside from clarifying the turns he needed to make on the back roads, she was quiet the rest of the ride. He parked at the far end of the hospital lot to give them a short walk in the fresh air before their appointment. She held tight to his hand as they skirted four rows of cars and, when they gained the sidewalk, gave a tug which brought him to a complete stop.

"What is it, sweetheart?"

"I am desperately afraid." A small sob accompanied the words.

He gathered her close. "We'll see what the doctor has found and go from there, shall we?" He felt her nod against his chest. "Whatever's happening, know that I love you with every fiber of my being." The words just slipped out. "Did I actually say that out loud?"

She chuckled and plucked the handkerchief from his breast pocket. "You did, and it was exactly what I needed to hear."

"And I mean it. We're doing this together, eh?"

She tidied her face, drew in some deep breaths, and in they went to the suite of offices that comprised Dr. Bowes' clinic.

The moment they emerged into the biting west wind, Lyssa circled his waist with her arm, and he wrapped her shoulders. "How do you feel about all of this?" he asked her.

"Embarrassed that they suspected I was anorexic."

"Which you are not, correct?"

"Correct, but still. Plus, really stupid that I ended up with malnutrition." She exhaled. "And mostly relieved because we have a plan that's as simple as eating the right foods—regularly, of course—and taking supplements and keeping up with daily hydration, exercise, sleep, and social connections."

A glance at his face showed the worry lines had melted away, and a smile played around his mouth. *Thank you, God.* "I'll ask Manda, but I don't think any of this was part of our education, at home or at school. I'm not saying that's an excuse, just saying it's stuff I didn't learn growing up. Did you?"

"Most of it, yes. And the rest by talking frankly with my physician about this problem or that. You feel your eating plan is manageable?"

"Totally. I welcome your support, and I am committed to making this a lifelong change. One day at a time."

He gave her shoulders a squeeze. "As your enthusiastic supporter, I know one bit of advice we shall put to immediate use." His voice was light and carefree. "Let's have a meal at the restaurant she recommended. Wharton's, was it?"

"Warfields. She told us to walk along the stream to Main Street and turn left."

The restaurant was doing a brisk business over the lunch hour. They were shown to a table at the front window that had just freed up. They both ordered the salmon salad. As soon as their waiter set a basket of hot bread and rolls before them, they dug in.

With his mouth full of rye bread, Kyle said something like, "Changes to spreadsheet."

"Let's take a look." She placed her iPad between them on the table and opened the spreadsheet she'd designed after her initial appointment. "It's pretty compatible with what she prescribed today. I need to add taking a multivitamin every day. Oh, and for the next three months, take higher doses of several vitamins and minerals."

With his notes from the visit in hand, he bent his head to her spreadsheet. "Shall I add some check boxes for your vitamins?" he asked.

"Yes, please. The special ones are potassium, D3, folic acid, and a B-complex."

When he saved the changes, she told him, "I am so grateful you want to be part of this. I almost forgot to add calendar reminders about getting blood tests every six weeks." She opened the calendar on her iPhone and took care of that.

"Done." She tucked away the tablet and the phone and reached for his hand. "Tell me what you think. I'll need to cook breakfasts and dinners whenever I'm in Tompkins Falls next semester, and it really would be easier to do that in our kitchen at the house."

He did a double-take. "I never thought I'd hear that from you."

"I know we both had strong reactions when we found out Billy Warren had created the kitchen and master suite. Please be honest, darling. Could you move back in?"

Their salads arrived, and she saw relief wash over his features.

She teased, "Not ready to answer, were you?"

"I'll trust the salmon to kick my brain into gear," he told her with a smile she couldn't read.

The next twenty minutes were given over to savoring every bite of the crisp salad, tangy dressing, and perfectly grilled salmon. And to emptying the breadbasket of its herb rolls, rye bread slices, and cheesy bread sticks.

"Did you save room for dessert?" the waiter asked.

Kyle raised his hands in refusal, but Lyssa said, "When we came in, I saw some kind of berry pie in the case. Is there a slice left? And I'd like coffee, too."

"There's one slice with your name on it. Shall I bring two forks?"

"Just coffee for me." When the waiter had departed, Kyle raised an eyebrow. "You've got your appetite back. It looks good on you."

"A good meal does a lot for my energy and enthusiasm. About the house—"

"I agree. If we're to move past the vandalism and the unpleasantness with Warren, the right thing for us is to return to our home. Together. And I will plan to be in Tompkins Falls with you as much as possible through the spring."

He was gripping the edge of the table, though, and his white knuckles told her how much this was costing him. He might never embrace the Finger Lakes as completely as she'd embraced his native Cornwall, but she needed this concession for the spring semester. "That will help so much, darling. And we'll schedule time in Cornwall, too, even before the summer break. And by fall, I'll be able to make Cornwall or London my home base. How does that sound?"

His answering nod came slowly. By the time he looked up, her blueberry pie and their coffee had arrived. "We'll sort out the UK arrangements over the summer, shall we? But short term, we should have the new furniture and dishes and such moved into the house before our flight on Sunday."

"I'll call the movers on our way to the architect's office right after dessert." She lifted her fork.

"Perhaps Natalie will help unpack the dishes and set up the kitchen," he suggested.

"And wouldn't it be nice to have Joel brandish his magic wand and fill the pantry?" She knew her eyes were sparkling. They always did when she and Kyle joined forces to get a big job done. "This is the best blueberry pie ever. You've *got* to try it." She pushed the pie plate to the center of the table.

"One bite. I'm getting half my usual exercise this week, and that must change."

While the elevator took them to the sixth floor of the architect's building in Rochester, Kyle smoothed Lyssa's waves off her forehead and planted a kiss. "You aren't nervous, are you?"

"No. We've been thinking about this for months, and we're in sync about what we want."

He stood aside for her to exit. She scanned the directional sign and pointed them to the right.

They'd barely enough time to remove gloves, scarves, and coats before the assistant showed them into Pamela Kriegstein's inner office. The architect held out her hand, first to Kyle and then to Lyssa. "Peter and Gwen Shaughnessy tell me you're building on a cove on Chestnut Lake and shopping for an architect."

He liked the woman's forthright manner and gave her extra points for not calling their friend Pete.

Lyssa spoke up. "We've brought some sketches that may help you see our vision. And Kyle has some photographs he's taken of our cove." He savored the way she called it 'our cove.'"

"Very helpful." Kriegstein motioned them to a large rectangular table and gestured for them to spread out what they'd brought. After disclaimers and a reminder about their time limit, Pamela invited them to brainstorm with her.

Within half an hour, he was satisfied they'd found their architect. Lyssa and Pamela had immediate rapport. Personally, he appreciated the architect's commitment to preserving the beauty of the setting.

"So our homework," he said as they wrapped up the discussion, "is to talk with Justin about a road or driveway access from the highway, which is a good mile away. I'll have that conversation before we leave for Cornwall."

"Sounds like we're going forward together?" Pamela asked with an expectant smile.

"Yes," they chorused.

Pamela committed to preliminary design documents for the February meeting, and Kyle pledged to have answers to their new questions.

With firm handshakes, they said their good byes, and the Penningtons paused just outside the suite for an embrace. "When it's right, it's right, eh?" But Lyssa's eyes were far away, and a smile curved her lips. "What are you thinking, my love?"

"That some good has come from having to delay our plans to fly to Cornwall."

He agreed, glad he'd made something good happen for her. "Indeed. And since we're having dinner with Justin and Gianessa tonight, shall we break the news about our new architect?"

"Let's. I'll give Gianessa a heads-up to smooth the way."

Kyle salivated at the tantalizing aromas that greeted them at the Cushman home two hours later. Justin ushered them inside and took their coats. Thankfully, there was no talk of murder during their meal of roast pork and a rainbow of vegetables and fruits.

Justin himself brought up the topic of their progress with the cove house. Though Kyle expected him to act huffy when they announced their choice of architect, Justin threw them a curve by saying, "Gwen and Peter set aside an acre on Cady's Point for themselves after she purchased twenty acres for Manda and Gianessa's holistic health center. Did you know that?"

Kyle dug way back in his memory to the days when he and Lyssa were dating in London. "That's the land Gwen purchased from someone you knew close by London, isn't it?" He waited for Justin's reaction. The pleased smile encouraged him. "It's a beautiful property, as you know, though I suspect designing a house on a rocky cove for a family with young children posed a challenge for their architect, eh?"

"Well said, Kyle," Gianessa said with a wink.

"Yes, you Penningtons are wise to base your choice of architect on that criteria." Justin raised his glass of sparkling water. "To Kyle and Lyssa's new house on the cove."

Kyle caught the look of relief on Lyssa's face as they lifted their glasses. The ring of crystal mingled with their "Cheers."

"That grand news," Justin continued, "made up for some disappointment in our effort to hire Marguerite's replacement."

Lyssa and Kyle exchanged worried looks.

Justin set down his glass and took his time centering the base within an embossed design on the tablecloth. "I was ready to suggest," he told them, "Lyssa rent her house to Danika McGregor for a semester to give her time to settle into Tompkins Falls. As it turns out"—now he fiddled with his spoon—"we'll have to use our adjunct to cover all of Marguerite's classes."

Lyssa moaned. "I was sure we'd be celebrating Danika's acceptance of your offer."

"Was the problem with the offer?" Kyle asked.

Justin harrumphed, and Gianessa supplied the answer. "She's reluctant to accept until the police have solved the two suspicious deaths."

"Sorry to hear that," Kyle said and placed a hand on Lyssa's back. "So the adjunct is the winner. Let's hope she does well by Marguerite's students."

"How—" Lyssa's question died on her lips when Justin shoved back his chair and vanished into the kitchen. Kyle was sure Lyssa's unasked question had to do with how the candidate knew about Drayton's and Block's deaths. He wanted the answer himself.

Gianessa patted Lyssa's hand and whispered, "He's really upset about this. Let's let him fuss with the coffee, and he'll have a different topic of conversation picked out by the time he comes back."

Although Justin was making plenty of noise stacking cups and saucers on a tray, Lyssa whispered, "So classes are covered, but who will be department chair?"

"Justin wants the interim dean to handle it."

Lyssa chuckled. "That would be Rand. How does he feel about it?"

"I don't think he's been asked yet. Justin has requested his presence on campus later this week." Gianessa mimed locking her lips, and Lyssa did the same.

Chapter 19

Wednesday morning, Lyssa opted to attend the Early Risers AA meeting in the back room of the Bagel Depot. It wasn't that she hadn't heard the reluctance in Kyle's voice when he'd offered to supervise the furniture deliveries at the Seneca Street house, but she knew she'd have more mental energy if she started the day with a meeting. Natalie was helping out and, besides, Lyssa would only be an hour late if she left right after the meeting.

She offered to grab bagels for all of them, but Kyle waved off the suggestion and told her to suit herself. She left him with a warm kiss.

After the meeting she suited herself by taking a seat at the breakfast counter. While she munched a raisin bagel spread with peanut butter, she drew out a much-folded sheet of graph paper stained with coffee. Though she'd been carrying it around the last two weeks to capture notes and organize her thoughts about the murder of Charles Drayton, it was badly out of date. Her first correction was to cross out *Emile Duval* and pencil in the man's correct name. She also changed *Jacqueline Duval* to *Vivienne*.

Her list of suspects was behind the times as well. She had starred *José*, but now she crossed off all of her fellow diners and did the same to the vague *Other Languages Faculty*. Hank had said his people had interviewed everyone a second time and cleared them of suspicion.

She'd never thought Vivienne or Stan Block was Charles' killer, let alone Natalie, so those names also got lines through their middles. "Wait," she said out loud.

"Need something, honey?" the waitress asked from a few positions away. Lyssa checked her coffee level and shook her head with a bright smile.

What was it Kyle had said at dinner last night? Justin had told them he would probably have to use the adjunct for Marguerite's spring classes because Danika McGregor wouldn't accept her offer unless and until the murders had been solved. And who could blame her?

Then Kyle had said something in jest. What was it? She couldn't think, over the noise of slurping coffee and conversations on either side of her. "Something about a winner," Lyssa muttered. The waitress splashed coffee in her mug. "Thanks," Lyssa said without looking up. *So the adjunct is the big winner?* Something like that.

The man on the stool to her right tapped his finger on the edge of her paper placemat. "You should get one of their glazed pecan buns, lady. No offense, but you could use a few more pounds on you."

"Seriously?" Lyssa answered him with a laugh. "That's very sweet of you, but my doctor has me on a strict diet that doesn't include pastries." The man snorted and shook his head.

She returned her thoughts to Kyle's phrase, the adjunct being the big winner. What did she know about the woman? As search coordinator, she had supported all the interviews and the big finale dinners for the candidates, but she'd only exchanged a handshake with Danika McGregor, and she'd never met or even talked with the adjunct.

She wished she'd been invited to the adjunct's dinner at the wildly popular farm-to-table restaurant in Canandaigua. Although the dean's assistant had reserved a small room for eight, only five people actually showed up. To be fair, maybe they were hustling to post grades. More likely they figured the adjunct didn't have a prayer of getting the job.

What was her first name? Nadine? Nanette? Lyssa blurted out, "Nicole!" and immediately apologized to her neighbor.

She fished her iPad mini from the depths of her tote bag. Her search of the campus directory told her the woman's full name, Nicole Dutois, but it didn't produce her photo or any further information, so she signed on to the campus intranet. There in full color was a professional headshot of an attractive thirty-something woman with honey brown hair cut in a shoulder-length swing style. *Oh my gosh, is it her?*

She texted the woman's name to Trooper Hank Moran, asking if they had cleared Nicole Dutois as a suspect, wondering if they'd even talked to her because she was just an adjunct. She left a ten-dollar bill on the counter and raced out of the Bagel Depot. On the way to her car, she called the head of Campus Security.

"Hey, Tony," she greeted him. "Will Nicole Dutois be using Marguerite's office if she's hired?"

"No *if* about it, Lyssa. She's over there this morning with a couple of guys from Maintenance shoving the desk around for her. She's making them crazy." He mimicked a woman's high-pitched voice. "Try it over here. A little at an angle. No, not that way."

"So it's a done deal that she's been hired full time?"

"I guess. Why do you want to know?"

Lyssa invented a reason. "I just want to—to congratulate her before Kyle and I fly out Sunday. Thanks, Tony." She put the phone on Bluetooth before seating it in its holder and heading for campus.

Her next call was to Rand Cunningham. "Hey Rand, where are you?"

"Hamptons. At my family's beach house, in exile here while the rest of them are celebrating together at the penthouse in Manhattan." She sidestepped the poor-me line about family dynamics. She'd heard all about his being disowned by the elder Cunninghams for choosing to use his expensive degrees for a career in higher education rather than a VP position in their successful public relations firm. "Where are *you*?" he asked.

"I'm on my way to campus. What can you tell me about Nicole Dutois?"

"She's a pain in the butt."

"I hear she's teaching all of Marguerite's classes for spring semester. Is the ink dry on that contract?"

"Yeah. Justin said she was holding out for a permanent spot for herself *and* the job as chair, but he wouldn't cave. She's a good teacher, but she hasn't finished her doctorate and has no people skills. No way could she chair the department."

Lyssa's phone beeped, and Rand said, "I just sent you the picture from her interview dinner, and you'll see what I mean. She's beaming and the rest of us can't wait to get out of the room." He rambled on about the windswept snow looking like sculptures on the beach below the house, but Lyssa tuned out and pulled over for a look at the picture he'd sent.

Nicole was wearing a cat-that-swallowed-the-canary smile. Even with high heels, she was only Becca's height, and Becca was maybe an inch shorter than Lyssa. "You there, Lyssa?" Rand asked.

"Uh, yeah. Just thinking about the years in grad school when I worked as an adjunct making pennies, without benefits." She almost said something about having coffee with him when he came to campus later in the week, but she caught herself in time. Gianessa had said it was confidential until Justin talked with Rand about chairing the Languages department, and she wasn't sure that had happened yet.

"Good experience, though," Rand pointed out.

"Gotta go, Rand. Thanks for all this. Happy holiday."

She continued to campus, wondering how Nicole felt, never getting a firm offer or health insurance. Sure it sucked, but would she *kill* for that? Lyssa shook her head. Those were reasons for a professor wannabe to keep going with her doctoral program and polish up her professional skills. Not reasons to eliminate the competition.

Besides, it made no sense that Nicole would poison the candidate who'd called himself Emile Duval and not do something terrible to Danika McGregor, the one who'd interviewed just before Emile.

Lyssa frowned at the irony. Danika had been a sure thing until Emile's phony resumé showed up on Justin's desk. Hank had cleared Danika as a suspect, hadn't he? He must have or Justin would not have made her an offer.

Which she'd refused. Emile, far from being the answer to Justin's dreams, had messed up their best hope, first by overshadowing Danika's candidacy and second by dying and scaring off Danika with his death.

She made the turn onto the campus roadway, parked in the faculty lot, and bent her head against the wind. She'd just stop by Marguerite's old office, congratulate Nicole, and maybe offer to shelve a few books for her. It was the right thing to do, and it might give her some closure about Marguerite's death.

Since Natalie's jovial supervision of the movers was spot on, not to mention much more effective than Kyle's curmudgeonly style—she'd even shown up with boxes of doughnuts and a seemingly endless supply of coffee, cream, and sugar—Kyle escaped to the small room upstairs with his phone and laptop. For an hour he made calls to various staff in London, trying to shut out the grunts, shouting, and occasional laughter from the first floor.

"Need your signature, Kyle." Natalie's voice carried up the stairs and broke through his concentration.

"Coming straightaway."

The sight of the fully furnished living room brought a smile to his face. "How clever of you to group furniture that way," he told her. Chairs and sofa faced each other on either side of the fireplace. "We'll have to have a friend over after the holidays, eh?" He winked at her.

"*Moi?* You've never done that. That would be nice." She pointed him to the paperwork. "Sign next to the arrow on each page, and this crew will be on its way. Two more trucks right behind them, ready to offload kitchen table and chairs and who knows what else. When is Lyssa coming?"

"I really thought she'd be here by now."

"Then I guess it's you and me, and I need you in the kitchen to tell me how you two organize your dishes and cookware."

"Happy to." He'd left his phone upstairs, but it was probably better not to be interrupted while placing Waterford goblets and dessert settings of Belleek porcelain. He noticed the sweat on Natalie's brow and the pinching beside her mouth. "We owe you a day at the spa after this, Natalie."

"Make that two days, Kyle." This time there was an edge to her voice.

What's keeping Lyssa? Ignoring a prickle of worry, he rolled up his sleeves and cast his eye over the assembly of boxes on the kitchen island, stacked two high and all stamped Fragile. For this, he needed a nice selection of Vivaldi. He plugged in earbuds and switched on his iPod.

Lyssa arrived at Nicole's office to find two burly maintenance men standing back from Marguerite's massive desk. They'd angled it into a sunny spot that would guarantee sunshine on Nicole's shoulders all afternoon and give her easy access to the floor-to-ceiling shelving units.

"Oh my gosh, that's so perfect, Nicole," Lyssa gushed. "How did you ever think of placing the desk there?" Not that Nicole had asked her opinion.

The thunderclouds on Nicole's face gave way to wide-eyed surprise. "And you are?"

"Lyssa Pennington. I coordinated the search for your position." She stepped aside as the men filed out of the room. Belatedly, her brain kicked in. Her enthusiastic approval of the desk's location had given them the opportunity to escape. That might have been a mistake.

Lyssa kept the smile on her face as her gaze swept the office. And there were the saddle-colored fine leather gloves sticking up from the pocket of a dark gray winter parka hanging on the coat tree. She glanced back at Nicole, who tipped her head, making her hair swing along her jawline. No doubt about it, she was alone with Charles Drayton's killer.

"Sorry I can't stay to help," she said. "I just came by to congratulate you, Nicole." She needn't have bothered with the lie. Nicole wasn't buying it. In fact, she had made good use of the seconds it took Lyssa to deliver the message.

She had circled around Lyssa and closed the office door, effectively cutting off Lyssa's escape. "Too late," she singsonged. "You know, don't you?"

Lyssa weighed her options. If Nicole attacked, she would fight back, but she doubted she had enough strength to win that battle, one more consequence of neglecting her health all semester.

Nicole might be shorter, but she was heavier by at least thirty pounds and her tight-fitting T-shirt showed well-toned arms. No, this situation called for brains over brawn. "I'm sorry, you're thinking I know what, Nicole?"

Lyssa smiled as she fingered the phone in her pocket. First, she lowered its volume. "Do I know that President

Cushman wouldn't agree to make you department chair? Yes, but you know, he'll probably reconsider once you finish your doctorate, don't you think?"

Nicole muttered. "Why would I want to do that? It's so boring."

Lyssa did a count of the phone calls she'd made on the way to campus. Just the two, right? Tony and Rand, in that order, so Tony's number would be second in her call history. She summoned up a mental image the screen.

Nicole was saying, "I know you saw me leaving the kitchen that night. You have to believe me, there wasn't enough poison in the bottle of wine to kill him. I never meant for him to die, just make him so sick and so mad he'd turn down the job."

Lyssa blindly pressed the screen of her phone just below halfway, hoping she was activating Tony's phone number. With the sound off she had no way of knowing if her call was succeeding. She had to assume it was going through. Now, she just needed to buy time. And pray her butt off.

"I'm really curious where you found strychnine," she prompted Nicole.

"Oh, you didn't know? I inherited a Victorian from my grandparents. One of the painted ladies on Elm Street. There's amazing stuff, like rat poison in the basement and Tiffany lamps in the attic. I didn't think I'd need to work at all, but it costs thousands to heat the place and to keep up with repairs." She shrugged. "I'll be fine now that I'm full time."

Seriously, that was her motive? Lyssa fought with herself to maintain the girlfriend voice while, she hoped, Tony was puzzling over the silent phone call he'd just gotten from her. Or could he hear some of the conversation? How did that work? Would he remember that she planned to stop by Nicole's new office?

"Like I said, Nicole, if you finish up your doctorate, you could have a faculty position anywhere." She glanced behind her at the books Nicole had arranged on the shelves. "You speak, what? German, Spanish, Italian, French, Russian?" *Oops.*

Too late, she realized those were Marguerite's books. Nicole's were still in boxes. Panic rose in her throat, and she sent up a prayer not to show her fear.

"Whatever." Nicole barked a laugh. "How can anyone compete with a superstar who also speaks Arabic and Chinese?"

This was not the moment to tell Nicole the man she'd murdered was a total fraud. "So what? You're brilliant, Nicole. You can learn any language you set your mind to." She shifted her weight from one hip to the other. "It's like I tell my students, we have to keep ourselves marketable."

Nicole had edged away from the door.

Should I run for it? A wash of chills down Lyssa's back warned her not to. Her enemy now stood in front of a low bookcase directly under the room's light switch, gripping something behind her back. Something she'd found on a lower shelf while Lyssa was pontificating about the benefits of further study.

She searched her memory. Marguerite had used that bookcase to show a few treasured reminders of her travels, like the colorful Provençal bowl on top, where she always deposited her office keys. *Help me, Marguerite.*

The bowl wouldn't make much of a weapon, but the pointed object Nicole brought into view from behind her back would. The foot-tall Eiffel Tower with all its intricate detail cast in heavy metal, an award Marguerite had been so proud to receive at a conference in Lyons. Everyone had teased her about having to pay extra because it put her suitcase over the weight limit.

With a malevolent chuckle, Nicole hoisted the award overhead with one hand, her arm muscles bunching. A cruel smile stole over her face. "Nice of Marguerite to keep this on hand, don't you think?"

A voice that sounded just like Marguerite's whispered to Lyssa, *Don't let her get away with this.* Lyssa gathered her strength and charged her tormentor, head butting her in the stomach. Nicole crashed back into the bookcase.

Lyssa groped for the door handle, found it, and gave it a twist. Before she could open the door, though, Nicole shot out her free hand, gripped Lyssa's outstretched arm and, with a strength far beyond Lyssa's, hurled her across the room, taunting, "Fool!"

Lyssa landed hard on one hip and slid on the polished hardwood. Her back and head smashed into the desk, and she cried out in pain.

Laughing and gripping the Eiffel Tower by its elegant neck, Nicole swung wildly at Lyssa's head. One half of the four-pronged base connected with Lyssa's cheekbone and the orbit of her eye. The searing pain nearly blinded her.

One good eye was all she needed, though, to watch Nicole retreat and dance into position for her next move. Now Nicole pointed the weapon like a spear, waving it back and forth, cackling with glee. *She's insane.*

Lyssa rose to her feet, limbs loose, just as Tony had taught her in self-defense class. Nicole sidled a few steps back and, holding the spear low, launched herself the full width of the room. Lyssa pivoted and, swinging around like a shot-put thrower, slammed her elbow into Nicole's breastbone. *Oh my gosh, it worked.*

Nicole lost her grip on the weapon and staggered sideways a few paces, one hand over her chest, fighting for breath. Lyssa kicked the Eiffel Tower under the desk out of Nicole's reach.

Now was the time to run for it, but halfway to the door dizziness hit her. *God, don't let me pass out.*

She was sure she was hallucinating as the door swung wide and three dark forms spilled into the office. The forms took substance as they rushed by her. Tony Pinelli and the two movers.

Tony twisted Nicole's arm behind her; she screamed as she dropped to her knees.

The three men subdued Nicole Dutois, despite her wild struggle, and Tony got a pair of handcuffs on her. The biggest of the movers sat on her back.

Lyssa was trembling from the flood of adrenaline. She sank to the floor and lay on her back, knees bent, dimly aware of two more men—these in uniform—joining the cluster around Nicole. One of them recited the Miranda warning.

Tony had backed away from the action to stand at Lyssa's side. When the officer paused his reading to ask, "What's the charge?" Tony answered, "Attempted murder of Lyssa Pennington."

"Tony?" She tugged at Tony's shirt. "She confessed to poisoning Charles Drayton using rat poison from her basement."

He squatted next to her. "Moran's on his way, and we'll let him handle that one. She's going to prison for a long time, honey. You just lie still until the EMTs get here. We'll have the pros take a look at your eye, okay?" He bent closer for a better look. "Jeez, how'd she do that to you?"

"Marguerite's statue." She pointed under the desk.

He knelt and peered under the desk. "I see it." His voice caught. "Think she murdered Marguerite, too?"

Chapter 20

Kyle didn't give a flying fig that Trooper Hank Moran filled the doorway to Lyssa's hospital room or that the lawman was glaring at him. "With all due respect, Hank, I've only just arrived, and I need a moment with my wife," he snarled.

"And I need her statement." Hank's voice was deadly calm.

"Guys, stop. We've got thirteen minutes until the nurse comes to kick you out. This is how it's going to go. First, take the testosterone down a notch, both of you. Agreed?"

Did my wife say that?

Kyle eyed Hank until he gave Lyssa a nod. Only then did he relax his own posture.

Lyssa continued, "Kyle's staying at my side unless he doesn't want to hear the details Hank needs."

Kyle inched his chair closer to the right side of the bed and folded his arms.

"And, finally, Hank, you get four minutes, not a second more. Kyle's timing you."

Kyle lifted his arm and stared at Hank over the dial of his wristwatch.

"Understood." Hank crossed to Lyssa's left side and flinched, probably at the evidence of her injury—a line of Steri-Strips and ugly black stitches along the ridge of her right cheek and another set above her eye, plus assorted contusions.

"Sweetheart, you need to keep the icepack on that eye."

Without a word, she put it back in place. "I'm ready, Hank."

The trooper asked for and received her permission to record her statement. He said for the record, to spare her undue strain, Tony Pinelli's description of her confrontation with Nicole Dutois was adequate for moment. "Mrs. Pennington, please confine your remarks to anything Ms. Dutois said pertaining to the murder of Charles Drayton."

Lyssa reached for Kyle, and he held her hand with the utmost gentleness. "Can you do this, love?"

She nodded and began by recounting the details she noticed as soon as she entered Marguerite's old office—Nicole's haircut and height, and the gloves and coat in plain sight. She stated those items were the ones worn by the bearer of the poisoned wine the night of the murder.

"I knew right away she was the person leaving the kitchen at Westerlee Hall, and Nicole knew right away I had made her. I tried to bluff my way out, but it wouldn't work. She told me she hadn't meant to kill Drayton, but I didn't believe her."

"Why is that, Mrs. Pennington?"

"Because she revealed means, motive, and opportunity."

Hank dipped his head, probably hiding a smile. "What did she say about the means of death?" he asked.

Lyssa told them about the rat poison Nicole had discovered in the cellar of the old Victorian she'd inherited. "She knew it contained strychnine and that the dose you'd use to kill a rat wouldn't necessarily kill a person. But she made a point of defending her actions by saying the poison was meant to make the candidate sick and mad, so he wouldn't take a job at Tompkins College."

Lyssa addressed opportunity by pointing out Nicole had access to the resumé s of both the candidates who'd been brought to campus. It wasn't a huge leap to conclude she had used the detail about Drayton's supposed hometown to choose the wine for him. She'd added the poison before bringing the bottle, uncorked, to the dinner.

When Hank probed into how Nicole would know exactly where to bring the wine, Lyssa pointed out it was common knowledge the dinner was planned for Westerlee Hall, and the layouts of all campus buildings were available on the campus intranet, so Nicole could easily plan her arrival and departure from the kitchen or dining room.

For the record, Lyssa repeated what she and Hank had already discussed. When Nicole had arrived in the kitchen, just ahead of Lyssa, the caterers were setting up, and the bottles of wine Lyssa had ordered were already on the counter nearest the dining room. Nicole had set her distinctive bottle a little apart and displayed a gift card that said the wine was for Duval, who they now knew was Charles Drayton.

Lyssa went on, "Her motive was hard for me to wrap my head around. Why would she want to eliminate Charles Drayton from the running but not make any move to eliminate the woman candidate everyone loved, Danika McGregor?"

"And did she tell you why?"

"I had to dig for it. To start, just before I got to campus, Rand Cunningham sent me a photograph taken at the end of Nicole's two-day interview. The expression on her face showed she was over the moon about how successful it had been. Rand said the committee didn't share that opinion about her chances for the job and, frankly, their dismissal of her showed in their faces in that picture."

"You'll forward me that photo?"

"Sure. But it's not just the photo, Hank. She seemed delusional about her qualifications for a full-time faculty job and for the department chair position. Nicole doesn't have her doctorate, which is mandatory for a tenure track position and for department chair. When I pointed out that was holding her back, she didn't seem to get it, said it was too boring to continue for the doctorate."

When Hank stayed quiet, Lyssa went on, "The candidate after Nicole was Danika McGregor, and everyone liked her. But, from what Nicole said, she didn't feel threatened at all by her."

"Threatened in what sense?" Hank asked.

"Less qualified than her as a contender for the job. Which was ridiculous. Nicole didn't come close to the woman's credentials or expertise with languages or her experience as a department chair. Honestly, the only thing Nicole seemed bothered by in either candidate was Drayton's claim to speak a bazillion languages."

At Hank's raised eyebrows, Lyssa said, "Her exact words were, '*How can anyone compete with a superstar who also speaks Arabic and Chinese?*' And, no, I didn't tell her Drayton's CV was a total fraud, including the stuff about Arabic and Chinese. And, by the way I don't remember him claiming to speak Chinese."

"Thank you for that. Anything else, Mrs. Pennington?"

"Yes, she mentioned how expensive it is to heat and maintain the old Victorian she inherited but said she should be okay now that she's full time." Pain creased her forehead. "Then it stopped being a conversation and got physical."

"And what signaled that change?"

Lyssa wetted her lips with her tongue. "She flaunted her weapon." Lyssa gulped. "It was that intricate casting of the Eiffel Tower Marguerite had received as an award."

"We'll stop there, Mrs. Pennington." Hank switched off his recorder and got to his feet. "I'm sorry for your ordeal, Lyssa. We're all grateful you held your own."

"Can you leave us now, please, Hank?" Kyle stood and started toward the door. Hank gathered his things and departed. Kyle shut the door behind him and stood with his hand on the latch, fighting against his rage. What had possessed her to walk into what she must have known could be a fatal confrontation?

When he looked back at her, she was silently crying. "I know you're angry with me," she told him. "When I feel up to it, we can hash it all out, but for now I've asked Gianessa to be your sounding board. She's expecting you to come to the house after you leave."

He wanted nothing more than a no-holds-barred argument with Lyssa, but this was hardly the time. She needed complete rest, but he needed to rant. And she knew it. "I'll call her."

"Thank you. There's time for one question before the nurse comes."

One? He had a thousand. And a million doubts. "Actually, here's one. How did you get on to Nicole as the killer in the first place?"

"It was what you said at dinner."

His stomach did a dive. Even though Lyssa hadn't said it as an accusation, it made him dizzy to think he'd had some part in her decision to confront the woman. "When? What did I say?"

"We were at Gianessa and Justin's, and you said the adjunct was the winner. You were right, but it didn't make any sense. Justin's offer to Danika McGregor was fabulous, I'm sure, but Danika put him off. Why?"

"You know why. She was well within her rights to hold off her acceptance until the two murders were solved."

"True, but how did she *know* two murders had been committed at Tompkins College since her interview?"

"I …" He remembered thinking the same thing.

She continued, "Justin claims his PR people whitewashed Drayton's death and kept the word 'murder' out of the media. And Stan Block's death wouldn't have made national news."

"I see your point."

"So who told her?" Lyssa pressed. "It could only be one person, the malevolent big winner, Nicole."

Neither he nor Hank had pursued that line of thinking, yet Lyssa had put the pieces together and solved Drayton's murder. He gave her one of his lopsided smiles. "You're too clever by half, my love. I shall see that Hank includes those insights in his interrogation of Ms. Dutois."

A click heralded the arrival of a male nurse who rolled a cart past Kyle toward Lyssa's bed. "Time for the guest to leave," he told them with a cheery smile.

Kyle promised, "I'll be back in a few hours. Call me if you need anything."

Hank Moran was still in his cruiser when Kyle reached the parking lot. A tap on the window got Hank's attention, and Kyle relayed the information Lyssa had given him.

Hank agreed to use it in his effort to get a confession of murder from Nicole. "Probably Block's murder, too," Hank added.

"Not likely." Kyle checked his watch. He'd promised to talk with Gianessa, and her time was at a premium.

"I'm not sure you're aware, Kyle," Hank was saying, "this Dutois woman threw your wife around Professor LaCroix's office. She's strong enough to have killed Stan Block and moved his body by rowboat without benefit of a motor. So I'll be picking apart her claim of innocence, and the police will be checking her property for a vehicle matching the description of the one your friend Natalie Horowitz saw at Block's cottage the night he was killed."

"Thank you for that." The image of Lyssa being thrown around had hit Kyle like a blow to the stomach. "Remember, though, both Natalie and Vivienne said the driver was a man. And the eyewitness who saw the boat going away from the crime scene and into the islands said it was a man rowing."

"Where are you getting that information about the man in the boat?"

"From Joel Cushman." Kyle got only a blank look in response. Surely Joel, who had been at Hank's house when the boaters returned with Stan's body, had made sure Hank knew about Phil Phillips' spotting the rowboat as it passed his house after the murder.

"Say more."

"Joel told me it was your neighbor Phil Phillips who alerted the boaters that he'd heard a boat splashing past his house with a man at the oars, taking it into the islands the night Stan was killed. That's what got them organized to search the islands for the missing boat."

"Did Phillips tell the police that?"

"I don't know what Phil told the police. I just know he told the boaters, and they told Joel when Joel was at your house after the boaters brought in Stan's body."

Hank's face had darkened with anger. Probably he hadn't been at the house when the boaters were there, so Hank was relying on the reports from the local police who had interviewed the residents on both sides of the crime scene, including Phil. And those reports were not giving him the full picture. He didn't blame Hank for being angry about the poor communication between agencies.

Hank asked Kyle, "What else did Cushman tell you about the person rowing into the islands?"

"Only that it was a man, that there was no motor running, and he was doing a sloppy job of rowing." Hadn't

Joel made an effort to communicate this to Hank? Nonsense, he must have.

"Your thoughts about who it might have been at the oars?"

"A couple of Stan's blackmail victims were strong enough to do the job, and you have their names. I would add Billy Warren, who was angry enough at his wife's memorial service to tear someone limb from limb. If he'd known or suspected that Stan Block was the one harassing his wife—"

Hank's laugh came right from his belly. "Still holding that grudge against Warren, are you?"

Kyle stood his ground. "I take exception to your words. I've seen Warren do enough reckless things in the past few weeks to keep my attention on him." He told Hank about Warren's prowling around the Pennington's house on Seneca Street and reminded him of the hit-and-run accident involving an SUV with children on board.

"There was no verification Warren was the driver," Hank told him.

Heat rose up Kyle's neck. "I made that report myself as the person who witnessed the accident and who came to the aid of the driver and her terrified young passengers."

"You made the 911 call?"

"Yes, and made a report at the scene to the officer who responded. Dansko, I think his name was. When you say there was no verification, are you saying no one followed up with the woman driving the SUV?"

The trooper growled deep in his throat.

"I take that as confirmation. And now I think of it, no one checked back with me, either, or asked for a signature on my statement. Was I remiss?"

"No. If what you say is true, the police should have asked you to come to the station to review and sign your statement."

Kyle flinched. "I assure you, what I've just said is the truth." He repeated the details of Warren's disregard of the stop signs, the impact that sent the SUV onto the grass, Kyle's own actions at the scene, and his words to the responding officer. He'd leave it to Hank to follow up or not.

Something else had occurred to him, and he thought he knew why Warren had been sneaking around Lyssa's house on Seneca Street even after the repairs had been completed. Perhaps he'd been keeping the beat-up Volkswagen Beetle in the Penningtons' garage, the one Natalie had seen behind Stan's the night of the murders. That garage arrangement had been disrupted when Kyle took an interest in moving back into the house. He kicked himself now for not taking a look in the garage while he was there.

"What are you thinking?" Hank's challenge broke into his thoughts.

He was thinking Warren must still have access to the garage at the home he had shared with Marguerite, and that's where he might have stashed the auto after moving it from the Penningtons' garage. "If I were investigating, I'd also want to check Marguerite LaCroix's garage for that old beat-up Volkswagen the women reported behind Stan Block's house the night he was murdered."

"But you're not investigating. Correct?" Without waiting for an answer, Hank powered up the window of his cruiser.

Just as well. Kyle was expected elsewhere.

Kyle's call to Gianessa brought him an immediate invitation to the elder Cushmans' stone-and-glass house perched high above Chestnut Lake. While Gianessa and the nanny put the twins down for a nap, Kyle waited at the wall of windows in the living room, drinking in the beauty of the lake on this cloudy bright afternoon, the water a finger of slate blue between snow-covered hills.

On a day like this, he could appreciate the beauty of the Finger Lakes. Lyssa, he was sure, had a visceral connection to it, much like his own to the north coast of Cornwall.

"Pretty day." Gianessa's melodic voice pulled him out of his musing. "You probably know I grew up in San Francisco, so I was a West Coast girl when I met Justin. After seeing the Pacific Ocean every day of my life, this lake didn't do it for me."

He laughed. "I don't know anything about your history," he said with his most charming smile.

"My past is not pretty. Due to my drug use, I lost my marriage and my precious little girl."

Why was she saying all this?

"Joel brought me here to reimagine the Spa at the Manse," she told him, "but that's a story for another day." She pointed down the hill half a mile to the cove where he and Lyssa planned to build their own stone-and-glass house. "Let's walk down and back."

"Uh." He looked down at his Italian loafers. "I have snow boots in the car. I'll just change footwear first."

They met in the driveway, Gianessa bundled in her LL Bean coat with the hood up, he with his boots on and a muffler wrapped round his throat. Lyssa had given him the scarf their first Christmas, two years ago.

As they trekked along a shrubbery border on the northern edge of the Cushman grounds, Gianessa chattered about the extension Justin was planning to their winding access road to provide a paved surface to the Pennington's cove. "I brought you this way because Justin and I both think it's the best route, and we want to know what you think before we bring in an engineer."

"I don't see a problem, unless you plan to take down these berry bushes to accomplish it. I hope you won't. They're valued habitat for your songbirds, you know."

Gianessa's musical laugh made him wonder why he was talking about bird habitats, hours after his wife had nearly died due to her own poor judgment.

"Perhaps we shouldn't be doing this at all," he went on "taking over your lovely cove, putting up a structure that will be visible from your home, and driving our cars inches away from nesting birds."

"Kyle—"

"Did you know there's a blue heron in that cove? Suppose he's forced to vacate once the construction starts."

"Kyle—"

"If it were up to me, Lyssa and I would be living in Cornwall instead of—"

"Kyle." She'd said his name at least three times, he realized.

"Sorry. It's not about the birds."

"Yes, I know."

"It's about what you said days ago. Lyssa and I get caught up in these quests for justice and lose all common sense. And now she's not just emaciated and dehydrated, she's lying in a hospital bed, propped up on pillows, and her face—her beautiful delicate face—is crisscrossed with stitches." He bent double and gave into the tears he'd been holding back.

Gianessa shepherded him to a garden bench out of the wind. "Let it out, Kyle. Then we'll talk."

When his tears and rage and expletives had run out, he fished out a handkerchief and dried his tears before his face froze in the bitter wind.

"Talk to me about you and Lyssa."

"I'm very sure neither of us did this sleuthing before we met each other. We were both focused on our own careers. And we've been good for each other in that regard. My company is on solid ground again, thanks to Lyssa, and she's doing work she loves and breaking new ground all the time with her teaching. Why isn't that enough? That and starting a family."

He folded the damp handkerchief six times over until Gianessa covered his hands with her own. "Stop."

He quit the handkerchief folding. "This latest quest"—he spat the word—"has cost her physically, and I am no help to her."

"Not true," Gianessa told him. "When none of the rest of us could get Lyssa to see she had a problem with her health, one that she'd caused herself, you got her to talk with Dr. Bowes, and to redirect herself. That is, we hope that's the result."

"She says one day at a time, and I support it." He knew Gianessa was correct, that he'd been to one to break through Lyssa's denial. It had been the same with his company. Only Lyssa could wake him up to the fact his second-in-command had been embezzling from him.

"You and Lyssa are good partners for the journey, and life is never going to be trouble free."

Snow was falling now, and he watched the flakes land and balance on the fibers of his cashmere coat. "Tell me something, if you can."

Gianessa gave him a nod.

"Why has Lyssa been so obsessed with this murder? Beyond all reason, Gianessa."

"I saw it, too, and it scared me. Let's be glad it's over now."

"Is it really over? I don't feel any closure around Marguerite's death or Stan Block's. But my question is, why couldn't she leave the investigation to the authorities?" Her met her gaze.

"You have the answer."

He cocked his head at her. "I don't believe I do."

"Think about it." She stood from the bench and, without a word of explanation, headed downhill. "Show me what you're planning for the house," she called over her shoulder.

Two hours later, as he pulled into Wegman's parking lot to pick up the feast he'd ordered for the two of them to share in Lyssa's hospital room, his phone rang.

In heaven's name, why was their new architect calling? "Pamela, what can I do for you?"

"Kyle, just wondering if you're committed to Billy Warren as the builder for your house on the cove?" Her voice was strained.

"Billy Warren? As our builder? No, not at all. I don't understand."

"Strange," she answered. "He called an hour or so ago and said you and he had a deal that he'd be your contractor and builder. He asked if I wanted him to arrange for the site preparation—percolation testing, survey, and so on. I tried calling you right away but your phone was off and I didn't feel comfortable leaving a message about it."

The snake. "I apologize, Pamela. That's complete fiction, and I'm ever so grateful you've called for clarification. I regret you were bothered by his prank."

Her laugh fell far short of lighthearted. "I take it there's bad blood between you?"

"Indeed and, at the moment, I'm not sure how to fix it, but I do take responsibility. I hope this hasn't put you off our project. Lyssa and I were very impressed with your response to our ideas, and we both want to move forward with you as our architect. Without Warren in the mix."

"Good. I feel the same, and I have two possible builders in mind, but we can talk more about that at our next meeting."

"Splendid, Pamela, thank you."

He sat for a moment after disconnecting, then glanced around. He'd steamed up the car windows. *Lord, what am I to do?* He switched on the defroster.

Peter Shaughnessy and Hank had both advised him to disengage from Warren before it became a feud, but apparently he'd gone past the point of no return. Peter was the obvious person to talk with. He swallowed his pride and called him, laid out the newest facts, and admitted, "I need your counsel, Peter. How can I undo this feud with Warren?"

Peter was silent too long for Kyle's comfort. Finally, he answered, "Kyle, I can't tell you why, but I want you to let the authorities take care of Warren."

"What—"

"And I *strongly* urge you to pour your energy into your family right now, especially your wife and your sister-in-law."

"I'm completely missing something. I don't understand why you're telling me that's the answer."

A whoosh of frustration came across the connection. "Just know that Gwen and I are doing exactly that, and we need you to join us in that effort. I can't stress enough that Manda needs support right now, from both you and Lyssa."

"Has something happened to Manda?"

"No, it's not that."

"Then what *aren't* you saying?"

"That's all I can tell you at this point, Kyle." Peter broke the   connection.

Chapter 21

Lyssa knew the moment Kyle pushed through the door to her hospital room he was running on emotion and none of it happy. His cheeks were tight and he couldn't quite meet her eyes. The balloons he was juggling and the bag of aromatic food didn't fool her one bit.

But not to worry. He'd been a grump many times when they'd dated. She had a magic formula for that.

With a bright smile, she told him, "You are the best. How did you know I was famished?" He mumbled something unintelligible, handed her the bag, and then secured the balloons to the leg of her nightstand.

She took a peek. "Two whole meals? Beef *and* grilled chicken."

"I thought we could share."

"Brilliant." That got her a long assessing look. "No, I'm not on drugs, just a half dose of plain old Tylenol."

While he fetched a robe for her, she rolled the table alongside the bed. She sat with her bare feet dangling over the side of the mattress and patted the spot next to her. "Sit here and we can both see the balloons."

"You like them? I got something right, eh?" It may have been a weak one, but it was definitely a quirky Cornish smile.

Somehow they were in each other's arms for a long embrace, both apologizing. "Seriously, how are the bruises?" he asked as he pulled back.

"I hurt a lot, but I got some sleep and that helped. And they tested the heck out of my eyes and said my vision would return to normal in short order." She winked at him with her undamaged eye. "However, I'm still seeing double, and I don't do well with the forks and knives or putting the toothpaste on the toothbrush. Feed me, and I'll be good as new."

"That's my girl." He dug into the bag and set up their feast.

After a few delicious bites with help from a spoon, she told him, "Justin sent me a surprise email just before you arrived."

"What about?"

"A few days ago he told me, when he first talked with Emile Duval at the start of Emile's two-day interview, Emile seemed familiar somehow."

"That's odd, isn't it?"

"You'd think so, but Justin finally realized Drayton Textiles was one of the first startups he considered investing in when his venture capital business was new."

"Twenty years ago now. Evidently Justin didn't invest?"

"Correct. He thought the focus was too narrow, that Charles couldn't succeed if he limited himself to women of a certain size."

Kyle chuckled. "Let me guess. Charles Drayton thumbed his nose at Justin Cushman, said *watch me*, and built an empire."

"Probably right. Anyway, Justin thinks Charles has been looking for a chance to get back at him all these years." The balloons set up a crazy dance as the blower for the heat clicked on.

"I'm siding with the balloons on this, my love. Justin's ego is making it all about him."

"Maybe. But if it's true about Drayton Textiles being one of Justin's early rejects, I'll bet Charles laughed out loud when he realized Justin was now president of the college where his wife's paramour had stashed the incriminating love letters. Hence, the elaborate hoax. If they could pull it off, they'd get the letters back *and* Charles could put one over on Justin."

"That's a long time to carry a grudge, eh?"

"True. But, to my thinking, it explains why the Draytons went to so much trouble to set up the charade instead of Vivienne quietly slipping into town and retrieving the letters."

He *hmmph*ed. "Interesting point. Keep eating, please."

When she'd nearly finished her half of the feast, he told her, "I got a strange call from our architect while I was gone."

When she heard about Billy going behind their backs to claim the job, she huffed, "I can't believe he had the nerve to do that."

"Pure spite, I'd say."

"Or maybe just entitlement. Manda says he's *the* most popular builder in Tompkins Falls." She reached for another roll.

"Hold on, here." His mock indignation made her laugh. "Are you thinking you're entitled to the last roll?"

"I was going to split it with you." She wasn't but she gave him the larger half. "Billy *has* done most of the work the Cushmans have ever needed, and maybe he sees the house on the cove as a Cushman job, not a Pennington job. Did you know Joel had Warren Construction's name on the grant they've just gotten for restoring the old mill buildings?"

"I should have. What's Joel got planned there?"

"Condos in one building, lower-priced apartments in another, a few eating places on the main floor and co-op style shops to encourage local artisans."

He was suddenly quiet, fork poised in midair.

"What's wrong?"

"I need to tell you about another puzzling conversation. When I blew off steam to Peter about Billy's interference, Peter gave me advice that I don't understand."

As he related Peter's message, word-for-word, her heart pounded. "Why did he think Manda needs support?" She heard the shaking in her own voice.

Kyle's arm came around her shoulders. "I wish I hadn't mentioned that phone call."

"I'm glad you did, and I need to call her. And honestly I'm too stuffed to finish all this."

While he set about cleaning up their containers and messy napkins, Lyssa reached for her phone. Before she could press Manda's number, though, a visitor announced himself.

"Something smells good in here." Justin Cushman lounged in the doorway, hands shoved in his coat pockets.

"We've polished it off, Justin. You're out of luck." Kyle tossed the garbage in the trash basket. "Sit down, be comfortable."

Something wasn't right with Justin. His shoulders, usually squared with confidence, were slumped, and the smile seemed frozen on his face.

"I won't stay." He ambled to the foot of Lyssa's bed and made no move to take off his coat.

"What's happened?" Lyssa stood from the bed and wrapped her robe tighter. "Is it something with Manda?"

"No, and what I have to say is not to be shared with anyone."

Kyle stood beside her, and she drew strength from his nearness.

"You both need to know that Joel and our attorney are at the police station with a friend."

"Who?" they chorused. "Why?"

Justin swallowed and told them, "Billy Warren has turned himself in for killing Stan Block."

"Whoa." Lyssa leaned against the edge of the mattress. "I didn't see that coming."

Kyle folded his hands in prayer and touched them to his mouth. He gave a silent prayer of thanks. Far from wanting to gloat, he felt compassion for the young man whose life had fallen apart in the past month. He told them, "Frankly, the way he's been behaving, I strongly suspected something was very wrong. Justin, can you tell us anything more?"

Lyssa held up one hand. "Wait. I don't think I can hear this right now, and I really need to call Manda."

"My dear, I am sorry for adding to your burden," Justin apologized. "I thought you both should know."

"Thank you, but maybe you can give the details to Kyle. Outside? Would that work?"

"Do you need a nurse, sweetheart?"

"No, really, I just need to talk to my sister." She gave him a hug, and he grabbed his coat with assurances he would return.

"Let's get some fresh air, old friend." Kyle led the way down the hall and out of the hospital. Cold wind smacked him in the face. Too late, he realized he'd left his gloves and muffler in Lyssa's room. He put the wind at his back and found a recessed spot with some shelter. "You first."

"I'm not surprised you were suspicious," Justin said, "though I have to say I was shocked. Joel told me you'd asked Hank Moran to talk with Phil Phillips about the man in the rowboat and to look more closely at Warren."

Hank hadn't wasted any time, and Kyle felt vindicated by that. "How did Joel know that?" As soon as he asked, he remembered Phil was not only Joel's sponsor but he was someone Joel watched out for and supported in his old age. Phil would know Joel's business inside and out, both personal and professional, and he'd have reported to Joel anything that might threaten that business. And this development definitely threatened his latest business venture.

"Phil called Joel as soon as the police left his house this afternoon. He hadn't confirmed or denied to the police if Billy was the man in the boat, but he admitted the man at the oars fit his impression of Billy. He'd been wondering about it since he saw the boat go by that night and, especially, when he heard the identity of the body on the island. Phil keeps up on all the gossip, and he knew Billy had reason to go after Stan, but he hadn't volunteered anything to the authorities because it was just speculation, and Phil gives a person the benefit of the doubt."

A swirl of wind sent Kyle deeper into their niche. "What did Joel think?"

"I don't know the answer. He didn't confide any of this to me until an hour ago." Justin shivered as another gust invaded their space. "Let's walk, it's warmer."

Kyle swore under his breath. He knew there was no dissuading Justin, even when he was wrong.

Fifty feet down the sidewalk, Justin picked up the story. Fitting together the pieces, Kyle realized Billy had come to Joel's office at the Manse within an hour of Kyle's conversation with Hank outside the hospital.

Billy had laid his cards on the table and confessed he'd gone to Block's cottage to give him a thrashing for terrorizing Marguerite. But Block had taken a fall during the fight and struck his head. Stan Block was dead and Billy panicked.

"He commandeered a boat," Justin continued, "but couldn't risk using a motor, and it was too cold to take the body any distance. He thought if he dumped the body in the islands, it would be months before anyone would find it. We both know the plan didn't work."

"How had Billy found out Stan Block was Marguerite's tormentor?"

"He wouldn't tell Joel that, and I suspect he didn't know for sure until he confronted the man. That's for the police to find out."

Kyle thought back to Warren's aggression toward Lyssa outside the chapel following the memorial service. He'd acted on two false assumptions on that occasion: that Lyssa had provided the pills and that the pills killed Marguerite. "Billy Warren is a man of action, not someone who waits for the facts to line up before he gets physical." Justin gave him a puzzled look, and Kyle explained his thinking. "Did Joel say what had spooked him into confessing?"

"From what Joel said, when the body and the boat were discovered the next day, he still wasn't worried because he'd worn gloves and hadn't left fingerprints, but when Moran's team showed up this afternoon and asked him for an alibi and looked through the garage window at an old beat-up car he'd stolen and hidden there, he knew he couldn't bluff his way out."

Kyle realized he'd been right about the car. "Why didn't they arrest him on the spot?"

Justin shook his head.

Kyle had to think about the reason. It didn't take him long. Evidently Billy's reputation, Joel's power in the community, and the weight of their combined grant—to rescue the derelict mill buildings from their current reputation as a drug haven and transform them into attractive and useful space—swayed the police's decision in Warren's favor. "So going to Joel for help was a smart move, but I wonder if Joel has the whole story."

"What do you mean?"

"I don't believe I told you or Joel about my confrontation with him at Lyssa's house or the accident that followed."

"Was this the confrontation when you refused his offer to use him as the builder for the cove house? He told me about that."

"I refused his offer based on his abuse of Lyssa at the memorial service. But what's important here, and I don't think you or Joel know this, is the accident he caused immediately after." He repeated what he'd said to Hank hours earlier. "Clearly, Warren had no regard for their safety or possible injury."

Justin glared at him.

"It's true, every word."

Justin halted. Shook his head. "I knew something was off. Did you file a police report?"

"I called 911, requested medical help, reported the violations, named Warren as the driver, and provided the license number of the company van. I only realized today that no one ever got back to me to verify anything or to formalize my statement."

Another blast of cold air went through the cloth of his coat, and he turned around. "Let's walk back to the hospital entry. Get out of the wind for a bit." Justin fell into step, and Kyle asked, "What did you mean, something was off?"

"Warren has a way of putting a spin on things to his advantage. We all do it for self-advancement. That's why I watch people's eyes. Sometimes his are shifty. Warren told Joel you claimed it was him driving the van when you alerted the police to the accident. But Warren swore to Joel someone else had taken the van that day without permission and never logged it in the book."

"We can assume that's what he told the police as well?"

Justin nodded. "And embellished it by saying you'd been hassling him ever since the argument outside the chapel."

Kyle swore under his breath. "And they believed a solid citizen like Billy Warren over a Brit, eh?"

"That's the way it is in this town. I wish you'd said something to me after it happened. Joel would have been all over Billy about it, and he wouldn't have gotten away with it."

"Poor bugger was taking one risk after another, wasn't he?"

Justin made a noise in his throat—disgust, Kyle thought. Before continuing, he checked the vicinity for anyone who might be listening. His voice low, he told Kyle, "My concern, to start, is that Joel's putting up Warren's bail."

Kyle did a slow burn and said sarcastically, "Lucky for Billy Warren."

Justin was silent, and Kyle wondered if they'd just moved to opposite sides of a very loaded issue. "Sorry, that was uncalled for," Kyle said. "I do have sympathy for the man. He's lost his wife, and his behavior since then is the direct result of that tragedy. I doubt I'd do much better under the circumstances."

"It's generous of you to say that, but I'm concerned about something else, something worse."

Kyle waited.

"Joel has also retained a defense attorney who comes highly recommended. I told him I thought it was a mistake to finance Warren's legal battle. Now I'm sure of it, and there's no way to keep Joel's decision a secret in this town. A large faction will conclude Joel is buying off law enforcement and the judicial system to protect his renovation project."

"He needs to know that Warren has not been truthful with him, Justin."

"I told him he's risking his reputation, but he wouldn't hear it. He's determined to see the mill buildings restored, and Warren Construction is hardwired to the multimillion-dollar grant."

"Justin, Joel is misinformed. If he moves forward—"

Justin clapped him on the shoulder. "Not your worry, Kyle."

The jovial tone put Kyle on alert. Justin had let it go too quickly.

"I'll chew on this, talk it over with Gianessa, and find a solution. You and Lyssa need a break from all of this. When are you leaving for the UK?"

"Sunday noon. Without fail." He added a mirthless chuckle. "I don't suppose you're trying to get rid of me, your old pal who has an inconvenient habit of blurting out the truth?"

Justin blustered, "Nonsense."

Kyle wasn't convinced. More pieces fell into place. Peter Shaughnessy must have known what was coming. Probably Manda had confided in her sponsor, Gwen, who'd talked it over with her husband, Peter. And that's why Peter had urged Kyle to leave Warren to the authorities and throw his support behind Manda. Did that mean Manda and Joel were on opposite sides of Warren's dilemma? It must be something like that. Lyssa would get it out of her sister.

For the moment, it was comforting that Peter and Gwen had declared their support for Manda and for Lyssa. There was no comfort, however, that Manda and Joel were at odds two months before the birth of their first child.

Kyle halted, aware there were more implications that he'd need to deal with. For one, Lyssa would be reluctant to leave for Cornwall if Manda was in crisis.

Justin had paused on the sidewalk, too, but went right on saying, "It appears that, once again, my softhearted nephew has been led into an intractable position by a less-than-scrupulous associate."

Justin was quite an actor when he chose to be. Kyle told his old friend, "It's a shame Joel didn't check the facts about the accident."

285

Scowling, Justin stepped closer, and Kyle fought the instinct to retreat in kind. "You do understand I will do *everything in my power* to support my nephew?"

Sweat beaded on Kyle's upper lip. The subtext was a warning to back off the police report he'd made about Warren's reckless driving.

He sent up a silent prayer, and the words came to him. Standing tall, he answered, "I completely understand that your loyalty must lie with Joel. And you have my assurance Lyssa and I will give all the support we possibly can to Manda through this difficult time."

Justin's lips were a thin line, his gaze searching.

Recalculating? Kyle made a show of consulting his watch. "I need to check on Lyssa. Thanks very much for the heads-up, old friend. Stay in touch."

He brushed past Justin and ducked into the lobby of the hospital, his hands shaking.

Lyssa looked up from her phone call when Kyle returned from his walk with Justin. He looked as thunderstruck as she felt talking with Manda. She grabbed for one of their leftover napkins and fished out a pen from the nightstand. "*Bizarre. Compare notes before you go?*" she wrote.

Kyle nodded and hung his coat on a hook by the door, then rubbed his hands together and blew on them. She hid a smile when she realized his gloves and scarf were still on the chair.

When she tuned in again to Manda, her sister was repeating the same worry she'd spoken at least three times. "The bombshell Billy dropped on us is affecting our health. Joel's handicap is so much worse when he's stressed. I want to be here for him, Lyssa, really I do, but I'm afraid for the baby." This time she added, "You are so lucky to be leaving for Cornwall. I wish I could come too."

This was a new twist. Until now, Manda had been worried Dr. Bowes would put her on bedrest.

Something stopped her from saying, *Come with us to Cornwall*. Instead, she told Manda, "That's not a good idea. I need total rest right now, Manda, and Kyle and I need the time together. Besides, I know you're really just trying to get me to stay in Tompkins Falls for the holiday, right?"

Silence.

"Manda, you've *got* to see your doctor. I can't go with you because I'm still in the hospital, and Kyle and I are leaving Sunday noon. It was nearly impossible for him to get those flights. Suppose there is something wrong with you or the baby? You *have* to see your doctor. Promise me you will."

Kyle was waving at her.

"You've got a million friends in AA. Gwen and Gianessa will do everything they can you for you. You just need to ask."

Now Kyle was pointing to himself with both index fingers. She laughed. "My husband's trying to tell me something and I can't make it out. Hold on."

"I may be able to drive if her appointment is Friday."

"Did you hear that? He's offering to drive you to the doctor's if—okay." She shook her head at Kyle. "Let us know if you change your mind. Love you, Manda." She put her phone down and reached out a hand. "Knowing you would even consider being at her side, she has finally agreed to call Dr. Bowes and get in to see her. But you're off the hook for driving her. I think it's a woman-to-woman thing."

He took a step closer, and she put her arms around his neck and exhaled. Deeply. Completely. "I've had enough Tompkins Falls drama. Manda says Billy is insisting it was self-defense when he killed Stan Block. Who in their right mind will believe that?"

"Anyone who wants Billy Warren not to go to jail, and that's a lot of people in this town. Including Joel, apparently."

She pulled back to look at his face. What wasn't he telling her? Maybe she'd just let him tell her when he was ready. Her worry was for the tension between her sister and Joel so close to the due date.

She rested her good cheek against Kyle's shoulder. "Manda is trying to get Joel to rescind his offer to pay for Billy's defense unless Billy gets real about what he's done. What did Justin tell you?"

He huffed. "Remember the accident I reported?"

"When Billy hit that carful of kids and took off?"

Kyle was nodding. "From what I can gather, Billy lied to the authorities, said someone else must have used the van, and that I had lied about him being the driver because I had it in for him. Joel and Justin both believed Billy's version." Hank had, too, but he'd keep that to himself.

Her stomach dropped. "Kyle …"

"I know, and I think Justin wants me to retract that police report. At least have Billy's name removed."

She felt herself growing faint. "Let me lie down."

"Sorry, love, I wasn't going to tell you any of this until we were home in Cornwall." He helped her onto the bed and fluffed the pillows. "Be honest here. Knowing what Manda is going through, do you want me to do as Justin is asking?"

"Falsify the police report you made after witnessing the accident? No."

"Good."

"Were you going to?"

"No."

She smiled up at him and touched her fingers to his mouth. "Thank God. Should I tell any of this to Manda?"

"She has enough to deal with already. Did I understand you to say you're not keen to have her come with us to Cornwall?"

"Correct. Do you think that's heartless?"

"I think your healing has to come first. And we need time together to recover from all these deaths and accusations and our setback with starting a family."

"I agree." Tears welled up.

"Lord willing, we'll have you out of here tomorrow morning, then two and a half days of rest, and we're on our plane Sunday noon." He stroked her cheek. "Manda is strong and resilient, just like her big sister, and you'll talk with her every day we're away, eh?"

"True. And you and I will go for walks." She closed her eyes with a smile. "Maybe a long walk toward the end of my holiday break."

Static preceded an announcement in the hallway. Visiting hours were over.

She pulled him close and clung to him for a long moment.

Chapter 22

Lyssa awoke at dawn the next morning when Kyle slipped into her room and deposited something on her chair.

"Hi." She'd startled him.

"Sorry. I didn't mean to wake you. How are you feeling?"

"Like I need a hot shower and a serious session with a toothbrush. What did you bring?"

"Your get-out-of-hospital clothes in a duffel you can use for your things."

"Sweet."

"Take all the time in the world. Sleep more if you want."

She made a face at him, and he laughed.

"I'll be downstairs settling our bill and rousting the attending physician to sign your release."

She drifted between waking and sleeping until the squeaks of the breakfast trolley sounded down the hall. It was time for that hot shower that she hoped would ease most of her aches and pains. She took care not to get her stitches wet.

As she toweled off she caught her reflection in the mirror and shut her eyes to the damage. Swelling all around the eye socket, bruises everywhere, worse on her left hip. It was no wonder her entire body hurt. She tried to remember how many days they had until their flight to the UK. Whatever, it would have to be enough.

She somehow managed to step into the pair of sweatpants Kyle had brought, shimmy into the tank top, and get the Cornwall sweatshirt over her head. By the time she'd balled up her rumpled johnnie and robe and dumped them in a corner, she was exhausted. And famished.

Right on time, the breakfast lady was sliding a tray from the cart onto Lyssa's rolling table. With a glance at the name on her badge, Lyssa put on a sunny smile and told her, "Good morning, Lucy."

"Ready for a meal, I hope." Lucy lifted the plastic cover on the plate to reveal two perfectly poached eggs sitting proudly on toast points, accompanied by melon slices. "Juice, of course, and a cup of coffee. Will that do until you get home?"

"Beautiful." But she couldn't make the fork cooperate.

"Trouble seeing with that eye injury?"

Lyssa was laughing as the fork danced around the egg. "The doctor said this might happen for a while," she told Lucy. She held one hand over her bad eye and stabbed the tines dead center in the yolk. "Got it."

Lucy took pity on her and cut everything into bite-size pieces before she went on her way.

While she savored her meal, she listened to the clatter and murmurs from the hall. Not everyone on the floor was well enough to go home today. If only she'd remembered to ask Lucy which day this was.

Hank Moran had left a voicemail for her during the night. Thanks to Lyssa's efforts, he had succeeded in getting a confession from Nicole Dutois for the poisoning death of Charles Drayton. Despite Tony Pinelli's speculation about Nicole being responsible for Marguerite's death, Hank said the city police had verified Nicole's alibi for the night of Marguerite's death, and the authorities were satisfied Nicole had no knowledge of the vial of pills in Marguerite's car.

Obviously, Hank was still looking for answers for that vial of pills. If he still thought Lyssa had given the pills to Marguerite, he hadn't said so. Regardless, Lyssa needed to know who had done it and why. Without that answer, there was a shadow of doubt hanging over her. Whose doubt, she didn't care. She honestly felt as if Marguerite had been haunting her, driving her to set the record straight and allow both of them—sponsor and sponsee—to find peace.

So how could she find out?

She'd had an idea once, but it was gone now. The doctor had explained she could expect to have temporary amnesia for the time before or after the attack. Before Nicole came at her with the Eiffel Tower, she'd been sitting at the breakfast bar at the Bagel Depot updating her notes.

She fished in her purse for the piece of graph paper covered with her messy handwriting, and there was her idea, written in pencil in a crowded corner of the paper, in the form of a question: could Marguerite have gotten the pills while she was in Brittany? It seemed like such a long shot, she doubted Hank Moran would be interested in pursuing it.

Lyssa thought back to Marguerite weeping and sobbing through some of their conversations as she came to accept her sexual orientation. Marguerite had often pressed the flat of her hand to her breastbone, circling incessantly to ease the angst and pain. Wasn't it possible Marguerite had made the same gesture in unguarded moments on the trip as she wrestled with the implications of her affair with Vivienne?

Could a motherly fellow traveler, like the mysterious Shirley, have taken note and tried to help?

Lyssa glanced again at her handwritten cogitations. An arrow led her eye to *Check M's FB for names of Brittany people*. She'd never gotten around to it. There was no time like the present. Kyle was somewhere downstairs, talking with the doctor about her discharge instructions and with the billing office about the charges for her care. That could take hours.

She turned on her iPad and got to work. She barely heard Kyle come into the room sometime later. "Catching up on your email, love?"

She looked up. "I've found her," she told him. "Remember the older couple in the back row of the Brittany snapshot? Shirley is the wife of your Scottish thriller writer."

Kyle felt a smile spread over his face. "I might have known you'd keep working on this. How long did it take?"

She checked the time. "An hour and a half."

"What say you pack up your things, and I'll see if I can find contact information for my thriller writer and his pill-toting wife, shall I?" Then we can hand it over to Hank, he was thinking.

"Brilliant." She handed over her device.

Minutes later he jotted something on an unused napkin.

Probably curious that the key clicks had stopped, Lyssa came to his side. "You found it? How?"

"The phone book for the West Highlands is online. She's listed, he isn't."

"Let's call her."

"Let's leave it to Hank."

Relief washed over her face. "But please tell him to tread lightly. I'm sure Shirley meant well."

"I'll tell him you said so."

She nodded and vanished into the bathroom with her phone.

He was still talking with Hank about a few loose ends when she reappeared. When his call was done, she told him, "Manda left a voicemail saying Joel would drive her to her doctor's appointment Friday afternoon. Is that tomorrow?"

"Tomorrow is Friday. And that's good, eh, that Joel is taking care of her and the baby in the middle of their crisis?"

She nodded and smiled. "Let's go home."

He grabbed the bag and started to open the door just as Lyssa's phone rang. "Justin," she told him, and they groaned in unison.

"Putting it on speaker, are you?" he teased. He was happy to support her in any way she wanted. He stashed the bag at the door and joined her on the edge of the bed.

Justin was calling to request Lyssa's presence at a showdown—his word—with Vivienne first thing in the morning. "Rand Cunningham will be with us, but I'm not sure where his loyalty lies."

"Rand is loyal to you, Justin."

"Perhaps, but he's escorting Vivienne from Long Island in his family's corporate jet. It seems Drayton Textiles and their supermodel, Vivienne, are among the Cunninghams' high-echelon clients."

"I repeat, Rand is loyal to you, Justin. You don't need me there."

"You've only to show up and speak the truth, my dear," Justin was saying. Kyle wondered if Justin had even heard her. Would she fight this battle?

"Hold on a second," she said and muted the phone.

Kyle said, "My take: he's pressuring Vivienne for a fat donation, and he needs the female perspective to sell her."

"He may not like what I have to say when I come face-to-face with Vivienne." She raised her good eyebrow. "Maybe I'll do it, but I won't use his script."

"Hold on. What are your thinking?"

"This is a chance to tell her the full impact of her behavior. Not just on me or the college." She nodded as if she'd come to a decision.

He wished she wouldn't do it. The encounter could be gut-wrenching, and she was so vulnerable right now.

"I'll do it on my terms, and I promise I won't let Justin bully me into 'one more thing.'"

Kyle narrowed his eyes but, before he could argue, she took the phone off mute.

The second she accepted, President Cushman outlined a task force he was creating to review adjunct pay and benefits. She rolled her eyes, and Kyle opened both hands, as if to say I told you so.

"Excellent, Justin. That inquiry is long overdue."

She actually sounded like she meant it, and perhaps she did.

"And do you know who's perfect to lead that task force?" she added.

"You, of course, my dear. Did I tell you I've learned of a conference for you in Norway next spring? Its theme is Excellence in Online Teaching and Learning."

There it was—the reward that would sweeten the deal so she couldn't refuse. Classic Justin Cushman.

But Lyssa was smiling secretively as she told her ultimate boss, "When I'm back for the spring semester, we'll talk about the conference. Now, back to my recommendation. I'm unable to take on any additional duties because I have a full course load that will be partially online, and I need to measure my effectiveness and fine-tune my online teaching style, per my agreement with you. In that regard, I've designed a classroom action research project so I can publish a paper and perhaps use it to inspire my colleagues at Tompkins College."

At the silence on Justin's end, Kyle beamed at her and gave her two thumbs-up.

She smiled and told Justin, "So, I'm respectfully declining membership on the task force and suggesting that Rand Cunningham is the obvious person to lead it. As interim dean, he has supervisory responsibility for most of the adjuncts who teach at Tompkins College and he's greatly respected by the departments under him. Further, by publishing the task force findings, he'll showcase Tompkins College as a cutting-edge institution. Don't you think?"

After a two-second hiatus, Justin said, "Good thinking. Be in my office by eight o'clock tomorrow morning." He ended the connection.

"Wow." She whooshed with relief. "I actually stood up to Justin."

"Good show, Mrs. Pennington."

Chapter 23

When Lyssa and Rand arrived promptly at eight o'clock Friday morning, Justin opened their pre-meeting with the good news that the woman candidate had accepted the college's offer and would assume Marguerite's position at the start of the semester, as they'd hoped.

Rand shook the president's hand and agreed to contact her before the day was out. Lyssa gave in to a moment of sadness at losing Marguerite forever, followed by genuine excitement at the promise of a new colleague, one who would take care of Marguerite's students.

"Shall we?" Justin motioned to the two straight chairs standing next to his cushy presidential chair. The stage was set for the showdown with Vivienne. He asked Lyssa to take the chair at the end, farthest from the door, because her injured face would only serve as a distraction during the negotiation.

She walked silently, cheeks hot, to her assigned seat with Rand right behind her. When she glanced at Rand, he rolled his eyes at her and mouthed, *Sorry.* She smiled back, glad for his solidarity.

"I see the guest gets the hot seat," Rand joked as he made himself comfortable. An upholstered armchair, not much larger than theirs, faced them.

Justin made no comment but briefed them on his agenda. Rand would speak first after Justin's introduction, followed by Lyssa, and then Justin would close the deal. His choice of words made it clear Kyle was right, Justin was looking for a donation from the wealthy widow, not trying to placate her in any way.

He gave both of them key phrases to use in their statements. She and Rand nodded and smiled. As soon as Justin turned his back, Rand touched her sleeve, leaned close, and whispered, "I've got my own agenda. You, too?" She gave him a silent high five.

Moments later, the office door opened and Vivienne was shown to her chair. Lyssa was struck by her sensuality and sultry beauty. Her form-fitting black silk dress revealed more cleavage than had ever been visible on the campus of Tompkins College. The costume was the antithesis of widow's weeds.

After briefly introducing Lyssa as "Professor Lyssa Pennington, hostess at your husband's fatal dinner," Justin said a few mild words of regret over the widow's loss, followed by stern words about the fraud the Draytons had perpetrated against the college. Vivienne pursed her mouth and turned hooded eyes on each of the three in turn.

Though she couldn't see the others' faces, Lyssa responded with a pleasant smile, wondering how Justin would handle the widow's melodrama.

Soon, Justin got to the point. "What we will consider, Mrs. Drayton, in lieu of prosecution, is a public apology for the hoax and some manner of restitution." When Vivienne opened her mouth to speak, Justin rose from his chair and towered over her. "I have the floor."

She shut her mouth.

Hands behind his back, Justin stepped toward Vivienne and passed within inches of her before hovering behind her shoulder. "Six of my faculty were traumatized by witnessing your husband's agonizing death, which would *never* had occurred if you and he hadn't carried out an *elaborate hoax* against this institution of higher learning in a *desperate attempt* to protect your reputations." By the end of his statement, he had made a complete circle around Vivienne, Lyssa, and Rand. He finished the exercise by standing behind his own chair.

"Even more serious than the impact on my faculty was the *ordeal* Professor Pennington suffered." He nodded in Lyssa's direction. She hadn't expected to be singled out so early in the meeting. Did he remember she planned to speak after Rand?

She briefly met Vivienne's cool gaze and nodded once. Evidently, she'd done the right thing, because Justin continued speaking.

"After planning and attending to every detail of the celebratory dinner for you and your husband—which, by the way, you blew off—Professor Pennington then suffered at the hands of the police, who did their utmost to pin the murder on her. I arrived at the interrogation in time to see her *collapse* on the floor."

Nausea hit her with no warning as the scene came back to her. She sucked in her breath. When she stole a look at Rand his eyebrows were raised at her, and she mouthed, *I'm okay*. She took a few more deep breaths as Justin went on.

"Not to mention the expense of bringing you and your husband to campus under false pretenses and having to manage the legal, parental, and media fallout that resulted from your charade." Again, Vivienne opened her mouth to speak, and he raised his hand to stop her and roared, "Do *not* think you can *weasel* out of this by saying you handled your own lodging arrangements or, worse, claiming the dreadful consequences were not your *intention*."

Vivienne shifted on her chair, raising one elegantly clad shoulder as a shield against the president's ire and fixing him with a smoldering gaze.

He pressed forward over the back of his chair until his face was on a level with hers. "In this world, Mrs. Drayton, you do not get credit for your intentions; you get credit for what *happens*. And what *happened* was murder, an atrocity committed on *my* campus that was *entirely* preventable. Charles Drayton's death was a direct result of your scheme as Mr. and Mrs. Emile Duval. Whether the law sees it that way or not, your actions are unacceptable to this institution and we demand recompense."

Vivienne blinked her heavily made-up eyes and composed herself. "I understand, Dr. Cushman," she said. "Let's speak privately, shall we, about your initiatives at Tompkins College?"

Without waiting for Justin's agreement, she directed her sultry amber gaze to Rand and gave him a warm smile that was just short of seductive. "Dr. Cunningham, my deepest thanks to you and your family for transporting me here and for treating me with respect through this difficult time." The implication was Rand was the only member of the trio to show respect to the grieving widow.

Her mouth opened to say something more, but Rand cut her off with a chilling, "My parents' firm provided the jet because you pay them the big bucks, Vivienne, and for no other reason." This was definitely not Justin's script.

Vivienne's cheeks turned deep red.

"Personally, I'm here at the request of President Cushman," Rand went on, "a man I greatly admire. When you have your private chat with him, you'll want to pay attention to his design for a scholarly research and learning center in the heart of the campus."

He reached out a hand to Lyssa and she gave him a million-dollar smile. Unfortunately, he squeezed her hand and she gasped at the pain. "Sorry," he whispered and added, "Do you need a minute before you say your piece?"

"Please."

Vivienne had risen from her chair and had her clutch bag in hand when Justin growled at her to take her seat. "Professor Pennington has something to say that you need to hear." The woman lowered herself onto her chair.

While Lyssa collected herself, Rand told Vivienne in a confidential tone, "You're probably not aware, Vivienne, that Lyssa was injured earlier this week in a confrontation with the person who murdered your husband. In flushing out the killer, she cleared *your* name. You owe her big-time for that. I'll leave it to President Cushman to give you one or two hints for paying that special debt."

For the first time, Vivienne looked uncertain. She studied the collection of rings on her fingers before addressing Lyssa. "I am profoundly grateful for your courageous action and deeply disturbed that you were injured." Touching as the words might have been, there wasn't a hint of sincerity in her delivery. "Maybe you and I can have coffee before I leave today?"

Lyssa turned the other cheek to give Vivienne the full effect of her stitches and bruises. Vivienne paled. "I don't think so, Vivienne. I'll say what I have to say in the sanctity of this office, and I'm confident neither of these gentlemen will repeat one word of it outside of this room." She narrowed her eyes at a startled Justin Cushman, who nodded. Once Rand had murmured his agreement, she returned her full attention to the woman.

"I was Marguerite's LaCroix's AA sponsor, and I supported her through the agony of accepting her sexual orientation and coming out to her husband." Rand inhaled sharply, and Justin sank onto his chair.

Lyssa took a calming breath and said, "I neither condone nor condemn her affair with you, but *three* deaths—hers, your husband's, and one of our security officers—all resulted from that mistake, and there is *no way* to erase those

301

consequences." The next words caught in Lyssa's throat and she had to swallow before continuing.

With a prayer for courage, she held her head high. "My husband and I plan to have children, and we decided last night, if we're lucky enough to have a little girl, we'll name her Marguerite because of our friend's courage and her brilliant spirit, *not* because of her indiscretion with you, a married woman who apparently has no moral compass."

She nodded to Rand and to Justin. Justin's eyes were wide with shock. "Thank you for allowing me to speak, President Cushman."

Justin retook control. With a harrumph, he told their guest, "I will be with you momentarily." To Rand he said, "Please escort Mrs. Drayton out."

Lyssa's head screamed with pain. She didn't care if Justin fired her for what she'd just said but, as the door closed behind Rand and Vivienne, her effort to remain dignified dissolved in a flood of tears. She doubled over with a sob. Justin was at her side with a fistful of tissues, and she welcomed his arm around her shaking shoulders. "Brava, Lyssa," he murmured.

When her crying had run its course, the office was silent. Justin crossed to the door, murmured something to his assistant, and turned back to her.

"Kyle is on his way here. Will you be okay alone for a few minutes?"

She looked up to see his hand poised on the doorknob. In spite of her nod, though, he hesitated, his eyes filled with worry.

"I'm okay, really."

"If you need me, my dear, I'll be in the conference room with Mrs. Drayton."

She rallied a smile. "Hold out for five million, Justin. And don't give her naming rights."

He chuckled and stood taller for his exit.

Peace settled over Kyle as he navigated the narrow gap between the Seneca Street house and the neighbor's fence. On the walk to the house, he hovered beside Lyssa, though she was managing perfectly well on her own. "Glad to be home?" he asked as they entered the kitchen.

"Yes. It feels different."

"How so?"

"When I've come to check on it, it has always felt lonely."

"The house did?" He didn't understand her sensitivities, but he knew they were very real to her.

She nodded.

"Maybe our friends are to thank for the change." He told her about Natalie's tireless work on the furniture delivery, the Pinelli brothers' insistence on scraping the bricks free of ice and snow, and the delivery Manda had arranged of staples for the pantry. "Gwen and Peter have left us a beautiful meal for tonight's dinner. There's more than enough for our lunch, too. Are you hungry?"

"A little. Are these from you?" She was eyeing a bouquet of pink roses on the island.

"From Gianessa and Justin." He helped her off with her coat. When he returned from hanging the coats in closet, she was fingering the petals of the single red rose in a vase on the kitchen table.

"That one's from me."

"Thank you." She met his kiss, her eyes sparkling with delight.

He set about making tea for them. As the water reached a boil, she left off inhaling the flower scents and scrounged in the pantry, emerging with crackers and almond butter.

"Appetizer?" She didn't answer, and he left her to her thoughts.

"I said what I needed to say," she told him. He must have looked blank. "At the meeting this morning."

It was the first she'd talked about it, and he hadn't probed. Justin had warned him it had been emotionally draining for her. "Justin called it a showdown. Was it?"

"Three against one. And you were right. The whole plan was to hit her up for a donation."

"No surprise."

"Rand and I weren't privy to the outcome."

"I understand from Justin that whatever you said was the knockout punch. He has enough now to move ahead with construction." Though she was intent on opening a box of crackers, he caught sight of a grin. "Justin said she argued for calling the new building the Drayton Center, but he quashed it."

"Good." Her voice was solemn. "It's always been his dream and it's only right for it to carry his name."

"I didn't realize you felt so strongly about it."

"I didn't either. I hadn't thought much about names before our walk yesterday." She set a plate of crackers, the just-opened jar of almond butter, and two knives on the island and settled on one of stools. A soft smile played around her mouth.

They'd walked the hall at the hospital, while waiting for a wheelchair to come available for her discharge. Somehow their path had taken them to the windows that overlooked the nursery. He'd blurted out something about Marguerite being a lovely name for a girl, and Lyssa had smiled more brightly than he'd seen in months.

"When you said that about Marguerite being a beautiful name," she told him now, "everything fell into place. In spite of the ugliness around her death, there are ways I can honor her as a person. Honor her trust in me, her commitment to the truth, and her remarkable capacity for inspiring young men and women."

He handed her a steaming mug of Earl Grey. "Perhaps her spirit lives on, eh?" They clinked their drinks and said "Cheers."

"Now it lives on in a good way. She would have continued haunting me until we found the truth."

"That's why you did all this?" he asked, and she nodded. So it was less about Hank suspecting her of having a hand in Marguerite's death or of killing Charles Drayton. She'd felt compelled to lay bare the truth so Marguerite could rest in peace.

Lyssa blew across the liquid. "Now that she's at peace, we can be, too. Do you feel it?" She watched him over the rim of the cup as she took a tiny sip.

Come to think of it, his breathing felt easier and his heart didn't ache the way it had for weeks. "I do, my love." He gave her his best Cornish smile.

She answered with that full-out laugh that would always sound to him like songbirds greeting the dawn.

THE END

About the Author

C. T. Collier grew up in Seneca Falls, NY, left the area for college and jobs, but always wanted to return to the Finger Lakes. Today she lives in a beautiful small city on one of the prettiest of the Finger Lakes, not unlike fictional Tompkins Falls on lovely Chestnut Lake. Most days you'll find her writing in her tiny office looking out on a woods populated with fox, deer, wild turkeys, and songbirds. In her career as a tech-savvy college professor she has been endlessly fascinated with campus intrigue. Entirely fictional, Tompkins College is no college and every college.

Learn more at https://drkatecollier.wordpress.com

Made in the USA
Columbia, SC
12 May 2018